A NARR

The captain had adm...
explain to the captain ab...

"Swords are no good," Benny had said one morning as they rested just beneath a manhole cover. "You need something with stopping power. A shotgun is just the thing, one that fires slugs. Big ones. Why I've seen albino 'gators down here that would go fifteen feet long."

The captain asked about crocodiles, but Benny professed not to know the difference between a 'gator and a croc.

"Crocs have a notch on the side of their blinkin' snouts," the captain explained. "It makes them look a little like they're ... smiling. And the one I'm looking for ... ticks."

"Like a clock?"

"Exactly like a clock."

"Never heard a thing like that. How would a croc get down here, anyway? Flushed down the toilet like the 'gators?"

"Not exactly," the captain said.

The truth was that the croc had learned a lot in its new environment, and one of the first things it had learned was how to hide in a crowd.

Only a few days after his conversation with Benny, the captain had found himself face to snout with the very creature he had sought for so long. The captain had smiled and raised the shotgun he had bought that very day, taken careful aim, and then Willem had dropped the flashlight.

There beneath the New York streets, the bulb had shattered, and the sewer tunnel had been plunged into darkness that gathered 'round the captain like a thick, damp woolen blanket. And then the captain heard the sound that had haunted his dreams for more years than he cared to recall:

"Tick ... tock. Tick ... tock."

—from "What a Croc!" by Bill Crider

urban NIGHTMARES

**Edited by
Josepha Sherman &
Keith R. A. DeCandido**

BAEN

URBAN NIGHTMARES

This is a work of fiction. All the characters and events portrayed in this book are fictional, and any resemblance to real people or incidents is purely coincidental.

A Baen Books Original

Baen Publishing Enterprises
P.O. Box 1403
Riverdale, NY 10471

ISBN: 0-671-87851-4

Cover art by David Mattingly

First printing, November 1997

Distributed by Simon & Schuster
1230 Avenue of the Americas
New York, NY 10020

Typeset by Windhaven Press, Auburn, NH
Printed in the United States of America

Contents

Dedicated to Jan Harold Brundvand

take her.

She went to the lockers to drop off her lunch. Then, she

Introduction

Josepha Sherman & Keith R.A. DeCandido

Are there *really* alligators in the sewers? Have people *ever* tried to microwave their pets or to bring strange-looking dogs up from Mexico? And does a maniac with a hook for a hand *truly* wander the night, looking for unwary teens to kill?

Well . . . yes and no. There really was one lonely alligator in brief residence in the New York City sewer system (it had apparently fallen off a ship and was quickly dispatched), and it's fairly likely that someone out there thought microwaving a wet dog was a good idea. Legends rarely develop in a vacuum.

But the veracity of the tales isn't what makes them so popular. For these stories are part of the ever-expanding world of urban folklore, the body of tales, beliefs, and rhymes that are usually told by "a friend of a friend" as *true*, but which are composed by no one and known by everyone. An urban folktale generally has a modern setting (although, despite the name, it need not take place in a city), and usually features a plot that seems perfectly rational at first, but proves totally improbable on closer examination.

Some of these tales have ancient antecedents: versions of "The Hook," for instance, date back to the thirteenth century. Others are in a constant state of evolution: Editor Sherman has watched a generic tale of a woman in an ice cream parlor getting so rattled by seeing a celebrity that she puts the ice cream in her purse evolve within a few months so that the celebrity becomes actor Paul Newman. Like any oral tradition, urban folktales add more and more elaborate details

1

with each retelling, sometimes due to faulty memory, sometimes to make the story more exciting (which is why these details often involve celebrities).

With this anthology, we add yet another layer, to wit, a story that uses the folktale as a springboard. *Urban Nightmares*, like many anthologies before it, came to be at a science fiction convention, with a convivial group of writers that included Lawrence Watt-Evans, Christie Golden, Laura Anne Gilman, and the two editors (all of whom, you'll note, have stories herein). The topic turned to urban folktales and the story possibilities behind them. Then someone (we're not really sure who) said, "This should be an anthology!" The next thing we knew, we had one, full of enthusiastic authors, many of them Hugo- and Nebula-Award winners, who loved the idea of taking their favorite urban legends—whether they be ones that frightened them as children or amused them as adults—and making new stories out of them.

And so they have, ranging from ancient stories gussied up for modern times to new twists on urban folktales we've heard many times before to new legends that have sprung up thanks to the Internet. We're sure you'll find them both disturbingly different and eerily familiar.

Happy reading.

And . . . pleasant dreams.

Gator

Robert J. Sawyer

Something scampered by in the dark, its footfalls making tiny splashing sounds. Ludlam didn't even bother to look. It was a rat, no doubt—the sewers were crawling with them, and, well, if Ludlam could get used to the incredible stench, he could certainly get used to the filthy rodents, too.

This was his seventy-fourth night skulking about the sewers beneath New York. He was dressed in a yellow raincoat and rubber boots, and he carried a powerful flashlight—the kind with a giant brick battery hanging from the handle.

In most places, the ceiling was only inches above his head; at many points, he had to stoop to get by. Liquid dripped continuously on the raincoat's hood. The walls, sporadically illuminated by his flashlight beam, were slick with condensation or slime. He could hear the rumble of traffic up above—even late at night it never abated. Sometimes he could hear the metal-on-metal squeal of subway trains banking into a turn on the other side of the sewer wall. There was also the constant background sound of running water; here, the water was only a few inches deep, but elsewhere it ran in a torrent, especially after it had rained.

Ludlam continued to walk along. Progress was always slow: the stone floor was slippery, and Ludlam didn't want to end up yet again falling face forward into the filth.

He paused after a time, and strained to listen. Rats continued to chatter nearby, and there was the sound of a siren, audible through a grate in the sewer roof. But, as always, he failed to hear what he wanted to hear.

It seemed as though the beast would never return.

The double doors to Emergency Admitting swung inward, and ambulance attendants hustled the gurney inside. A blast of ice-cold air, like the ghostly exhaling of a long-dead dragon, followed them into the room from the November night.

Dennis Jacobs, the surgeon on duty, hurried over to the gurney. The injured man's face was bone-white—he had suffered severe blood loss and was deep in shock. One of the attendants pulled back the sheet, exposing the man's left leg. Jacobs carefully removed the mounds of gauze covering the injury site.

A great tract of flesh—perhaps five pounds of meat—had been scooped out of his thigh. If the injury had been another inch or two to the right, the femoral artery would have been clipped, and the man would have bled to death before help could have arrived.

"Who is he?" asked Jacobs.

"Paul Kowalski," said the same attendant who had exposed the leg. "A sewer worker. He'd just gone down a manhole. Something came at him, and got hold of his leg. He hightailed it up the ladder, back onto the street. A passerby found him bleeding all over the sidewalk, and called 911."

Jacobs snapped his fingers at a nurse. "O.R. 3," he said.

On the gurney, Kowalski's eyes fluttered open. His hand reached up and grabbed Jacobs's forearm. "Always heard the stories," said Kowalski, his voice weak. "But never believed they were really there."

"What?" said Jacobs. "What's really there?"

Kowalski's grip tightened. He must have been in excruciating pain. "Gators," he said at last through clenched teeth. "Gators in the sewers."

Around 2:00 A.M., Ludlam decided to call it a night. He began retracing his steps, heading back to where he'd come down. The sewer was cold, and mist swirled in the beam from his flashlight. Something brushed against his foot, swimming through the fetid water. So far, he'd been lucky—nothing had bit him yet.

It was crazy to be down here—Ludlam knew that. But he couldn't give up. Hell, he'd patiently sifted through sand and gravel for years. Was this really that different?

The smell hit him again. Funny how he could ignore it for hours at a time, then suddenly be overpowered by it. He reached up with his left hand, pinched his nostrils shut, and began breathing through his mouth.

Ludlam walked on, keeping his flashlight trained on the ground just a few feet in front of him. As he got closer to his starting point, he tilted the beam up and scanned the area ahead.

His heart skipped a beat.

A dark figure was blocking his way.

Paul Kowalski was in surgery for six hours. Dr. Jacobs and his team repaired tendons, sealed off blood vessels, and more. But the most interesting discovery was made almost at once, as one of Jacobs's assistants was prepping the wound for surgery.

A white, fluted, gently curving cone about four inches long was partially embedded in Kowalski's femur.

A tooth.

"What the hell are you doing down here?" said the man blocking Ludlam's way. He was wearing a stained Sanitation Department jacket.

"I'm Dr. David Ludlam," said Ludlam. "I've got permission." He reached into his raincoat's pocket and pulled out the letter he always carried with him.

The sanitation worker took it and used his own flashlight to read it over. "'Garbologist,'" he said with a snort. "Never heard of it."

"They give a course in it at Columbia," said Ludlam. That much was true, but Ludlam wasn't a garbologist. When he'd first approached the city government, he'd used a fake business card—amazing what you could do these days with a laser printer.

"Well, be careful," said the man. "The sewers are dangerous. A guy I know got a hunk taken out of him by an alligator."

"Oh, come on," said Ludlam, perfectly serious. "There aren't any gators down here."

✧   ✧   ✧

"Thank you for agreeing to see me, Professor Chong," said Jacobs. Chong's tiny office at the American Museum of Natural History was packed floor to ceiling with papers, computer printouts, and books in metal shelving units. Hanging from staggered coat hooks on the wall behind Chong was a stuffed anaconda some ten feet long.

"I treated a man two days ago who said he was bit by an alligator," said Jacobs.

"Had he been down south?" asked Chong.

"No, no. He said it happened here, in New York. He's a sewer worker, and—"

Chong laughed. *"And he said he was bitten by an alligator down in the sewers, right?"*

Jacobs felt his eyebrows lifting. *"Exactly."*

Chong shook his head. *"Guy's trying to file a false insurance claim, betcha anything. There aren't any alligators in our sewers."*

"I saw the wound," said Jacobs. *"Something took a massive bite out of him."*

"This alligators-in-the-sewers nonsense has been floating around for years," said Chong. *"The story is that kids bring home baby gators as pets from vacations in Florida, but when they grow tired of them, they flush 'em down the toilet, and the things end up living in the sewers."*

"Well," said Jacobs, *"that sounds reasonable."*

"It's crap," said Chong. *"We get calls here at the Herpetology Department about that myth from time to time—but that's all it is: a myth. You know how cold it is out there today?"*

"A little below freezing."

"Exactly. Oh, I don't doubt that some alligators have been flushed over the years—people flush all kinds of stuff. But even assuming gators could survive swimming in sewage, the winter temperatures here would kill them. Alligators are cold-blooded, Dr. Jacobs."

Jacobs reached into his jacket pocket and pulled out the tooth. *"We extracted this from the man's thigh,"* he said, placing it on Chong's cluttered desk.

Chong picked it up. *"Seriously?"*

"Yes."

The herpetologist shook his head. *"Well, it's not a gator*

tooth—the root is completely wrong. But reptiles do shed their teeth throughout their lives—it's not unusual for one or more to pop loose during a meal." He ran his thumb lightly over the edge of the tooth. "The margin is serrated," he said. "Fascinating. I've never seen anything quite like it."

Ludlam went down into the sewers again the next night. He wasn't getting enough sleep—it was hard putting in a full day at the museum and then doing this after dark. But if he was right about what was happening . . .

Homeless people sometimes came into the sewers, too. They mostly left Ludlam alone. Some, of course, were schizophrenics—one of them shouted obscenities at Ludlam as he passed him in the dark tunnel that night.

The water flowing past Ludlam's feet was clumpy. He tried not to think about it.

If his theory was right, the best place to look would be near the biggest skyscrapers. As he often did, Ludlam was exploring the subterranean world in the area of the World Trade Center. There, the stresses would be the greatest.

Ludlam exhaled noisily. He thumbed off his flashlight, and waited for his eyes to adjust to the near-total darkness.

After about two minutes, he saw a flash of pale green light about ten feet in front of him.

Jacobs left Chong's office, but decided not to depart the museum just yet. It'd been years since he'd been here—the last time had been when his sister and her kids had come to visit from Iowa. He spent some time looking at various exhibits, and finally made his way into the dinosaur gallery. It had been fully renovated since the last time he'd seen it, and—

Christ.

Jesus Christ.

It wasn't identical, but it was close. Damn close.

The tooth that had been removed from Kowalski's leg looked very much like one of those on the museum's pride and joy—its Tyrannosaurus rex.

Chong had said there couldn't be alligators in New York's sewers.

Alligators were cold-blooded.

But dinosaurs—

*His nephew had told him that last time they were here—
he'd been six back then, and could rattle off endless facts and
figures about the great beasts—*

Dinosaurs had been warm-blooded.

It was crazy.

Crazy.

And yet—

*He had the tooth. He had it right here, in his hand. Ser-
rated, conical, white—*

*White. Not the brown of a fossilized tooth. White and fresh
and modern.*

Dinosaurs in the sewers of New York.

It didn't make any sense. But something *had taken a huge
bite out of Kowalski, and—*

Jacobs ran out of the dinosaur gallery and hurried to the
lobby. There were more dinosaurs there: the museum's rotunda
was dominated by a giant Barosaurus, rearing up on its hind
legs to defend its baby from a marauding allosaur. Jacobs
rushed to the information desk. "I need to see a paleontologist," he panted, gripping the sides of the desk with both arms.

"Sir," said the young woman sitting behind the desk, "if
you'll just calm down, I'll—"

Jacobs fumbled for his hospital ID and dropped it on the
desktop. "I'm a doctor," he said. "It's—it's a medical emergency.
Please hurry. I need to talk to a dinosaur specialist."

A security guard had moved closer to the desk, but the
young woman held him at bay with her eyes. She picked up
a black telephone handset and dialed an extension.

Piezoelectricity.

It had to be the answer, thought Ludlam, as he watched
the pale green light pulsate in front of him.

Piezoelectricity was the generation of electricity in crystals
that have been subjected to stress. He'd read a geological paper
about it once—the skyscrapers in New York are the biggest
in the world, and there are more of them here than anywhere
else. They weigh tens of thousands of tons, and all of that
weight is taken by girders sunk into the ground, transferring
the stress to the rocks beneath. The piezoelectric discharges
caused the flashes of light—

—and maybe, just maybe, caused a whole lot more.

✧   ✧   ✧

"Son of a gun," said David Ludlam, the paleontologist who agreed to speak to Dr. Jacobs. "Son of a gun."

"It's a dinosaur tooth, isn't it?" asked the surgeon.

Ludlam was quiet for a moment, turning the tooth over and over while he stared at it. "Definitely a theropod tooth, yes— but it's not exactly a tyrannosaur, or anything else I've ever seen. Where on Earth did you get it?"

"Out of a man's leg. He'd been bitten."

Ludlam considered this. "The bite—was it a great scooping out, like this?" He gestured with a cupped hand.

"Yes—yes, that's it exactly."

"That's how a tyrannosaur kills, all right. We figure they just did one massive bite, scooping out a huge hunk of flesh, then waited patiently for the prey animal to bleed to death. But—but—"

"Yes?"

"Well, the last tyrannosaur died sixty-five million years ago."

"The asteroid impact, I know—"

"Oh, the asteroid had nothing to do with it. That's just a popular myth; you won't find many paleontologists who endorse it. But all the dinosaurs have been dead since the end of the Cretaceous."

"But this tooth looks fresh to me," said Jacobs.

Ludlam nodded slowly. "It does seem to be, yes." He looked at Jacobs. "I'd like to meet your patient."

Ludlam ran toward the green light.

His feet went out from under him.

He fell down with a great splash, brown water going everywhere. The terminals on his flashlight's giant battery hissed as water rained down on them.

Ludlam scrambled to his feet.

The light was still there.

He hurled himself toward it.

The light flickered and disappeared.

And Ludlam slammed hard against the slimy concrete wall of the sewer.

"Hello, Paul," said Dr. Jacobs. "This is David Ludlam. He's a paleontologist."

"A what?" said Paul Kowalski. He was seated in a wheel-chair. His leg was still bandaged, and a brace made sure he couldn't move his knee while the tendons were still healing.

"A dinosaur specialist," said Ludlam. He was sitting in one of the two chairs in Jacobs's office. "I'm with the American Museum of Natural History."

"Oh, yeah. You got great sewers there."

"Umm, thanks. Look, I want to ask you about the animal that attacked you."

"It was a gator," said Kowalski.

"Why do you say that?"

Kowalski spread his hands. "'Cause it was big and, well, not scaly, exactly, but covered with those little plates you see on gators at the zoo."

"You could see it clearly?"

"Well, not that clearly. I was underground, after all. But I had my flashlight."

"Was there anything unusual about the creature?"

"Yeah—it was some sort of cripple."

"Cripple?"

"It had no arms."

Ludlam looked at Jacobs, then back at the injured man. Jacobs lifted his hands, palms up, in a this-is-news-to-me gesture. "No arms at all?"

"None," said Kowalski. "It had kind of reared up on its legs, and was holding its body like this." He held an arm straight out, parallel to the floor.

"Did you see its eyes?"

"Christ, yes. I'll never forget 'em."

"What did they look like?"

"They were yellow, and—"

"No, no. The pupils. What shape were they?"

"Round. Round and black."

Ludlam leaned back in his chair.

"What's significant about that?" asked Jacobs.

"Alligators have vertical pupils; so do most snakes. But not theropod dinosaurs."

"How do you possibly know that?" said Jacobs. "I thought soft tissues don't fossilize."

"They don't. But dinosaurs had tiny bones inside their eyes; you can tell from them what shape their pupils had been."

"And?"

"Round. But it's something most people don't know."

"You think I'm lying?" said Kowalski, growing angry. "Is that what you think?"

"On the contrary," said Ludlam, his voice full of wonder. "I think you're telling the truth."

"'Course I am," said Kowalski. "I been with the city for eighteen years, and I never took a sick day—you can check on that. I'm a hard worker, and I didn't just imagine this bite." He gestured dramatically at his bandaged leg. But then he paused, as if everything had finally sunk in. He looked from one man to the other. "You guys saying I was attacked by a dinosaur?"

Ludlam lifted his shoulders. "Well, all dinosaurs had four limbs. As you say, the one you saw must have been injured. Was there scarring where its forearms should have been?"

"No. None. Its chest was pretty smooth. I think maybe it was a birth defect—living down in the sewer, and all."

Ludlam exhaled noisily. "There's no way dinosaurs could have survived for sixty-five million years in North America without us knowing it. But . . ." He trailed off.

"Yes?" said Jacobs.

"Well, the lack of arms. You saw the T. rex skeleton we've got at the museum. What did you notice about its arms?"

The surgeon frowned. "They were tiny, almost useless."

"That's right," said Ludlam. "Tyrannosaur arms had been growing smaller and smaller as time went by—more ancient theropods had much bigger arms, and, of course, the distant ancestors of T. rex had walked around on all fours. If they hadn't gone extinct, it's quite conceivable that tyrannosaurs would have eventually lost their arms altogether."

"But they did go extinct," said Jacobs.

Ludlam locked eyes with the surgeon. "I've got to go down there," he said.

Ludlam kept searching, night after night, week after week.

And finally, on a rainy April night a little after 1:00 A.M., he encountered another piezoelectric phenomenon.

The green light shimmered before his eyes.

It grew brighter.

And then—and then—an outline started to appear.

Something big.

Reptilian.

Three meters long, with a horizontally held back, and a stiff tail sticking out to the rear.

Ludlam could see through it—see right through it to the slick wall beyond.

Growing more solid now . . .

The chest was smooth. The thing lacked arms, just as Kowalski had said. But that wasn't what startled Ludlam most.

The head was definitely tyrannosaurid—loaf-shaped, with ridges of bone above the eyes. But the top of the head rose up in a high dome.

Tyrannosaurs hadn't just lost their arms over tens of millions of years of additional evolution. They'd apparently also become more intelligent. The domed skull could have housed a sizable brain.

The creature looked at Ludlam with round pupils. Ludlam's flashlight was shaking violently in his hand, causing mad shadows to dance behind the dinosaur.

The dinosaur had *faded* in.

What if the dinosaurs hadn't become extinct? It was a question Ludlam had pondered for years. Yes, in this reality, they had succumbed to—to something, no one knew exactly what. But in another reality—in another *timeline*—perhaps they hadn't.

And here, in the sewers of New York, piezoelectric discharges were causing the timelines to merge.

The creature began moving. It was clearly solid now, clearly *here*. Its footfalls sent up great splashes of water.

Ludlam froze. His head wanted to move forward, to approach the creature. His heart wanted to run as fast as he possibly could in the other direction.

His head won.

The dinosaur's mouth hung open, showing white conical teeth. There were some gaps—this might indeed have been the same individual that attacked Kowalski. But Kowalski had been a fool—doubtless he'd tried to run, or to ward off the approaching beast.

Ludlam walked slowly toward the dinosaur. The creature tilted its head to one side, as if puzzled. It could have decapitated Ludlam with a single bite, but for the moment it seemed merely curious. Ludlam reached up gently, placing his flat palm softly against the beast's rough, warm hide.

The dinosaur's chest puffed out, and it let loose a great roar. The sound started long and loud, but soon it was attenuating, growing fainter—

—as was the beast itself.

Ludlam felt a tingling over his entire body, and then pain shooting up into his brain, and then a shiver that ran down his spine as though a cold hand were touching each vertebra in turn, and then he was completely blind, and then there was a flash of absolutely pure, white light, and then—

—and then, he was there.

On the other side.

In the other timeline.

Ludlam had been in physical contact with the dinosaur as it had returned home, and he'd been swept back to the other side with it.

It had been nighttime in New York, and, of course, it was nighttime here. But the sky was crystal clear, with, just as it had been back in the other timeline, the moon perfectly full. Ludlam saw stars twinkling overhead—in precisely the patterns he was used to seeing whenever he got away from the city's lights.

This was the present day, and it was Manhattan Island — but devoid of skyscrapers, devoid of streets. They were at the bank of a river—a river long ago buried in the other timeline as part of New York's sanitation system.

The tyrannosaur was standing next to Ludlam. It looked disoriented, and was rocking back and forth on its two legs, its stiff tail almost touching the ground at the end of each arc.

The creature eyed Ludlam.

It had no arms; therefore, it had no technology. But Ludlam felt sure there must be a large brain beneath that domed skull. Surely it would recognize that Ludlam meant it no harm— and that his scrawny frame would hardly constitute a decent meal.

The dinosaur stood motionless. Ludlam opened his mouth in a wide, toothy grin—

—and the great beast did the same thing—

—and Ludlam realized his mistake—

A territorial challenge.

He ran as fast as he could.

Thank God for arms. He managed to clamber up a tree, out of reach of the tyrannosaur's snapping jaws.

He looked up. A pterosaur with giant furry wings moved across the face of the moon. Glorious.

He *would* have to be careful here.

But he couldn't imagine any place he'd rather be.

Sixty-five million years of additional evolution! And not the boring, base evolution of mice and moles and monkeys. No, this was *dinosaurian* evolution. The ruling reptiles, the terrible lizards—the greatest creatures the Earth had ever known, their tenure uninterrupted. The way the story of life was really meant to unfold. Ludlam's heart was pounding, but with excitement, not fear, as he looked down from his branch at the tyrannosaur-like being, its lean, muscled form stark in the moonlight.

He'd wait till morning, and then he'd try again to make friends with the dinosaur.

But—hot damn!—he was so pleased to be here, it *was* going to be a real struggle to keep from grinning.

She of the Night

Laura Resnick and Kathy Chwedyk

She walked into my office—and into my life—just as I was contemplating closing five minutes early and heading down to Joey's Bar to see if my credit was still good there.

Business was slow. To tell the truth, clients had lately been about as plentiful as honest politicians, and there were moments when I almost regretted turning down my brother-in-law's offer, right after the war, to partner him in a fishing tackle and bait business out on Staten Island. After all, he worked regular hours and made enough to keep a decent roof over my sister's head. They ate three squares a day—roast chicken every Sunday—and were saving up to buy a house.

Meanwhile, I . . . ah, I made my living, if you can call it that, by snooping around people's private problems, ferreting out the sorry little secrets of their sorry little lives: a broken wedding vow; a few bucks pocketed from the cash register; the real dirt on a fortune-hunting lothario; a runaway girl who didn't want to go back home. Truth is, I was just starting to agree with my brother-in-law's notion that this was no life for a grown man . . . when *she* walked in.

The sun was just disappearing somewhere beyond New Jersey, and the room was lost in shadow. Since I figured I couldn't count on charity from the utilities company, I hadn't even turned on my desk lamp. (In fact, if I didn't get a new client soon, I'd be doing business from a park bench before long.) The setting sun—and the neon sign from the hotel across the street—gave the room a red-orange glow. It looked like

15

fire dancing over her skin. It looked so good, I still didn't turn on a light.

She was exotic in a way that fan-dancers and silent screen stars only tried to be. Earthy, like the girls in Sicily, where we landed before fighting our way up through Italy inch by bloody inch. Beautiful, like . . . well, not like anything I'd ever seen. Hair as black and shiny as polished obsidian hung down her back. Her kohl-rimmed eyes were almost that dark, and her unpainted lips glistened like she'd just been well-kissed. She wore a black evening gown of some shimmery, clinging material, the like of which I'd never seen before. It left her arms bare and hugged her body like a jealous lover. The slit only went up to her knee, but it was enough to make me forget what few social graces I had ever possessed. She wore an ankle bracelet that matched the thick gold ornaments twining like snakes around the smooth, ripe flesh of her upper arms. I stared like a hungry dog about to be served its first meal in a week.

She was the one who finally broke the silence: "Mr. MacPherson?"

"Yes." I stopped staring long enough to stand up and offer her a seat. She glided forward and slid into the chair, moving as smoothly as water. "How can I help you, Miss, er, ma'am . . ."

Now that she was closer, I could see she was no spring chicken. But, who cared? She was a woman of a certain age, as the Frenchies would say; like a vintage Rolls Royce, she had many a smooth, comfortable ride left on that elegant chassis.

Her head swayed slowly back and forth, chin stuck out. "My name is Lilith."

"Lilith," I repeated. "That's, uh, very pretty."

She nodded once to acknowledge the compliment. Those dark, unblinking eyes held my gaze with an intensity that tied my tongue into a knot and made my mind go blank.

Well, maybe it was her gaze; or maybe it was the way that dress clung to her ripe curves like a second skin.

Calm and poised, unlike most people seeking out my services, she began, "This is a delicate matter."

It usually was.

"It involves a man?" You only had to look at Lilith to figure it *had* to involve a man.

"Yes," she replied. "A man who has taken advantage of me." I nodded and urged her to tell me everything, assuring her that talking to me was like confiding in a priest. There were, of course, a few big differences between me and a priest, but we could get around to that later. I leaned forward in anticipation.

Her husband, Hugo Adams, had ditched her for a younger woman, one of those adolescent, dewy-eyed, adoring types whose idea of a creative outlet was trying on lipstick samples at the cosmetics counter at Woolworth's. Her name was Evie. She followed Hugo around as if they were joined at the hip, and hung on his every word.

The guy probably didn't know how to satisfy a real woman, I thought smugly. Why else would he leave a classy dame like Lilith for a snot-nosed kid?

After Adams left Lilith, he tried to talk her into giving him the mink coat he'd bought her as an anniversary present right before he left her. No doubt, Lilith said wryly, it was a guilt offering. His new wife had seen Lilith wear the coat, and she was obsessed with the thing. Evie insisted that if Adams truly loved her, he would get it for her. After all, he had bought and paid for it. Evie found a receipt from the furrier's shop among his belongings that said so.

Adams offered to buy Lilith a new coat—a more expensive one—if she would just give up the mink.

"Of course, I refused. It's *mine*. I've *made* it mine, and no one else can have it." Lilith spoke the words with passionate, possessive intensity, but with more dignity than you'd expect of the usual scorned woman. "That coat . . . is extremely precious to me."

Adams's child-bride whined and pouted and nagged until he was desperate to appease her.

"In the end," Lilith concluded, "he stole it from me."

I rubbed my chin, feeling the rough stubble of a five o'clock shadow. "So you want me to get the coat back for you, is that it?"

"Precisely."

If there was one thing I hated even more than eating boiled cabbage, it was disappointing a beautiful woman.

"Look, I'm sorry ma'am . . . uh, Lilith. The problem is, Adams bought and paid for this coat. He has the receipt for it, and possession of it." I shrugged apologetically. "Even if you could prove that Adams gave you the coat—"

"I can prove it's mine," she snapped.

I found myself staring at the way the fading orange-red light shifted and played on her skin. She almost seemed to glow, like some half-dreamed creature of the night.

Coming to my senses with a start, I turned on a desk lamp. The sudden intrusion of bright light startled her. She jumped so fast that I scarcely even saw her move. One moment she'd been sitting in the chair; the next, she was hovering by the door, her chest rising and falling as she tried to recover her poise.

Even now, I noticed, she didn't blink.

"Sorry," I said. "I didn't mean to—"

"That's quite all right, Mr. MacPherson." She glided forward, but didn't sit down again. She looked twice as good in the light, I discovered.

I returned to the matter at hand—but it took some effort. "You say you can prove the coat belongs to you. How?"

"It would be too late by then," she muttered.

"Excuse me?"

She frowned slightly. It was the first time her face had shown any expression, I realized with surprise; her voice and body conveyed far more than her face.

After a long pause, she said, "Actually, offering proof would be . . . extremely awkward."

"Well, then—"

"So I would like to hire you to buy the coat back from Hugo for me. I'll offer him double what he paid for it."

"Why don't you just buy it from him?"

"Because a man is never reasonable when dealing with his ex-wife, Mr. MacPherson." There was a terrible bitterness in her voice. "Not when he has a pretty young wife to impress."

"I'm sorry," I found myself saying.

"I have the money here in cash." She reached into her shiny evening bag and pulled out an envelope stuffed with money. Then she pulled out an additional $250 and gave it to me. "I'll pay you another two-hundred-fifty if you succeed," she promised.

"That's . . . very generous." The money swayed my judgment. I accepted the job. Even if I couldn't get Adams to cooperate, this $250 would keep the wolf from the door for awhile. I didn't bother to wonder where Lilith had gotten the money. The lady obviously had her sources. That gold jewelry she wore looked like it was worth more than my brother-in-law made in a year.

Lilith placed her hands on my desk and leaned over. I didn't even try to keep my eyes on her face this time. "Bring me my coat by this time tomorrow evening, Mr. MacPherson, and I promise you I'll be generous with more than my money."

To be honest, I was willing to bodily assault Mrs. Adams to get that coat back.

Unfortunately, Adams wasn't prepared to be any more reasonable with me than he was with his ex-wife. It didn't matter how much Lilith was willing to pay for the coat he had originally given her, he was simply too infatuated with his new wife to try to get it back. Watching him whine and sweat while we talked in his office the day after Lilith had come to see me, I wondered what the hell she had ever seen in the guy. There's just no figuring women, is there?

"Maybe you could swipe the coat the next time your wife goes out," I suggested, "and let her believe it was stolen. Then you could buy a replacement with the money Lilith—"

"My wife wears it every time she goes out."

"This time of year? Isn't it a little warm for—?"

"Nonetheless, she wears it everywhere she goes," he said fretfully. "Always."

"Likes it that much, eh?"

"I told Lilith I'd get her a new one as soon as I could, but she simply wouldn't see reason."

"So you stole it from her."

"I retrieved it," he said defensively. "And Lilith went positively berserk. You'd think I had taken away her first-born, the way she was acting."

"What is it about this particular coat?" I asked him, never having seen it.

"Damned if I know." Adams shook his head. "*Women.*"

I kind of had to agree with him on that score.

He leaned forward. "You seem like a decent fellow, MacPherson, despite your profession. So, let me give you a word of advice that I wish someone would have given me."

"What's that?"

"Be careful around Lilith." His eyes focused intensely on something quite distant from me and his stuffy office. "She's not like anyone else. She is . . . lawless. Outside of the normal order of things."

"Thanks for the tip." I put on my hat and left.

We met towards evening in an overgrown corner of Central Park, just as Lilith had instructed me. Shadows lengthened and snaked through the trees, sliding silently around their dark trunks, creeping sinuously across the ground as the sky gave up the sun. Born and bred to city life, I've never understood what some people find so appealing about grass, mud, and trees crawling with worms and insects. If Lilith didn't want to travel all the way downtown to my office once again, why couldn't we have met in her apartment, or in a coffee shop? Why did she insist upon meeting here, in the midst of New York City's sorry attempt at wilderness?

I didn't enjoy having to tell her that I'd failed to get the coat back. I *especially* didn't enjoy doing it surrounded by those squatting trees and crawling shadows. Too much strong coffee and too many cigarettes on an empty stomach can make a man a little jumpy, after all.

"I *must* have that coat back!" Lilith hissed furiously when I finished breaking the bad news.

"Where are you going?" I asked as she whirled away from me, her hair flying around her like a dark cape.

"To find Hugo!"

"Lilith, wait—"

"I can't!" she insisted. "Not any longer."

I could see this wasn't going to be easy. Dressed exactly as she had been the night before, she glided swiftly through the tall grass and shadows, weaving a path in and out of the trees. I followed, occasionally stumbling as darkness descended, and tried to make her see reason.

It was a black tie, charity affair in a millionaire's penthouse overlooking the park, but Lilith walked right past the security guard with a disdainful sniff when he asked to see her invitation.

When he tried to insist, she turned a look on him that made

him cringe against the wall. A trick of the artificial light made her eyes appear to glow red.

She spotted Adams and his child-bride before I did, and approached them with a single-minded concentration they obviously found unnerving.

The new wife—a petite, dimpled blonde—wore the long, honey mink coat open down the front to partially display a wispy blue chiffon frock and a lot of pale, chubby flesh. She wore a diamond choker so thick it made her neck disappear.

Evie licked her lips nervously.

"He's mine," she said triumphantly as she placed a possessive hand on her husband's arm. "I'll never give him up."

Lilith gave her a slow, malicious smile.

"My dear, you are entirely welcome to Hugo. He's served his purpose. It's the coat I want."

"You can't have it!" Evie cried. "Tell her, Hugie!"

"Lilith, you have no business here," Adams said in a voice about an octave higher than usual. "If you had any decency you would leave before you cause a scene."

"Give me the coat and I'll gladly disappear from your life," she said calmly. "Deny me, and I'll become your worst nightmare."

"You already *are* my worst nightmare." Sweat glistened on his forehead and upper lip.

People were whispering and staring, titillated by the sordid little scene.

"Ah, my friends," Lilith said sweetly, looking around at them. "A few months ago, *I* was the beautiful woman on his arm. The discarded wife is *such* an embarrassment, isn't she?"

A distinguished man in a tuxedo, obviously the host, bustled forward with two security guards in tow.

"Lilith, you'll have to leave," he said quietly.

"Not quite yet, Leo, darling," she said. "Not until I get back what he stole from me." She glared at Evie. "Does it please you to wear the coat he bought for another woman?" she taunted her. "I'll give you some fashion advice, Evie. Big, bushy furs make squabbish little twits like you look fat."

"Hugie, make her stop!" Evie's pink, round cheeks puffed up with anger, and her blue eyes were narrowed to bad-tempered slits. "You're just jealous."

"You are a tiresome little fool," Lilith said, staring at Evie so hard the girl started to squirm. "Give—me—the—coat!"

I swear Lilith didn't lay a hand on her, but suddenly Evie was shrieking in a high-pitched, whiny voice.

The kid had a great set of lungs and a serious adenoid condition—not an attractive combination. People were backing away from her in distaste.

"They're biting me!" she screamed. "She is doing this to me! I know it! Hugie, make her stop!"

Evie was quivering and shuddering and batting at the sleeves of the coat, which seemed to be pulsing and wriggling of their own volition.

"My babies!" cried Lilith triumphantly. "At last!"

Lilith threw Evie to the ground and tried to wrest the coat from off her back. Adams grabbed Lilith's arms and tried to pull her away from his wife.

"Hugie!" wailed Evie.

The coat lay wrong-side out, half-way off Evie, and I saw the snouts of little creatures poke through the thick satin lining. Tiny, pointed pink tongues flicked in and out of ghastly little fanged mouths.

"My darlings," crooned Lilith. She threw Adams off as if he had been nothing more than a pesky insect. He landed against the wall, nursing his wrist.

By then, women were screaming, sirens were blaring, and all holy hell was breaking loose.

Lilith had sunk to the ground and was gathering the little serpent-like creatures into the infested fur as if to keep the hatchlings warm. Whimpering, Evie had backed away from Lilith and the creatures until she was halfway under the refreshment table. Her bare arms were red from little scratch and bite marks.

Adams lurched to his feet and carefully stepped around Lilith. I didn't pay much attention to him because I was staring at Lilith and the ghastly little creatures, and I figured he was only going to comfort his wife.

Instead, though, he grabbed a flaming chafing dish from the buffet table and threw it at the coat. The thing immediately ignited and the air was filled with the sounds of a thousand screams being torn from a thousand tiny throats. I grabbed Lilith and threw her to the ground under me just in time to save her from going up in flames with them.

"My babies!" she cried out in anguish.

I'm no lightweight, but she lifted me bodily and shook me like a dog before she dropped me to the floor.

She seemed to grow in stature, and her eyes glowed blood red. Her hair stood up on end and crackled with static electricity.

"You should have let me die with them!" she cried, stretching her arms toward me. "My precious hatchlings! I thought at last I'd found a way to hide my eggs from those who would kill them, but that man and this pathetic creature he calls wife have defeated me again.

"Hear me now, mortal," Lilith continued, turning those glowing eyes on her ex-husband. "Someday I will bring my children into the world, and they will feed upon your seed until your kind is destroyed. I will have my revenge."

Evie's doughy face dissolved into huge, gulping sobs, and Adams enfolded her in his arms.

"There, there, precious," he said, patting her on the back. "She can't harm us now."

An evil grin stretched Lilith's mouth.

"You don't think so?" the demon woman said, lifting one eyebrow. "You haven't seen the last of me yet. Either of you. You think she's so perfect and submissive? Your adoring little wife is going to bring you a lot of grief someday. And you are going to deserve every minute of it."

"Hugie, I would never hurt you," Evie whimpered. "She's just mean and jealous because you love me."

"I know that, darling. You stay away from us," Adams said to Lilith, quaking with fear.

"Go away!" wailed Evie. "You don't belong here."

"Gladly," said Lilith in contempt. "Mr. MacPherson, will you escort me?"

She was magnificent. In the midst of the very chaos she had caused, she was more poised and dignified than any of them. Every hair on her beautifully sculpted head was back in place. Her arms glittered with gold again, and for the first time I noticed the sinuous forms had golden heads with ruby inset eyes and pointed snouts. I didn't understand what had happened; as I gazed into Lilith's eyes and saw the open invitation there, I didn't care. Gingerly, I crooked my arm and she placed hers within it. I adjusted my steps to her graceful, swaying walk.

"Look, ah, Lilith," I said as we passed the security guard's station again. It was empty, and when we went out the door we could hear sirens blaring. People who had been in the penthouse were talking excitedly to several police officers. No one attempted to stop us as we crossed the cordoned-off area and went into the park.

"Yes, Mr. MacPherson?" she replied politely. She sounded so *normal*.

"I don't quite understand . . ."

Her hand was cool and smooth as she touched my cheek. "You don't *need* to understand."

"But what were those . . ."

I lost my train of thought as she concentrated the full power of that unblinking gaze on me. I suddenly couldn't even remember what I'd been trying to say. The street lights glowed on her lush skin, and her smile made me tremble with anticipation.

"Come," she whispered, taking my hand. We left the world behind as she led me back into the time-shattering shadows of the park after dark.

She lay down in the cool darkness beneath a massive oak tree and enfolded me in her embrace. I felt as if my body had been drained dry by the time she was through with me.

"MacPherson," she murmured when it was over. She touched my face again. That fleeting caress seemed more intimate than what we'd just done. "The instrument of my revenge."

I stared at her in the dark. Her eyes seemed to glow red again.

"Revenge?" I repeated, feeling uneasy.

I wished I could believe that Lilith was one of those women who screwed the first man who came along to even the score when their husbands had done them wrong. It wouldn't be flattering, but I could live with that. However, this seemed like more than a grudge. Well, let's just say, I felt in my bones it wasn't that simple.

"Your holy book describes it well enough," she said, "but I don't suppose you've read it. Mortals don't seem to pay as much attention to such things as they did when the world was young. Fortunately for me."

"Uh, Lilith," I said as her shadow fell across me again. Her passionate embraces were like water flung on a drowning man, but, unable to help myself, I fell under her spell again. And again after that.

The whole time she was talking. Reciting something just under her breath. Although I only caught snatches of it, the intensity in her voice both scared and enthralled me.

"Wild cats will meet hyenas there," she whispered as her dry, rough tongue flicked against my ear, "satyr will call to satyr, there Lilith too will lurk and find somewhere to rest."

There was more, but the words didn't make sense, and my mind was clouded and lost in the wonder of her.

Dawn was breaking when I opened my eyes. At first I didn't see her. She was standing next to the trunk of a massive tree, and the texture of her dress blended in so perfectly with the roughened, dark wood that her head seemed to be suspended on the air in front of it.

"Ah, you live, after all," she said, smiling. "You are a strong one, then."

Dazed, I managed to smile back, even though every muscle in my body burned like fire.

"I must go," she said, without regret or apology.

"But . . . will I see you again?" I asked.

"You'll see me again, mortal," she promised. The expression in her eyes was fierce and triumphant. "You'll *all* see me again."

To my horror, she seemed to shrink, and her head grew narrow and rather pointed. The black scales shimmered in the moonlight as she sank to the ground. Her arms and legs had disappeared.

"Lilith," I whispered.

The graceful dark serpent slithered sinuously past me and slowly sank into a hole into the ground.

Stunned and disbelieving, I sat for a long time staring at the spot where she had disappeared. I felt so weak I thought I would die there, but after a while I found the strength to drag myself to my feet. Something crinkled in my breast pocket when I reached for a long-overdue cigarette.

Two-hundred-fifty dollars in cash. I'd spent the first $250. She'd made the final payment, even though the coat she'd wanted so badly was toast.

For services rendered, I thought wearily. I felt groggy. As

if I had been drinking nonstop for a week, and this was the mother of all hangovers.

It was only after I was back at my desk in my shabby office that I remembered the rest of what she was saying while she lay with me in the dark.

"The snake will nest and lay eggs there, will hatch and gather its young into the shade; and there the vultures will assemble, each one with its mate."

I knew then why she had paid me. She didn't need the coat anymore or the hatchlings that had perished when Adams torched it.

Thanks to me.

Lilith would come back, all right.

I wasn't sure I wanted to be alive when she did.

The Spider in the Hairdo

Michael A. Burstein

The metal shell, small enough to fit in a human's hand, landed gently upon the pavement. After a long minute, during which the occupant's sleeping consciousness established that its hundred-light-year journey was at an end, the shell cracked open. The two halves of the shell, built to withstand the cold, hard vacuum of empty space, fell apart perfectly and rattled against the ground. They wobbled for a few seconds, then were still.

The spider emerged from the shell and felt the air around it, warm and humid. It stretched its eight long legs and let its black body fur stand up on edge, probing the sunlight shining above. Briefly, it extended its needle-shaped proboscis from the mouth in its underbelly, stopping it before it hit the ground. Its body felt fully functional.

Immediately, images flooded the spider's mind, images meant to be triggered as soon as the spider was free of its shell. The spider shuddered at images of a home planet, far away, threatened with destruction. It paused at images of its own race threatened with extinction. Finally, it contemplated the images of a last-ditch effort to save its own kind, and to spread its people among the stars.

The spider now remembered why it had been sent out as one of millions, so long ago. The stimulus that had triggered the opening of its shell on this particular planet was electromagnetic radiation, a definite sign of intelligence of some sort, intelligence that could be bent to the spider's will.

It scurried away in search of an easily manipulated human mind.

✧   ✧   ✧

Peggy hated Mondays. It meant going back to school and, although home life was no great shakes, school wasn't much fun either. Especially now that, as a ninth grader, she had been forced to attend a new school, a long bus ride from her home. Why couldn't she have been sent to Forest Hills High School with all her friends from Russell Sage? No, she had been sent to Hillcrest, in Jamaica.

This morning, she had managed to avoid her tormentors when walking from class to class. Lunchtime, now, and as always, she waited until the hallway was empty before heading to her locker for her bag lunch.

She had just started to work the combination lock when she heard Roxanne's voice. "Hey! Fatgirl!"

Damn. She must have gotten wise to Peggy last week, when Peggy made a point of going to the lockers late. Peggy stopped fiddling with the lock and began a quick trot in the direction away from Roxanne's voice. "Hey! Come back here, girl!"

Her bookbag, an old blue one from L.L.Bean, fell off her shoulder as she ran. She skidded to a stop and backtracked to retrieve it.

Unfortunately, that gave Roxanne the time she needed to catch up. Before Peggy could pick up her bookbag, Roxanne grabbed her arm, lightly. Peggy noticed that two of Roxanne's friends were with her, jeering. "Hey, Fatgirl, didn't you hear me?"

Peggy squirmed. She hated the way Roxanne and her cronies all called her by that name. She wasn't fat, just plump. "Roxanne, go away."

"Aw, c'mon, I just wanted to say hello."

"Yeah, right. Just leave me alone." She twisted her arm free.

Roxanne spat at her, getting her blouse wet. "I don't know why they couldn't keep you losers in Forest Hills." With that, she walked away, her two leeches close behind.

Peggy watched them walk away, and wiped away the beginnings of tears in her eyes. If only they would leave her alone. She bent over, picked up her bookbag, and hooked it over her right shoulder.

She didn't notice the spider that had crawled into her bookbag.

✧   ✧   ✧

The spider had found the perfect host. A body small in stature, but wide in girth. Someone isolated from her community, feeling dejected, depressed. . . .

Vulnerable.

It needed to get closer to her, physically closer, for a period of a few days. That was the only way it could ensure the survival of its race. But how could it stay unnoticed on the skin of the creature for such a long period of time?

Delving below the level of language and conscious thought, the spider probed the creature's unconscious mind. It began to grasp more fully the social pains of the creature, and realized a way it could work this to its advantage. The spider readied itself for a direct onslaught into the creature's mind, to bend her to its will.

Dinner was always a chore. As an only child, Peggy had to bear the total brunt of her parents' questions. Sometimes it made her too sick to eat.

Her mother passed the meatloaf. "So how was your day at school, sweetheart?"

Her father passed the potatoes. "Meet any nice guys yet?" He laughed loudly.

Peggy poked at her food. "Everything's fine," she mumbled.

Her mother passed the peas. "You know, your father has a point. When I was your age—"

Peggy interrupted her. "Mom, may I be excused?"

Her mother paused in passing the gravy. "But, honey, you haven't finished your—"

"Mother, I don't feel well. I need to lie down. *Please?*"

Her mother nodded. "Okay, hon, but I'll leave your plate in the fridge in case you feel better later."

"Thank you." Peggy jumped out of her chair and ran down the hallway to her bedroom. As soon as the door was safely shut behind her, she collapsed onto her bed, squeezed one of her many teddy bears, and began to cry.

After she had let it all out, she sat up in bed and reached over to her night table for a tissue.

"I wish I were more popular."

I can help you with that.

She jerked her head around. "Who said that?"

Just think of me as a friend. I can help you with your problem.

She turned her head around, a little more methodically. There was no one near her. "How?"

Advice. What makes other kids more popular?

She shrugged. Perhaps it was just her own mind, helping her focus on her problems. "I dunno. Looks, clothes—"

There you go. Looks. Why don't you change yours?

She laughed bitterly. "It's not that easy. I've tried losing weight."

It doesn't have to be something elaborate. Perhaps something simple, like—like your hair.

"My hair?" Peggy's hands flew to her hair, and she pulled a strand in front of her face to examine it. It always struck her as being a dull brownish sort of color. She wore it long and straight, just because she could never think of what else to do with it.

Why not surprise them at school with a new hairdo? Something—retro. That would get their attention.

Peggy nodded, slowly. "Yeah. That might work. But what—wait! I know."

She rushed into the living room and pulled one of her parents' old photo albums down from the shelf. She paged through it. "I remember Mom showing me a picture once—there!"

The photograph, yellow on the edges, showed a picture of her mother at the same age Peggy was now, fifteen. She wore a purple sweater and a long white skirt with an embroidered poodle. But her hair! Her hair was coiffed up in curls that wrapped around themselves, forming an unfinished cone with the top of her head at the base. A beehive hairdo, that was what they called it. No one wore those anymore.

"What do you think?" Peggy asked out loud.

Perfect.

The next afternoon, once the usual annoyances at school were over, Peggy headed to the Kevork hair salon just off Queens Boulevard. She had brought the photograph of her mother along to show the hairdresser exactly what she wanted.

The hairdresser looked at the photograph, then at Peggy. She chewed on her gum, blew a bubble which popped, and studied Peggy's hair. Peggy shuffled and lowered her eyes to the linoleum floor. She already felt out of place, with the middle-aged women around and the speakers playing Muzak. The hairdresser wasn't helping.

Finally, the woman spoke. "Why wouldja want to do this for?"

"I want to be popular," Peggy whispered.

The hairdresser barked a laugh. "This ain't the fifties, kid. Go home." She handed the photograph back.

Peggy felt dejected and embarrassed. She turned on her heel to leave, when she heard the voice. *Don't listen to her. She doesn't know what she's talking about. Stand your ground.*

Peggy turned back to face the hairdresser. "I want a beehive. Will you do it? If not, I'll go somewhere else."

The hairdresser sighed. "Okay, kid. The customer is always right."

It took about an hour to do Peggy's hair, an hour which passed very quickly for Peggy. Neither she nor the hairdresser noticed the tiny spider which crawled into the hairdo just as the hairdresser was putting the finishing touches on the style. As the last curl in the hair was made, the spider was securely locked in.

The cost was forty dollars. Fortunately, Peggy had managed to steal a fifty from her mother's purse that morning. She paid the hairdresser and strutted out the door.

"You'll knock 'em dead, kid," the hairdresser called to her as the door swung closed.

Peggy ran all the way home, constantly patting her hair to reassure herself that the beehive was still there. She panted, breathless, as she ran into her house. "Mom! Dad! Take a look!"

Her mother emerged from the kitchen, her father from the living room. They both stopped short when they saw her.

"What do you think?" Peggy asked, turning all the way around. She could feel herself blushing with anticipation.

"Oh, Peggy, I don't *believe* it!" her mother exclaimed. Her father just laughed, louder and longer then she had ever heard him laugh before.

"I mean," her mother continued, "a *beehive* hairdo! Why on *Earth* would you go and do something like that?"

She stared her mother right in the eyes. "To make me more popular."

Her father laughed more at that, tears streaming down his cheeks. "I remember when your mother got one. But Peggy! No one gets them anymore."

"Well, *I* did. And I like it." She jutted her jaw out, defying her father to contradict her.

Her mother glared at her father, who stopped laughing. "Oh, Peggy," she said. "That's not going to make you popular. Those went out with poodle skirts."

Don't listen to her, said the voice. *The hairdo is perfect.*

"It's perfect, Mom."

Her mother shrugged. "Whatever you wish, honey. Come, it's time to eat."

After dinner, Peggy went straight to bed, her neck on the pillow and her head against the wall so as not to disturb her precious new hairdo. She was so excited about her new hairdo that it took her a long time to drift off to sleep.

The spider burrowed deep within the hairdo, exploring the warmth of its new, very temporary, home. It crawled around for a few hours, enjoying the sensations of another being's hair tingling against its body, and ingesting nutrients from the chemicals with which the hair had been treated. When the host went to sleep, it got to work.

The spider crawled down to the bottom of the hairdo, and found the tiny open spot of skin on its host's scalp, the point from which hairs whorled outward. Very gently, the spider settled its legs around this spot, so as to maintain stability as the host moved around. Slowly, it extended its proboscis out of its underbelly. The point of the needle, covered with one drop of a green sticky liquid, pierced the skin of the host's scalp with ease.

Exuding what, to the spider, was a sigh of pleasure and contentment, it began pumping liquid into the host's scalp, emptying its eggsac as gingerly as possible.

The host slept on, peaceful and oblivious.

The next morning was Wednesday, and Peggy woke up early. She had a slight headache, but her eagerness to show off her new hairdo overcame any thoughts of staying home. She tapped her feet impatiently waiting for the city bus, and when it let her off at the stop half a block away from Hillcrest, she ran to the school door as fast as her feet could take her.

She went to the lockers to drop off her lunch. Usually she

waited until just before homeroom, when Roxanne and her friends would be elsewhere, and sometimes that made her late for class. But this time, Peggy made a deliberate point of going to the lockers early.

Naturally, Roxanne was there. Pretending to ignore her, Peggy walked up to her locker and opened the combination lock, all the while humming. There were other kids around as well, and as she secured her lunch she noticed that slowly, conversations died out, and everyone went silent.

Peggy pasted a big grin on her face, and turned around to see everyone's reaction.

It was not what she had expected. Most of the kids stared at her, with their jaws hanging open or their heads shaking. A few looked puzzled, and whispered to their neighbors.

Finally, Roxanne maneuvered her way through the crowd, her two companions close behind. She studied Peggy's hair intently, then burst out, "Girl, whadja go and do that for? You look like a beauty school reject."

She began to laugh, and her companions joined in. Soon the entire crowd of Peggy's peers were laughing at her.

"I thought it would look good," Peggy heard herself say. That just made them laugh louder.

Then the voice comforted her. *It does look good.*

"It does look good," Peggy repeated aloud.

It will make you popular.

"It's going to make me popular." She turned on her heel and walked off to homeroom, holding herself as high as she could.

In the end, the only people she managed to impress with her hairdo all day were her teachers, or at least the older ones. A lot of the kids had teased her, and some adults had gently suggested that she change it back. But, as she went to bed that night feeling more tired than usual, she knew that her beehive hairdo would make her the most popular girl in school, in just a few days or a week. The voice told her so.

The spider continued to inject the green sticky liquid into the host, but at a slower pace. It moved from spot to spot on the host's scalp, as each injection point became too inflamed to hold its proboscis steady. But the spider had a problem. It had not anticipated how weak this host became in such a

*short time. Another night or two of injections would be nec-
essary. The spider reached into the host's dreams as she slept,
projecting images that would ensure that she leave its home
intact for that long.*

The next day, Peggy's headache felt a lot worse. During her
morning English class, Ms. Carberg expressed concern about
how pale she looked.

"I feel fine," she lied. In truth, she felt a little dizzy.

"I don't think so, Peggy. I'm sending you to the nurse's
office."

Peggy knew the nurse, Ms. Matthews, because she also
served as her Health Education teacher. She made Peggy lie
down on a couch, but Peggy kept her head and hairdo upright.
Then Ms. Matthews stuck a thermometer in her mouth and
looked at it after about a minute.

"It's a little high. Are you feeling all right?"

"Well," Peggy said, "I have been getting these headaches."

"Hmm." She reached into her desk drawer and took out
a small plastic bottle. "I'm going to give you two aspirin to
take. If you start feeling any worse, you should consider going
home."

"Okay." Peggy slowly lifted herself off of the couch and
stood up. She quickly sat down.

"I'm still a little dizzy, I guess."

Ms. Matthews nodded and gave her the aspirin and a paper
cup filled with water. Peggy swallowed the pills and handed
the empty cup back. Then she closed her eyes, getting her
breath back.

"You know," Ms. Matthews said, "it could be your hair."

Peggy's eyes flew open. "What?"

"Well, perhaps your beehive is a little tight. Maybe we
should undo it."

"Undo it? Well—" A wave of fear swept through Peggy,
strengthening her resolve. She heard the voice in her head.
Do not undo the hairdo.

"No!" She jumped up, feeling recovered. "Leave my hair
alone!"

"Peggy, relax." Ms. Matthews reached out and took her hand.
"If you don't want to undo your hair, you don't have to."

Peggy pulled her hand away. "Don't touch my hair!"

Ms. Matthews held up her hands, palms forward. "I won't, I won't. Are you feeling better now?"

Peggy nodded, slowly. "Yeah, I guess so."

"Better get to your next class, then."

For the rest of the day and on Friday, the other teenagers tended to ignore Peggy. Except for Roxanne, of course, who ribbed her, mostly about her hair. But Peggy ignored her, as she knew that the hairdo would eventually make her popular. When going to bed both nights, she thought about undoing it, as Ms. Matthews had suggested; but each morning, she awoke with a firm resolve to keep every hair in place.

The headaches did cause her problems over the weekend, though. She had trouble concentrating on her work. So instead of going out or doing anything after finishing her homework, she slept for twelve hours straight on both days, and that seemed to help when Monday morning arrived.

By her afternoon Geometry class, however, Peggy once again felt weak. She usually paid close attention at the beginning of class, when Mr. Hakner sent students to the blackboard to work out last night's homework, but this afternoon she wanted to do nothing but zone out. Unfortunately, it was not to be.

"Peggy, will you do the next problem, please?"

Peggy sighed. Couldn't Mr. Hakner see how lethargic she was feeling on this particular afternoon? She pulled her body up and began walking to the front of the room.

Roxanne stuck out her foot and tripped her. Peggy stumbled and almost hit the floor, but recovered. She steadied herself, but still felt dizzy.

"Peggy, are you okay?"

"Yes, Mr. Hakner." Peggy glared at Roxanne and walked the rest of the way to the blackboard. She heard someone chuckle and say, "Must be that hair, weighing her down."

Just ignore him, said the voice.

Peggy picked up a piece of chalk and began working out the proof. Suddenly she felt even weaker and more unsteady.

"Peggy, are you okay?" Mr. Hakner asked. "You look pale."

"No, I'm fine, I—" Peggy said, and the room dissolved in a sea of bright colors. Her last thought just before she fainted was a flash of concern for her hairdo.

✧   ✧   ✧

Slowly, Peggy awoke, not realizing she had been unconscious. She didn't recognize the bed she was in or her sur-
roundings, and she tried to lift her head. Weakness and pain
claimed her, and her head thunked back down to the pillow.
Strands of her hair fell loosely around her shoulders. It took
a moment to register, and when it did, she tried to scream.
But no noise came out.

Oh no! They've done it!

Groggily, she reached her hands up to her head, barely
noticing a tube and needle inserted into her left arm. Her
hairdo! Her beehive hairdo! It's undone!

True, the voice in her mind called from what seemed like
far away. *It is all over. I have failed.*

Turning her head, Peggy saw a nurse call button hanging off
the bed. They must have put her in the hospital. Despite her
weakened state, she managed to reach over and push the button.

A nurse entered a moment later. "Good, you're awake," she
said, smiling. "Let me go get the doctor." Peggy tried to ask
the nurse to stay for a moment, but the nurse left quickly,
before she had a chance to speak.

The doctor entered a few minutes later, along with her
parents. Her father held back, but her mother leaned over and
kissed her. "Sweetheart, are you all right?"

Peggy found her voice; she had started to feel better while
waiting. "What happened?"

Her mother looked at the doctor, who moved closer and
sat down next to her. "First of all, Peggy, everything's going
to be all right. You just had an infection, that's all."

"An—an infection? What about my hair?"

"Ah. Well, Peggy, we found a spider living in your hairdo.
Somehow it got trapped inside and couldn't escape."

A spider? Disgusting! "Where is it now?"

"In the lab. It's still alive. We're studying it to see what
other bugs it might be carrying."

"Other bugs?"

"I mean bacteria. The spider seems to have infected you
with whatever it had. We found a series of red welts on your
scalp, probably due to the spider biting you. That's how you
got infected."

Peggy nodded slowly, and sat up. "How long do I have to
stay here?"

The doctor clasped his hands together and wrinkled his brow. "Technically, you're cured, but this is such a bizarre case that I'd like to keep you here for observation for a few more days."

Peggy agreed. As soon as they left her alone to get some rest, she spoke out loud. "What do you mean, you have failed?"

You wish to know? the voice asked.

"Yes."

I can tell you now. It no longer matters. It paused. *I was not just a voice in your head. I am the spider they found.*

Peggy shuddered. "Go on."

The spider explained to her what it was, and about its mission. Finally, Peggy spoke. "You mean, you were going to turn me and everyone else into spiders?"

Yes.

"Including Roxanne and the girls at school?"

The voice hesitated for a moment, then replied: *Yes.*

Peggy sat up, hugged her knees, and started to cry. "I hate them. I wish they were dead."

The voice said nothing as Peggy dried her tears. Then she asked, "Can you help me with that?"

Yes.

"Good," Peggy said. "You'll have to help me find where they've put you."

Peggy snuck out of bed and the spider directed her to the lab. When she found it, she shivered at its ugliness. Still, she found the inner strength to pick it up and put it in her hospital gown pocket. "I hate spiders," she explained to it. "But I hate Roxanne more."

Peggy stayed in the hospital two more days, keeping the spider safely away from everyone, especially the doctors who were anxiously searching for it. After dinner with her parents on the night she returned home, she took the spider upstairs with her to bed, and put it on her pillow. She lay her head down next to it.

"Please wait until I've gone to sleep," she said, looking right at it.

The spider lifted a leg in acknowledgement. *Yes. And thank you.*

Peggy's last thought before she drifted off to sleep was that she would finally have her revenge.

❖   ❖   ❖

As Peggy slept, the spider deposited eggs into her body, piercing her all over instead of just on the scalp. The tiny eggs coursed through her bloodstream and found their way into every organ, every tissue, and every cell. Out of respect, the spider made sure they left her surface intact. They hatched into larvae, which ate away at her body, enlarging and engorging themselves, until they were ready to emerge.

Peggy's mother went to wake her daughter the next morning by knocking on her bedroom door. "Peggy, time to get up. How are you feeling?"

Peggy didn't answer.

Frowning, Peggy's mother opened the door and entered the room. Her daughter lay on the bed, under a blanket.

"Peggy, it's time to get up," she said. She pulled the sheet down to expose Peggy's body, and what she saw made her blood run cold.

Peggy lay there, apparently lifeless. Her skin, covered with a thin sheen of glistening green slime, rippled as if something underneath was anxiously trying to break free.

Peggy's mother recovered from her shock. She bent over and gently poked her daughter on the shoulder. "Peggy?"

Immediately, a thousand tiny spiders burst free from the hole she had accidently poked in Peggy's shoulder. Peggy's mother jerked back her finger and screamed. She watched in frozen horror as other spiders slipped out of Peggy's body through the holes in her ears.

She backed off and glanced at Peggy's head. Peggy's eyes slowly sunk into her face and disappeared, and spiders crawled out of the empty sockets. Then, with a sound like paper being ripped apart, the shell that was Peggy's body cracked open. Her skin collapsed into a pile of dust onto the bed. The spiders crawled out onto her bed, fell to the floor, and spread everywhere. Peggy's mother tried to flee, but she was overcome immediately, her screams stifled by spiders crawling into her nose and mouth.

Quickly, the spiders moved off in all different directions to begin spreading their race across this planet. But one spider set off slowly, with its own mission, given to it by the human girl that had helped it save its species. It set off to find its host's tormentor, Roxanne.

Sit!

Lawrence Watt-Evans

Big Bill Benson took another big bite of his sandwich and glowered over the top at his manager, Ken de Carlo. If Ken looked past his client, he had a view out the deli window of yellow taxis and grey city streets. The city was a lot less intimidating, but Ken met Bill's glare head-on.

Bill swallowed the bite, then said, "I been doin' all that stuff you told me. So how come nobody knows who the hell I am yet?"

Ken spread his hands. "Hey, come *on*," he said, "give it a little *time*! Have a little *faith*!"

"I *been* givin' it time," Bill said. "I been poundin' other guys into the canvas for a year and a half. It's about time I got somethin' back besides chump change."

"You're getting there, Bill!" Ken assured him hastily. "I swear you are! Boxing takes a little career-building, that's all. You'll be a household name before you know it."

"Sure I will, Ken." Bill put down the sandwich and leaned across the tiny butcher-block table. "You know how many times I've had people point at me, or come up to me in the street, 'cause they recognize me? You know how many times I've had people ask for my autograph?"

"Well, there you go, Bill!" Ken said happily. "They . . ."

"Do you know *how many* times, Ken?" Bill interrupted, his tone now threatening enough that the white couple at the next table glanced over uneasily.

"Ah . . . no, not exactly . . ." Ken stammered.

"*None*," Bill shouted. "Not one goddamn time. There ain't a dude in this whole damn city knows who the fuck I am!"

"No, no, that ain't it!" Ken assured him hurriedly, raising his hands in dismay. "You don't *understand*, Bill! They just can't believe it's *you*."

"Like they'd care if they did."

"Sure they'd care! They just don't recognize you."

"What, I look just like everyone else?" Bill gestured at his broad face and the half-shaven skull above. "I'm six foot four, three hundred pounds . . ."

"Yeah, but you know, most people aren't good with faces, Bill—especially white folks, you know they all say they can't tell one brother from another."

"They're full of lyin' shit," Bill growled.

"No, no, they *mean* it! Listen, listen, lemme tell you about something I heard, happened a couple months back."

Bill picked up his sandwich. "Okay, Ken, you tell me." He took another bite.

"Okay, there was these two little old Jewish ladies here in New York visitin' family, and they had money, y'know, so they were stayin' at a nice hotel on Central Park South, right?" Ken said. "They'd been livin' somewhere out in the Midwest or somewhere, but not isolated or anything, I mean, they watched TV and went to the movies and all."

"So they weren't hermits. Go on."

"Okay, so they get in the hotel elevator, and just before the door closes they see this hand catch the door, and it's a black hand, and they've been livin' in some lilywhite suburb somewhere, they don't know from homeboys, so they get a little worried, and the elevator door opens back up and this dude steps in, great big strong-lookin' dude, really big, and he's got a dog with him, and the man and the dog get in the elevator, see, and these two old ladies they sorta scrunch back in the corner tryin' to stay outta the way. And the bad-lookin' dude turns and says, 'Siddown!' And the two old broads from flyover country drop like they been hit with a brick, sittin' on the floor of the elevator so as not to piss off this big mutha. And he starts laughin', and says, 'Not you, ladies, I meant the *dog*.'" Ken looked at Bill expectantly.

"Yeah, yeah," Bill said. "So it's a funny story. I think I maybe heard it before. So?"

"So that's not the point, Bill! The point is, the ladies get up, and the big dude apologizes, and asks where they're stayin', and they tell him they're stayin' there at the hotel, and that night when they're eatin' their dinner in the hotel they ask for the bill, and the waiter tells 'em it's been taken care of by Mr. O'Neal, and they look around, and there's the dude from the elevator wavin', and they realize it's Shaq!"

"Like they wouldn't recognize Shaq. Come on, Ken . . ."

"No, it's *true*, Bill, I swear! White folks don't recognize no one!"

"Bull. Listen, I heard that story when I was a kid, 'cept it was Reggie Jackson. Or maybe George Foreman or Magic Johnson or Bill Cosby or some other big famous dude. I maybe believed it when I was ten, but I ain't ten, Ken, and I ain't buyin'."

"No, it's *true*, Bill—just some of the details got messed up, maybe."

"No, it *ain't* true, and you know why? Because even if the old broads from the ass end of nowhere didn't know Shaq or Reggie or whoever it was from a hole in the ground, ain't nobody stupid enough to sit down on the floor of a goddamn *elevator* like that when some dude's bossin' his *dog*."

"Sure they are, Bill! You know how scared white folks get about us brothers any time there ain't a cop right there! You get some timid bitch alone with you in an elevator, you can tell her to play dead, and she'd drop!"

Bill shook his head, then dabbed away a bit of mayonnaise. "Nope," he said. "Wouldn't happen."

"Sure it would!"

Bill leaned forward. "You mean you think that if I borrowed my sister's pit bull and got in some elevator at the Ritz-Carlton with some rich bitch and said, 'Sit,' she'd put her ass down on the carpet right there in the elevator and to hell with gettin' her fancy dress dirty?"

"Yeah, that's what I'm tellin' you!"

"Then I'm tellin' *you*, Mr. Business Manager de Carlo, that you're . . . fulla . . . shit." He jabbed Ken's chest with a finger to emphasize each of the last three words.

"Yeah? Well, why don't we just try it and see, wiseass?" Ken had risen out of his seat, and the two men were almost nose to nose, glaring at each other across the table. They'd been

in this position half a dozen times before, and every time Big
Bill had backed down—he *looked* tough, and he was good with
his fists, but he wimped out every time Ken called him on
stuff like this. Ken waited confidently for him to back down
again.

"You're on," Bill said. "I'm gonna get Brenda's dog and go
into some hotel and wait for some white pussy to get in an
elevator, and we'll just *see* what happens—and what a lying
sack of shit you are!"

Ken blinked in astonishment. "Come on, Bill, you aren't
gonna do . . ."

"The hell I ain't!" Bill shouted back. "I'm gonna do it, and
I'm gonna prove you're full of it, Ken, and when I do you're
fired! I'll find another manager, or maybe get myself a regular job somewhere like Ma wanted . . ."

"Wait a minute!" Ken interrupted, desperately trying to think
of some way to hang onto his meal ticket. "Now, wait one
goddamn minute! You're gonna fire me if *one* white broad has
the stuff to stay on her feet? Is that fair? Maybe you're gonna
pick some goddamn Marine or somethin'!"

"Oh, right, like the Marines been recruitin' little old ladies?"

"Then maybe she's too goddamn deaf to hear you! No, no—
one bitch ain't a fair trial, and I don't care *who* it is!"

"So how many you think gonna be fair, Mr. Manager?"

"Maybe half a dozen . . ."

"No way."

"Three tries, then," Ken said. "You give it three good tries,
and *one* of 'em will sit for sure!"

He prayed he was right. Three would at least give him a
little longer to think, and maybe to talk Bill back to him.

Bill considered Ken for a moment, then said, "You're on.
Three tries. None of 'em get down and you're history. One
of 'em sits and you keep your job."

"And you do what I tell you for the next goddamn year!
Give me some time to work with you, if you wanna be famous!"

"Six months."

"All right, six months—that'll be enough, anyway!"

"Don't matter anyhow," Bill said, holding out a hand to
shake on the deal. "Won't none of 'em so much as duck."

"Ha!" Ken said, ideas already starting to percolate. "You'll
see!"

✧   ✧   ✧

He would never have admitted it, would have laughed at
or pounded on anyone who suggested it, but Big Bill was
nervous. He was about to deliberately try to intimidate an
innocent white woman, and not back home in the 'hood but
in a fancy hotel, where she might call the management, and
the management might call the cops, at the slightest excuse.

In his granddaddy's day that could've gotten a man lynched.

It was one thing when he was sitting on the stoop with
his homies and some bitch walked by, and something else
altogether here, with the potted palms and mirrors and chan-
deliers.

He looked at the people milling about the lobby, and saw
a fine blonde fox in a tight grey suit heading toward him—
or rather, toward the elevators; he was waiting beside the
elevator doors, trying to look casual.

She didn't have anyone with her. She was about as good
a test case as he was likely to get. He glanced down at Killer
and said, "Come on."

Killer immediately got up and trotted forward, then paused
and looked back at Bill as if asking, "Where to?"

At least Brenda's dog was behaving himself; Bill had worried that maybe the damn dog would piss on his shoes, or bark
its head off, or something, but so far Killer had been a perfect little choirboy.

The blonde was already stepping into an elevator; Bill
hurried, but had to catch the door with his free hand to keep
from getting hit as it closed.

That sort of ruined his entrance, but he tried to ignore that.
He was supposed to look bad, he reminded himself; he growled
quietly, as if angry at the elevator door.

He glanced back at the blonde; she was ignoring him,
staring blankly ahead. He looked down at Killer, who looked
back up calmly.

"Siddown!" Bill barked, more loudly than he had actually
intended.

Killer dropped his fanny to the carpet instantly.

The blonde glanced casually over at Bill, but showed no
sign of moving otherwise.

Bill looked back and met her gaze. She didn't look scared;
she looked cool as Christmas.

He felt stupid.

"Talkin' to my dog," he said.

"Of course," she said. She looked down. "What's his name?"

"Killer."

"I didn't know the hotel allowed dogs."

"Ah . . . they make exceptions."

"How nice. Here's my floor."

Bill stood and watched as the door closed behind her and the elevator started back down toward the lobby.

"Told Ken it wouldn't work," he said. "And she didn't know who the fuck I was, either." He shrugged. "That's one down, anyway."

The woman in the lobby must've been fifty if she was a day, Bill thought. She had skin like wrinkled, spotted leather and lemon-yellow hair that looked about as natural as Tang, and she talked like a cowboy—if she wasn't really from Texas she was doing one hell of a fine imitation. She'd been talking with the man in the dark suit for fifteen minutes, while Bill stood behind the potted palms with Killer at his feet.

Finally, though, she slapped the suit on the sleeve and turned away with a grin.

Older woman, out-of-towner, traveling alone—here was a perfect second try.

Bill timed his move better than before; he and Killer stepped onto the elevator just before the Texan. For a second, Bill wondered how to count it if she decided not to get on alone with a big black man after all, but she never even slowed down.

He reached over and pushed a button at random, starting the elevator toward the twenty-eighth floor. The doors slid closed as the woman pushed a button.

Bill looked down at Killer, then said, "Siddown!" in his best do-it-or-die voice.

The woman turned and asked, "You talkin' to me, boy?"

Bill stared at her, and his feigned anger was suddenly genuine. Nobody had dared call him "boy" since he was twelve. "What if I am?" he demanded.

Suddenly her purse was hanging open on one arm, and her other hand held a big black gun, pointing straight at his face. "Then you'd better tell it to Mr. Colt here," she said.

The anger was suddenly mixed with fear.

"You ever hear of the Sullivan Act, lady? You can't carry a gun in New York!"

"You ever hear of the Second Amendment? I've got a right to protect myself."

"Seems to me the cops might think that's their job."

"Seems to me the cops might not care what some big black bruiser thinks, when it's his word against mine. If he's still alive to talk, and not shot in self-defense." The gun never wavered.

Killer growled warningly.

The gun still pointed straight at Bill, but the woman looked down at the dog.

"That yours?" she asked.

"You see anyone else in here?"

"Well, shit," she said. The gun dropped until it hung loose in her hand, pointing at the floor, then she stooped and gave Killer a quick pet, rumpling his ears. "Didn't know they let dogs in here, or I'd've brought Rusty. Why'n't you say you was talkin' to him?"

"Why'n't you watch who you call 'boy'?"

Before she could reply the elevator stopped, and the doors opened. She stood up.

"My floor," she said, glancing at the indicator. She stepped out, tucking the pistol back in her purse.

As the doors closed she turned, smiled, waved, and said, "You got guts, boy, talkin' back with a gun in your face!"

Alone in the elevator Bill said, "Shit." He slumped against the wall and wiped sweat from his face with his sleeve, trembling as he did. Then he looked down at Killer.

"Thanks," he said. "But next time, speak up sooner, y'hear?"

Killer wagged his stumpy little tail and panted, tongue lolling.

"I coulda been killed!" Bill said.

Ken nodded. "Sure. It's a mean ol' world out there—which is why those two broads from Iowa sat down for Shaq."

Bill snorted. "That's still bull, Ken. I tried it twice and neither one of 'em was half as scared as I was!"

"So you picked some tough broad from uptown and a crazy Texan. Why not give it a *real* try?"

"I hung around that lobby all day, Ken—didn't see any little old ladies."

"So try a different hotel. If I'd known where you were going I'd have suggested it sooner. Maybe one that don't cost so much—you won't get anyone doing the town on her Uncle Harry's pension in a place like that."

Bill shook his head. "I've had enough—and I told you, they didn't budge. You were wrong, and I'm gonna find me a new manager."

"C'mon, Bill! You said three tries—don't welsh on me! Gimme a fair shot! I'll let you count those two if you do the third one right."

Bill stared at Ken for a moment, then shrugged.

"Oh, hell, one more try."

Ken smiled up at him.

"You'll see," he said. "And I know just the place—they get the old ladies from Podunk by the busload."

Bill had to admit that Ken was right—the hotel he had suggested did, indeed, have half a dozen blue-haired fossils in the lobby at any given time.

And sure enough, after just twenty minutes two of them came in from the street and headed for the elevators, unaccompanied by bellmen or other escorts. Bill gave Killer his cue, and the four of them, man, dog, and two women, boarded the elevator almost simultaneously.

When the doors closed, Killer looked up expectantly.

"Sit!" Bill snapped.

The two old women looked at one another, then sat down—one quickly, the other creaking a bit as she settled.

Bill stared down at them in astonishment.

They looked uneasily up at him.

The story called for him to laugh now and tell them to get up, but Bill was too flabbergasted; he just stared.

"Did we do it right?" one of them asked tremulously.

The pieces fell into place suddenly, and Bill smiled—not a *nice* smile at all.

"You did fine, ladies," he said. "You can get up now."

"Well, thank *goodness*," the stiff one said, as she struggled to rise. Bill bent and gave her a hand.

"How much did he pay you?" he asked, once she was upright.

The women glanced at each other, clearly unsure if they were supposed to admit anything.

Then one of them shrugged. "Twenty dollars each up front," she said. "Another hundred if it comes out right."

"I'm glad to have the money, because New York's so expensive," the other one whined, "but I didn't understand *why* he wanted us to do it! Is there a camera hidden in here somewhere?"

"Don't you worry 'bout it," Bill said. "You just take your money and have a good time. Where'd Ken say he'd meet you?"

"Back in the lobby, in ten minutes."

Bill nodded. "Well, that's fine." He pushed the STOP button, then L. "We'll wait for him there."

Bill watched from the corner behind the desk as Ken gave the two old ladies their money; then, as soon as the bills had been tucked out of sight in the two oversized purses, he stepped out into the open.

"Hello, ladies," he said. Then his voice turned cold. "Hello, Ken."

"Bill!" Ken forced a smile. "What a surprise!" He looked at the women, then back at Bill, groping for words.

One of the women said, "Well, we were just leaving, and I'm sure you two have things to talk about."

"I'm sure we do," Bill said, not taking his eyes off Ken's face.

The two scurried away like late-for-work commuters, leaving the two men standing face to face.

"Ken, you *are* a lyin' sack of shit, and *worse* than that!" Bill said. "You think I'm stupid? You think you can con me *that* easy?"

"I think I should've hired a couple of broads who can act better, is what I think," Ken said, recognizing that the game was lost. "Look, Bill, I can explain. I just can't bear to see you throw your *career* away by firin' me, not when you're so close . . ."

"Oh, fuck that. You're fired, Ken. Now, excuse me while I take Brenda's dog home; I guess tomorrow's soon enough to find a new manager." He beckoned to Killer, then started away.

"Bill!" Ken called after him, "that's not fair! I swear, you *are* famous! You're right on the edge! Just stick with me a *little longer*, please . . . !"

Bill didn't listen.

The little restaurant was just around the corner from the hotel where he'd fired Ken, but Bill tried not to think about that as he ordered dinner. He was splurging, a little solitary celebration of getting rid of the man who'd been running his life for so long, and Brenda had highly recommended this place.

Tomorrow he'd make a few calls, talk to some old friends, and see whether he could find a *real* manager, someone who could get him on track to a title bout.

Right now, though, he was going to blow some of his savings on a fancy dinner, and then go get a few beers and try to wash the taste of Ken's little scam out of his mouth.

"Look! It's him!"

Bill looked up, startled; was there a celebrity here he hadn't even noticed?

Then he saw that the voice came from the door of the restaurant, where two very familiar old white broads had just entered. One of them was pointing at him.

He sighed, and waved to them.

The two leaned their heads together and whispered for a moment, and then, a bit hesitantly, came over to his table.

Bill waited. He supposed they'd want an explanation of just what that mess this afternoon had been about.

Then, as they approached, one of them pulled a little book from her purse.

"We didn't get a chance to ask you before, what with one thing and another," she said. "Could we have your autograph, please?"

Bill blinked up at them in surprise, then smiled broadly.

"Sure," he said. He accepted the proffered pen, and opened the book, thumbing through it looking for a blank page.

As he did, a thought managed to penetrate his shock. Maybe Ken really had been right all along. Maybe he *was* right on the verge of the big time. Maybe he owed Ken an apology and another chance.

Or maybe Ken had put them up to this.

But it didn't seem his style, to try another con after the first one flopped. Bill dismissed the idea. He uncapped the pen as he smiled broadly, then placed the book on the table, ready to write.

His first autograph, his first taste of fame—he savored it, and tried to think of something clever to write. He looked up at the two women for inspiration.

"We just *love* basketball, Mr. O'Neal," one of the women burbled happily. "And we thought you were *wonderful* as the superhero in that movie!"

The Hook

Kristine Kathryn Rusch

When my daughter heard the story, she was ten. Her first sleepover, far from home, at her friend Anne's cabin on Lake Nebagamon.

I've been there; I can picture it.

Eight girls clustered together on the screened-in porch. Carly is tired; she has spread out on the porch swing, her back against the slates, a musty blanket pulled over her legs. Nights on Nebagamon are cool, the rusty smell of the lake nearly overpowering. Moths bat against the screens, and mosquitoes squeeze through the tiny square holes. Buzzing and absent-minded slaps accompany the crickets harmonizing outside. The girls are armed with two buckets of popcorn, smores, and three brands of sugared soda that my wife and I don't allow at home.

They use a flashlight because Anne's mother won't allow a campfire on the lawn. The girl with the light shines it on her face, close so that her features are distorted, and tells a scary story. Most, in Carly's opinion, are dumb, like the one about the guy who sleeps in a haunted house, sees something white at the foot of his bed, grabs his gun and shoots off his own toe. I think she doesn't understand the story; she says she understands it too well. She believes the man deserved what he got for sleeping in a haunted house in the first place.

She forgets—or perhaps she's too young to know—that all our houses are haunted, in one way or another. Each girl tells

51

a story, some tell two, and none of them frighten her. None of them except the Hook.

You've heard about the Hook. These days, it seems everyone has. Some books on urban legends say the tale was devised in the 1950s to scare teenagers away from parking, to prevent them from having inexpert sex in the crowded back seat of their parents' car. It doesn't seem like the sort of story to scare a ten-year-old, particularly a naive one. Carly's friends laughed, not the response the teller wanted. But Carly, sensitive, aware Carly, remained awake all night, staring at the star-filled night sky, slapping mosquitos and listening for the scrape of a hook against metal, afraid that a murderer was on the loose, afraid that he would come for her.

Children are so attuned to the world around them.

I could not comfort her when she came home. I couldn't even hold her. I left her to the warm, enveloping arms of my wife, who gazed at me over our child's head with something akin to sympathy mixed with something closer to anger.

You see, the tale of the Hook is not, as urban folklorists would dream, a myth designed to stop teenagers from illicit behavior. Nor is it simply a tale children tell in the dark. The Hook has its basis in fact. I should know because it's my hook two teenagers found embedded in the door of their car that hot August night.

My hook.

My escape.

My crime.

A murder no one sees fit to remember. Crimes of passion I can never forget.

If she finds this record, my wife will be angry. It is, in its own way, a confession that will blow our lives apart. She will have a right to her anger, since she has kept me safe for more than forty years. Carly is the child of our old age; an accident that happened because we thought my wife was going through menopause. We discovered our mistake too late; the symptoms of menopause became the symptoms of pregnancy, and we found ourselves the parents of a child we felt inadequate to raise, but one we couldn't part with. Carly is not our future, but our redemption, and because of that, it is her discovery of our secret, however obliquely, that forces me to write this.

I work in the room we call my office but which is really the attic. Its sloping ceiling follows the roof line. Two small windows open on either end. Through them, I can see the yard and the neighborhood beyond. So quiet, so suburban. So seemingly safe. What would my neighbors say if they knew the truth of my past? What would I say if I knew the truth of theirs?

No one is allowed up here but me. The books that line the walls are my books, the desk my desk, the stereo my stereo. This is the only room in the house with a lock on the door. We made the decision decades ago, when we learned that I needed privacy almost more than I needed freedom, that I needed a place to hide when pressures got intense, that I needed a prison to bar me from society on those days when I frighten everyone—including myself. I type with my left hand, sixty words a minute with the thumb, forefinger and pinky. A virtuoso performance that my professorial colleagues at the university never cease to marvel at. The prosthesis is obvious at moments like this. The rest of the time, it hides beneath the long sleeves of my dress shirts, the even longer sleeves of the dark suits my wife buys and dry cleans. I come home each night dusted with chalk. Sometimes a line runs across the back of my jacket. My wife shakes her head as she brushes me off, my daughter laughs at my clumsiness, and I find joy in those details, joy in the way life's small pleasures add up into even greater ones.

There are days I don't even think about my past.

There are days.

But not many.

On the tenth of October, 1954, I murdered Delbert Glaven. I sliced open his throat with the hook at the end of my right arm.

I was fifteen years old.

On the twelth of October, 1954, I was arrested.

On the sixteenth of October, 1954, I escaped from jail with the help of two friends, one of them a deputy sheriff. They returned my blood-stained hook to me, and attached it with electrician's tape before I disappeared across the countryside.

❖　　　❖　　　❖

On the thirty-first of October, 1954, the sheriff's department found my hook imbedded in the door of Edna Wilson's Nash Rambler. Mrs. Wilson's son, Tom, was hysterical with terror. His girlfriend, one Anna Mae Connelly, spoke not a word, not about her disheveled clothing, nor the bruise on her left cheek, nor the child she birthed and abandoned exactly nine months later.

Edna Wilson's Rambler, if it still exists, is about half a continent away from Lake Nebagamon. Half a continent, and forty years away. The world has changed. I have changed. I speak in sentences now instead of fragments. I have good diction and use middle-class English instead of the slurred dialect of that long-ago time. I look in the mirror and see nothing of the tall, gangly boy I had been. Nowadays six feet is not such a great height. Many of my students tower over me and, if the genes tell, my daughter will too. The world has light in it now, while I think of the past as darkness, unrelieved darkness.

Yet my past catches up to me in stories little girls tell in that darkness, a flashlight distorting the features of their cherubic faces.

October nights are cool in the south. Cool and damp, with a touch of frost, a touch of winter-to-come. Southerners hate the winter. They think they suffer through it more than the rest of us, that their delicate skin, used to sweltering summer nights, heat so thick it is a live thing, makes them even more susceptible to cold.

They are wrong, for they have a protective layer that inures them to everything. Cold, pain, emotional distress.

Everything, and nothing at all.

I grew up in New Orleans (Nawlins, as I called it then, before the precise pronunciation and flat vowels of the Midwest coated my voice), and had never been farther north than Slidell until I was thirteen. That year, I ran away from home, thinking that life in cosmopolitan New Orleans had prepared me for everything.

It had not.

It had certainly not prepared me for cross-country travel, with a pack on my back, a hook taped to my arm, and an APB notifying every peace officer within shouting distance of my presence. I slept on the ground, and woke with hard frost on my face. I hoarded the fifty dollars cash them good old boys gave me, and only twice did I venture into the small towns that lined my back-country route.

Twice was once too many.

On October 31st, I went into a town whose name I learned only later, when the news reports appeared. I went in for some food and a jacket if I could find one, and a night on a bed provided by the Sisters of Charity, or whatever mission was operating in that dark place in those dark days.

I had thought I was far enough north to escape the news. I had thought no one would be looking for me outside of Louisiana. I was young, I had never seen a movie, read a book, or watched television. I thought I was invincible.

I was wrong.

When I left the general store, my pack heavier for the cans of pork 'n beans, and the packages of jerky that would carry me through, the store clerk called the local sheriff. He and his dogs never found me, but the radio station interrupted its programming every fifteen minutes with a bulletin about the "deranged escaped murderer with a hook" who was haunting the countryside.

I heard the first report from that Nash Rambler's radio, a tinny announcer's scared voice filtered across an unnamed lake on Halloween night.

But I get ahead of myself.

The story, as my daughter relates it, is this:

A couple is parking on an abandoned road near a lake. They have the radio on and hear a special bulletin about a crazed murderer with a hook for a hand who has escaped from the local penitentiary. The bulletin says anyone who sees such a man should flee, and then report to the police.

The announcement makes the girl nervous.

"I think we should leave," she says to her boyfriend.

"Nonsense," he says. "What are the chances of the murderer turning up here?"

The girl reluctantly agrees. She lets the boy kiss her some

more, then, unable to shake the feeling, says, "I really think we should leave."

The darkness of the woods, the silence, the seclusion are getting to the boyfriend as well. "All right," he says. He starts the car, puts it in reverse, and backs away, all in one motion.

It is that motion, he says, that saves his life. For when he gets home, he finds a hook hanging off the passenger side door.

Truth.
Perspective.
It all changes with time.
What I remember is this:

The moon was full. I had made camp beneath a large tree near the edge of a lake. The water lapped against the shore and, despite the air's chill, the night sky had a beauty I had never noticed before.

There had been a frost two days before, and all the bugs were dead.

I had seen no animals.

I was alone.

Except for the car across the lake.

The car didn't bother me. It was a Nash Rambler, and its driver was obviously young. The blaring radio had announced the car's arrival long before I heard the crunch of tires on gravel. The car parked near the water's edge. The windows were steamed, the chassis shook, and I knew the two occupants were much more interested in each other than they were in me.

Besides, I got to hear Opry music, mixed with some early rockabilly. I had escaped the law once again. I had a meal of jerky, mixed nuts, and freshly baked bread. Everything seemed perfect.

Until I heard the slap.

I didn't know it was a slap until the second one, followed by a thud, and a woman's voice screeching in anger mixed with terror. I bent back over my meal, telling myself it wasn't my concern. But the third slap, ending with the trailed off scream, decided me. That, and the bulletin cutting into the wailing guitars.

The bulletin about me, the escaped convict. It didn't matter that I was merely accused, nor did it matter that I had escaped, not from a penitentiary, but from a jail. What mattered was my crime, and the fact that I had killed a man by slicing his neck open with what passed for my hand.

It made me sound crazed.

Perhaps I was.

I crept along the lake's edge, not caring that my feet broke brambles, that the echoes, carried across the water, announced my presence. The radio was too loud, the couple in the Rambler too preoccupied with their struggle to notice me.

Until I rapped on the window with the pointed end of my hook.

Here it all gets jumbled. Every time. Perhaps a shrink could separate it out. I cannot.

My hands on his shoulders. Hands. Shoulders. Yanking him back. He turns, face shrouded in darkness. Lit by the dials on the dash. Air steamy. She gazes up at me, the prettiest girl I've ever seen, despite the cut lip or perhaps because of it, gazes at me with fear and thankfulness and relief.

I pull him off. He falls to the pavement. She gathers her ripped clothes together, slides up the hood. He slams and locks the door. She reaches for the passenger side. He turns the key in the ignition. I circle around, grab the passenger door, as he shoves the car in reverse.

Mud slicing through the air.

Mud.

Hands.

Awful ripping pain.

Awful bone crushing pain.

And I am on my knees in the dirt.

On the pavement.

In the wilderness.

Near the laundry.

My right hand cradled against my chest.

The blood seeping from the rips in my stump.

It is, some say, the devil's own luck. My future wife finds me, drags me to her cabin, hides me when the law comes searching for me. They find my camp, my stuff. They question her, and she says nothing. She is a young woman, on her own at her parents' second home, proving that she can spend a weekend alone.

She keeps me there for nine months, sneaking in from town to feed me. She nurses me to health, and plans our escape. We go north, get new identities, enroll in college, become real young people with no pasts and important futures. We marry but do not procreate.

Except by accident.

My wife saw everything, or so she says. She heard the scream, came to the clearing, saw me pull open the car door, yank the Wilson boy up so hard he hit his head on the rear-view mirror. The girl scrambled up, grabbing her clothes, while he recovered, slammed and locked the door. I ran to the other side, grabbed the door handle as the car peeled backward, covering me in dirt and leaves and blood.

She did not know I was wounded until I passed out.

When I awoke, she had already decided that I was falsely accused, a hero, a man who deserved her love and loyalty for the next forty years.

But she did not see it all. No one has seen it all, or knows it all, not even them two good ole boys who busted me out of jail. Busted me out for guilt, because they couldn't stomach seeing me going down for something we all did.

When I am feeling rational, I pass it off to hormones.
When I am feeling truthful, I know it is more.
Much more.

Too much beer and not a little loneliness. That's what I remember from those days. That, and discovering that my buddy Scott actually worked for the sheriff as a sometimes deputy, as a more-often janitor. Scott swore not to tell that I was a runaway, and I swore not to tell that he carried a non-regulation gun and a then-illegal Swiss army knife hidden in his sock.

I would like to say it was their idea. Or, barring that, I would like to say we all came on the idea at once. But it built over time. Scott said he knew of a place that hired out women by the hour, and with his connections, his gun, and his badge, we could get one for free.

But only one, he thought. So we decided to share.

The night blurs into a haze of cigarette smoke and Okie music, a bar with a pool table and no patrons and too much beer. A girl with the face of an angel, whose no somehow became yes, and whose escape outside became an enticing dance, leading us to the promised land.

Scott started, taking her on the hood of a green Ford, while the other guy, whose name is lost to traitorous memory, had one hand over her mouth. She squirmed and pounded and screamed, and somehow that seemed right to me, impatient me, so I grabbed Scott by the shoulders with my two good hands and pulled him off, shoving him aside so that I could take my turn.

And as I did, I didn't even notice the headlights in my face, or the fact that the girl started to scream. I just thought the other guy was getting ready for his turn. But the hands on my shoulder weren't his. They belonged to Delbert Glavin, the girl's brother, who pulled me back and beat me black and blue, and stomped on my right hand so hard he broke all the bones from my wrist to my fingertips.

The doctors couldn't save it. They cut it off. And gave me the hook instead.

Delbert's sister disappeared, and no one discussed the incident for the shame of it. He didn't press charges—how could he when it was clear—in those unenlightened times— that just by being in that bar she was asking for it?

And so when I got out of the hospital, I somehow thought the wrong was visited on me and not on him, and certainly not on the girl whom we saw as nothing more than a piece of ass, nothing human certainly, nothing with any more feeling than a blow-up doll bought mail order.

So I tracked Delbert Glavin down, used my new weapon to rip open his throat, and let the law come after me.

And my friends saved me, as I knew they would.

So what was I doing, opening that car door, crazed murderer that I was? Hero's journey, Campbell would have said, from ignorance to enlightenment. God, the Christians would say, had given me a second chance to redeem myself, and I took it, saving a poor girl from the very thing that caused it all.

But I remember the emotion, the charged adrenaline that shot through me when I heard that scream, and the blurred memories that still combine when I think of this. And I wonder, hands on shoulders, why I was pulling the Wilson boy aside.

I think altruism became part of my nature when pain ripped through my right arm a second time. Only a fool would fail to realize that no moment of hideous pleasure was worth the price of a hand. Only a fool would need to learn that lesson twice.

I've been a good, fine upstanding man for forty years. A man who minds his own business, a man who looks the other way when he needs to, a man who leads his life and no one else's. I have been unusually blessed.

Or unusually cursed.

This daughter of mine will be a world-class beauty. I have kept my distance from her, hoping to protect her from that thing which is her father. And I can continue to do that until she is old enough to go out on her own. Then she must make her own choice, live her own life, in the world that spawned me.

And I fear for her.

Oh, I fear for her.

Because she is bold, and she is bright, and she will not heed warnings told by schoolgirls in the dark.

And she needs to.

They all need to.

I know.

And that knowledge is punishment enough.

Doggedly

Josepha Sherman

They think me no more than a dog, this warm, friendly family of adult male, adult female, immature younglings. They feed me what a dog would eat, groom my smooth, sleek coat as they would a dog, call me their "good boy" and "protector."

And why should they not? Protector is what I am, fierce, devoted.

Indeed.

Oh, I have heard others of their kind wonder at me, even condemn me since I have the appearance of a breed known for its fierceness: Doberman. But my family merely laughs. "What, Duke hurt anyone? He's as gentle as a pup and bright as they come. Makes a wonderful babysitter, too."

I do, I do, indeed, though they have never yet trusted me with the youngest one, the one who is still helpless and unripe. They have never trusted me alone.

Yet. The adults are restless, saying such things as, "When did we last have a night out?" "A night without the kids?"

They hunt through all their paper sources, their voice sources, for one of their kind to serve as "babysitter," as the foolish term states. They find a youngster, immature female, though my senses tell me she is at the edge of ripening, and in her mind is swirling hotness and thoughts of an immature male. I play with these thoughts, strengthen them.

And there is the call, just when my adults are to leave, the cancellation of service that means my judgment was accurate and the immature female has been overwhelmed by other thoughts than work. Panic, yes: They have "tickets," things that cannot be "refunded." They will stay home—no, they will lose money. But the children! They will stay home—but they were looking forward so strongly to this night alone! They will forget the "tickets," just have dinner—but who will watch the younglings?

So obvious, so very much that. I insinuate myself under the adult male's hand, letting him pet my coat, look up at him with *trust* and *honesty* and *gentleness* radiating from my eyes. Not the slightest hint of harm to me, and not the slightest hint of resistance from him. He has no choice, the adult female has no choice. They must trust me. Besides, they argue to each other, the older two younglings are old enough, surely, to be left alone for just this short, short time. And the dog, the dog, sweet, trustworthy dog, will guard them.

Indeed.

They give in. Uncertainty still quivers in their minds, but the adult male and female find themselves dressing for the outside world, giving their younglings frantic instructions the younglings barely hear.

And I? *Go*, I tell them silently. *Go*.

At last they are gone. I am alone with the younglings. I do not harm them, no, I do nothing but act the friendly canine they believe me. Time, trust, these are more important.

The older younglings are too boisterous with the adults away. I send sleepiness to them, and am pleased to be restored to peace as they settle into slumber. The youngest still rests in its crib, all unaware of me as I scent its unripe state: hardly a being of their species yet, this one.

So. Now I shall act as the guardian, settle down with head on paws. This is quiet, and that sometimes can be as fine a thing as the hunt.

I rest. Even, I drowse; this form I hold has its whims.

Intruder! I come wildly awake, springing up, aware of my lips drawn back over my fangs as I scent, stalk, find.

This, too, has taken other shape than its own. This one looks very much like an adult male, the shape taken, no doubt, to make it easier to pass through the streets and use the fingered hands to pry open windows that had been locked. But this is not the thing it seems.

Nor does it fail to recognize me. In its taken shape, it can speak, and I hear, "Well met."

I speak, not with words, though the other hears me sharply enough, *"Not as well met. My territory."*

"Mine, now, dog-thing." But then it laughs, awkward imitation of the species-form it wears. "Or both. Enough here to share."

"No, I do not share. Leave."

Its eyes glint with fire not from this here-and-now. "You are in dog form. Inferior form. I wear the dominant species shape."

"And poorly."

"Really? Foolish dog-thing." It holds a metal shape, and my senses tell me sharply, *weapon, iron-spitting weapon.* Such is common in this realm; no problem for the intruder to find or steal it. "Ah, you know what this is. Noisy, primitive but very deadly. Something a thief might use."

It aims at me. I wait, muscles tensed. It thinks the dog-shape weak. It does not know the savage strength within. It shoots; I leap, now, up before it can fire again. My jaws are strong. Catching wrist and hand, I clamp down, hear bones snap. It shrills pain, an alien sound. It loses its disguise and I see, as I knew was there, fangs, talons. I bite again and the weapon goes flying. I am hit across the head and fall, spitting out a severed claw. Roaring, the other lunges at me and we fight in true, right, fury, rending, tearing. We hit the crib in our frenzy, knock it aslant, and the unripe youngling wakes and adds its terror to our fight.

"You hear? You hear?" the other spits. "My prey, my hunting ground!"

It hurls itself on me, crushing me to the carpeted floor. I cannot breathe, see, think. I will be destroyed and it will take this so-carefully nurtured territory—

"No! My territory!" I scream in my not-voice. I twist, bite, rend, I snap at its throat and almost, almost tear it. The other convulses free, but not before I catch its hand again and bite down with all the will within me. There, there! I have severed fingers! The other pulls free, keening in pain, and something breaks within it. It turns and flees, shape abandoned, one more shadow in the darkness.

It will not return.

And I? I cannot dislodge one taloned finger from within my throat. I choke, coughing, trying to breathe. At last I collapse on the floor, panting, knitting my torn flesh back together but unable to dislodge the talon.

That is when the adult male and female come rushing in. They see me, the slanted crib, the howling youngling and its bewildered, blinking other siblings. For a moment I am the center of hysterical blows and shouts: They think, fools, fools, that it was I who tried to slay their younglings! I struggle, cough, cough again—and at last the cursed talon is dislodged.

There are twin cries of horror from the adult male and female. They see the talon as a finger, no more. And now they look around the shattered room and see where the iron-spitting weapon lies.

"A burglar! There was a burglar in here! Oh you brave dog, you chased him away!"

Now, of course, I am a hero. I would wish merely to be alone to rest, but no, I must be petted and hugged and begged for forgiveness. Forgiveness! As though I care what they think of me.

No, I am a hero, and much is made of me. There is a time of confusion after this, of strangers rushing in, going over the room with care, hunting traces, evidence.

Of course they find nothing. Nothing, I think, that they could recognize.

At last, at last they all grow weary. The strangers leave, the room is still once more. All sleep, save me. I alone remain awake, musing.

The intruder was a fool. Worse, a glutton. One does not rush such things; one waits for a meal to grow to proper ripeness. As I will wait.

I rise, patrol my territory.

My family.

My prey.

My Brother's Keeper

Mike Resnick and Jack Nimersheim

God, I'm tired. (That's not an idle expression. Are You listening, You pompous bastard?)

How long has it been since I've rested? Days? Weeks? Months? It feels like decades. More likely, centuries.

The petitions come with ever-increasing frequency. Their young voices are a constant chorus, an endless torrent of pleas, drowning out the peace forever denied me.

"I wish someone would teach that bully a lesson."

"I wonder how he'd feel if somebody pounded him to a pulp."

"If only I had a big brother to stand up for me."

The phrasing may differ, but the requests are always the same. And it is I who must respond to each summons, answer every request. Such is my duty; such is my curse.

Damn! There's another one. Oh, well. No rest for the wicked—yet another idiom steeped in irony.

Kyle Patton felt extremely satisfied with himself as he swaggered down the sidewalk of West Holland Boulevard. The sun warmed his smiling face. A gentle breeze cooled the sweat from his tan, muscular body. He'd had a good day: a towering three-run homer in the bottom of the sixth inning that turned an anticipated defeat for his high-school baseball team into a surprise victory; the congratulations of his teammates; the gratitude of his coach; the cheers from a hometown crowd; Jenny Firth's promise to reward his heroics later that night with a special "surprise," provided he could borrow his father's Grand Cherokee and then find a nice, quiet, secluded spot out by Tucker's Pond.

Yep. A damned good day.

Ripping off that dweeb's *Starter* jacket behind the bleachers after the game was mere icing on the cake of Kyle's insatiable ego. Of course, it would never fit him. Too small. Every fancy jacket he'd ever peeled off the quivering frame of a skinny underclassman was too small for him to wear. But then, wasn't that the point of the exercise? Who'd be so stupid as to pick on someone his own size? Or bigger? Certainly not Kyle, that was for damned sure. Kyle was smart. Smart enough, in fact, to have figured out that offering his newest acquisition to Jenny—and it *would* fit her—might just procure him a second surprise, out in the moonlit fields of Old Man Tucker's dairy farm.

Kyle was still swaggering, still smiling, when a large hand wrapped itself around his mouth and pulled him, none too gently, into the alleyway that separated Karen's Boutique from The Daily Grind Croissant and Expresso Shoppe.

My hand.

"That's a nice jacket you're carrying, kid," I said. Kyle didn't know me from Adam—excuse me, make that from Cain—but he didn't have any trouble recognizing my threatening tone. (Why should he have? He'd spent endless hours perfecting a similar inflection in his own speech patterns.) "Looks a little small for you, though," I continued. "I wonder why that is?"

I released Kyle's mouth, grabbed his left shoulder, and spun him around.

The late afternoon sun could not penetrate the narrow space in which Kyle and I squared off against one another. It wouldn't have mattered if it did. Had we been standing in the light, he would almost have vanished in my shadow. I stood eight inches taller than Kyle, and outweighed him by close to seventy pounds, all of it muscle built over a longer period of time than Kyle would ever know.

"What do you want?" Kyle managed to stammer, stumbling even farther back into the shadows of the cramped alleyway.

I'd heard that question so many hundreds, thousands, even millions of times.

"What I want is peace. And He'd grant it to me, if it weren't for punks like you. As long as you and your kind—*my* kind—exist, I remain here, an eternal balance to the scales."

Of course it didn't make any sense to Kyle, who by now had retreated so far into the alleyway that he was cowering against the half-filled dumpster next to the door that led to the kitchen of The Daily Grind.

"Since I can't have the peace I crave," I continued, my voice almost a whisper, "I must content myself with the retribution that He insists is my responsibility." I stepped toward Kyle, feeling the usual combination of rage and resignation welling up within me. "So get ready to cough up the jacket, kid, along with some blood and a couple of teeth from that perfect smile."

Kyle Patton never made it to Tucker's Pond. He spent most of the evening at the North Shores Medical Clinic, lying on a gurney, thanking God for the availability of local anesthesia and a capable oral surgeon. That night he spent at home, alone, thrashing about his bed, cursing a painkiller that seemed incapable of outlasting the pain it was designed to kill.

Jenny Firth *did* go to Tucker's Pond that night, accompanied in a last-minute roster change by Wade Bannister. Wade played center field on the team and earlier in the afternoon crossed the plate just ahead of his good friend, Kyle Patton, when Kyle knocked out that game-winning dinger. Wade made it all the way to third base with Jenny—still ahead of Kyle, but not the home run he'd hoped for.

A coat! Amazing, that the children of today visit harm upon one another over something as inconsequential as a coat. Other trivial objects trigger violence, as well.

Last week—or maybe it was last month; time has very little meaning at this late date—the call came from a playground. I materialized just as one child toppled another from the upper rungs of a ladder attached to a tall metal slide. I heard the smaller child's femur snap as he fell heavily to the asphalt. I saw the satisfaction in the larger child's eyes as he stared down at his victim, a cruel sneer playing across his young face. Those youthful features bore no sign of the innocence normally associated with adolescence, nor the slightest sign of regret for the pain he'd caused.

Of course there wasn't. Otherwise, I would not have been summoned—although, now that I reflect upon it, "summoned" is probably not the right word. No disembodied voice issues forth from the heavens, demanding my presence. Rather, I'm *drawn* to youthful conflict, like a moth to the proverbial flame. My involvement is implied, not imposed.

"Am I my brother's keeper?" Those are the very words I once used; the Bible got *that* right, anyway.

Give the Old Man credit. He possesses a marvelous sense of irony. Because now that is precisely what I am, what *He* made me. On my eternal shoulders rests the responsibility for defending those children who are too small, or too weak, or too frightened, or too meek, or too gentle, or too genteel, to defend themselves. A fearful child calls, and I respond. Whenever the big abuse the small, the strong mistreat the weak, I appear—always bigger, always stronger ("More able-bodied," He once proclaimed, again demonstrating the ironic wit few realize He possesses) to balance the scales.

For example, Kyle Patton saw me as someone taller, more powerful, more agile, than he was. That bully on the playground perceived a different me, younger than the persona I assumed earlier this evening—and nowhere near as well developed physically—but still old enough, and strong enough, and big enough, to evoke within him the same fear he relied upon to intimidate others.

The specifics of my appearance and abilities change continually, calculated each time to counterbalance the current circumstances, whatever they might be. The pattern of my intervention, however, remains constant. It is always the same.

At least it was, until that day at the park. I felt myself taking shape, becoming solid, drawn to the baseball diamond. It was dark, and if there had been a game, it had long since broken up.

There were two big kids, almost men, in leather jackets, beating the hell out of a younger boy. I'll give the boy this: he didn't scream for help, and he didn't cry out when they pummeled him. He just took it stoically. He knew better than to fight back, since they would have just beaten him even worse.

I walked over, unseen.

"That's enough," I said.

The larger of the boys turned and landed a roundhouse on my jaw. I didn't flinch.

"Don't you know that hurts?" I said, landing the same blow on his chin. He spun like a top, then collapsed.

I grabbed the second boy by the throat and held him a few inches above the ground as he gasped for air, and then, for the first time, my eyes fell on the face of his victim.

I set the boy on his feet.

"Go!" I said firmly.

He stared at me dumbly.

"Take your friend and go," I said, "or I shall teach you the meaning of pain, and before I am through with you you will know why men fear the night."

He gulped, helped his groggy companion to his feet, and both of them ran off into the shadows.

"Thank you," said their victim.

I turned to him, and saw the face I had been sure I would never see again: the clear blue eyes, the perfect nose, the light blond hair.

"*You!*" I hissed.

He stared at me, afraid to say anything.

"That face has haunted me for millennia!" I said. "Every time I struck another child, it was you I was hitting. Every time I sent them running off into the dark, it was *you*! Why have you come to torment me?"

"I don't know anything!" said the boy, almost in hysterics. "Please don't hurt me!"

"I have already killed you once, when the world was young," I said. "*Can* I kill you again?"

The boy began blubbering incoherently in terror.

"Why, after a thousand thousand generations? Why now?" I demanded.

And suddenly the crying stopped, the terror left, and it seemed that he had been possessed by something coldly rational.

"I am not here to torment you," he said in the voice that still haunts my every moment. "You have paid your penalty. It is time to make your peace with God, and to rest."

"God has sent you?"

"How else could I be having this conversation with you, my brother?"

"And what does He want of me?" I asked.

"Only that you beg Him for His divine forgiveness."

"I begged Him for that ten million full moons ago," I said. "When I wandered cold and alone in the land of Nod, I confessed my guilt and asked for His mercy." I paused. "You see what it got me."

"Ask Him again," said my brother. "This time He will listen."

"Has He no memory of what I said?" I demanded. "Can God not recall my confession and my plea?"

"He is God," said my brother, as if that answered everything.

"Then go to Him and tell Him that He must ask for *my* forgiveness, for the punishment He gave me is totally out of proportion to the crime I committed."

"You took my life."

"Have you any idea how many men have taken the lives of other men? Do they all wander the Earth, meting out punishment to those who perform acts of force? I don't think so, or the world would not be overrun by violence."

"No," admitted my brother. "You are the only one. The others have other punishments."

"So I am the only one condemned to right wrongs and defend the defenseless?"

"It is not a condemnation, my brother. It may have felt like a punishment, but it is a high calling that has cleansed your soul. Otherwise I would not be here to present God's offer."

I considered his words for a long moment.

"I will stay here," I said at last. "*Someone* must avenge the children."

"God will send another," said my brother.

"He may say so, but He is not to be trusted," I replied.

"Blasphemy!"

"Nonsense," I said. "We are what we are. You were made a victim, and I was made a killer. If I were not avenging acts of violence, I would be perpetrating them."

"But this need not be!" protested Abel. "God loves you!"

"If God loves me, I shudder to think what He does to those He merely likes!"

"You are an evil man!"

"You noticed," I said. "But by killing you, I find that I am doing the Lord's work. Isn't that ironic?"

"I shall curse your name as long as I live, Cain!"

"That won't be as long as you think, my brother," I said, approaching him with a grim smile on my lips.

It was over in a matter of seconds. The police will round up the usual suspects, and they may even convict one of them of my crime, but since I have no true existence, no fingerprints, no thick file in their headquarters, they will never know what truly happened.

Just before I vanished, I felt *His* voice inside my head:

Thou hast broken thy covenant with Me, Child of Perdition! From this day forth, until Judgment Day, thou shalt be an outcast to My kingdom, and thy only existence shall be as the Children's Avenger!

Blessing or curse, it all depends on your point of view. Retribution is the one job for which I am perfectly suited. Even as I write these words, I find I am being drawn to the alleyway behind the grocery story on Oak Street.

I can hardly wait.

Disney on Ice

Ellen Guon

FADE IN

LOS ANGELES, CALIFORNIA, LATE 1980s

ESTABLISHING SHOT—LOS ANGELES—DAY

INTERIOR SHOT—APARTMENT

We see a young woman, her apparent age around 23, seated at her desk. Next to her, the computer printer is just finishing printing a letter.

CLOSE ON THE LETTER

The letter is addressed to a story editor at Disney Television. We can read the first few lines, in which the screenwriter is offering her services to the studio in spite of the fact that there's a Writer's Guild strike in progress.

ANOTHER ANGLE ON THE YOUNG WOMAN

She reaches for the letter in the printer's tray, and gazes at it for a moment. Then she crumples it up into a ball and tosses it into the nearby trash can.

CUT TO:

You've heard the stories, I'm sure. Everybody has. That Walt Disney was cryogenically frozen after his death, and that his body is kept in a room underneath Sleeping Beauty's castle in Disneyland. Set up in a display case, so his blank, frozen eyes can still survey his empire. It's a great story, especially if you want to spook someone out on a late night trip to Disneyland.

Me, I know the truth.

It started on an awful day during the Writer's Guild of America strike. Except that it wasn't an awful day, really, any more than all of the days that had preceded it. For months, I'd been working as a temp flunky for Feature Animation, in the old warehouse building on Flower Street. Just a few minutes' drive away from the main studio lot and the strikers. Another day sitting at a desk, doing mindless drone work for countless hours instead of pitching ideas to television editors and writing scripts. To be followed by an evening of sitting at home, staring down in the Past Due notices on my bills and another nasty letter from a collection agency.

My boss dropped another of his Memos of Death on my desk. "Make sure that the Camera Room gets copies of this," he added, walking away. "You forgot them last time."

Right. As though it mattered. I think his last memo was asking people to suggest decorating ideas for the company picnic. I photocopied the memos and began walking the copies through the building, dropping them in in-boxes and on people's desks. The door to the Camera Room was closed, predictably enough. I knocked and waited for a reply before entering.

The camera room was bathed in a warm, red glow, making everything look very surreal. I handed the two guys their copies of that asinine memo, then glanced up at the usual photograph of Walt hanging over the camera flatbed.

"Looks kinda like the Devil, doesn't he?" one of the cameramen said, smiling.

"He sure does," I said. "Have you heard that story with him being cryogenically frozen?"

"Who hasn't?"

I was walking back to my desk when it suddenly hit me. What

if Walt Disney had made a deal with the Devil? What if Disney had been cryogenically frozen when he was dying . . . at that point, would he be alive or dead? Technically, he'd probably still be considered alive. That'd be a great trick, to make a deal with the Devil and then cheat him out of his due by never really dying.

I had this image of Walt Disney, frozen like a chunk of ground beef at the supermarket, his glassy eyes open and staring, still trying for some semblance of a commanding presence. And a frustrated Devil standing there with clenched fists, outraged at being cheated of his prize.

It was a kernel of a great idea for a story. Unfortunately, with the Writer's Guild strike, no one was paying for great stories anymore, not unless you were willing to walk across a strike line. And I wasn't willing to do that.

At least, not yet.

Another few hours of work, then it was time to walk out of there and drive home, past the line of screenwriters striking at the main studio. Every day, I'd see them there, holding their signs, waving at the cars driving past. I'd drive past them on my way home, then drive past them again in the morning, on the way to the job that I hated.

I just couldn't do it anymore. I had to earn a living as a writer. I had to be something, or this would slowly drive me crazy. Something had to break, before I did.

Tomorrow, I had decided, would be different. Tomorrow I would walk up to the gate, walk past those strikers and onto the studio lot. I'd be writing again. I'd be earning my living as a writer, not as a flunky. All I had to do was walk past the strikers and through the gate.

It wasn't like I didn't have to go to Disney tomorrow, anyhow. I walked through a door into the hallowed Disney Empire every day. This wouldn't be any different. I'd just be walking through as a writer, not a temp flunky.

Liar, a small voice whispered to me silently. *Liar liar liar* . . .

I could do it. I'd only have to do it once. After that, we could conduct business by phone, fax, email. I wouldn't have to do it again. Christy, Katherine, Larry, and Joe, they'd all be in the line, but I'd just ignore them and walk right on past.

What would they do? What would they say?

I knew what they'd say. That I was being an idiot. How could

I sell my soul so cheaply, for a script or two? A few grand for killing my conscience forever. And what if it didn't die? What if my conscience lingered to haunt me, like some fading ghost that doesn't have the strength to hurl objects around the room, just lurking and whispering in the background?

What would Disney have been paid in exchange for his soul, if he had really sold it to the Devil?

Or . . . look at the alternatives. I could leave L.A. and go someplace new. I could get out of screenwriting forever. And I was sitting at a desk, one step away from walking away from here forever.

I'd been invited to a party at Marv's that evening. A lot of my friends would be there, television writers and comic book writers. I wasn't in the mood for partying, but it was better than staying at home. Besides, surrounded by the people whose ideals I was going to betray, it'd be a good place to decide this whole thing, once and for all.

I drove past the last few strikers, now folding up their banners and carrying their signs to their cars. I drove through the rush hour traffic all the way across the San Fernando Valley, and pulled up at Marv's just as it was getting dark. Not too many people were there yet; I got a beer and found a quiet corner of a couch in the living room.

It wasn't quiet for long. Katherine found me there, even as I was trying to fade into the background. She looked good; standing out in the sun was brightening her fair hair, making it much closer to blonde. I knew she could tell something was wrong with me, though, by the look in her eyes. "How's it going? Doing anything interesting?" she asked.

I nodded. "Yeah. I'm starting on a spec script. I had a great idea, a story about Disney being cryogenically frozen to avoid paying the price for a deal with the Devil."

"Hmm, get ready to be sued within an inch of your life when you try to sell it. Roy & Crew will *not* be amused." Katherine was an ex-Disneyite, too . . . she'd been there for about six months, and knew the mentality.

"Well, it doesn't matter anyhow," I said, taking another sip of beer. "It's not like I can sell anything now."

"The strike won't last forever. You know that, even if you don't believe it now." She stood up and waved hello at someone across the room. "Excuse me a sec, okay?"

"Sure."

"Ah, here you are. I've been looking for you."

I started at the sudden words from behind me, and turned quickly to look. There was a man sitting down next to me.

"Good evening," the stranger said. "I'm sorry I startled you." He was impeccably dressed, even for such a casual party, in what was clearly an Armani suit. Just the shoes were worth a few hundred bucks, more than I'd make in a week as a production flunky. He looked like your typical Hollywood guy, with the ponytail, a single earring, and the flip phone bulging from his suit pocket. Dark hair and intense blue eyes. A producer, or an agent.

"You aren't a writer," I said. "None of us starving writers can afford to dress like that."

"No, I'm not a writer," he agreed. "I'm here for business, actually. I came here to talk to you." He smiled, showing even white teeth. "I'm with an agency." Then he dropped the agency's name casually, the way I'd expect a rich person to drop a Waterford crystal that they didn't want anymore.

I blinked. "You're really here to see me?"

"Of course. Though I didn't expect to have to track you down at a party. I like your idea for the Disney story, by the way."

"You do?"

"You should make the Devil very charismatic, of course. Incredibly handsome. A fitting opponent for Disney. It's a good story, I can probably sell it." He leaned against the back of the couch and took out a cigarette from an expensive case. "I know all about you, girl. You're a production flunky at Disney right now because you can't get any more writing work. You're afraid that you'll never amount to anything. But you will, because you have that burning spark inside you. You're the kind of person I'm always looking for."

"All I want to do is write," I said. "I just want to walk into a store and see the kids watching my episode on the row of television sets, or see the posters for my movie up in front of Mann's Chinese. You probably get a hundred people like me every week."

The stranger nodded thoughtfully, and then blew a cloud of smoke in my direction. "No, you're different. I can make it happen for you" he said.

I felt faint. He was serious about me, this guy from a top agency. "What's your cut? Ten percent? Fifteen percent?"

"I don't do bits and pieces, none of the small stuff," he said. "If I represent you, it's for everything. Career guidance as well as contract negotiations. You'll have to dedicate yourself to what I'll make of you. Because I," he said, "am the person who can make your dreams come true."

I couldn't help but laugh. "God, that's a tacky line. Now I really believe you're an agent."

He smiled, though I noticed that the amusement didn't quite reach his eyes. "You need me. You need me very much. And I need people like you." His voice grew quieter. "I know about your old agent, the one you don't talk about. I know how he told you that to get a writing job, you'd need to spend a weekend with the producer. I know you smiled and made a joke about it, and then went home and cried."

Stunned and more than a little angry, I just stared at him. Finally, I found my voice again. "Who did you talk to? Katherine?"

"Does it matter? Everyone talks. You're a good writer but not known well enough to get a good agent, which makes all the difference in this town. You're not a Scientologist or anything special that'll help you get through the doors. You've been told who you have to sleep with to have a screenwriting career, and you don't want to do it."

I couldn't look at him. "I wanted to be a writer, not a whore. Why is that so hard?"

"Because the world doesn't care. You have to not care, either. Do what it takes to survive, to succeed. It's you or them." He ground up the cigarette in a nearby ashtray. "I don't waste my time on people who aren't willing to pay the price. I only pick the winners. You're a fighter. I need people like that. You're willing to do almost anything to succeed. You almost walked across the WGA strike line. By tomorrow, you might actually do it. I respect that."

"You do?" I stared at him in shock. "I thought it was the most loathsome thing I'd ever contemplated in my life."

He shrugged. "It's just getting the job done. And you can do it."

"How about ethics? Integrity?"

Somehow, his blue eyes became even more intense. "This

is Hollywood, girl. Those won't get you far. Talent isn't enough. You need contacts, and luck, and the right attitude. You've sold a few scripts, started to get a career off the ground, but you won't amount to much of anything here. This town will eat you up and spit you out."

"I've already learned that," I whispered.

He smiled. "Take my card. Think about it. Call me." He handed me the card, then walked away without another word.

My head was spinning from the conversation, the sudden change in my possible fortunes. A major agency pursuing *me*? What a concept.

The next day, I sat in my car for a long time, looking at the strikers. All I had to do was get out and start walking. They probably wouldn't even say anything to me. Just start walking and keep walking, right past them through the studio gate.

I got out of the car, and I walked across the street to the strike line. Christy was there with her white cardboard sign in one hand and a Pepsi in the other.

"Hey there, lady!" She waved me over. "Want to keep me company for a while?"

I managed to smile. "Sure. You're looking good."

"Yeah, it's the Pepsi. Caffeine is my best friend. I'm tired, not getting enough sleep. Stressed. The money's starting to run out. How about you?"

I shrugged. "Same old, same old. Doing production flunky work while I wait for this to end. Something's got to break soon."

"I know. Any day now."

That was what everyone had been saying for the past month. We spoke for another few minutes, then I headed back to my car.

I couldn't do it. Not after talking with Christy, and seeing the rest of them, looking exhausted and worried and desperate. I couldn't do it, not today.

That's when I saw him. He was parked across the street in a black convertible BMW, wearing bright mirror shades. His face was shadowed, but I knew it was him. The agent.

He couldn't be there for me. He was probably waiting to be fashionably late for a high-powered meeting with Eisner or Katzenberg. I didn't go up to talk with him. It didn't feel right. But I still had his card in my wallet.

I could almost feel his eyes on me, like a physical touch. What in the hell was he doing here?

That afternoon, I gave notice at Disney. I don't think anyone noticed, even my boss. He just sort of shrugged and asked me for the phone number of my temp agency.

I boxed up the few personal items I'd brought into the office, and walked out to the parking lot. It was still sunny and warm, a beautiful day. I wondered whether any of the WGA strikers had brought suntan lotion with them. If I was walking the strike line, it'd be in shorts and a bikini top. Why waste that good L.A. sunshine?

It would be hypocritical beyond belief to go see my friends now, having made the decision to cross the line tomorrow. But a day like this was meant to be spent outdoors. I decided to make a different pilgrimage of sorts.

I drove to the Forest Lawn cemetery in the Burbank Hills, overlooking the Disney studio lot and the water tower with the Mouse. This was the place, if my research had been right. I parked at the bottom of the hill, and began walking.

If you had to be buried someplace, this place wasn't so bad. The cemetery was green, despite the long drought. And pleasant, in a morbid sort of way. Most of the cemetery was graves marked with plaques laid flat on the ground, so it looked more like a park than anything else. Further up the hill were mausoleums, mostly gaudy but a few tastefulness. I started searching in the high-rent district or the cemetery at the top of the hill.

Surprisingly, it was only a few minutes before I found it. A large mausoleum, with numerous people buried in it. A simple metal plaque with a name on it, and some dates. I gazed at the plaque, not certain what I wanted to be feeling at this moment, then I noticed someone walking toward me from the road.

It was the agent. He walked over the trimmed grass, taking the shortest possible path toward me, not caring where he set his feet. Anyone else would have detoured around the gravesites, not walked across them, but not this guy. "I thought I'd find you here, after hearing you talk about your Disney story," he said, leaning against the stone wall. "So, have you made a decision yet?"

"I don't know," I said. "I just don't know."

He smiled. "If you work with me, things will happen. You know that. You'll be amazed at how quickly it'll happen."

"You wouldn't talk percentages with me back at the party. Will you do it here? What will your services cost me?"

"We'll figure that out as we go. To start with, you know what you have to do. Just . . . do what you have to do to succeed. You can start by walking across the Writer's Guild strike line tomorrow."

"I've thought about it," I admitted.

"No, you've decided to do it," he countered. "You're going to do it tomorrow. That's why you quit your job today."

"What is it with you?" I asked. "Why do you keep following me? How do you know every detail of my life?"

"It's my business to know people. You'll do all right. Tomorrow will be hard, but after that, it'll get easier. You'll see."

"I just don't think I can do it. I don't think I can walk past my friends in the line. I can't be that cold."

"You can do it. Everybody does it."

"No . . . not everybody. There's Katherine, we used to work together at Marvel Productions, she was just a secretary but now she's making it as a writer. She's like me, she's not Guild yet, but she will be soon. She's standing out there on the line with everyone. And Misty in Oklahoma, she's sold her first fantasy novels, she's going to make it big. She's working like crazy, working full-time as a programmer and writing half the night. She's going to make it, all on her own. She isn't hurting anyone to do it. She's just doing it."

The agent blew a cloud of gray smoke in my direction. "You have to be willing to succeed at any cost. If you don't, you fail."

Maybe it was a trick of the smoke, but suddenly he looked very strange. Through the gray haze, I saw him differently for a moment. His blue eyes looked ancient and cold, with no hint of warmth in them, like an actor forgetting to play the part for a moment.

At that moment, I knew who he was.

"No, I can't do it," I said. "There are some prices I'm not willing to pay."

He should have just walked away. But from his tone, it was also obvious that he wasn't willing to quit, not yet. "You know what you're giving up, don't you? I won't come back for you. I won't waste any more time on you. If you say no, that's it. It's over. You'll never get this chance again."

"I know," I whispered.

"I've seen a lot of kids like you," he said. "Some small amount of talent, but lacking the drive and brains to succeed. Stupid. With the words 'Not going to make it' written in burning letters on their foreheads. You'll be waiting tables and typing some executive's letters for the rest of your life. That fire, that creative spark, that's not enough by itself. You think that's all you need, but you're fooling yourself. You're giving up your dreams for a little self-righteousness. You think that'll keep you warm at night, when you read in *Variety* about the people making the major deals, living the dream that you walked away from? You're giving that up, and for what? Nothing. Absolutely nothing."

"But I won't hate myself," I said. "And I won't owe anything to someone like you."

"Stupid," he said. "Noble, but stupid. Goodbye, kid." He started to walk away.

"Wait!" I called after him. He stopped, and looked back at me.

"There's something I have to know," I said. "Did he do it? Did Disney cut a deal with you?"

He smiled. "That would be telling," he said.

I watched him go. He didn't look back.

Now what? Tomorrow, I didn't have to go to Disney for more drone work. I was done with that. Tomorrow I could do anything I wanted. I had a little time, until the money started to run out. Some time to think and make decisions. I needed a change.

Oklahoma, maybe. My novelist friend had offered me crash space at her house for as long as I needed it. Oklahoma would be a big change for the better. I could learn how to write novels instead of half hour toy commercials with storylines.

So I'd be walking away from my screenwriting career, but so what? It was time for something new.

"You seemed like you were having quite an argument with that young fella," someone said from a few feet away. I turned to see one of the cemetery employees, leaning on his rake. He was a very old man, wearing a grass-stained jumpsuit, with an old baseball cap pulled low over his eyes. He must have been in his eighties, at least.

"It was nothing," I said. "Nothing at all."

"You know, young lady, you're not the first person to come here," the old man said. "Seen lots of people come here. Guess a lot of folks don't believe that Walt Disney is really dead."

"They think he's frozen," I said. "That's what everyone thinks."

"He picked a good spot for himself," the groundskeeper observed. "I think he must have gotten very tired, toward the end. Probably just wanted to get out into the sunshine a little, find some quiet, restful place for himself, away from all the crowds, everyone who wanted a piece of him. A place where he could look out over his empire. Don't you think?"

I looked away, down at the Disney buildings below, the water tower with The Mouse painted on it, the tan buildings of the soundstages. I glanced back at the groundskeeper, who was watching me closely, with those bright, mischievous eyes. The old man, smiled, wiped the sweat from his eyes, and walked away.

Those eyes . . . no, it couldn't be . . .

No. I don't want to know. Some things, it's better not to know. I'd rather just believe.

I could have run after that old man, but I didn't. Instead, I started the long walk down the hill, just thinking about it all. So, did Disney make a deal with the Devil? I don't think so. Is he cryogenically frozen at Disneyland? Definitely not.

Is he buried at Forest Lawn?

Well, maybe.

Am I going to make it through this awful time?

. . . Yes. Yes. I think I will.

EXT FOREST LAWN CEMETERY — DAY

The young woman walks away from the stone mausoleum building. The man in the expensive suit is standing off to one side near a row of trees, unseen.

AGENT
(quietly)
That's another one for you, Walt.

He gets into the convertible black BMW and drives away.

CAMERA PULLS BACK

As the man drives away, we watch the woman, now a tiny figure in the immensity of the grassy cemetery ground, walk down the hill towards the city below.

FADE OUT

The Release

S.M. & Jan Stirling

Don winced as the flat, harsh light from the fluorescent lights stabbed suddenly at his eyes.

"What are you doing?" he asked Lisa in a sort of stifled scream. His heart had almost choked to a stop in horror.

"No windows," she said calmly, whipping the black ski mask over her head and shaking out her blond hair.

God, she's cool, Don thought with admiration.

"They're over here," Lisa said, moving gracefully towards a row of glass cages.

"Crocodiles?" Don asked in surprise. *I'm risking jail for these?* The only reason he was involved with the animal rights group was to get close to Lisa. The only reason he was risking his whole life doing this was to impress her. *Because frankly this animal rights stuff is bullshit.* He'd been in the group six weeks and he was starting to dream about steak. "Reptiles," he muttered in disgust. "Why did it have to be reptiles? They're only one step up from bugs."

"They are helpless innocent animals with as much right to live free as you or I," Lisa said severely, glaring at her partner with stunning blue eyes.

"Maybe so," Don said petulantly, "but they're disgusting and they stink."

Lisa blinked. It was unusual for Don to disagree with her. But she rallied quickly. "Don't get speciest on me," she told him. "We have to rescue these animals." She glanced around. "Here," she said dumping disks out of a plastic box. "We'll use these. And they're alligators. Not crocodiles."

I don't care what they are, I'm not touching those slimy things with my hands, he thought as he reluctantly took the box.

There were six of them and they were as white as maggots, with pale amber eyes. One of them yawned, revealing a peppermint pink mouth and a fringe of tiny but mean looking teeth.

Then he spied a pair of heavy gloves and what looked like hot-dog tongs. *Oh, thank God*, he thought. He lifted the lid of one of the tanks and laid it aside without looking at what he was doing. It knocked several sealed beakers to the floor.

"Good idea," Lisa said.

"What?"

She swept the glassware on a lab table to the floor with her arms.

"Lisa! For God's sake! Stop that. you don't know what's in those jars, it could be something dangerous." *It could also bring the guards down on us. You're making a hell of a racket*, he thought.

"I don't care," she said defiantly. "Knowledge gained by torturing animals is evil and should be destroyed."

So, like, we shouldn't have insulin or polio vaccine? he thought.

"Don't you have the courage of your convictions, Don?" She knew he didn't, knew exactly why he was with her tonight. *Not that I care, if he does the right things for the wrong reasons the results are the same*. And there was the off chance that he might learn. *Not that I'm holding my breath*.

She's magnificent, Don thought. He couldn't take his eyes off the way her bosom rose and fell beneath the tight black sweater. *What the hell, I don't have polio*. "You're right," he said fatuously. "Go ahead."

While he packed the baby gators in the emptied diskette boxes she smashed vials and bottles, emptied the refrigerator, danced on diskettes and hammered a scissors into the hard drive with an alabaster paper weight.

They finished at the same time.

"I'm jealous," he said aloud, admiring the destruction.

"I saved you one," she said reaching into the refrigerator. She put the little bottle in his hand.

"Thanks." He grinned and dropped it.

She leaned over the smoking puddle of broken glass and presented a quick kiss on his mouth for a reward.

"C'mon," she said.

They were slipping through the hole they'd made in the fence when they were suddenly blinded by powerful flashlights.

"Hold it right there," a harsh voice demanded from out of the glare.

"No!" Lisa declared. "You have no right to torture and kill these innocent creatures!"

"Over there," Don said, indicating an open manhole with a safety barricade around it.

They retreated at a run and slipped through the triangle of orange saw horses with their flashing lights. Don looked down into the black hole they guarded apprehensively.

"We can't let them catch us," he said.

Lisa glared at him. "We can't let them catch *them*," she said, meaning the alligators. She took a deep breath and dropped into the hole.

Don's heart dropped with her. *My God!* he thought. Some of these holes were eighteen feet deep. He heard a splash below.

"Come on," Lisa said impatiently.

Don looked around and there was a hand reaching out for him. With a yelp he stepped forward into blackness.

The senior security guard looked into the hole, then at the man next to him.

"No," that man said.

"Me neither," agreed his senior.

Don was a fastidious man and being up to his neck in sewer water was hideously disgusting to him. All he could think of was the myriad diseases that were slipping into his body through every orifice. In fact, he was already feeling downright sick.

"Lisa!" he called.

"I'm right here," she said. "Turn over onto your back. Just relax and float, go with the current."

He didn't appreciate her coolness anymore. Now he thought that she was too stupid to realize the danger they were in.

"Where are your gators?" she asked, very concerned.

"I'm fine, thanks," he said through gritted teeth. "I've got them."

"Well, hold them up. I don't want them to drown."

Given that they were being swept along in pitch blackness in water of unknown depth he felt this was a bit much.

"They're made to swim," he said. "Maybe we should let them go."

"Are you crazy? Do you know how many diseases you can get down here?"

Jesus! he thought. *I'm trying to forget.*

"Lisa," he said insincerely reasonable, "If we don't get out of this water soon *we're* going to be an endangered species. I'm freezing and I'm going numb. Be a shame if they drowned because they were trapped in their boxes after we die."

She was quiet for a moment. *I'm cold too*, she thought. *Maybe he's right.* Hard as it was to believe. But even stupid people were right sometimes.

"Let's wait a bit," she said.

They drifted for what seemed an eternity in the darkness. Don grew colder, his hands were like chunks of frozen meat. *Why don't I just deep six these little bastards?* he wondered. *What's she gonna do? Sue me?*

It was then that they hit the sand bar.

"Oh, God," Lisa said, and placing the boxed gators high upon it, she then grabbed at it with clumsy hands, dragging her freezing body upwards through sheer determination.

Don was right behind her and she saw with gratitude that he'd kept his reptilian burden. They flopped onto their backs and looking up saw a sewer grating above them.

"You're right," she said at last, her speech slurred. "We have to let them go."

Oh, thank you Mother Nature, he thought sarcastically. He didn't offer to help when she crawled over to the boxes. He noticed that neither of them had thought to call for help. *Oh right. Like someone in New York City is going to respond to cries for help coming from the sewer.* Waste of energy even thinking about it.

Lisa crawled back and flopped down beside him.

"I think we're dying," she said. "Something in one of those vials . . ."

I told you not to break things, he thought. *But no-oo, evil knowledge must be stamped out. You stupid bitch.* He wanted to say it to her, but he was too tired to try. He couldn't move anymore, not even a finger. *Great, I finally get to lie next to the most beautiful woman I've ever seen and I'm paralyzed. It doesn't get much better than this.*

Lisa had expected the alligators to take to the water the moment she freed them. But instead they were coming towards the two humans. *Probably looking for warmth, poor things,* she thought. *Boy are you guys headed in the wrong direction.* She wondered why she wasn't shivering. She was so cold.

Don felt the little clawed feet begin to climb his leg, but he couldn't move his head to look. Slowly, though, the little beady eyes lifted over his hip.

It's so little, he thought, almost pitying, realizing how vulnerable it would be to rats, *so helpless.* The gator cracked its tiny jaws and hissed suggestively. *So hungry.*

How *You* Can Prevent
Forest Fires . . .

Keith R.A. DeCandido

"Cassie, *what* are you doing?"

I wanted to ignore the voice. I knew it was my younger sister, and I did not want to talk to her. Or to anyone else, really. But she hadn't gone away when I ignored her any other time in the last eighteen years, so I was pretty sure that wouldn't work this time either.

I looked up to see her standing in the doorway of the bedroom she and I used to share before my twin brother Paul moved out. Her right hand occupied itself by twirling her not-naturally-blonde hair. "Well, gee, Sunni," I said, "I'm checking over the stuff in my dive bag. I'm wearing a bathing suit. It's a beautiful Saturday morning. What do you *think* I'm doing?"

"You're going diving, aren't you?"

I sighed. "Your grasp of the blindingly obvious remains strong." I turned my back to her, hoping that now she'd go away. Kneeling down next to the big mesh dive bag, I went on checking to make sure it was all there. Wetsuit—check. Fins—both here. Knife—present. Mask, hood, and snorkel—yup. Buoyancy Compensator jacket and regulator—all there. First aid kit—yes. Sunscreen—no. Damn. Have to stop at the drugstore.

"Cassie, you *can't* go diving."

I snarled, but did not look at my sister as I made sure the dive computer had fresh batteries in it. She could insist on staying, but I was damned if I'd give her the satisfaction of looking at her. "Why not?"

In a tone that implied a "duh!" Sunni replied, " 'Cause there are *forest* fires!"

My sister had made a lot of leaps in logic in her life, but none so high, so far, and so graceful as this one. I gave it a 9.2.

Realizing I wouldn't get any peace until she finished whatever loopy train of thought she was on, I turned, put my hands on my hips, and glared at her. "Sunni, what're you talking about?"

"Don't you know how they put out forest fires?"

"With water, generally," I said, throwing her "duh!" right back at her.

"Don't you know how they *get* the water?"

"It can't be that hard. Three-quarters of the world is covered in it, y'know."

"They've got these, y'know, *helicopters* with these really *big* scoops, and they scoop up the water and dump it on the fires."

I suppose it was possible. I guess. All I really knew about forest fires was that they were bad and that there'd been too many of them near here lately—both north of us, near L.A., and east of us in New Mexico and Arizona. We hadn't had any fires here in the San Diego vicinity, at least, but that didn't stop us from getting drought warnings.

Sunni wasn't finished. "And every time they do this, they always find some *divers* in the forest, *burned to a crisp*."

Make that a 9.5. "Who told you this?" I asked as I zipped the bag up.

"That skanky guy you've been hanging out with—he told me when he came over last week."

"You mean Xcott?"

"Yeah, him. And that ditzy girlfriend of his."

That would be Geena. And yes, his name really is Xcott, which is pronounced the same as Scott; it's just spelled with an X. We're both victims of ex-hippie parents—in fact, that's why my boyfriend Gary introduced us. His parents named him Scott-with-an-X; mine named me and my twin Castor and Pollux (yes, I know that "Castor" was a guy, please don't get me started) and named our younger sister Sunflower.

Xcott was also my mentor in diving. When I first saw that

copy of *Ocean Realms* in Gary's dorm lounge, I realized that I just had to become an underwater photographer. See, I've always loved taking pictures, but never found a subject I liked to photograph—until I saw that amazing shot of a sea anemone that was taken in Bonaire. Then I knew what I had to do.

Or, at least, I thought I did. Xcott was the one who told me that I couldn't just go underwater with a camera. I needed to get certified as a diver (Sunni, who thought the whole thing was stupid, said *certifiable* would be a better word) and get a ton of equipment. It still didn't take that long for two reasons: One, we live in La Jolla, California, about six seconds away from the beach. Two, I have very rich, high-powered-lawyer parents. They seem to figure that they've built up a huge karmic debt from spending their "sordid youths" (their words) sticking us with names like Castor, Pollux, and Sunflower. So they will indulge virtually every whim we have. When Paul decided to quit college and wander the roads "looking for America," our parents sent him off with their blessing and a wad of cash. When Sunni decided she just had to have a Jaguar, she got one. And when I realized that I had to be an underwater photographer, which included a big shopping list of equipment, that list was filled.

Xcott showed me all the places to dive in the area, he taught my certification course at the dive shop he co-managed with Geena, and he was my buddy on my first few dives. He also introduced me to Dina Rosengaus, a tall Russian woman who, as it turned out, was the one who took that picture of the anemone in *Ocean Realms*. She showed me all the tricks of underwater photography, and how it differs from the above-water kind. (Dina also turned me on to a source for a wetsuit that would actually fit. I'm 5'11", and they just don't make wetsuits for amazons. Of course, except for Dina, every female diver I'd met was 5'2" and petite, so there probably wasn't much of a demand.)

I moved past Sunni to the bathroom (one of three upstairs) that doubled as my darkroom.

"*Cassie*, you're not *lis*tening to me! You *can't* go diving!"

"Sunni, you didn't actually believe him, did you?"

Inevitably, she followed me into the bathroom. "Of *course* I did. He's been diving, like, for*ever*, he *knows* this stuff. You said so yourself."

I had, too—mostly when I first started diving, and Sunni kept asking me thousands of times if this "jerk friend of Gary's" knew what he was doing.

"Well, he was probably pulling your leg," I said as I gave the underwater camera—same as a regular camera, mostly, except for the waterproof casing and the huge strobe light attachment—a once-over.

"I *still* don't think you should go diving until they put that *fire* out."

I once again barrelled past Sunni and went back into the bedroom. She followed, not giving up. "Cassie, I—"

"Sunni, look," I said, whirling around and putting on my best I'm-your-older-sister-and-I'm-six-inches-taller-than-you-dammit voice, "I have had a really fucked-up week, okay? I've been completely submerged in that stupid Keats paper, and when I haven't been doing that, I've been taking shit from Liverakos." Dr. Liverakos was the professor to whom I was a teaching assistant at the University of California, San Diego's Revelle College, where I'd been a grad student for a year. "It looks like next week is going to be even worse. So today, I'm finally getting a chance to take a break from all of it, and I'm going diving. Period, end of discussion."

And with that, I turned my back on her, packed away the camera in its bag, hefted it and the dive bag, and for the third time barrelled past my sister.

"Okay," Sunni finally said to my back as I went downstairs, "but if you get killed, *I get your room!*"

It's really hard to describe how much I love diving. Most non-divers just don't get it. I mean, I tell people I'm a diver, and they nod and say, "Oh yeah, I've gone snorkeling a few times myself," like that means anything. Saying you know about scuba diving because you've gone snorkeling is like saying you know about skydiving because you've jumped off a low tree branch.

I'll never forget my first real dive. When you train to get certified, you start out in a classroom, then you go into a pool, then finally in open water. The pool diving didn't excite me, and I almost gave it up, but then Xcott took me into the Pacific for the first time.

The freedom is amazing. I mean, yeah, you have to keep

track of your bottom time and your air intake and your surface intervals and all that, but after a while you do that as easily as you walk on land. And you don't think about it, and you just enjoy the freedom. You can move any way you want, you can go over things and under them, and the water covers you like the world's biggest flannel blanket.

But the best part is the fish. So many different shapes, sizes—and colors! The colors are just incredible. There's nothing like it on land. And they just love to dart around you and toward you and under you and over you, and I swear some of them actually pose for my photographs. And then there's the kelp forests, which just have to be seen to be believed.

So, of course, the dive that day was incredibly boring—I just saw a few flounder and a bunch of starfish. It just made me crankier. Probably my last chance to dive for at least a couple of weeks, and none of the fish wanted to come out and play. Not even a sea otter to frolic with.

Eventually I'd had enough. I swam up toward the surface, taking a safety stop at about twenty feet below the surface. (Safety stops are three-to-five minute pauses during your ascent to give the body a chance to shed any excess nitrogen that's built up during the dive; you don't always need to, particularly after a dive this short, but I don't like to take chances.) About two minutes into the stop, I saw a quick glint of something that reflected the sunlight. I turned to see a curved piece of metal coming toward me. In a moment of sheer lunacy, I thought it was a scoop. *Oh my God, Sunni was right, I'm gonna get scooped up and dumped on a burning Sequoia. . . .*

Then I came to my senses and actually looked at the thing. It was a hubcap. As it floated slowly downward, I got grumpier—partly because I hated finding crap like that in the ocean, mainly because for a minute there I actually believed Sunni's bullshit story.

Afterward, I angrily tossed the dive bag into the back of my pickup truck, said goodbye to Geena and the other folks at the dive shop, and went home. Things looked up immediately—Sunni's Jag wasn't in the driveway, so she was probably off with her dippy friends pretending to study while really cruising for guys. With Mom and Dad in Las Vegas on business for the weekend, it meant I had our big house to myself.

The pictures I took were all of real dull subjects, so developing them would have depressed me, and the absolute last thing in the world I wanted to do was tackle Keats. So I turned on the computer and checked the scuba diving list on the Internet that Xcott and Geena had spent ages talking me into trying out. I finally gave in a month earlier, and also joined a commercial online service that had a scuba section on it, including weekly live chats on Saturdays.

So what's the first message I download? Somebody asking about the helicopters with their scoops that dump water and divers on forest fires. This guy's question resulted in about twenty-five replies within an hour of the original post, all with the same pissed-off tone, all saying, basically, "Don't be stupid."

Except for one guy. His e-mail address was something cutesy like SEALION@whatever-it-was.com. He kept insisting that it was true, that his wife died that way. Nobody paid any attention to him, but, thinking about it, no one ever paid any attention to him, no matter what he said. And he'd posted quite a bit in the past month. I thought that was pretty mean, really. I mean, his wife *died*.

My boyfriend and his suitemates were throwing a party in their dorm for no real reason that night. ("We're seniors," he said, "we're supposed to party." I don't remember ever acting like that when I was a senior.) But he told me it would start at nine, which meant it wouldn't get going until at least ten-thirty, so I figured I could hang out in the scuba chat room.

Within minutes, I was having a great time gabbing with Anna Bronstein, the sysop, and four other people about how hard it is to photograph parrotfish.

Then a guy with the user ID SEA.LION joined the chat.

\<SEA.LION\> Hey there. Are you the same C.ZUKAV who's on the scuba list?

I blinked, then typed, "Yup, that's me."

\<SEA.LION\> Cool. I just joined up here. Good to see a familiar face.

It was the same guy, I realized. The one who said his wife died by being scooped.

But everyone on the list said that was just a joke.

I decided that Mr. Sea Lion had been trying to razz the guy who asked the question on the list, so I didn't bring it up in the chat.

At close to eleven, I finally logged off. SEA.LION hadn't said a lot, and none of what he did say mentioned his wife or scoops. And nobody really responded to the few things he did say. This made me feel better for some reason. I announced that I was heading off to my boyfriend's party, and everyone said goodbye.

We live walking distance from UCSD, which is why I never bothered to get a room on campus. Seemed stupid to give up one-fourth of a huge house for one-half of a dorm the size of my parents' walk-in closet. So I hoofed it to Revelle College's senior dormitory for the party.

I grabbed a beer from the plastic garbage can by the door that was full of ice and Budweiser cans. I couldn't see Gary, but I did see Xcott. I said hi, told him about my dull dive that morning, then asked him why he told Sunni that dumb story.

He laughed. "Oh, man, I'm real sorry, Cass, but Sunni's, like, so easy, y'know?"

Geena walked up just then. "Who's easy?"

"Cass's sister." After Geena fixed him with a very nasty look, Xcott quickly said, "I mean she's, like, easy to *tease*. Remember, we got her with the forest fire story?"

That brought a smile to Geena's face. "Oh yeah, she bought that one with a credit card." (Geena always came up with metaphors that sounded wrong somehow.)

I felt reassured after that. Then I asked, "Hey, you seen Gary?"

Xcott frowned. "Not in the last few minutes."

I wandered around for a while, but no sign of Gary. His roommate, Mike, was acting like an asshole in the middle of the room. Half a beer, and Mike was completely plastered. The other four guys who lived in the suite were nowhere to be found—probably off at someone else's party.

Finally, I gave up and went into the bathroom.

That's where I found Gary. He was liplocked with some bimbo. Neither her hair color nor her chest were the ones she was born with.

I stood there with my mouth hanging open. I couldn't actually say anything, but I just kept standing there. They didn't even notice me for something like five minutes. Then Gary came up for air and saw me standing there.

"Oh, uh, hi Cass. How you doin'?" He sounded very drunk. "Didn' hear y'come in. Oh, sorry, this's Bambi. Bambi, this's my friend, Cassie. Sheeza grad student."

Bambi. Her fucking name was *Bambi*. My boyfriend was making out in the bathroom of his suite with a woman named after a fucking cartoon character, and his reaction is to introduce me to her! As his "friend."

"You goddamn pissant pus-eating slime-caked insectoid Neanderthalic fucking *shithead*!"

Then I threw my beer can at him.

My memory is hazy on what happened next. I think I yelled at him a little. He acted all innocent. Bambi looked confused (probably still trying to figure out what *Neanderthalic* meant).

Then I stormed out. I think I knocked Mike on his ass when he got in my way. (It's easy when you're 5'11" and really pissed.)

I don't actually remember walking home, but I must've. The next clear memory I have is logging on.

Sure enough, the scuba chat was still going on. However, the only two people in the room were SEA.LION and Anna the sysop. This scrolled by just after I came into the chat room:

<SEA.LION> They finally found her in the forest. Right there in the *middle* of the forest. In full scuba gear. I mean, how else did she get there?

Oh God.

I didn't type anything until Anna prompted me:

<A.BRONSTEIN [Anna]> Hey there, Cass. How was the party?

Thank you, Anna, for changing the subject. "Lousy," I typed. "My boyfriend is the scum of the earth."

We went on for a while about how men are pigs. Mr. Sea Lion didn't say a word until he finally left the room without even saying goodbye. Some others joined the chat, at which point Anna, good sysop that she was, steered the topic back onto diving stuff.

When I left, I checked the e-mail on my UCSD account. There were four. One was from Gary, time-stamped from before the party, which I deleted without reading. Two were from the scuba list. The last was from the Sea Lion. "Sorry for leaving so suddenly," he said. "I just wanted to warn you to be careful. With all the fires over in your neck of the woods, diving might be risky."

I don't know what possessed me, but I actually replied to this. I decided to play dumb, and ask what possible connection there could be between diving and forest fires.

After I sent it, I regretted it, but it was too late.

Maybe he'd ignore it.

I went down to the kitchen, yanked open the freezer, and was relieved to find that Sunni hadn't touched my tub of chocolate chip cookie dough ice cream. I put a depressing Nick Cave album on the CD player, ate ice cream, and tried to come up with imaginative ways to kill Gary.

I didn't get a reply to my e-mail to Mr. Sea Lion for two days, but when I did, it was a doozy.

I'd spent Sunday holed up in my room with Keats. Sunni tried talking to me at one point, but I gave her a real nasty look, and she stayed away from me for the rest of the day. I spent Monday on campus, helping Liverakos, and being surly to anyone who came within ten feet of me.

Monday night, I logged on and found a pile of scuba list e-mail, another e-mail from Gary (I didn't delete it—yet—but I didn't read it, either), and one from the Sea Lion.

He wasn't kidding. He hadn't been pulling anyone's leg. His wife really was found in full scuba gear in the middle of a forest fire that had been put out in Canada somewhere.

The e-mail he sent went on for several pages. It went into all kinds of specific detail—where his wife was found, where she'd been seen last, stuff like that—most of which I glossed over.

My first thought was: *It's true. It's all true.*

My second thought was: *Get a grip, stupid. You don't know who this guy is. You don't even know his real name.*

He's probably just a psycho. There are lots of them on the net.

I closed the file and read the rest of the stuff from the list. It was a typical day's worth of messages: Lucienne had just gotten back from the Cayman Islands and posted the beginning of her trip report; Greg's dive computer turned out to be a lemon, and he posted full brand information so people could avoid it; Glenn and Brandy asked for hotel recommendations in Key West, to which half a dozen people had replied; and the schmuck calling himself "The Regulator" kept the flamewar about solo diving going for another day. All typical, ordinary, normal diving talk. No scoops. No charred corpses in forests.

Then the phone rang. We have a dedicated modem line, so the call didn't kick me offline, but it took me a minute to locate the cordless—I barely made it before the machine kicked in. "Hello?"

"Cass, it's Geena. You seen Xcott today?"

"Uh, no, why?"

"'Cause I haven't seen him since noon, that's why. His gear's all gone, though."

I sighed. "Geena, are all the boats still there?"

"Uh, I think so—lemme check."

I heard Geena put the phone down, and I put my head in my hands. She didn't even think to check the boats. Worse, if Xcott's not around, she's supposed to be managing the dive shop, and she doesn't know if all the boats are accounted for?

"Well, the boats are all there," Geena said when she got back to the phone, "but Manfred just told me that Xcott had been talking about doing a beach dive. So maybe that's where he is. Sorry to've bothered you, Cass."

"Hey, no big deal. Hey, did you read Lucienne's trip report yet?"

From there, we spent half an hour doing scuba gossip. Geena was still pretty worried about Xcott, since he obviously went off somewhere without telling her. I thought at first that that was pretty mean—what if something happened to him? But then, I didn't always tell Sunni or my parents where I was going all the time. Hell, half the time, they'd only know I was gone because the truck wasn't in the driveway.

By the time we got off the phone, it was almost ten.

Liverakos had some kind of family thing Tuesday, so I had to handle his sophomore lit class by myself—and it started at eight-thirty. So I got undressed and climbed into bed.

At one, the phone rang. I'd kept the cordless in my room, so it woke me up. "Mfginer?" I said, the closest I could come to, "Why the hell're you calling me at this hour?"

"Cass, it's Geena!" She sounded completely nuts—the way Sunni sounded when she broke a nail. "Xcott *still* hasn't come back! Marty and Nic said they saw him do a beach dive at six, and he hasn't come back yet. We gotta find him—can you get down to the shop?"

"Uh—"

"And bring your dive light!" And then she hung up.

I stared at the phone for a while, not sure that this wasn't all part of a dream.

After a minute, I realized that it wasn't, and that I'd never hear the end of it if I didn't go down to the shop. Besides which, I'd never get back to sleep.

I clambered out of bed, put on a bathing suit, started to go downstairs, remembered I'd need my gear, went back upstairs, grabbed the dive bag, started down again, remembered Geena asking me to bring the dive light, went back up again, rummaged through my closet, found the light, put it in the bag, then went down a third time.

The television sounded from the living room. I went in to find my father channel surfing, various bits of paperwork all over the floor around him. He did this when he had to stay up late working—take occasional TV breaks.

"Where you going, hon?" he asked, hitting the "mute" button on the remote.

"Dive shop," I said, and realized that I sounded like the walking dead. I was not in any shape to dive, much less search for someone who probably had already finished his dive and gone home and didn't bother to call Geena. Or maybe he was seeing another woman. It's all the rage these days. Maybe he and Gary had a contest to see who could cheat on their girlfriends more successfully. Or maybe Nic and Marty saw someone else on the beach. Why wasn't I in bed like a sensible person?

"Isn't it a little, uh—late for that?"

"Some kinda crisis. Gotta go help."

My father frowned. "Well, okay, but be careful. And remember, it is a school night."

I nodded and started to leave. My father gave me a final concerned look, then de-muted the TV.

"*—fires are now under control. One body was found in what was left of an oak tree, apparently wearing some kind of r—*"

"*—nd, there can be only one. May it be Du—*"

Suddenly, I was wide awake. "Go back!"

"What?" my father asked.

"Go back to that news thing on the fires!"

He flipped the channel. "*—e'll have more on the latest fire to hit Southern California in a little while. Up next, Headline Sports.*"

Then it cut to a commercial.

"What was it he said?" I asked. "The body was wearing what?"

"I'm not really sure. Why?"

"Did he say 'rubber'?"

"I don't think so. Cassie, are you okay?"

I shook my head. This was insane. "Never mind, it's nothing. Really."

Of course it was nothing. That was just a story. A myth. It didn't really happen. How the hell would they get the scoops onto the helicopters anyhow? It was crazy.

I went out to the driveway, tossed the dive bag into the bed of the truck, got in and pulled out.

"*They've got these, y'know,* helicopters *with these really* big scoops, *and they scoop up the water and dump it on the fires.*"

"*Cass's sister. I mean she's, like, easy to tease. Remember, we got her with the forest fire story?*"

"*Oh yeah, she bought that one with a credit card.*"

"*They finally found her in the forest. Right there in the middle of the forest. In full scuba gear. I mean, how else did she get there?*"

"*One body was found in what was left of an oak tree . . . .*"

No. It was stupid. Xcott was probably off drinking somewhere. He had not been dumped on a forest fire.

I pulled into the dive shop parking lot. Several other regulars had shown up and were piling into one of the shop boats. Geena looked the most worried, but everyone seemed kinda nervous. That's when it hit me that Xcott could still be lying dead underwater somewhere. And the cops wouldn't be any help—he hadn't been missing long enough. Just because he hadn't been scooped didn't mean he wasn't in trouble.

So a bunch of us went out in a boat. One guy who's name I couldn't remember was fiddling with the tuner on a radio.

"—orest fires continue to rage—"

Then the guitar riff from some Eric Clapton song or other came on. "There we go," he said. "Always better to dive with classic rock."

We each took an area where we would look for Xcott. When we got to my location, I got onto the platform, held my mask and regulator to my face, and started to step forward.

"Uh, Cassie?"

I turned back toward the radio fiddler. "What?"

"You *may* want to put your fins on first."

Great. I can't even remember to put the stupid fins on. As everyone laughed at me, I got off the platform, put on my fins, and then stepped off the platform into the ocean.

I felt like I was being smothered. Tonight, it wasn't a flannel blanket, it was a pillow someone had shoved onto my head. I turned the dive light on and started looking.

Every time the light shone off something metal, I panicked, thinking I was going to get scooped. At one point, I almost lost my regulator, which would not have been a good thing. Then I'd drown and everyone'd be searching for *me*. Then Gary could feel guilty. Might even be worth it for that.

Christ, Cass, get a grip!

I didn't find him. That's probably because he wasn't there to be found. This whole thing was a waste of time that was just keeping me from getting a good night's sleep. If Xcott did turn up alive, I'd probably kill him.

We each agreed to search for an hour. After I'd been down for forty-five minutes, I headed back up for the surface, giving myself time for a safety stop.

As I trod water twenty feet under the surface, the water started churning. I looked up, pointing the light upward. Between that and the almost-full moon, I could make out some kind of shape right above the water.

I squinted, trying to figure out what the shape was.

After a minute, I realized that it was a helicopter. Panic

started bubbling in me—the water churned more as the 'copter moved closer to the water—

—and then it pulled away. The water grew calm again.

If I hadn't been wearing a wetsuit, I would've put my head in my hands. The 'copter was probably there for some legit reason. Maybe Geena had a friend with access to one and had asked him or her to help look for Xcott.

Whatever it was, it didn't have a scoop and wasn't about to dump me on a forest fire. This is the last time I dive when I'm half-asleep.

Five minutes had passed, so I prepared to swim back up to the surface.

That's when the tentacle grabbed my foot.

I looked quickly down and saw a massive thing that was all scales and teeth. It started pulling me closer. Three days worrying about a scoop, and I get attacked by some kind of crazy sea monster!

My regulator came loose as I started to scream. . . .

Cold Shoulder

Susan Shwartz

Just that evening, the crowd of parents and Pep Club in Roper Stadium had cheered as their team, huge in shoulder pads and helmets, dashed out of the tunnel onto the field whose floodlights extinguished the moon. After the game, Tommy wandered out by himself onto a battered football field lit only by the tunnel's humming fluorescent lights. So what if he'd kicked the winning field goal? It hadn't kicked down the wall between himself and the rest of the world. When the crowd had seen who'd made the point, it had stopped cheering, and some creep had whistled.

Everyone in town knew Tommy Foreman had gotten Laura McKelvey in trouble. She had lots of friends; and everyone was still pretty mad and taking it out on him.

Last year, people had waited around for him. But the band was all packed up, and even the cute-but-dumb drum majorette who twirled twin sabers had gone off too. Tommy wandered off across the ploughed-up football field. He kicked at the dark soil that his cleats had turned up when they'd torn at the grass. You could still see the chalk of the yard lines in some places. Programs and a few leaves blew in the vacant stands. He shivered and hunched his shoulders against the October wind.

Time was when girls saved their best smiles for him and boys clustered about, back-slapping, when he'd show up at dances with his arm around Laura. Now, they looked at him as if he were a preacher's kid who'd gotten drunk and spit up in church. The story was Laura had gone out to California to stay with an aunt, but if you believed that, you probably were dumb enough to believe in Santa Claus and the Tooth Fairy. Everyone knew when she started getting sick in the mornings, then spending too much time in the nurse's office. When she fainted during a Pep Rally, folks were sure. Wasn't as if he'd talked, it wouldn't have been nice, but all the guys knew they were doing it.

The night she'd told him, he could scarcely understand what she said, she was crying so hard. "What're we gonna do? Tommy, they kicked me off cheerleaders, said I was a bad example . . . and . . ."

"What's the matter, Laura?" he'd asked. She'd interrupted *Death Valley Days*, his favorite Western, but she was a sweet kid, the cutest girl in school, and she let him inside her.

"Tommy," she whispered, and he knew that if her folks hadn't been in the house, she'd have been wailing. "I'm gonna have a baby!"

He'd gulped and let the phone fall. *Now, what do I do?* His life closed in on him so he couldn't breathe. By the time he picked up the receiver again because he'd finally thought of something stupid to say, she'd hung up.

Then her father had called Pop. When the shouting stopped, Pop called him in and demanded, all head-of-the-family, *Son, what're you going to do now?* and Mom said it was all the girl's fault for leading a good boy on.

Turned out there was going to be a big family council at McKelvey's. "Go put on your suit," Mom told him, for all the good that would do.

Mrs. McKelvey didn't even have so much as coffee out. (Mom raised an eyebrow. Whenever people came over to *their* house, she had the dinette table set with a white cloth and the good china and the cake stand out.) Laura sat by her mother, looking down at her saddle shoes and crying. She was plainer than Tommy had ever seen her. Mr. McKelvey and Pop didn't shake hands, and none of the grownups lit cigarettes. The TV in the living room was off.

It would have been different if they were getting engaged. Then it would have been all smiles and girlfriends' envy and talk about the darling little baby. Babies were darling if a girl had a ring. Otherwise, they were little bastards-pardon-my-language, and the girl's reputation was ruined.

"You all know what's happened," Mrs. McKelvey started the ball rolling. Tommy was surprised. He'd have thought the men in the family should take charge. After all, Tommy had always taken charge with Laura—though see what it got them! "The question is what we're going to do now."

Everyone stared at Laura and Tommy. His ears got red till he felt like a jack o'lantern.

"I think the boy should do the right thing," said Mr. McKelvey. "He'll finish school. With luck, they won't kick him off the team. Laura can do her GED at home—their home."

What?! If Tommy had been holding a cup or glass, he'd have dropped it. Maybe Laura was ready to get married, but he was too young.

Mom cut in. "I think you should get rid of it."

Pop's jaw almost dropped to think Mom would say something like that. The couple times they'd talked he'd told Tommy women don't have morals, for all that Mom was so big on the whole family's going to church. Maybe she knew she and his sister Linda—Tommy'd kill her if she got herself into trouble!—needed it even more than the rest of the family.

Laura's dad's neck swelled up like a Thanksgiving gobbler.

"Not an AB," her mother said, glaring at Mom. "Sometimes it doesn't just kill the baby, but the girl too. Hasn't my poor baby had enough?"

Pop looked kind of sick, and Mr. McKelvey looked like only the width of Pop's shoulders was keeping him from punching out Mom. Some people just have no manners.

"She could have the baby and put it up for adoption," said Mrs. McKelvey. "We'd say she was going to my sister's for the school year, but . . . "

Tommy blinked. How could the woman talk like that? First, about killing a baby, then about Laura's maybe dying, and now about giving away a baby—his son, maybe—as if it were a kitten no one wanted.

"Don't give it away!" he blurted.

"What am I supposed to do?" Laura cried. "I'm a nice girl, I can't just bring a baby home like one of those . . . those funny-looking girls in *National Geographic* with the funny hair and no tops on so they can feed their babies and don't use proper bottles. What do you think I am?"

"Well, I think that's pretty obvious," said Tommy's Mom, sweet like poison, and Laura started crying again.

Mr. McKelvey looked at Tommy narrow, sizing him up to see if he could work, maybe, and said again, "I still think the boy ought to do the right thing."

"I'm doing the right thing!" Tommy cried. "I got a future ahead of me. I have to make something out of myself."

"So do I," Laura said. She was fighting in her own weepy way.

"You already did," Mom said, and Tommy knew there'd be no peace in the house if he brought Laura home to Mom.

Aside from Laura being about to be an unwed mother and all, the heck of it was she'd been just the sort of girl you wanted to bring home. What's worse, he knew the time would come when he'd be looking for a nice girl. After he'd gone to school, gotten one of those big executive jobs with a bigger desk so he could make all the money he'd need. The mills were okay for summers, but Pop wanted him to be Someone. Then he'd have a boat, and the nice girl could stay home with the babies while he took the boys out on the boat.

Girls. They had to go and spoil things, then cry and want you to fix it just because. It was Tommy's whole life at stake.

But this was Laura after all, and she'd been so sweet. Mom always said Tommy had a soft heart, just look how good he was to his sister Linda, making sure the boys treated her right.

"Look," he said in a softer voice, "maybe I can't get married now, but in a couple of years. . . . Just don't give it away. . . ."

His voice had stopped cracking a couple of years ago, or he wouldn't be in this fix; but it cracked now.

Laura collapsed sobbing onto the couch.

"Why, you little bastard." Mr. McKelvey started for Tommy, his fists up, and then Mrs. McKelvey had left Laura crying onto a cushion and hung onto him, crying herself; and Mom was crying, and Pop pulled them all out of that house and bundled them into the Buick and back home.

Tommy hoped he'd never have to live through another evening like that.

That was all anyone had said, but the word went out, and Tommy's bank account with his summer money from the mill got confiscated; and Pop, half-embarrassed, half-proud, had the talk with him he probably should have had a whole lot earlier about urges and using rubbers.

Everyone else gave him the cold shoulder, though.

Tommy sighed and walked out the gate of the stadium. Pop's Buick was mostly off-limits now since his parents figured that's where Laura got into trouble. His own junker was up on blocks 'cause there was no way he could afford to put in the 8-cylinder engine he wanted.

Past Ohio Ave. Down to Elm Street by the Drugs. No one was there, sitting on the stone walls, leaning against the lamp post, except for the cop ("you call him 'Officer'"), Ol' Man Adams who stood in a circle of light.

"All alone, son?" he asked. Adams had known them all since they were kids.

Then, he saw it was Tommy and his face changed. Tommy almost groaned. Jeez, not him too!

"That was a fine goal you kicked tonight, Tommy," said Officer Adams.

"Thanks, sir," he said, just like nothing was wrong and he was the perfect, golden boy again.

Adams shook his head. "They're giving you a bad time, are they?" Tommy didn't want to talk about it, but at least someone would talk to him as if he didn't crawl on the ground. "I've seen it before. Kid goes a little wild—young blood, you know—makes a bad mistake, and next thing you know, town's too hot to hold him."

"Aw gee, Officer," Tommy said, looking down and kicking at a pebble. Guys like Officer Adams thought it was "manly" when a boy stood up straight and called them "sir," until they started in on him. So he looked down and acted awkward when he knew he didn't have an awkward bone in his body. His body did what he told it to.

Did he tell it to knock Laura up? Tommy blinked. It was the first time he'd thought of it like that.

Well, he guessed was glad he knew he could have kids now, but this one had sure bought him a lot of trouble.

"You want to hear what I'd do if I was you?" Adams was asking.

Tommy knew he had to nod his head *yes.*

"I'd tough it out and finish school this year, then go into the Service. With those shoulders, you'd be a cinch for the

Marines. Come back with a uniform on your back and money in your pockets, and everyone'll let bygones be bygones. Maybe even that nice girl . . . you know it's a shame about her, Tommy. . . ."

The Marines had sent Unk to Korea. He said he was so darn cold there (but he didn't say "darn") that all the *jo-sans* in Seoul couldn't warm him up. Linda had asked what a *jo-san* was and been sent to do homework, but they let Tommy stay. Unk had even given him a beer.

"You're not listening, are you, Tommy, lad?" asked Mr. Adams. "Too wrapped up, are you? Well, when you stop feeling sorry for yourself, think about it."

Tommy sighed and walked away, forgetting to stand up straight. Maybe he should have married Laura after all. He'd tried to do the right thing. When he'd tried to write her and say he hoped they could be friends, his letter came back marked "Addressee Unknown." The story was her parents were moving out of town.

Cripes, she'd looked so pretty at the junior prom in that white strapless formal, almost like a wedding dress, she giggled; but Reverend Nieman wouldn't let brides in his church wear strapless dresses. He'd given her white orchids from his summer job money that he'd earned working in the mill, and she smelled of baby powder and that gunk that comes in a blue bottle that all the girls are crazy about.

He couldn't help himself. After the prom, they'd gone parking at the old Catholic graveyard. Didn't seem respectful to do it at the Presbyterian one near the church. One thing led to another, and that strapless dress didn't help. He had it down around her waist and all those ruffles of her long skirts way up over her knees, so he could see that soft skin between her stockings and her panties with the lacy garter belt, all shining in the dashboard lights. She let him touch her there, then even higher; and he kept pleading with her to let him . . . let him . . . oh god she was so beautiful . . . let him . . . just let him . . . oh god he loved her, he loved her, it felt so *good* in that minute when his knees went weak and he felt like he did when he woke up sticky in the mornings and had to go wash himself.

She hadn't known how to make him stop. He didn't think he could have even if she'd really tried. She'd spent the whole ride home crying and putting Kleenex in her underpants so the blood didn't get onto all those stupid white ruffles. She said she'd tell her mother she had an accident, one of those things that always happened to girls and that his sister giggled at with her friends when they looked at *Seventeen,* which might as well have been the Bible for the way they talked about it, and flipped past the Kotex ads real fast.

The shower after the game had felt good. For all the cold shoulders Tommy had got that evening, he felt good too. He wished they hadn't sent Laura away. He wished he had her here, right now. He'd have her skirt up around her waist again in a minute, and she'd let him.

Why'd she have to get in trouble anyhow?

He walked toward Gypsy Lane a little stiffly, like he had to pee and his pants were too tight, but feeling better than that.

Then, he saw the girl walking toward him on Ohio Avenue.

She was beautiful. She was so gorgeous she wasn't even Veronica in a town full of bouncing Betties but something totally different. Better. She looked like Audrey Hepburn in that soppy thing they'd had to sit through when they let Mom pick out the movie for her birthday. She even made Laura, all gussied up for the prom, look like a hick.

"Hi!" he said, expecting to get the old high hat the minute she saw it was ol' Poison Tommy.

"Hello," she said, smiling. He had never seen her before in his life, but that smile—he wanted to make her smile again.

"I don't think I've ever met you. After all, if I had, I'd have to be blind, deaf, and dumb not to remember. What's your name?"

She turned that amazing smile on again. "Mary . . . "

Mary Martha? Mary *Myrtle*? Sure as God made little green apples, no parents on earth could have been dumb enough to name this gorgeous thing "Myrtle."

She laughed like the glockenspiel at half time when the band marched down the field.

"Mary Myrta. You say 'Meer-ta.' "

Oh, foreign. That explained it. She was one of those new immigrants. Not Mill people, though. They lived over by Brier Hill way. The girls from Brier Hill were supposed to be easy and a lot of fun, but some of them didn't just have brothers, they had old men who worked with molten steel, and it didn't do to get them mad.

If her folks were immigrants, well, you didn't come more American than he was. He looked at her again, real close this time. She sure didn't go to Roper High. Maybe she went to Villa Maria, that queer place girls went to if they were Catholic and wanted to be nuns or big brains. Wasn't as if it was a real school. It didn't have teams and there were no boys. Maybe it was okay for foreigners, who were queer that way, like the Jews who'd started settling here. Their girls were bossy, and their boys weren't much for sports, but all the Jew kids made Honor Roll. Pop said none of those boys would ever be let into the mills to work as long as white men had sons and nephews, and Tommy could be thankful for that.

Oh, this girl was so pretty, and Tommy was lonely and still kind of excited. Maybe he did want to get married real young after all. Maybe he'd have his very own war bride, and *he* wouldn't have to join the Marines to get one, either. Those foreigners kept their girls at home so much, he'd just bet this little Mary Meer-ta was a great little housewife already.

"Did you miss your ride home from the game?" he asked her. She had to have. Next, he'd ask her if she'd seen him make the final point. He'd offer to walk her home; a pretty girl like her shouldn't be out all alone in the dark.

She smiled at him, her dark eyes huge in her pale face. "Ride . . . game . . . I forget . . . "

"Daydreaming, were you?" he asked. "Well, it's night-time now. I haven't got a car, but I can walk you home if you like. Or if it's far, we can go to my house and Pop will drive you."

Or maybe a miracle would happen and Pop would let him take the Buick. Another miracle.

"It's not far," she murmured. Then she shivered. "I'm cold. May I wear your sweater, please?"

Funny about that. Tommy didn't feel all that cold, though his breath was steaming, along with other parts of him. She had to be foreign. No American girl would be bold enough to ask to wear his letter sweater. It meant she was his girl. Linda had begged to stitch the big orange and black **R** on it when he'd won it. She blushed and said it was practice for when she had a home of her own, and Laura, who was going to wear it, smiled and said she could. After the stuff with the baby and all, he'd found the sweater in a brown sack on his front porch. Mom had had it dry-cleaned so it didn't smell of baby-powder and Evening in Paris anymore.

Tommy draped it over her shoulders. He was feeling kind of squirmy—those urges again. Thanks to Pop's advice, he even had a rubber in his wallet. She was foreign. Maybe she didn't know enough . . . he should be so lucky!

But the girl was talking now. Strange stuff, not just about the game and the weather, but how the evening made her feel. That poetry-type stuff, what a guy had to listen to before girls let you kiss them.

"Which way do you live?"

She pointed with her chin, and he walked her home like she was the reverend's wife. One of the pretty little houses down where Gypsy flows into Logan, with a lot of trees and bushes. He'd done enough yard work to see, even in the dark, they were well tended. A light was on in the front porch, and a faint mist rose about it.

Well, wasn't she going to ask him in, or put up her face or anything?

"Well," said Mary Myrta, "thank you for walking me home."

And put out her hand as if she wanted to shake his. For all the world as if she were one of the guys!

He took the offered hand and pulled her toward him for that kiss he'd been imagining the last five blocks.

She tugged it free. "I just *met* you," she blurted and ran up the shallow stairs of the stone porch and inside. He saw a tall rectangle of light gleaming indoors. Then, as the door shut, it turned dark. The porch light switched off, leaving him standing there in too-tight pants like a jerk.

He was almost all the way home when the night wind made him remember. He'd left his letter sweater with Miss Mary Myrta, world-famous tease. Well, he was going to get it now, and tough if it woke up her mom and dad. They were probably up watching Jack Paar like all the old folks.

Walking fast, whistling because it was so quiet, he returned to the brick house and knocked. He knocked for a long time. After awhile, the door opened, just a crack, and what had to be Mary Myrta's parents peered out, suspicious-like. Tommy could see inside the house. Foreign, all right. There wasn't even a proper TV across from the man of the house's

Barcalounger in the living room—not even a Barcalounger. Just books and dark wood and a few queer pictures.

He gave the parents his best shy grin. "I'm Tommy. I walked your daughter home after the game. She was wearing my sweater and forgot to give it back. It's cold out."

The parents—dark-haired, pale-skinned like their girl— stared at each other like they were turned to stone.

"You're the Foreman lad, aren't you?" asked the father. "I've heard . . . heard much about you. You're the one that got that girl in trouble, aren't you?"

His voice had an accent. Maybe they were commies. Pop says next to George Patton, Senator Joe McCarthy is the greatest American of this century, and they both got brought down by queers.

"What does he say, Walter?" asked the girl's mother. "He asks for our daughter?" She drew a sharp breath like she was going to scream, and her hands went out. Tommy stepped back a little.

"Hush, Giselle. We left that behind us in Europe too." Gently, he pushed her behind him. "Tomas—" he said Tommy's name with that queer accent— "Foreman. I know boys like you from Europe with your fair hair and your blue eyes as if the light shines through your skull to the sky with nothing in between. Blond brutes who come and take what they want and kick with their hobnailed boots."

What was this old crazy man saying? You wore cleats, not boots, to play football.

"Go home," he said. "Go home and pray for a good heart. *No*, Giselle. I *told* you. Let it die. Let it rest in peace." He turned back to Tommy.

"Son, you've got a bad reputation for being careless and hurting people. But I can't think that you're as deliberately cruel as the boys we saw in Europe. Our daughter is dead—" he hurled the word at Tommy like a football. "She died a year ago today, on her birthday. In a car crash with another beautiful American blond boy. We don't have your sweater. I wish we did."

"Go home," the mother said. "Go home and pray for a good heart. Marry that nice girl you hurt. If she'll have you. Spend the rest of your life making up to her the pain you cost her. I shall pray you choose right, but don't ever come back here. Good *night!*"

That . . . that jerk had practically called him a Nazi! Tommy had half a mind to march back and tell him that his father was in the VFW, and him and Mom always voted Republican. But the door slammed *that's-that*! and all the lights went out in the house. Sneaking about and hiding in the dark, that's all people like that were good for. Why, Tommy had a good mind to . . .

It was getting really cold out. Tommy walked away, whistling to show he didn't feel bad, not that the girl was dead, not that her father had ordered him off. Anyways, he didn't believe it, not one little bit. So they thought they could warn him off—bad dog! bad! In that case, they had another think coming. He'd tell Pop, and Pop knew people in the Mayor's office. But before he went home, he'd do something to show that Tommy wasn't some pansy that some commie traitor could push around.

Besides, he really wanted his sweater back.

He looked up at the moon. *Now what?* he asked it.

The light bulb went off in his head, just like in the comics.

Running back to the house, he slipped inside and "borrowed" the keys to the Buick. Pop would kill him if he knew, but with luck, he'd be back in no time. He let the car coast out of the drive so Pop wouldn't hear it, then fired up the ignition and headed off to the Catholic cemetery. It was wicked to go there, so wicked you felt like doing anything you wanted; and you did want.

Laura had been scared the first time they went there, but he'd told her it was safe, they were in the car, and pretty soon, he'd gotten so hot that the windshield had steamed up and she wasn't scared any more. Leastways not of the cemetery. The Buick smelled of baby powder and that blue stuff the girls all liked.

Tommy was starting to feel all hot and bothered, but it was cold, even with the car heater on, and the place was creepy with statues and crosses like one of those bombed-out cities in the pictures of Europe.

Now he was here, he had to go through with it. He parked the car and got out. *Really* creepy. It was way too late in the year for lightning bugs, but cold greenish lights flitted and darted across his path, dancing like they were leading him somewhere.

He puckered up to whistle, then stopped. Whistling in a graveyard was about the worst luck there was . . .

Since he didn't have a better idea, he followed the lights. Might as well go that way as any other and at least, he wouldn't fall and break a leg. Bad enough he risked catching his death of cold, as Mom would say.

The place was full of old willow trees, branches drooping on the ground or lashing in the wind. The next gust blew some of the branches of one of the largest trees aside. It was all so Creature Features Tommy had to laugh. And when the little lights flared up, showing Tommy a small, even humble tombstone, he wasn't surprised. The grave was decorated with a bouquet of autumn flowers, he forgot the name.

And on the headstone, neatly folded, was his sweater.

Well, in that case, Mary Myrta wasn't going to need it any more, now, was she? Tommy reached out to pull the sweater off the stone the way he might tug the towel off a girl at the beach. She always protested, then gave in.

He felt a sudden tug. When he looked up, Mary Myrta was standing by the tomb, holding onto an arm of the sweater. She looked sad and angry and remembering, all at once.

Idiot! Tommy scolded himself. *Scared of a girl!*

"It was cold," he said, "and you'd taken my sweater. I wanted it back. I worked hard to earn it, and it means a lot to me."

"Did you go to my parents and inquire?" the girl asked with that odd accent of hers.

Tommy nodded.

"You dared!" she hissed. "And . . . "

"Your father told me to go away, and your mother to pray for a good heart. Your father told her that . . . something . . . was left behind in Europe, but I don't think she believed him."

Mary Myrta smiled. To think that just that evening, Tommy had tried to get her to smile. He stepped back, but didn't let go of his sweater. His. He'd earned it.

"You are quite right, Tommy. Mother didn't believe him. And neither did I. But you should have listened. How can such a smart boy have been such a fool? A fool about everything, Tommy, not just about Laura. Everything. And what's worse, one who thinks he's always right."

"Hey!" Tommy protested. "It's cold out. I let you wear my sweater 'cause you were cold."

"Every chance, Tommy. First Laura, and then, if you'd had time, me. You don't learn, and now school's over. I'm sorry, Tommy."

Her dark eyes grew huge and cold as Sputnik in outer space.

"Mary, will you for Pete's sake cut that out? You're giving me the willies! And I'm freezing!"

Mary Myrta smiled coldly.

"You won't have to worry about the cold for long, Tommy. I promise you."

How could he ever have thought her an easy mark?

Boy, are you dumb! He had time for that one last thought before Mary Myrta's eyes grew huge and even colder. Rime frost covered his own eyes, and his blood froze. His body toppled onto the grave, with the clatter of snapping icicles. then sank into the faintly mounded earth at the base of the headstone.

A little steam rose from the sweater that lay on the ground, and it unraveled. The orange and black strands of the **R** on the pocket writhed in mute protest in the chilly air for just a little longer.

Tommy would never have to worry about being cold again. Or, for that matter, about anything else.

Payback

Barbara Paul

I knew it was going to be a rotten day the moment I saw the *Dallas Herald* had cut off my dangling participles.

Grrrr. Three times a week the *Herald* prints my column: "Good English for Americans" by Molly Showalter. That morning's column was a summary of what I saw as the Seven Deadly Sins of modern grammar (subject-verb disagreement, like that). It was meant as an introduction for my next seven columns, one Deadly Sin per column; the seventh was dangling participles. But that last Deadly hadn't made it into print. I'd been edited down to six Sins.

Nobody gives up a Deadly Sin without a fight; I punched out the number of the *Herald* city desk and got Marty Hicks, still on from the night shift. "Marty, what happened to my participles?"

A pause. "All right, I'll bite," he said. "What did happen to your participles?"

"They were cut," I snarled. "I do a column about the seven most common grammatical errors and you cut one of them out?"

"They must have needed the space," Marty said vaguely. "Come on, Molly—you've been writing for newspapers long enough to expect that sort of thing. They do the best they can."

"Doesn't anyone read what's being cut?"

"I'm sure they do. Do another column about the missing thing, the participles."

I reminded him I'd already turned in the next seven columns, one of which was about participles. "But today's column makes me look dumb," I insisted. "I say 'Here are seven danger spots' and give them only six."

"Oh, I doubt that anyone noticed." Real concerned, he was; I would have made Marty's head start sprouting feathers if I could have.

"What about syndication?" I demanded. "Did the cut version go out to the syndicate newspapers?"

"No no no," Marty assured me. "They always send out your original copy. I'm sure they did this time, too." This was getting me nowhere; I muttered a useless curse and hung up.

All that before breakfast. I made a note to do a column on the use of "they" as a method of accountability-avoidance.

Griselda turned up her nose at Sheba Savory Duck in Meaty Juices, her favorite last week. Her dry Friskies were untouched. I opened two other cans of cat food, but she wasn't having any of them, either.

"That's it, Griselda," I told her. "Four kinds of food are out. It's that or nothing." She meowed to be let out, throwing me a dirty look over her shoulder as she left without saying a word.

My newspaper had abbreviated me and my cat was mad at me. Two bad omens.

But the toaster obeyed instructions and popped up two golden-brown halves of an English muffin. (You can't get real bagels in Dallas.) Already the heat was shimmering in the street outside the kitchen window; it was going to be a scorcher. I ordered the air-conditioning to turn itself on.

I took my second cup of coffee in with me to the computer. My e-mail led off with a couple of solicitation letters— *Get rich quick using your computer! Only a small investment fee to get started!* I deleted them both.

Then the bad news started. A University of Texas graduate student I paid to do research for me had quit school and was joining a rock band. My auto insurance was cancelling me because I'd had the nerve to put in a claim when somebody ripped off my tape deck. An online shopping mall swore my order was shipped a month ago and suggested I contact the Post Office. A muchpromised treasurer's report for the Dallas Journalists Association that I headed just hadn't gotten written, too much to do, you know how it is, ha ha ha.

None of which did anything to improve my disposition.

Oh, a pox on all of 'em. Only one thing to do when every little thing starts going wrong: bury yourself in work.

So I started a new column, one about the bewildering new practice of connecting verbs to short adverbs with a hyphen ("I told him to hurry-up"), a nefarious habit that was spreading like wildfire. My scorn would be blistering. I sat before the computer with my arms folded, watching as my thoughts appeared on the screen.

My coffee cup was empty. I couldn't make a fresh cup appear out of thin air. Some people with The Gift could do that, but I had to go through the step-by-step spellcasting process to brew a fresh pot of coffee. I'd forgotten to use a blocker and had to erase the words of the spell from the computer. It wouldn't do to have words like *argha, mene ti makless* appear in the middle of a column about grammar.

Now, before you get the wrong idea, I'm no devil-worshipper who meets in a coven with others for the purpose of performing unspeakable acts. The witches who go in for that sort of thing are *weird* and I want no part of them. No, my powers are limited—rather more so than I would wish, but there you are.

My vanishing spells are shaky; there are a number of people I wouldn't mind seeing disappear, but I'd never been able to make the spell work on something the size of a human being. The largest thing I'd ever made vanish was a tom cat that was giving Griselda a hard time. Also, I'm not very good at long-distance spells; more than a couple of city blocks and you can't count on them. And my ability to cast forgetting spells? Fergit it. It's why I'm no good at spellcasting over the telephone; I can't make the people I talk to forget they'd heard me mumbling incantatory phrases at them.

But there are compensations. I can make a broken-down car start. I can fix a VCR. I can rewire a faulty light switch without touching it. My computer never gives me trouble; it wouldn't dare. I think of myself as a technowitch.

So I'm limited in what I can do, but I'm pretty good within my limitation. Another thing I'm good at is meeting deadlines; I wrapped up the rough draft (very rough) of the new column and stored it to polish later.

The phone rang; it was Elizabeth next door. "I'm sorry to disturb you, Molly," she began, "but I'm wondering if you'd take a look at my microwave oven when you have a minute. It's stopped working altogether and I don't know if it's worth repairing or whether I should just buy a new one. Maybe you could advise me."

Translation: *Come fix my microwave for me.*

"You're so good with mechanical things," she finished apologetically.

I hesitated, but then said I'd be over in a few minutes. I liked Elizabeth; she was a middle-aged lady, a widow, and a good neighbor. But lately she'd begun suspecting that I had something going for me that other people didn't have. I don't believe she'd actually thought *witch* yet; after all, it was almost the twenty-first century and this was Dallas, not Salem. But she knew something was different. I'd have to be very careful around Elizabeth from now on.

I grabbed a small tool kit I keep around for appearance's sake and headed next door. The first thing I saw in Elizabeth's kitchen was Griselda, sitting on the window sill watching the street outside.

"I hope you don't mind," Elizabeth said, "but I've been giving Griselda part of my omelet in the mornings. She does love it so."

That was one mystery solved; I never kept eggs in the house. "No, I don't mind."

"She likes ham better than cheese," Elizabeth hinted.

I had to grin; Elizabeth worried about Griselda more than I did. My neighbor was in her early fifties, nice-looking in an old-fashioned way, and as calm and even-tempered a being as I had ever met. I'd never seen her angry or excited. Frequently when Griselda was fed up with me, she'd go to Elizabeth to be soothed.

"Let's take a look at this thing." I turned the microwave on its front and removed the bottom panel. Not much to see there, but I made sure I was blocking Elizabeth's view. "Well. That might be your problem right there."

Elizabeth moved closer. "What is it?"

"This little doohickey seems to have slipped off the whatsit right next to it. Let me see if I can get it back on." I pretended to work on it, muttering to myself all the while. (What

I was muttering, if you must know, was an old healing spell that I'd upgraded to include mechanical objects.)

Elizabeth was trying to watch but I hunched up a shoulder. "Where in the world did you ever learn to do these things?" she asked.

Loaded question; what was she really asking? "From my brother," I lied. "He was always tinkering. Let's try it now." I plugged in the microwave and set the timer for thirty seconds. It worked perfectly, of course.

She sighed. "You know, I started to take it in for repairs rather than bother you. But, Molly, I couldn't even pick it up." She looked at her hands. "No strength left."

I tried joshing her. "What are you talking about? Why, you're in your prime!"

She shook her head. "Once you pass fifty, little things you've counted on all your life begin to desert you." She forced a smile. "But you won't have that problem for a long time yet. You have a ways to go before you hit fifty."

Fifty, huh. What Elizabeth didn't know was that I had a granddaughter older than she was. And a daughter who was very good with anti-aging spells.

We chatted a while; and when I started to leave, Griselda jumped down from the window sill and followed. We left with Elizabeth's soft thank-yous in our ears.

Why didn't you tell me you like omelet? I asked Griselda.

I don't have to explain myself, she replied.

Snooty cat.

Inside, a message was waiting on my answering machine; someone named Bobbie Jo Miller in the *Herald's* legal department asked me to drop by her office as soon as I could—some question about my contract.

Now what? It was only a little before noon; plenty of time for something else to go wrong today. Might as well go in and see what this Bobbie Jo Miller wanted.

Leave the air-conditioning on, Griselda instructed.

I did. I noticed the mail hadn't arrived yet; it kept getting there later and later in the day. On the drive into town I did some pondering . . . about my daughter and my granddaughter, whom Elizabeth had unknowingly started me thinking about.

Thanks to my daughter's skill in anti-aging, we all three

looked to be in our late twenties—which made it a tad difficult to live together as a three-generational family. That was not really a problem, as we saw one another frequently. But we could never stick around in one place too long before people started noticing we never seemed to get any older. You can use plastic surgery as an excuse only so many times. So we'd have to leave Dallas eventually. Pity; I was just getting used to country-western music.

The room in the *Herald* building that used to hold the legal department was now packed with microreaders and cabinets full of spools. I went into the newsroom. Every time I saw the *Herald*'s newsroom, I wanted to conjure up an enormous vacuum sweeper and suck up every piece of paper in the place. Newsrooms are all messy, everywhere, but the *Herald* surely outdid them all. I was surprised to see Marty Hicks at the city desk; his shift ended hours ago. "What are you still doing here?" I asked him.

He was slumped down in his chair, dark circles under his eyes. "I'm just holding the fort until Jack gets here," he said. "He had to meet someone at the airport."

"You look beat."

"I am." He yawned, as politely as he could manage it. "Molly, I'm sorry about your, er, infinitives."

Participles. "Not your fault. Marty, I have to see someone in the legal department, but I'm not sure where it is now."

"Oh, right down that hall." He pointed, and yawned again. "Let me guess—Bobbie Jo? She's been on the payroll only one week and already she's had half the staff in."

I went down the hall to the legal department, which was one big room with three desks in it, only one of which was occupied at the moment. Behind the desk sat a thirtyish woman who one glance told me was a Good Old Girl. She wore a gold satin cowboy shirt and more make-up than a Dallas Cowboys cheerleader.

I went up to her desk and said, "Are you Bobbie Jo Miller? I'm Molly Showalter."

"Molly!" She sparkled at me as if she'd just been sitting there waiting for me to show up and brighten her day. "Oh, I am *so* glad you came in! You don't know how I've been *wantin'* to meet you!" Bobbie Jo came around from behind her desk and made sure I was seated comfortably. She pulled up another chair to sit opposite me, no desk separating us. Cozy.

"Something about my contract?" I asked.

"You know, I just *love* your column," she burbled, not hearing. "I read it every single *day*! I wouldn't miss it for the world."

It wasn't published every single day. "Thank you."

She leaned toward me, trés confidential. "You know something? You and I are *neighbors!*" *Neighbors* had three syllables, the way she said it. "I almost died when I looked up your phone number and saw we lived on the same street!" A big Texas laugh. "Looks like we're goin' to be seein' a lot of each other."

Looks *as if*. "We are?"

"Yes!" Yay-yuss. "My hubby and I just moved here from Austin, and we took a house that's about *two blocks* away from you. The pink stucco with the cactus hedge?"

I knew the one she meant. I mumbled something like *Welcome to the neighborhood* and listened to her chatter on about a barbecue she was planning to hold to meet her new neighbors, all the while emphasizing more words than a schoolgirl. I didn't like Bobbie Jo Miller. She wrinkled her nose when she laughed and tossed her hair at the end of every third sentence.

Finally she was convinced she'd established an atmosphere of friendly-neighbors-just-chatting and got around to the reason she'd summoned me. "I don't know what's *happened* to office help these days," she said with a sad little shake of her head. "These girls can't type worth *spit*. Did you notice in your contract that *Herald* is spelled with two e's—*twice*? And Showalter is spelled wrong once!"

I'd noticed. "So?"

"Don't you see, Molly? That makes the contract void."

I stared at her. "Bullshit."

"No, honey, it's not bullshit." Same sad little shake of the head. "I can cite you a hundred cases where contracts were declared void because the name of one of the contractors was spelled wrong. And here both names are spelled wrong!"

I sighed. "So have the contract retyped."

"Well, that's just the thing. Since we're goin' to have to redo

the contract anyway, wouldn't this be a good time to renegotiate the terms?"

Uh-oh. "To what end?"

"Well, Molly, your column is so popular—and it's a *wonderful* column, it *deserves* to be popular—and all those other
newspapers have picked it up and you're makin' a *bundle* out
of syndication . . . seems to me the *Herald* doesn't need to
be payin' you as much as it does."

I ground my teeth. "I see. *You* decide how much money
it's okay for *me* to earn." The emphasis habit was catching.

"Now, honey, don't be like that. I got it all figured out.
All you need is *fourteen more papers* to pick up your column
and you'll be makin' every *bit* as much as you're makin' now."
Bobbie Jo got up and went behind her desk. "I got the numbers right here."

"Forget the numbers," I snarled. "You're using a few typos
as an excuse to screw me out of money that's rightfully mine.
When did the *Herald* start welching on its contracts? Are we
going in for sleaze law now?"

She got a glint in her eye. "Now, Molly, that wasn't nice."
Like all Good Old Girls, Bobbie Jo was hard and unyielding
under that folksy, friendly exterior. "I'm sorry you're takin' it
that way, but we're just goin' to *have* to renegotiate our agree-
ment. There's no way *around* it, Molly."

"You can talk to my lawyer." I got up to leave.

"Now, honey, don't go away mad!"

But I did.

I went straight from the *Herald* building to my lawyer's
office. He was out of town.

Wasn't this turning out to be one lulu of a day? My
researcher and my auto insurance both abandon me, my Dallas
Journalists Association treasurer fails to come through once
again, my online-shopping-mall order is lost, my newspaper
is trying to do me dirty. And my lawyer's out of town.

On the way home, I had a flat tire.

I picked up the mail and charged into the house. Griselda
took one look at me and disappeared; she can read my moods
pretty well.

The message light on the answering machine was blinking.
Bobbie Jo's cheerful tones said, "Molly, honey? I'm worried

you and I got off on the wrong foot. How's about we try again?
You come to our *barbecue* Saturday night—I want you to meet
my hubby. Anytime after seven. Now, you be there, you hear?"

I heard. I'd go to her barbecue . . . when pigs danced on
the moon. What was the fool woman playing at?

Forget her. I was too irritated and upset to eat; I poured
a glass of iced tea and sat down to open my mail.

And got another shock.

It was my Visa bill; it said I'd charged $285 at Neiman
Marcus. That couldn't be right. I'd been in Neiman's only once
in the past month, when I'd gone shopping with my daughter.

I thought back over what we'd done. It was my daughter
who'd wanted to do the shopping; I was only along for the
ride. But let's see, I had bought a scarf that was on sale—
but that was only about twenty bucks. And I'd paid for our
lunches at the café, two salads. My total bill shouldn't have
been any more than about thirty-five dollars.

I called Neiman's billing department and said there'd been
a mistake.

"Oh, dear," replied the concerned voice on the phone—
Terry or Kerry, she'd said, I didn't quite catch it. "Let's just
check your purchases, shall we?"

"Let's."

"Here we are." Terry or Kerry had found the right computer screen. "Ladies' Accessories, $20." The scarf. "Café,
$265."

"*What*?!"

"That does seem like a lot to eat," she admitted. "Let me
call up the café bill." A pause. "Ah, I see what it is. Two salads
with drinks, $15. And the recipe for the Neiman Marcus
cookie, $250."

I was stunned. I remembered now; my daughter and I had
both wanted a sweet taste after our salads but not a big dessert,
so we'd asked for the Neiman Marcus cookie listed on the
menu. It was a good cookie, mostly oatmeal with just the right
amount of melt-in-your-mouth chocolate and crunchy nuts. It
was so good that I'd asked the waitress if I could have the
recipe.

The waitress had been very apologetic when she said
Neiman's didn't give its recipes away. So I'd asked if I could

buy it. Yes, she'd said, all of Neiman's recipes were for sale. How much? I'd asked. Two-fifty, she'd replied.

"That's where the mistake is," I told Terry or Kerry on the phone. "The recipe was two dollars and a half, not two hundred fifty."

"No, ma'am, that's no mistake. The Neiman Marcus cookie recipe sells for two hundred fifty dollars."

"But that's absurd!"

"I'm sorry, ma'am, but you did sign the charge slip."

"Well, we were in a hurry and I guess I didn't look too closely. But two hundred fifty dollars for a recipe? What if I returned it?"

She was sorry again. "We have a no-return policy on recipes, Ms. Showalter. You see, people could copy the recipes and then bring them back, and, well, we just have to make it a final sale. No returns."

I fumed and fussed and even screamed a little, but she wouldn't budge. No return, no adjustment to my bill. I slammed down the receiver in disgust.

Griselda had come out of wherever she'd been hiding and was sitting by my feet. *Temper, temper,* she admonished.

Did you hear all that?

Yessssss. What are you going to do?

I didn't know what I was going to do—but I sure as hell was going to do something. I couldn't just let that pass. *I'm open to suggestion.*

Griselda had one. *Hit them where it hurts, in the pocketbook. Eliminate the demand for their expensive cookie. Make sure nobody else ever asks to buy the recipe again.*

I thought that over. *You mean . . . pass it on to other people? Give it away?*

Griselda purred.

Oh, that was brilliant! I'd give that damned recipe to so many people that no one would ever get stuck with a bill for it again! *Griselda, you're a genius!*

I know.

I reached for the phone and called Terry/Kerry at the billing department. Once last chance. "If you don't make a satisfactory adjustment to my bill right now, do you know what I'm going to do? I'm going to give your precious recipe away. That's right. I'm going to give a copy to every single person I know,

and then I'm going to ask them to give copies to every single
person they know."

A gasp. "I wish you wouldn't do that."

"Then adjust my bill."

"I can't!"

"Then kiss your little cash cow goodbye. That recipe is going
out today."

"I really wish you wouldn't do that!"

"I'll bet you do," I chortled and hung up.

Then I got to work. I scrabbled through my drawer of loose
recipes and came up with the right one. Next I pulled up my
list of online addresses and set the server for a mass mailing. Then I told the story of exactly what had happened, being
careful not to exaggerate or use emotion-laden words. Finally,
I gave them the recipe.

The Neiman Marcus Cookie

2 cups butter	4 cups flour
2 tsp soda	2 cups sugar
5 cups blended oatmeal°	24 oz chocolate chips
2 cups brown sugar	1 tsp salt
1 8-oz Hershey Bar (grated)	4 eggs
2 tsp baking powder	3 cups chopped nuts
2 tsp vanilla	(your choice)

°Measure oatmeal and blend in a blender to a fine
powder.

Cream the butter and both sugars. Add eggs and vanilla;
mix together with flour, oatmeal, salt, baking powder,
and soda. Add chocolate chips, Hershey Bar, and nuts.
Roll into balls and place two inches apart on a cookie
sheet. Bake for 10 minutes at 375 degrees. Makes 112
cookies. (Recipe may be halved.)

So far so good. But I could make it better. Watch the
technowitch in action.

Now, an electronically-carried spell isn't like a virus. A virus
can't be transmitted in a text file, which was what an e-mail

letter was. But a real, honest-to-badness witching spell could be embedded in text, sent off through cyberspace, and made to work its magic on the first person who read the message. I wanted to embed a compulsion spell, with time-delayed reinforcers. No one who read the letter would be able to resist passing the word.

Two hundred fifty dollars for a recipe! Pah.

Embedding a spell in e-mail isn't easy. You can't just murmur words and be done with it. You need talismans and totems and some rather nasty ingredients. You need to go through all sorts of gyrations and ritualistic rigmarole while chanting backwards. One false step and the whole spell collapses. You don't undertake an embedding spell lightly.

But finally it was done. Still, I hesitated before sending the letter out. Maybe I should test it first? I called Elizabeth next door.

Before she got there, I altered the story slightly; I changed *my daughter* to *my friend*. I told Elizabeth I wanted her opinion on something I'd written before I sent it.

She sat down at the screen and began to read. She hadn't read far when she exclaimed, "Why, that's outrageous!" She finished the letter and went back and read it again. "Neiman's did that? That's . . . that's incredible!"

"Believe it."

"Oh, I do believe it, Molly!" She got up and began to pace agitatedly around the room. "What could they be thinking of, to charge that much for a cookie recipe?" Her face was red, and her voice kept climbing up the scale. "I never heard of such a thing! I don't know if I'll ever go back to Neiman's, when they pull stunts like that!" she declared furiously, clenching her fists.

This was the calm, unexcitable Elizabeth who never got angry? Wow, that was some spell I'd fashioned. "Then you don't think I'm doing the wrong thing?"

"Absolutely not! You're doing exactly the right thing! People should know about it. Molly, give me a copy of that recipe—I want to tell my friends!"

I printed out a dozen copies for her—and then, at her request, a dozen more. "Ask them to tell *their* friends."

"Don't you worry, I will." She gathered up her copies of the recipe and left the house muttering to herself. The hardcopy I'd given her wouldn't carry the embedded spell, of course; but that didn't matter. It had started.

I changed *my friend* back to *my daughter* and sent the letter off through an anonymous forwarding service in Sweden that I use. Then I went online and posted the story (under a pseudonym) in six different news groups; more than that would have looked suspicious. Then I set up a new web page and put the story there—no graphics, no bells and whistles; just the facts, ma'am. Embedded spells work just fine online.

Then I called my daughter and my granddaughter and told them what I'd done. We shared a laugh at Neiman's executives, who were bound to start wondering why people kept repeating the story. Heh heh heh.

By then my stomach was complaining about no lunch, so I fixed something for Griselda and me. While we were eating, I told her about Bobbie Jo Miller, how she was trying to weasel out of a contract commitment and how she'd moved into that pink monstrosity surrounded by cactus in the next block.

Check her out? Griselda asked.

Yes, please. I need some way of getting at her.

As soon as I've finished eating.

She took her time, and of course there was the washing ritual to go through. But then I let her out and watched her trot away to see what she could find out about Mrs. Bobbie Jo Miller and her "hubby." Bobbie Jo might not be home from work yet, but patient Griselda would wait.

I was feeling better, now that I'd actually done something about Neiman's and their blasted recipe. It was only four o'clock; maybe I could do something about the other things that were bugging me.

So I called the store that maintained the online shopping mall and pointed out that their web page said delivery would be made by UPS (insured) whereas they'd sent my order Parcel Post (uninsured). I told them that if they didn't replace my order within ten days, I was going to take legal action. I was hastily assured that wouldn't be necessary, and a new order would be shipped tomorrow. By UPS.

One down.

It had finally dawned on me that insurance companies don't cancel policies through e-mail; they send you some sort of legal form through regular mail. So I called my auto insurance company next—and received profuse apologies from the harried-sounding man I talked to. It seemed that a recent employee had just been given the sack; in revenge he'd sent e-mail to as many policyholders as he could telling them they'd been cancelled before someone caught him and put a stop to it.

So that was all right.

Next I called the treasurer of the Houston Journalists Association and told him he was out of a job. I ordered him to send me all his records, including bank statements. A few more phone calls and the Association had a new treasurer.

The University of Texas grad student who'd been doing my research but now wanted to be a rock musician—I couldn't do anything about him. I was going to lose that one.

But all in all, the day was ending a heckuva lot better than it began.

It was another three hours before Griselda came home, but she was grinning from ear to ear. *Good news?* I asked. *What? What?*

Relax. Your problem is solved. Do you know what Bobbie Jo has been doing the past few hours? Interviewing husbands.

Huh?

Actors. She hired one of them to impersonate her husband at the barbecue Saturday night.

I don't understand. Where's her real husband?

She doesn't have one. Bobbie Jo came to Dallas determined to earn a reputation as Superwoman. Ultra-efficient in the office, the perfect hostess at home. So, an attractive, adoring husband catering to her every whim is an essential part of the picture.

I was flabbergasted; the woman must be nuts. *Why a husband? Why not just introduce him as a boyfriend? Or fiancé? Less chance of getting found out.*

Griselda tilted her head. *Boyfriends and fiancés can be transient. Having a handsome, sexy man permanently dancing attendance shows she can do the woman-thing as well as the career-thing. Bobbie Jo signed the actor to a long-term contract.*

By then I was rolling on the floor laughing. *Handsome and sexy, huh?*

Oh, yesss. A mature hunk. You'll like him.

There were two ways I could go. I could attend the barbecue Saturday night and announce before everybody that the man Bobbie Jo had introduced as her husband was in fact an out-of-work actor she'd hired for the occasion. Or I could keep my mouth shut and let Bobbie Jo know I was in on her little secret and use that knowledge to negotiate my new contract upward. Well, I had until Saturday to decide. And if you think I let the word *blackmail* make me lose any sleep, you've got another think coming.

In fact, I slept like a log that night, and dreamt of dangling participles.

The next morning I laughed out loud when I saw my e-mail included six letters repeating the story of the Neiman Marcus cookie and its recipe. It was working—oh yes, it was working! Oddly, one of the letters had changed *flour* to *flower*.

About mid-morning Elizabeth came over, bearing a plate of cookies. "I couldn't resist trying out your expensive recipe," she said. "They smelled wonderful while they were baking. Here, have one."

Best cookie I ever ate.

Author's note: *The story of the Neiman Marcus cookie is pure malarkey, of course; but like all such urban legends, it has a way of persisting. Neiman Marcus gives its recipes free to anyone who asks for them and in fact has included several on its web page (http://www.neimanmarcus.com).*

My Father's Son

Ed Gorman and Larry Segriff

We only ever talked about death once, my brother and I, and I remember him telling me that he planned to be a sailor, and have his ashes cast over the water. Our grandfather had been an admiral, and my brother Kevin had been much taken with a life at sea.

He didn't live long enough to reach Annapolis, of course. That's why I was back with my family. I was attending Kevin's funeral. He'd been killed two days earlier in an automobile accident. He'd turned eighteen three weeks before his death. Annapolis had been only two weeks away.

We'd had some practice at it, my mother and father and I, this dying business. My sister Rita had died two years earlier, at age fifteen. She'd drowned in the swimming pool at the country club.

Many of my aunts and uncles made a great point of this at both the funeral home and the graveyard, how I was the only child left now, and how I must therefore carry on all those exalted traditions that the family at large cherished so much—traditions that allowed them to feel just a little bit better than the lesser mortals with whom they'd been forced to live.

Afterwards, at the estate house where my folks had lived for the past twelve years, I started knocking back scotch to make the whole thing tolerable. I kept remembering Rita's funeral, and what Kevin had said that night when the last of the mourners had left.

"It's not over, Bro," he'd said to me.

I'd asked him what he meant, but he'd merely looked at me with his big, brown eyes, seeming far older than his years, and said again, "It's not over, Bro, and I just can't get over this feeling that I'll be next."

I'd comforted him as best I could, but he'd been right, and I couldn't help wondering if he'd been right about the rest of it, too: that our parents were responsible for it all.

My father smiled bravely about my drinking. "You sure it's a good thing for a young doctor like yourself to be seen hitting the bottle quite so hard, David?"

"Doesn't bother the young doctor if it doesn't bother you," I said.

My mother had joined him. "You're slurring your words, honey. You don't want everybody to think you've got a drinking problem, do you?"

They were a beautiful couple, my mother and father, her tall and elegant and patrician, him dark and intense but in a safe upper-class sort of way. He took his intensity out on the stock market and yachting.

We were in the den. They were speaking softly. They didn't want to draw any attention to themselves or to me. The smiles stayed on their faces the entire time.

"You've never been very good with alcohol, David," my father said, "any more than poor Kevin was any good with girls."

And that's when I snapped.

Just couldn't take his bullshit anymore.

"Do you know how fucking sanctimonious you sound?" I said. "Did you ever think that if you and Mother had been better parents we might have turned out to be better children?"

The room was frozen now. Faces eager for scandal and the misery of others turned to watch me prove that I did indeed have a drinking problem.

"You two weren't home three nights a week when we were growing up," I said. "You were always out with your fucking society assholes!"

I'd never said any of this before to them. I wanted it to feel good, finally baring my soul and all that, but as much as one part of me got a definite thrill out of humiliating them, another part of me heard the adolescent whine and self-pity in my voice . . . and was sickened by it.

"Please, David, please," my father said, taking me by the elbow and leading me from the den.

I watched all their shocked faces watching me. I didn't like them any better than I liked my parents. They were all the same sort of smug, arrogant people that had infested our particular clan since the Revolutionary war.

"A little something for your scrapbooks," I said as my father continued to steer my mother from the room.

And with that, I hurled my scotch glass into the fireplace, where it smashed with the pleasingly singular sound of breaking glass.

Some of my aunts probably required smelling salts.

I awoke with the terrors, something I'd been doing a lot lately. Where am I? How did I get here?

A few times, I'd asked the most terrifying question of all: Who am I?

Dusk was rose and maudlin in the window. Far away, dogs barked and children laughed in the waning moments of their outdoor day. I wanted to be one of them, a little boy having frantic fun in the gathering night, just before Mom called me in.

My parents' house.

I'd been drinking.

There'd been an argument. I could see my mother's face. Humiliated. I could feel, like a lingering sore, the spot where my father had seized me by the elbow. All my aunts and uncles watching. Horrified. Then I heard the sound of glass breaking as my drink smashed into the fireplace. . . .

I threw up in the bathroom, came back and slept for a couple more hours.

Night.

Silence.

I sat on the edge of the bed, wondering if I was going to throw up again.

Then Dr. Tomkins's voice was inside my head: "David, you're a damned good intern, but you're going to get kicked out of this hospital—and out of the profession—if you don't make your peace with the bottle."

He'd said that to me less than two weeks before. Then, the day before yesterday, I'd found that the venerable Dr. Tomkins hadn't just been trying to scare me. I'd shown up with a wee bit too much scotch on my breath and he'd fired me on the spot.

Night.

Silence.

I went into the bathroom and threw up again. Then I took a hot shower, changed into a newly dry-cleaned shirt and slacks, and went downstairs.

The house was empty. The maid had cleaned everything up. It shone perfectly once again, just as my mother liked it.

I was in the kitchen, fixing myself a ham sandwich and coffee when Millie came in.

Millie and I had never liked each other much. I'd always had fantasies of those French maids you read about in paperbacks. You know, the sleek and nimble kind who always teach naïve young Americans about life as it really is.

Millie could have been a professional wrestler. In her starched gray uniform, and shined black oxfords, she had the beefy biceps of a prison guard, and the baleful brown gaze of a serial killer desperate for some action. She'd been with the family ever since my father had come into that strange inheritance back when I was twelve years old.

She glared at me now with vast contempt. "I picked up the glass in the fireplace."

This was her way of obliquely stating her moral superiority. Not only had she not thrown the glass, she'd even cleaned it up.

I sat there eating my ham sandwich. "I'm proud of you, Millie. Where are my folks by the way?"

"The club."

"Ah."

"Your mother left you two one hundred dollar bills on the desk in the den."

"I suppose I should say thank you and be very grateful for that."

Millie and I hadn't had one of our verbal battles in a long time. And the mood I was in, I was ready.

Then she said, "I almost forgot."

"Forgot?"

"Your brother left something for you." Her icy glare again. "He was such a good boy."

Meaning, of course, that I wasn't a good boy.

But how could I argue? Despite our upbringing, there'd been a fundamental sweetness to him, a sweetness I was in no danger of claiming for myself.

But she said nothing more. Just disappeared.

I finished my ham sandwich, rinsed out my cup and put it in the dishwasher, and then started toward the den to collect my guilt money. Mother had always been especially good at leaving money when she felt she wasn't spending enough time with us. I remember my sister standing in the doorway—she couldn't have been much older than five or six—clutching a ten dollar bill and crying because our parents were going to Europe for three months. I thought about that a lot during her funeral.

Millie was back with a large manila envelope.

"Kevin gave you this?" I said.

"Yes."

"Did he say why he didn't give it to our folks?"

"He asked me not to even mention it to your folks."

"That's strange."

"I thought so, too." She pushed the envelope at me. "Anyway, here it is."

I smiled at her. "Did you steam this open and peek inside?"

"I don't find that funny, sir."

"No," I said. "I don't suppose you do." Then: "Is there plenty of brandy in the den?"

Her glare was downright ferocious. "They knew you were coming home, sir, so they stocked up on alcohol of every kind."

Even I had to admire that one. I laughed and said, "I'd definitely have to give you that round, Millie. No doubt about it."

But I wasn't even sure she'd heard me. She'd turned around and walked away, down toward the darkness at the far end of the hall. Millie liked to keep the house as dark as possible. Secrets rest most comfortably in the shadows, and I'd always suspected that my family had more than its share.

My parents got home just as the day's first dogs were

barking, and just as the round red sun began to appear behind the waning night sky.

I'd been alternating scotch with coffee since opening my brother's final gift to me so I was in pretty good shape to do what I needed to do.

I waited until they were in the kitchen—Mother always liked to fix Father a hangover breakfast the way she'd done during Father's Princeton years—and then I strolled out carrying a fresh drink and tossed the brick of thousand dollar bills on the butcher block table where Millie prepared the evening meal.

As soon as they realized what it was exactly—the paper bank band around the brick of bills was an odd gray color, and very distinctive—as soon as they realized I'd learned their terrible secret, my mother said, "Kevin told you, didn't he?"

"Not told me," I said. "Left a letter for me."

I waved the letter at them and then set it down next to the brick of bills.

My father picked it up, scanned it. He'd already looked gray, the booze having taken its usual evening toll. Now he looked positively ashen.

"You mean you really believe this?" my father said. "This nonsense about a curse and everything?"

My mother went as cold and still as a statue. "What curse?" she asked.

He didn't answer her. He merely smiled at me, trying to show, I suppose, that he considered me so foolish that only a sardonic smile could possibly do me justice. "My God, David, you're a medical man."

I stiffened at that. "Yes," I said. "That's true. I am a medical man." I paused before going on. "Have you ever wondered why I drink?" I asked. "I drink because I'm a medical man. I drink because of all the kids I've seen, struck down by cars like Kevin, or drowned in a swimming pool like Rita, or given AIDS by their mother before they were even born. I drink because of all the patients I've watched fight a losing battle against a disease. But mostly, Father, I drink because of those rare, miraculous cures, when someone I *know* should be dead in six months instead lives on for years and years. I drink because I don't understand why these people live, and so I cannot duplicate that miracle for those who truly deserve it."

My hands were clenched, my voice ragged and harsh, and the desire for a drink had never been so strong as it was in that moment.

"Don't you see?" I asked him. "It's precisely because I *am* a medical man that I have to believe in miracles . . . and in curses."

My father looked at me, and for the first time in a long while I saw a hint of softness in his eyes. "There is no curse, son," he said. "Rita's and Kevin's deaths were tragedies, but that's all they were."

"They just died by coincidence?" I said.

"Of course by coincidence, David," he said.

I nodded to the brick of bills on the table. "You spent the money."

He glanced at my mother and then looked over at me.

"We had some financial difficulties when we were about your age," he said. "We found ourselves—without funds."

My father would never use a nice, simple, vulgar word like "broke." Not when talking about himself. They hadn't been broke, they'd simply been without funds.

"What curse?" my mother asked again. This time, there was steel in her voice.

I picked up the letter my father had just dropped on the table, the letter in which Kevin had detailed the whole strange story, and started reading it out loud. According to what Kevin had written, one night, a few years ago, he'd overheard our father sobbing in the den. He listened to Father say that they should never have spent the money. He kept referring to "the letter." Kevin had no idea what Father was talking about. But then, after Mother and Father went to bed, Kevin snuck down to the den and found a handwritten letter from one of my father's friends. The man's business had been going under so he began dealing drugs in a major way. He was a respected financier, after all. Who would suspect him? His partner was a Jamaican. One night the Jamaican man was to deliver three million dollars in cash to buy a huge supply of heroin. But my father's friend cheated his partner. He hired two masked men to rob the Jamaican and turn the three million over to the financier. Everything went as planned. But after a few weeks the Jamaican realized that he'd been betrayed. He went to the financier and told him he knew who was behind the robbery. The financier denied it. The Jamaican knew that he would probably never see the money again but he said that his grandmother, a houngan of the old voodoo ways, had hexed the money. Whoever spent it would bring death on himself and his loved ones.

The financier bought himself a fine boat and kept the money hidden in it. One night he invited my father out to the marina for a drink. But when my father reached the boat, he found the financier dead of an apparent heart attack. The financier had been counting through his millions in the briefcase. My father read the financier's letter about how he'd come by the money—and the hex that had been put on it—but my father took the money anyway, and hurried off the yacht. He figured that people were always finding large amounts of drug cash in strange places—he figured that every once in a while somebody kept the money and didn't turn it over to the police.

"About the time I was twelve," I said, "you and Mother told everybody that you'd come into this mysterious inheritance. But what you really came into was the three million you took from the financier. Only the hex was true. Two people died—my brother and sister. They died because you spent the money."

"Is it true, Frank?" my mother asked. "Was there a curse on that money? Is that why Rita and Kevin died?"

My father ignored her. "Not 'spent,' " he corrected me. "Invested." He looked at my mother and smiled. "I'm afraid I didn't do very well with the money I'd inherited from my own parents. This time I had your mother handle the money, and she did much better. That's why you spent the second half of your boyhood enjoying a luxurious life. She invested about a third of it and it made us very, very wealthy." He smiled. "Two of the original three million are still in the wall safe. Sort of like our good luck charm."

"So you don't see any connection between spending the money and the death of your children?" I said.

"Oh, be serious," my father said. "We were devastated when your brother and sister died, but we never thought for a moment that it had anything to do with any stupid curse."

All over America, people were finding large caches of drug money in garages, ditches, and the back seats of cars. Most of them had the good sense to turn the money over to the police.

But not my father. Not my parents.

My mother looked at him long and hard for a moment. The only sounds were the crackling of the fire, the tinkling of the ice in my drink, and the harshness of her breathing. Without another word, she turned her back on him and left the room.

I just shook my head. "You made your fortune on drug money, and you killed your kids doing it, and you absolutely don't give a damn, do you?"

"You really need to watch your drinking, David," my father said. "It's really getting out of hand."

I slapped him then.

Ever since I got home I'd sensed that neither of my parents were unduly saddened by the death of my brother. Why should they be? They had each other, and the grand, glorious traditions of the family to uphold, and they also had many millions of dollars.

My father surprised me by being quite composed. After the echo of my slap had died in the silent kitchen, he said, "You couldn't have resisted the temptation either, son. You would've spent the money, too."

"The hell I would have," I said. "I would've turned it over to the police."

"That's your self-delusion, David," he said. "Of all three children, you were always the greediest. You always wanted the very best." He offered me his sardonic smile again. "In that sense, you were very much like your mother and me."

He stood looking at me then, and I suddenly realized that my parents were strangers. I felt no kinship with them. None at all.

"Your brother and sister," my father said, "they could've handled being poor. But you were miserable all the years we didn't have money." Then: "Now that you know the combination to the safe, I half-expect you'll try to steal some of it from me."

Then he went back to his breakfast.

I slept until late in the afternoon and then went out and ran two miles.

After taking a shower, I came downstairs and went looking for my parents.

I found them in the den, dressed to go out for the evening, brandy snifters in their hands. There was a stiffness between them I'd never felt before, and I wondered what else might have died that day.

"I'll be leaving in the morning," I said. "I'm going to go back and see if the hospital'll reconsider."

My father shook his head.

"You've tried giving up the bottle before, David," he said. "And I'm sorry to say that I don't recall any triumphant results."

In the doorway, Millie said, "If you'll excuse me, ma'am, I'll be going into town now."

"Very well, Millie," my mother said. Her voice was weak, a hollow echo of its usual strength, and I could hear the booze in it already.

One night a week, Millie went into town and stayed with her rheumatism-crippled older sister. I hoped she was nicer to her than she'd ever been to me.

After Millie was gone, my father said, "I just want to make something clear to you, David. Whatever else you might think of us, we really did love our children."

I smiled at him and said, "The sad thing is, I think you really believe that."

I spent most of the night checking my wristwatch and congratulating myself every time fifteen minutes passed without me taking a drink. I was quite proud of myself. I hadn't been this dry since high school.

I spent half an hour in my brother's old room without quite knowing why. Somebody had to mourn the poor bastard. I guess it had to be me.

A lot of memories were in the very air of the room. I could hear his kid voice and see his kid grin and hear all his kid plans for when he got to be a grown-up. He wasn't ever going to make it. Not now.

I drifted downstairs. I tried to tell myself that I was just taking an informal tour of the house. Maybe I'd slice myself a piece of chocolate cake. Millie was a bitch but she was a great cook.

I passed the den twice without going in. I kept thinking of what my father had said, about how I was like them, like my mother and father, that I needed a lot of money, too.

The third time I passed the den, I went in. I tried not to even look at the sailing ship painting, behind which was the wall safe. Kevin and I had long ago watched Father open the safe. We were able to learn the combination, too, even though as kids we'd never dared to use it. Spying on our father had been a kid lark. These days, knowing the combination had other implications.

Two million dollars, my father had said. Their good luck omen. Unless you happened to be my brother and sister.

I walked over to the painting, grasped its edge, and swung it away from the wall.

The large round face of the safe sat there like the most beautiful girl in the world.

She was hard to resist.

I put my fingers to the dial, the combination numbers singing seductively in my ears.

So easy. Just open it up. Throw all the money in a bag. Clear out before my folks got back. They'd know I'd taken it but so what? What could they do about it without admitting how they'd come by it?

I started to turn the dial. 28 R. Then stopped myself.

I thought of Rita and Kevin and of how I'd loved them. Sister and brother. Two of the nicest kids you'd ever want to meet. And then I thought of the money in the safe. And I didn't want any part of it.

I went on up to bed.

And couldn't sleep.

I tried to think about Rita and Kevin and all the good times we'd had together. But somehow I couldn't sustain those memories very long. Because, hard as I tried to forget it, I kept thinking about the den. About the safe. About the money.

And then mercifully, before I was forced to admit that my father had been right about me, I went to sleep.

I'm not sure what time they rolled in. Very late, of course. They put on some music in the living room and, for a time, it woke me up. But then I drifted back to a deep sleep.

The fire was part of the dream.

Rita and Kevin and I were up in the attic of the place we'd lived in when we didn't have so much money. We were experimenting with cigarettes. And Mother smelled the smoke and came screaming up the stairs.

She was screaming again.

Only it wasn't part of the dream. I was in my pajama bottoms and trying to roll out of bed. The smoke was already heavy and gray and gagging.

I was glad I wasn't drunk. I was sensible enough to get on all fours and crawl out of my room to the hallway.

By now, both my mother and father were screaming, pleading for help from anyone, anyone.

A part of me wanted to save them, rush in there and smash open their windows, and drag them out to fresh air.

But another part. . . .

It wasn't easy getting down the hall, and then belly-crawling down the long stairs leading to the first floor.

But I made it.

And somehow I managed to crawl my way into the den, too. The smoke wasn't quite as thick down here as it was upstairs.

I picked up a costly Louis XIV chair and smashed out several windows. Then I grabbed one of my father's briefcases and went to the safe.

I was choking the whole time I worked the safe and jammed the money into the briefcase.

And they were still screaming. Upstairs. Getting more and more hysterical.

When the briefcase was full, I scrambled to one of the French windows, pitched my load out to the grass, and then climbed out.

I cut myself badly on the knives of glass that jutted from the window frame.

Rumble of fire trucks. Crying sirens. And still the screams and pathetic wails of my parents trapped up on the second floor. I buried the briefcase in a shallow grave in the woods on the west edge of our estate.

I made it look good for the fire officials. I was on my hands and knees when they arrived and I kept threatening to run back into the fiery, collapsing house to save my parents.

But of course there would be no saving my parents. Not now.

I'm writing all this down in case I die, and in case somebody finds this briefcase filled with good green Yankee currency.

Did a curse really kill my sister and brother? My mother and father?

I'll find out soon enough.

I had decided against playing it safe. As the only survivor, I stood to inherit all their stocks and bonds and fancy real estate, but I didn't want any of it. At least, not yet—not until I had the answers I needed. I'd set it up in a trust fund. If I made it back, their money would be there waiting for me. If not, well, I'd arranged to have it go for a scholarship fund at Annapolis in Kevin's name.

I wanted to think my reasons were humanitarian—that I couldn't allow that money to carry its curse to other unsuspecting victims—but I knew that wasn't the whole truth. It was much simpler than that. My real reason was simply that I had to know who was responsible for Kevin's death.

That was why I was on this cruise ship to Jamaica, with nothing but a briefcase full of money to keep me company. If there was no curse, I'd have a great time and, eventually, return home to my millions. And if there was a curse, well then the money would end up back where it began, bringing the curse home.

The nightmares are pretty bad, I have to say that. I guess you don't come by two million dollars this way without paying some sort of price. I see my sister in her open casket, I see my brother being lowered into the earth.

And, as much as I hated them, I hear my mother and father crying out for me to help them.

Tonight, the seas are calm as I lay in my bed writing this down.

My father was probably right. I shouldn't even be thinking about things like curses and hexes.

I'm a medical man, after all.

But more than that, I am my father's son.

The Remaking of Millie McCoy

Christie Golden

Millie shoved the last piece of luggage into her car and closed the trunk with a *thump*. She licked dry lips and for a moment just stood there, overwhelmed by the enormity of what she was about to do.

Millie McCoy, she of the short, mousy brown hair, the thick glasses, the skin pale as paste and the size twenty dress, was about to drive, alone, into Mexico. She was going to sit on a beach—in a bathing suit. She was going to eat food that was far too spicy. She was going to a place where she couldn't even speak the language.

What in God's name was wrong with her?

She had just turned forty. That was what was wrong. She had just turned forty with nothing to show for it but an ever-increasing waistline, a job that paid well but bored her to tears, a pleasant but empty apartment, and a car of the sort that her parents would drive. And on that morning, when she had risen and looked in the mirror, she hated what she had seen.

So Millie McCoy was going to Mexico. Maybe all that would change was that her fat, pale flab would become fat, sunburned flab. But it would get her out, get her away. Make her do something instead of getting up at six, working till five, eating a Weight Watchers frozen dinner and a half-gallon of Haagen-Daaz, watching whatever was on TV and going to bed by eleven.

Her heart thudded rapidly. For the first time since she had conceived this wild idea, staring at a travel poster at a local

149

Mexican restaurant while downing the special, Millie realized
that what she was feeling was not fear—but anticipation.

"It's now or never, Millie," she told herself. She walked
purposefully to the front of the car, opened the door, and eased
her bulk into the driver's seat. She checked the glove com-
partment for the umpteenth time, making certain that the
Mexican auto insurance she'd bought a few days ago from
Sanborn's Mexican Insurance was in the car and not on the
kitchen table. Ditto for the title, her birth certificate, all the
documentation she'd need. She placed her hands on the wheel,
in the proper ten-and-two-o'clock position, took a deep breath,
and turned on the ignition.

All went smoothly at the border crossing. She was glad she'd
gone ahead and bought the insurance through Sanborn—their
express window saved time and trouble. The guards seemed
utterly disinterested in her. So much the better. Millie McCoy
had gone all her life without attracting attention, and she didn't
want to start now. The guard waved her through without even
asking her to stop, and Millie went from the safe, familiar
Arizona she'd grown up in into the hedonistic, wild allure of
Mexico.

Her first full day, Millie did nothing but sit on the beach,
lathered with 45 SPF sunscreen and reading a novel entitled
Love's Wild Something or Other. She forgot the title if she
put the book down for more than a minute. It was like any
one of a thousand other romances, with the pretty heroine
(blonde in this book) and the equally pretty hero (dark-haired
in this book) in a clinch on the cover. But Millie didn't mind.
It was comfortable, predictable, reassuring.

For lunch, she lumbered over to the little thatched hut that
served sandwiches and drinks. Mariachi music blared cheerfully from a set of speakers. She ordered what she always ate
for lunch—ham and cheese and a Coke. With a side order
of fries and ice cream for dessert. The slim, dark youth who
bartended gave her an odd look.

"*Señora*, you have come all this way to Mexico. Do you
not wish to try something a little more—" He gestured, then
looked at her pleadingly.

Millie blushed. "No, thanks. That's fine."

He sighed and shook his head. "We have only roast beef

sandwiches, *señora*, *lo siento*. And no fries—just potato chips."

"That's fine," said Millie. The boy—and he was one, only about seventeen or so if that—looked at her with a mixture of confusion and, she thought, pity, then set about getting her meal.

She ate slowly, chewing every bite thoroughly. Between swallows, she glanced around. The beach was gorgeous, she had to admit—almost more interesting than *Love's Wild Something or Other*. It stretched in luxurious whiteness to meet the blue-green ocean. Palm trees swayed in the wind that was cooling, but never violent. The sun shone benevolently, and Millie glanced down at her pudgy thighs. Only a slight glimmer of pink. Thank goodness for SPF 45, she thought. Further down the beach, the surf beat against rocks instead of yielding sand. For a wild moment, Millie wanted to walk over there and see what strange alien creatures had been trapped in the calm tidal pools. Would she find shrimp, transparent and tiny? Beautifully colored fish? A little octopus, perhaps, its eight tentacles tentatively probing for a way out?

"*Señora*, I cannot let you go without offering you a margarita."

The boy's accented, smooth voice jolted Millie out of her reverie. A margarita? At *lunch*? "Um, no, no thank you. Delicious lunch. *Muchas gracias*."

She rose, hastily, knocking over the stool which fell to the soft sand with a muffled sound. She groaned, inwardly, and closed in on herself even more. Like a crab, she scuttled back to her chair on the beach and lost herself in the novel.

The second day, she was pink, but not red. Nonetheless, she dragged out the floppy straw hat she'd bought at the hotel boutique yesterday, plopped it on, and wore a T-shirt and long skirt when she headed out into the bright Mexican morning. It was hotter today than it had been yesterday, and more humid. Dutifully, Millie bought a large bottle of water at the food hut, even though it meant having to face the handsome young bartender again.

"*Buenos dias, señora!*" he greeted her. "You gonna try something other than a sandwich for lunch today?"

Millie forced a smile, though it felt like the grinning rictus of a corpse. "No, I don't think so." Then, on impulse, she added, "But I might have a margarita to go with it."

The youth laughed delightedly, turning to his companion and jabbering rapidly in Spanish. The other man, older and mustached, laughed deeply. The boy turned back. She had expected ridicule, but his chocolate brown eyes were kind.

"*Que bueno, señora*. We will make a Mexican spirit out of you yet!" And he winked.

Millie blinked. It had been years since anyone winked at her—winked in a friendly fashion, not as a joke, not as a cheap laugh at the expense of her obesity or homeliness. She paid for the water and walked off toward the beach, not really seeing where she was going. Goodness. If that was all it took, then she'd have started ordering margaritas at lunch a long time ago . . .

The beach was more crowded today than yesterday. She had a problem finding an appropriately shaded spot, but managed it. Somehow, though, the lust-driven characters in *Love's Wild Something or Other* didn't hold her attention as they had yesterday. They seemed—two-dimensional. Unbelievable. Their torrid scenes of passion failed to set her heart racing.

Maybe she wouldn't read all day today. Maybe she'd . . . oh, she didn't know, go for a walk and explore that tidal pool after all. First, though, lunch. She ordered a sandwich, and this time the boy prepared it cheerfully and without question.

"The very best roast beef sandwich in all of Mexico, *señora*."

"Call me Millie," she said, quite unexpectedly. Her eyes grew enormous at her own daring. But the boy only laughed, placed his hand to his brown, smooth chest, and said, "Very well, *Señora* Meell-ee. And you must then call me Miguel."

She smiled and raised the margarita in a toast. She drank it slowly, then bought another bottle of water. Armed with sandwich, chips, and water, she turned and strode with purpose down the beach.

Millie was barefoot, and the water lapping at her ankles as it ebbed and flowed was very pleasant indeed. Maybe tomorrow, she thought, giddy with adventure, she'd actually go *swimming*. She hadn't been swimming in the ocean since she was a child. She laughed to herself. It must be the margarita.

She found a flat, sun-warmed rock and spread out her towel, folding it carefully so that all the edges lined up neatly. Then she sat down, unscrewed the bottle cap, and took a long, thirsty drink. The long hike—well, long for her, at any rate—in the hot sun had tired her.

She was finished with her bag of potato chips and well into her sandwich when she had the sensation that she was being . . . *watched*.

The hairs along her chubby arms and the back of her neck prickled. Silently, she cursed her temporary insanity. Hadn't she read that Mexico was not the safest place in the world? That a woman should never, ever, venture out alone? Even though she was a short distance away from a great many people, she suddenly felt very isolated. She closed her eyes, opened them. Sweat beaded along her upper lip.

"Who—who's there?"

Silence. Her mouth was dry, dry as the stones, dry as the sand. She swallowed hard, tried again.

"Who's there? Show yourself?"

Again, nothing. No, wait—there it was, a faint whisper, scarce heard above the relentless noise of the surf. She turned—and saw it, perched on a rock about two yards away.

The creature was cute, in a horrendously ugly sort of way. Its fur was brownish-gray and coarse-looking. Something had happened to its tail, for all the fur had been pulled off and it lay, naked and somehow vulnerable-looking, twined about the little animal's body in a protective fashion. Rounded ears were flattened against the wedge-shaped head. But the eyes, bright and black, watched Millie with intelligence gleaming in their depths.

Relief flooded Millie. Not a murderer. Not a rapist. Just a small little animal.

On an impulse, she broke off a bit of her sandwich. The ears came forward and the creature crept toward her, its body quivering, ready to bolt. The nose sniffed. Millie lifted the bit of food over the creature's head and at once it sat up on its hind legs, begging. Ah, a dog then, albeit a dog unlike any she'd ever seen. She'd have to ask Miguel about it. She lowered the food to the dog's muzzle and it took the morsel with surprising delicacy, gulped it, and eagerly cocked its head, ready for more. The more she looked at it, the less ugly it seemed. And its behavior was downright endearing.

Millie finished giving it the rest of the sandwich, and by the time the food was consumed the dog—she'd have to give it a name, wouldn't she, couldn't just keep calling it "the dog"— had mastered begging and had even learned to roll over on command. Smart little thing.

"You are so cute," she told it in a baby-voice. It responded to her tone and ducked its head, its little beady eyes locked with hers, body quivering with pleasure. When she held out her hand, the dog sniffed it, then rubbed its head against her palm.

From that moment, Millie McCoy was lost. There they were, the two of them in Mexico, the native dog and the imported human. Both were misfits. Both were—let's face it, Millie thought grimly—ugly. And they had found each other here, on the gorgeous beaches of Mexico's west coast, where the bodies of the beautiful reclined, covered in scented oils and baking slowly to honey-gold perfection.

After a while, she rose, dusting sand from her bottom. The dog looked up at her quizzically. "All out," she said sadly, spreading her hands. It was silly, wasn't it, to read human expressions in animals, but she thought it looked disappointed. "But I'll be back, I promise." She bent with an effort, patted the animal on the head once more, then gathered her stuff and returned to the beach.

She dropped her things off at her hotel room and redressed, slipping on shoes and taking her pocketbook with her. She could hardly believe it, but she was going into town.

Piedra Azul was a smaller town, and Millie was relieved that she'd listened to the travel agent and set her vacation here, in a relatively out-of-the-way place, rather than the crowded beaches of Acapulco or Mazatlan. Of course, she couldn't have driven to either of those places from Arizona, and that was a primary consideration. Millie wanted to be able to bolt if she had to.

She parked on the street next to a wharf. There were a few other tourists ambling along the narrow, twisting road and venturing into shops with names like Los Castillo and La Estrella. The wind shifted, bringing to her nostrils the fragrance of pastries from a bakery, along with the more powerful scent of fish. From somewhere, the sound of the ubiquitous mariachi music wafted out. She shaded her eyes, glancing about, then sighed. She should have known better than to hope she'd find a "pet store" in this little town.

Nestled amid the shops with signs in Spanish and English declaring "We Take Visa" was what appeared to be a small grocery store. There was a cart of fresh fruit outside. Mindful of the admonishment from her travel agent not to eat fruit off of carts, Millie passed by regretfully and entered the store.

A bell chimed to announce her presence. A ceiling fan turned lazily, doing nothing to stir up the stifling heat. It was dark inside and she blinked, adjusting her eyes.

"*Buenos dias, señora*," came a voice. "Help you?"

She smiled at the thin, tall, elderly man who appeared from nowhere. "*Gracias*," Millie replied. Then, groping for the words, "*Donde esta . . .*" what was it . . . "*la sena un perro?*"

The man stiffened abruptly and his eyes flashed. In heavily accented but good English, he replied, "We do not serve dog meat, *señora*. You Americans have these ideas and cannot let them go, it seems!"

Mortified, Millie abandoned the attempt at broken Spanish and exclaimed, "Oh, no, no, I meant, do you have dog food—something to feed a pet!"

At that the man's eyes widened and he laughed. "Ah, *señora*, you asked for a dinner of dog." He waggled a finger at her, all smiles now. "You need to take a lesson, *verdad!*"

Relief flooded Millie and she giggled too. She and the storekeeper smiled at one another in a relaxed, friendly fashion.

"So," he said, "you have *un perro, si?*"

"Well, not really. It's kind of a stray . . . I've been feeding it."

"We have a lot of those running around here. You should be careful—they can bite, you know." He moved to the back of the store and Millie followed.

"Oh, not this one. He's a little sweetie." She paused. "I've never seen a chihuahua, but he's really tiny, so he might be one."

The man shrugged, pulled a bag of Purina Dog Chow off the shelf and handed it to Millie. "Probably all kinds of dog in the little one, if he is a stray. Do you need a bowl?"

Half an hour later, armed with Dog Chow, a bright red

bowl, a leash and collar (the smallest size they had), and several chew toys, Millie returned to her car. She was surprised how good she felt. The kindly shopkeeper was probably right—her little canine friend probably wasn't pure anything. In fact, it didn't look like any dog she'd ever seen. But then again, she'd seen a lot of things south of the border that had been alien to the Millie McCoy who'd never ventured past Arizona.

She was in a hurry to sneak some food to the dog—she had decided to call it Miguel, after her friend at the snack hut—and was so intent on getting to the rocky part of the beach that she carelessly stepped on someone's towel.

"Hey!" cried the towel's owner. An apology on her lips, Millie looked down—and her breath caught in her throat.

He was gorgeous.

Blonde hair bleached almost white by the sun. Skin warm and golden and slick with oil. Broad chest with a few tufts of golden hair. A tiny little Speedo that left very little to the imagination. He looked like a Greek god, and was glaring up at her now, blinking without his sunglasses.

"Oh, gosh, I—I'm so sorry!" yelped Millie. She clutched her beach bag, filled with goodies for little Miguel, to her ample bosom like a shield. She immediately leaned over and attempted to straighten the towel. The heavy bag swung down her arm and bopped Apollo in the nose. "Oh, god, I'm *sorry* . . ."

For a moment, blue eyes flashed anger at her. Then they crinkled at the edges and she realized Apollo was laughing. "No, no, it's okay, really," he said, waving back further no doubt disastrous attempts to help. "It's nice to run into someone who speaks English around here—and I do mean 'run into.'"

Millie felt her face—her homely, fat, sunburned face—fill with blood. She could think of nothing to say.

Fortunately, she didn't have to. Apollo chattered on and on for a bit, extolling the Mexican sunshine but deploring the Mexican accents ("thick Spic, I call it," he said), then asked abruptly, "So, you here by yourself?"

Millie nodded.

"Me too. My, uh," he laughed uncomfortably, "my girlfriend ditched me. But the plane ticket isn't until next Tuesday, so I'm kinda stuck."

Millie nodded.

"You want to have dinner this evening?"

Millie's eyes grew enormous. "I—uh—"

"Oh. You've got plans, then?"

"No! I mean, uh—" She hesitated, then plunged ahead. "Sure, I'd love to have dinner with you." My God! Was it really her saying this? "My name is Millie. Millie McCoy."

"I'm Bob Cunningham." Apollo-Bob stuck a hand up toward Millie, who grasped it and pumped it experimentally. The hand was calloused, strong, warm in hers. *Oh, my*, Millie thought to herself.

"You staying here?"

Millie nodded. "Room 213."

"Great. Seven okay?"

"Great," Millie replied, repeating him.

"Pick you up then." Apollo-Bob flashed a white, perfect, Colgate-with-fluoride grin at her, then rolled over onto his stomach and closed his eyes, letting his broad, gleaming back pick up more Mexican sunshine.

For a second Millie stood over him, then realized the conversation was over. A little abrupt, perhaps, but what did she care? She had a date with possibly the most gorgeous man on the entire beach.

She was smiling all the way to the rocks, where the smile grew upon sight of little Miguel, perched where she had left him, waiting trustingly for her.

"Hello, sweetie!" Millie made haste to place down the bowl and shake some Dog Chow into it. Miguel fell upon the food and began devouring it, his odd, furless tail twitching. His teeth were quite yellow, Millie observed, but when he paused and glanced up at her, she found his ugliness charming her all over again.

She reached to scratch his ears as he lowered his pointed muzzle to the food again. "We've beaten the odds, you know," she whispered to him, glee warming her voice. "You've found me, you ugly little puppy you, and I think you're just the best. And I've found Bob Cunningham!"

On an impulse, when the dog had finished, she scooped him into her arms and then tucked him into the bag. He peered up at her, curious, but made no attempt to escape.

"I've got you now, sweetie, and I'm not letting you go!" Millie said. "I'm going to smuggle you across the border, you see if I don't."

Unspoken was her deep, secret, shameful thought: And if I fall in love with you, you ugly little thing, then maybe Apollo will fall in love with me.

They had dinner at the hotel's restaurant. Loud disco music thumped and a glitter ball swung garishly, for all the world as if the year were still 1977. The food was mediocre at best, and Millie and Bob had to almost scream at one another to be heard. Millie was a little disappointed. After her courageous foray into the town, she had looked forward to an evening at a cozy, quaint little Mexican place run by an owner as friendly as Miguel or the shopkeeper from whom she'd bought the Dog Chow. But Bob seemed to like the glare and glitz, and he dove into his steak with gusto.

Millie's stomach growled at the appetizing smell of the T-bone. She could pack a steak away with the best of them, but she'd settled for grilled chicken. She didn't want to eat like a pig in front of Bob.

He did most of the talking. At first, Millie was more than content to listen, to drink in the words of this surfing, sand-haired deity, and to smother a smile of glee that he was sitting not with some trim, bikini-wearing babe but with her, with *her*, Millie McCoy!

But as the meal wore on, Millie found herself liking less and less the things Apollo-Bob had to say.

She didn't like the words "spic" and "wetback" used to refer to the locals. She especially didn't like it when the offensive words were preceded by adjectives like "stupid" and "shifty" and "thieving."

She nursed her black coffee while he chattered on, dropping her eyes from the gorgeous visage of the man sitting opposite her and staring at her spoon as she stirred. Something inside her hurt, terribly. It was disappointment. He ought to have been at least as beautiful on the inside as he was on the outside. Instead, Apollo-Bob Cunningham revealed himself with every word to be an unmitigated, racist jerk.

No Prince Charming. And therefore she couldn't be Cinderella.

Silently, Millie mourned for the Bob that might have been. At last, the bill came. Millie held her breath. She had a terrible fear that he'd ask her to dance, and she couldn't. She simply couldn't get up there and, as the singers urged, "shake her groove thing" in front of all these people. Fortunately, Bob seemed as disinterested in the gyrations going on on the dance floor as Millie. "It's getting late," he said, glancing at his watch. "Let me walk you back to your room."

Millie suddenly felt very, very apprehensive. "Oh, that's fine, I can even see it from here—"

"Nonsense. Couldn't let you go all by yourself."

Sand crunched beneath her sandals as they walked beneath an almost-full moon back to her room. Now, for the first time, he was silent. She didn't feel like talking, either. She just wanted this bitterly disappointing evening over with as soon as possible.

She unlocked the door, turned around. "Thank you for—"

That was as far as she got.

Bob's mouth crushed down on hers, hard, painful, brutal. His hands grabbed her upper arms, digging deep into the sunburned, doughy flesh and he propelled her inside. He broke off long enough to kick the door closed. Millie gasped, trying to protest, but then Bob's mouth was on hers again. His tongue shoved deep into the recesses of her mouth, almost choking her.

Millie fought back, adrenaline lending her strength. How could she have been so stupid, so blind? She had muscle, but she had far more flab than muscle. Bob was lean and hard and easily overpowered her, even though at over two hundred pounds she outweighed him. Millie began to cry, furious at her own stupidity, hot tears slipping past her tightly closed lids as she helplessly pounded on him as he lay heavily on her on the bed, as he ripped her blouse and shoved a careless hand down her skirt.

"That's it, fight me, bitch," he panted, his breath hot in her ear. "You're all the same. You want it, don't you, you fat whale of a—"

Suddenly he screamed, right in Millie's ear. Millie cried out, too, for the pain was agonizing. Then she gasped a deep *whoop* of breath as the pressure of Bob's body was suddenly removed. He lay beside her, frantically slapping at his lower legs.

There, hanging on for dear life, his little black eyes intent and his oddly pink ears flattened against his gray head, was Miguel. The first few blows did nothing to dislodge the little creature, whose yellow teeth were buried deep in Bob's toned, tanned calf. But finally one fist slammed into Miguel, and he went flying to land on a heap on the floor.

Millie gasped, her hands to her sore, bruised mouth. Swearing, Bob advanced on the small form. He raised a foot to stomp on the little beast, crush Miguel's tiny ribs, break his brave heart—

Millie fumbled for the bedside lamp. She grabbed it, stumbled off the bed, and brought the lamp down across Bob's back. He fell, fortunately not on top of the still-unmoving Miguel.

He wasn't bleeding. She'd just knocked the wind out of him. She loomed over him, an obese avenging angel, while he caught his breath and stared up at her fearfully.

"You bastard!" she cried. "You label an entire country as lazy 'spics,' you try to rape me because I'm fat and ugly and must be so damn desperate I won't say no, you hurt a tiny little dog who's just trying to protect me, and you shouldn't have to, you shouldn't have to, because you're gorgeous and, and perfect, except you're really not, you're hideous, *hideous* inside, and you better get out *now*, you piece of *shit*, because I'll slam this thing down on your beautiful empty skull, you hear me?"

He heard her.

He scooted past her on hands and knees, scrambling to his feet as he reached the door. He tugged it open and ran out into the night. Millie realized with a smirk of satisfaction that he hadn't even bothered to zip up his fly.

Millie fell to the floor. "Miguel!"

For a moment, it looked as if her brave little friend was dead. Then he twitched, his whiskered muzzle quivering, and opened his eyes.

"Miguel!" She cradled him to her, gently. "Oh, you brave, brave thing . . . "

Beautiful, he was. As full of sweetness and charm as Bob had been empty of it. His courage in attacking her would-be rapist had sparked something inside her.

She wasn't Cinderella. She'd never be.

But there were other fairy tales, that didn't rely on a Prince Charming to transform the heroine. Fairy tales that relied on a beast, instead—an ugly beast with a heart of gold . . . .

A thought came to her. Bob might come back. And he might bring friends. "We've got to go." She rose, ignoring her own pain, and began to throw things into the suitcase.

Within half an hour, she was packed, checked out, and on the road. She had wrapped Miguel carefully in a soft skirt and tucked him into a corner of the trunk. "Only until we're safely in the U.S.," she reassured him. He obliged by promptly falling asleep. As she sped up Mexican Highway 8, she prayed that the border crossing would be as easy going out as coming in. Normally, this was what was known as a "free zone." Cars could simply drive right through. This time, though, her heart sank into her toes. Apparently, there was a problem.

She pulled up, rolling down her window. The guard did a double take, staring intently at her face, then asked to see her ID and insurance. Millie handed it over, hoping that he wouldn't notice how much her hands were trembling.

"*Señora*," said the guard bluntly, "you have been beaten."

Millie closed her eyes. Of course. By now, Bob's heavy hand would have caused her face to swell up quite a bit. She'd been so worried about getting away with Miguel she'd ignored the pain.

"Who did this to you?" His eyes were sad, resigned. Suddenly Millie knew what he thought he would hear—some white tourist's cry of injustice against a Mexican man rather than her husband or boyfriend.

She thought of happy young Miguel, who had coaxed her into a margarita. Of the friendly shopkeeper. And then Millie McCoy thought of Bob, the California dreamboat who had turned out to be far, far worse than any so-called "macho" Mexican. She smiled in secret triumph as she replied, gazing levelly at the guard. "*Un americano, señor.*" She paused, and added with an anger that surprised her, "*un gringo.*"

For a long moment, he stared at her. She did not look away.

Finally, he nodded. He handed her back the insurance. "Put some ice on that, *señora*. And kick the *gringo* in the *cajones* if you see him again."

And then he smiled, and for just a moment, he looked almost exactly like the boy Miguel.

He waved her through.

The first thing Millie did the next morning was bathe Miguel in a good flea bath. He submitted gracefully, and when she had finished, his coarse gray-brown hair was soft and fluffy. She picked him up and buried her face in his fur, chuckling with affection.

"Now," she told him, "to the V-E-T."

Miguel sat quietly in her lap as they sat in the waiting room. She realized that she would need a small pet carrier for subsequent visits, as the other dogs and cats seemed to intensely dislike the little guy. Miguel did nothing except burrow even more closely into Millie's lap.

Her name was called, and she followed the vet, a Dr. Whelan, into the room and placed Miguel on the table.

The vet stared. Her eyes grew enormous. "Good God," she breathed.

Millie's heart lurched. "What? What's wrong with him?"

Dr. Whelan continued to stare. "I'll put it down immediately," she said.

"What?" Millie yelped. "What are you talking about? Does he have rabies?" Oh, God, no, she prayed silently.

Slowly, the doctor raised her eyes to meet Millie's. "Ms. McCoy," she said, deliberately. "This is not a dog." She paused, licked her lips, composed herself.

"This animal is a rat!"

Melissa McCoy, once known as "Millie," slowed down, bit by bit, until she came to a stop. She reached for a towel and mopped her sweat-dampened face. Her long, thick hair was caught up in an efficient ponytail and held back from her face with a sweatband.

An hour. Good for you, she told herself, reaching for a large bottle of cold water and gulping thirstily. Tonight, she'd go to the gym to work out with Elaine and Susan and finalize plans for their weekend backpacking trek.

She caught a glimpse of her reflection in the mirrored wall as she stepped off the treadmill, and smiled at herself. Melissa McCoy, forty-one, and as healthy and happy as she could be. Her own eyes sparkled at her and she gave the lean, shapely woman in the mirror a friendly wink. She positively enjoyed mirrors these days.

The mirrored tiles had appeared six months ago; the treadmill, ten. The whole apartment had undergone a major change reflecting the owner's, particularly the spare bedroom which was now a bright, airy artist's studio. The refurbishing of the apartment had come from the money bought with the products of that studio. Melissa had ditched her boring job right after she'd returned from Mexico, shortly before she'd bought the treadmill.

She'd lost, she guessed, somewhere around eighty pounds. But that wasn't the number that interested her. More important were the numbers one-twenty over eighty, her current blood pressure; twenty-five, the miles she could hike in a weekend. Numbers like those. She wasn't a spectator of life anymore—she was a participant.

She stepped into the kitchen, still breathing heavily from the hard workout, and busied herself with dinner: bread fresh from the bread machine, spinach pasta with homemade sauce, a green salad, and for dessert, strawberries with a dollop of Cool Whip Lite. While fixing her own dinner, Melissa did not neglect to prepare a meal for someone very special—someone who had changed her life, turned her from Millie McCoy into Melissa, helped her follow her dreams and create a few new ones. Someone who had brought the sunny spirit of Mexico into her heart and turned her around with its rays. Someone the world found abhorrent, but who had helped her remake herself.

Pouring Purina Dog Chow into a bright red plastic bowl, Melissa placed it on the kitchen floor. And as Miguel, the rat from the barrio, ambled into the room, eyes bright and nose twitching with anticipation, Melissa stooped to pet her best friend, and thought him the most beautiful thing in the world.

Along Came a Spider . . .

Laura Anne Gilman

The bright pink wrapping screamed out from the pastel greens and grey-whites. Even the package was thicker, chunkier. Just the right size to fit snugly into a ten-year-old's palm. Newt's own palm was itching.

Digging into the left pocket of his windbreaker, he hauled out a handful of change. Frowning, he carefully picked out the piece of lint and counted the pennies, nickels and dimes, then looked back at the display in front of him. The neatly-lettered cardboard taped to the front of the rows of candy mocked him silently. Not enough. Almost—but not enough.

The bell over the store's door clanked, and a group of girls from the junior high swept past him, heading for the magazine rack. One girl's arm brushed him, and he stumbled forward. Putting his hands out to keep from falling, Newt felt his fingers close around one of the shiny pink packages, pulling it into his empty palm, pushing it under the elastic of his windbreaker sleeve.

He hadn't meant to do that. Hadn't thought to do it. Couldn't believe he'd done it. Heart pounding somewhere around his Adam's apple, Newt didn't dare swallow for fear he'd choke. Sweat crowded under his armpits, and the air in the small five-and-dime suddenly became stifling.

Shoving the change back into his pocket, he jerked his shoulder so that the old woman at the counter couldn't see his face, flush with a shameful excitement he didn't understand, and hurried out the door. The clank of the bell overhead sounded an accusation to him. Thief. Thief.

He emerged into the early May sunlight, blinking owlishly. Much of Newt, in fact, was owlish. Round eyes set in a round, peach-colored face, framed by shaggy brown hair that without too much imagination could easily be mistaken for tiny fluffed feathers.

Feeling the object of his haste sliding under his sleeve, Newt stepped out of the shade of the store's awning and onto the curb. Looking both ways, he crossed the street, passed the pizza place on the corner, and hurried along the sidewalk. He went under the railroad bridge, past the library, and turned left, breaking into a full-out run once he entered the park behind the low-slung brick building. Short legs pumping, he felt the sweat spread from his armpits, all the way down his back.

Clutching the end of his sleeve to prevent the package from slipping out, he followed the path past the shallow duck pond and landed in a flushed heap under a willow tree that was wider around than Newt could reach. He felt safe there, protected by the bulk of the tree.

Shifting to avoid the bumpy roots snaking above ground, Newt unclenched his fingers slowly and allowed the package of gum to fall out onto his sweaty palm. It lay there, looking too innocent to be the cause of his sudden descent into crime. Newt swallowed hard, fighting the urge to go back to the store, to admit his guilt, or perhaps just to drop the gum back into the display and slink out, head down and in disgrace.

Slowly pulling the strip in the direction the arrows pointed, Newt tore off the top of the package and stuffed the debris into his jeans pocket. His mother always told him not to be a lit-terbug. Unwrapping the first cube of gum, he popped it into his mouth, jaws chomping down against the elastic resistance.

A burst of sweetness hit the inside of his mouth, bring-ing saliva out, softening the gum further. A few more rota-tions and he was ready for the ultimate test of every new bubble gum. The Blowing.

Gathering the electric-pink mass at the back of his mouth, Newt pushed it into place with his tongue, flattening it with his teeth and tongue. Letting his breath fill it slowly, the way his father taught him, Newt crossed his eyes trying to watch the bubble grow. They were right, he thought triumphantly. It *did* blow easier than any gum he'd had before. But the bubble wasn't big enough for Newt. Grabbing the pack, he unwrapped another chunk and stuffed it into his mouth. Then a third. Finally, he was satisfied with the size of the bubble growing in front of his nose.

Sitting with his back against the textured bark of the tree, Newt watched the clouds shift by, felt the late spring sunshine on his face, and blew bright pink bubbles until the last of the guilt dissipated under the simple pleasure of perfect bubbles. After a while, the taste of the gum also began to fade. He removed the wad from his mouth, looked at it, then just for the hell of it bit a small portion off, chewed and swallowed it. It tasted worse going down, sticking briefly in his throat before dropping into his stomach.

The rest of the gum he pushed with his thumb into the ground, the brown dirt sticking to the pink like flies on flypaper. Pulling out the remaining gum, he unwrapped the last two chunks and shoved them into his mouth, The burst of sugary taste took his mind off the queasy feeling in his stomach from the gum he'd swallowed.

That queasy feeling returned quickly when the steady drone of a baseball game in the diamond behind him was interrupted by the familiar sound of bicycle chains jangling and male voices yelling. Newt closed his eyes and prayed silently that they wouldn't see him. No such luck.

"Hey brat!"

Newt opened his eyes to see Robbie's face inches from his own. Robbie had the same owlish look as his younger brother, but adolescence hadn't been kind, adding a veneer of acne to the surface. His eyes, the same soft brown, held a malicious spark that Newt was all too familiar with.

"What're ya up to, brat?"

The three boys clustered behind Robbie were laughing, expecting some kind of show. Newt cringed inwardly, knowing what that "show" would involve. Robbie wasn't cruel, not really. He'd never hurt Newt, not physically, and their folks just told them to go to their rooms, and maybe didn't give Robbie his allowance. No big deal. But it was never fun either.

Robbie looked back at his cohorts; they were clearly expecting something impressive. Newt didn't dare blink, certain that the moment he did the attack would come. His mouth was dry despite the gum still in his mouth, his chubby fist still closed around the forgotten wrappers. The crinkling sound startled both brothers.

"Oh man."

Newt didn't like the gleam on his brother's face. Didn't like it a bit.

"You bought that?"

Newt nodded dumbly, ignoring the tickle of guilt at the base of his skull. "Uh-huh."

"Idiot. I hope you didn't swallow any."

Newt's round eyes grew rounder. "Nuh-uh!" A pause, then he ventured, frightened, "Why?"

"Spiders."

Newt blinked. He couldn't help it. He hated spiders. Robbie knew that. Robbie was just teasing him. Wasn't he?

"Yeah." That was Paul. Paul was a jerk. Newt wouldn't believe Paul if he said that water was wet. Besides, how could spiders be in a piece of gum? They were joshing him.

"Spider eggs," Mike clarified, as though reading his mind. Mike was a thin towhead, tall enough to pass for an adult. And he knew stuff. Lots of stuff, like movie trivia and bad words in three different languages.

"I don't believe you," Newt said, but his voice was unconvincing.

"S'true," Paul went on. "There were spiders in the plant where they make the gum, and they were living in all the machinery. Nobody thought to clean them out. And they laid their eggs in the gum. Yuck."

Glenn, who had hung back from the others, spoke up then. Newt hoped for a fleeting second that he would say they'd been lying, that it was all a joke and go on and chew your gum.

"If you swallowed any—" and he paused for added effect "—you know what'll happen, don't you?"

Newt shook his head, fearing the worst.

"The eggs'll hatch in your stomach. They'll feed on whatever's down there. Then they'll creep up your throat, all of them in one long black line. While you're sleeping, coming up and out of your nose . . ."

"Gross!" Mike said, and Robbie made a gagging noise.

"But you didn't swallow any, did you brat?"

Newt shook his head, his eyes wide with horror.

"Then you've got nothing to worry about."

Laughing, they got back on their bikes and rode off towards

town. Newt stared after them until they turned the curve in the path and disappeared from view, then looked down at the crumpled wrapper in his hand. Spitting out the gum in his mouth, he held it between two fingers and examined the well-chewed mass carefully. It didn't look like there were eggs there. But spiders could be real small, couldn't they? So maybe their eggs, you'd need a microscope to see them with.

Dropping the pink wad with a disgusted twist of his wrist, Newt stood and brushed the dirt off the seat of his jeans and walked away hurriedly.

He felt kinda sick, in his stomach.

Newt's father usually looked like a spectator at a tennis match, trying to follow both his sons' conversations at the dinner table. But tonight, Newt let his brother get all the attention. He sat in his usual chair, on the right-hand side of the table, and pushed food around on his plate while Robbie went on and on about the deer they'd seen, riding their bikes home that afternoon. Newt's mother said that there wasn't enough food for all the deer, that's why everyone was spotting them along the roads this summer.

Newt wished he'd been the one to see the deer. He'd have given it all his salad. Although he didn't think a deer would want to eat his pork chop. He cut the meat into even smaller pieces, frowning glumly. His mom had been home today, so there was bound to be dessert. Chocolate pudding, maybe. But he couldn't work up any enthusiasm for it. His mouth felt cottony, no matter how much Hi-C he drank, and his tummy felt like he'd swallowed a bowling ball, all heavy and full.

He was sure that Robbie and the others had been joshing him. Even if there had been spider eggs in that gum, and Newt shuddered at the thought, they couldn't hurt him. Could they? But the counselors at camp last summer had warned them not to swallow the watermelon seeds. Said they'd never digest, that you'd grow a watermelon vine in your stomach. And apple seeds. Everyone knew that you weren't supposed to eat apple seeds. Robbie took a moment's pause in the conversation to lean over the table and say, in a sing-songy whisper, "There was an old lady who swallowed a spider, to eat the fly, who wiggled and jiggled and tickled inside her . . ."

Newt felt the food he'd barely managed to choke down rise

again, and he shot from the table like dogs were after him, barely making it to the bathroom in time.

Newt looked at the clock for the fifth time in half as many minutes. Fifteen past midnight. He couldn't remember the last time he'd been up this late, without it being a special occasion. After he'd barfed during dinner, his mom made him go to bed, sure he was coming down with something. She'd brought him lemon water, and he'd managed to keep that down, and then his dad had tucked him in and told him to get some sleep. But he couldn't.

Being sick wasn't all that bad, he supposed. Everyone was really nice to him. Robbie'd even stopped by, standing in his doorway between TV shows, and told him a couple of dead baby jokes before their dad chased him off. Gross. Newt hoped he could remember them when camp started.

But now the house was quiet, only the low mutter of the TV from his folks' room and the sound of his dad maybe making a late-night snack in the kitchen. It should have been comforting. Instead, it just gave him time to think about stuff he didn't want to think about at all.

Newt stared up at the ceiling of his room, the only light from the glow of his alarm clock. Everything else in Newt's room was yellow. Newt hated yellow. He liked purple. But his mom wouldn't let him have a purple room. They let Robbie choose his own colors. It wasn't fair.

Newt's lower lip thrust out, and he hugged that injustice like the stuffed cat Robbie had told him to grow out of already. But it wasn't enough to take his mind off the fact that the shadows on the wall had fat bodies and long creepy legs. Or the tightness in his belly that had nothing to do with food, or being sick.

When he opened his eyes next, the clock's fluorescent hands were on the three and the five. He'd never been up this late, not even when his dad took them to the cabin, woke them up real early to go fishing. The house was too quiet now. The TV was off. Everyone was asleep. A car passed somewhere, not on their street, but other than that the only sound was Newt's own breathing. He put a hand on his chest, to reassure himself that it was really his own breathing, and not—what?

Then it happened again, the Thing that had woken him up, and Newt whimpered involuntarily, his fingers clenching on the cotton blanket. His tummy *shifted* somehow. Like he had gas. Like . . . something was pushing from inside.

Newt whined inaudibly, like their old poodle used to when she was upset. If he could have gotten his body to move, he would have been cowering in his parents' bed, covers pulled over his head, and who cared how Robbie'd tease him in the morning! But he couldn't move, as though someone had tied him down to the bed like in those horror movies they'd watched last month.

He strained again, trying to escape, and almost passed out. The pain was low down, under his belly button. Short, sharp scrapes and twists in his guts. Like needles in his belly. Like needing to use the bathroom really bad. He could feel himself strain, and worried that he'd wet his bed like some little baby, but nothing came out. Another cramp hit him, and he tried to curl into a ball on his side. Fire flashed from his knees to his chest, and Newt bit his tongue with the pain. Then it was gone, and the release was almost worse than the pain had been, waiting for it to come back.

The inside of his skin itched, and he shuddered like a horse shaking off flies. His mouth fell open, the jaw muscle slack as though he'd been given novocaine. Newt felt a stickiness in his throat, a heavy weight like honey flowing up. Tears trickled from the corner of his eyes, and snot pooled in his nostrils. Something twisted low down inside, and he shuddered again. There was a final *push* from deep in his gut, and Newt erupted in a hacking cough that lifted him off the bed and into a half-sitting position. That action freed his voice, and Newt wasted no time in screaming at the top of his lungs. A high-pitched, girly scream, but Newt didn't care what he sounded like, just so long as someone came. Now!

He continued coughing, willing to put up with the flow of things out his mouth so long as it meant they were getting out of *him*.

The light flicked on, and his dad burst into the room, followed immediately by his mom, her nightshirt on backwards. The coughing subsided, and he fell back onto the bed, turning his face piteously towards them.

"Oh my God!" His mother rushed to the bed, sitting beside him and cupping his chin carefully so that he had no choice but to look up into the light. He squinted away from it, seeing spiky shadows even in the illumination. The paralysis broken, his voice came back in a torrent, words falling out of his mouth in an incoherent rush. Something salty fell on his lips.

His father came out of nowhere with a washcloth in his hand. His mother took it from him, ignoring Newt's babbling as she dabbed at his upper lip. Newt paused long enough to see it come away red. There was an instant of silence, and then he burst into tears.

"There, there," his father soothed him, one hand heavy on his shoulder. "It was just a nosebleed. See? Nothing to worry about. Just tilt your head a little, and we'll get you all cleaned up."

The voice was familiar, comforting, but Newt wasn't buying it. "Mama?"

She smiled at him, but he could see the worry in her face. "There was something in my throat!" It came out garbled, even he couldn't tell what he'd said. Newt tried to stop snuffling long enough to explain, to tell them what had happened. It was really important that one of them understand that he wasn't a baby, to cry over a little blood. But she wasn't listening either, making cooing noises, and wiping the blood and snot away from his sweat-streaked face. And slowly, unwillingly, his tears faded down into watery hiccups, and the shadows thrown by the overhead light were just shadows, and his parents' words sounded right, and reasonable, and soothing.

Letting them place another pillow under his head, and pull the covers up over his body, Newt suffered his mom to kiss his forehead and his dad to ruffle his hair, and gave them a weak smile as they paused by the door.

"Do you want us to leave the door open?"

Newt hesitated, leery despite his exhaustion, and then nodded. Anything was better than being alone in the dark again.

"Okay. Goodnight, sweetie."

Letting his head sink back into the pillows, Newt closed his eyes and prepared to sink into sleep. Maybe he was coming down with a fever after all. His body felt like it was made of lead, so heavy. . . .

Overhead, in a corner, a large spider spun a web that shone pink in the light from the hallway.

The Hook of Death

Billie Sue Mosiman

I don't know what sins I've committed that sent me to the cold wasteland of Antarctica. Brian, the radar tech, and I have often sat mulling over steaming cups of the blackest coffee we could make to figure how we came to be stationed at McMurdo Sound. Being a government employee means taking a risk on where in the world you might wind up, but two years duty at McMurdo seems the cruelest punishment. And for my friend, Brian, the deadliest.

He has done something unforgivable and they have sent a team from the FBI to check us out. Tomorrow the plane should land and they will take Brian away. If I had the strength to argue, I'd beg them to take me too.

It's the isolation that either makes you mad or kills you. They tell me a few years ago another recruit went insane and had to be locked up in a supply room for months before they could ship him out. If he'd been allowed to run amok, they feared he would have murdered everyone at the base. Another time at a Russian base in this region, two men argued over a game of chess and one buried an ax in the other man's head.

If only we had locked Brian away . . .

It began with stories. The days and nights are interminable here. Once our stations are secure and all the work complete, the hours stretch out before us like years until the next day can begin. Brian came from Alabama. He had a soft drawl and a sunny smile. We had struck up a friendship early on. He had been at McMurdo for two years already when I shipped in. Since I was a replacement in Brian's sector and new and raw, he took me under his wing. The first year of my exile, we played games to pass the time. Cards, dominoes, darts. Brian nearly always won. He was quick-witted and able to see patterns inside of patterns, giving him the edge in most competitions. After a while, when it appeared I'd never improve and he would always be the victor, he suggested that I might like to hear some of the old tales he had heard or experienced as a boy in the rural south.

"Sure," I said, happy to be freed of the role of loser. "I'd love to hear some stories."

During the first few months after work, we'd take our coffee mugs over to the heating vent in the corner of the radar room where it was quiet and warm. Brian told me about watching his grandfather pick cotton on the farm, the ice cream socials during warm summer evenings, many hunting and fishing stories involving detailed descriptions of rifles, frog gigs, chasing coons up trees, the proper way to tan hides, and the best bait for catching bass and catfish in country fishing holes.

It passed the time. It was Time that was our greatest enemy. Men on the base used obsessions to get them through the endless empty hours. I knew guys who kept mice (shipped to them through the mail from a supplier in South Dakota), cataloged music tapes, put together endless model car kits, wrote daily letters home, or watched old movie videos over and over until they knew all the dialogue. It was like prison, each man to himself, trying to pass the days. Telling stories was just one more way to beat down the loneliness.

I noticed after several months of swapping stories, that just as in the playing of games, Brian was the better storyteller. I came from Chicago, raised by a single mother and had no extended family. Just to stay alive my mom and I had to work hard. Who had time for family stories?

Then one week a couple of months ago Brian said, "I could tell you strange tales you might not believe."

"Strange? Like how strange?"

"Well . . . like ghost stories and odd murders. But the best of all is the night Betsy Ann and I were out parking and there was this man . . ."

"What man?"

"He had been around our little village ever since I could

remember. No one had anything to do with him. They said he'd been to Vietnam and lost his arm and it made him crazy. He was always carrying on to anyone who would listen how they sawed off his arm at the elbow in the POW camp to try to break him."

"Well shit."

Brian shrugged. "I don't know if it's true. He might have lost it in a fire fight, shrapnel or something, who knows. Most people thought he was so damn nuts that anything he claimed couldn't be true. I used to go to sleep at night and have nightmares about someone sawing off the guy's arm. His name was Folcum. I don't know his first name, I don't know if anyone knew it. He lived alone in a cabin in the woods and didn't have a lot to do with anybody. They all just called him Folcum as in 'Here comes that Crazy Folcum again.'"

"So he had just one arm?"

"No, he had two. I mean, he had one and then he had a hook. They'd fitted his missing limb with one of those mechanical things that had two metal fingerlike appendages on the end of it. He could open and close them to pick up things. The two contraptions curved when they were closed so they looked like a hook. He'd wave that at the kids around the country store to scare them."

"So what happened when you were out parking with your girl?" This sounded like an urban legend to me. I'd heard of the one about the man with the hook and the parked lovers. I couldn't quite bring myself to disbelieving Brian's story, though. It hadn't seemed to me that he'd told me lies before so why would he tell me one now?

"Well, I was sixteen and Betsy Ann was just fifteen. Her folks wouldn't let her go on dates yet, but they let me drive her to church on Sunday nights. I'd come early and say we were going to stop for an RC at the store before church. We never did. Instead we took that extra half hour or so to turn down a little-used road that led to the old baseball diamond, park under the pines, and make out like bandits. By the time we got to church we'd be so flushed and horny, we'd have to avoid the preacher's eyes for fear he'd know what we'd been up to.

"One Sunday night in late winter we had the windows rolled up against the cool evening and we're sitting in the front seat with our tongues in one another's mouths and I had Russian hands and roving fingers. Betsy Ann was one hot babe and I was hoping eventually she'd let me have her, totally, you know?

"Anyway, we both hear the scrape of metal against the backseat door handle on the driver's side. I was driving my dad's old four-door Galaxy.

"It's real dark under the pines, can't even see the stars and there was no moonrise yet that night. We stop in the middle of a kiss, our lips frozen fast as popsicles to one another and when Betsy Ann pulled away, we heard it again.

"'What's that?' she said, and for the life of me I couldn't imagine. All I knew was suddenly I was too afraid to turn around and look back there. 'It's nothing,' I said, trying to believe it myself.

"Betsy Ann was looking back now so I forced myself. I didn't see anything, but it occurred to me the sound we'd heard could have been made by Folcum's weird metal hooked hand grabbing hold of the door handle.

"I told Betsy Ann that she could see for herself it was nothing. Time was running out for us to be at church, so I pulled her over to me and had just gotten my hand on her breast when the sound, louder, came again. I jerked around in the seat and saw . . . nothing."

"That's damn creepy," I told Brian. "Was it Folcum?"

"It sure was. I don't know what he was trying to do, scare us or get into the car with us, but I started up the car quick and took off. I saw his silhouette behind us in my rearview. Him and his awful arm."

"So what happened then?"

Brian hung his head and contemplated his coffee mug. He looked aged in the dim light. He looked to be struggling with bad memories and was about to change the subject when he said quietly, "Folcum caught Betsy Ann walking home from the bus stop the next day. He dragged her into the woods at the edge of the road and . . . and . . ."

I knew I didn't need to hear this. I resisted the urge to stand up abruptly and leave the radar room before he could finish.

"They found her three days later. She'd been strangled and mutilated. She'd managed to tear off a snippet of the shirt Folcum was wearing. It was clutched in her hand. When they went to pick him up, they found him not wearing the mechanical arm. He always wore that thing so they went searching for it in the house and found it had been bent all to hell. It wouldn't work anymore. And there was some of Betsy Ann's blond hair caught in the pincers like he'd tried to hold her head down by her hair."

"Jesus, that's awful, Brian. It must have shocked your whole community."

Brian looked up and a sly, ferret look came into his eyes. "While Folcum was out on bail, he disappeared." Brian smiled and a shiver of apprehension ran up my spine.

"He left the state or something?"

"Naw. He left the planet. I caught him out behind his house and dragged the bastard down to the creek and held his head under until he stopped fighting. I threw his stupid hook arm into the deepest part of a fishing hole and I guess it's still there today."

"You killed him?" I whispered.

Brian stood up and stretched. "Bedtime," he announced. "I've told enough stories for tonight."

I couldn't sleep for thinking about Brian being a killer. I understood the grief and pain his girlfriend's death must have given him, but take the laws into his own hands? Hold Folcum's head under water until he died? That was some cold business.

But then Brian called all these tales "stories" and maybe he just made them up.

It wasn't until he really lost it and went berserk at the outpost that I truly believed he was capable of murder and had probably killed Folcum, just as he claimed.

It was weeks after he'd told me about the man with the hooked arm that Brian started acting weird. He stopped telling me stories and clammed up tight. He didn't want to play cards or watch videos with me. He started keeping himself in his quarters and when I went to see about him, he was gruff and unfriendly. I asked him, "What's got into you? What's wrong?"

He said he had headaches, they were killing him and the McMurdo Sound medics wouldn't prescribe anything stronger than aspirin. Radar techs have to be careful about what medications they take. No one wanted them seeing flying saucers or incoming missiles on the screens.

I left him alone and started reading an Edgar Allen Poe collection I'd ordered from a book club. I worried about Brian, but if he didn't want my company, I was not about to force it on him.

The shift radar techs started coming to me and asking if I knew what was wrong with Brian. I was his friend, I should know what was up. He'd been saying he heard things and couldn't keep his mind on the radar blips. Couldn't they hear it, he asked them over and over, that awful scraping sound, like someone outside the hut dragging something metallic along the corrugated metal sides? They couldn't hear anything of course. They feared Brian was losing it and might have to be shipped out on the next available transport.

I braced Brian that night in his quarters. The entire base was constructed of Quonset huts made of corrugated metal and fully insulated on the inside. Nevertheless you could still hear the wailing of the cold winds out there and once in a while the creak of shifting ice or the thunder of a far off avalanche falling into the Sound, but I knew that's not what Brian thought he was hearing. He'd become obsessed with Folcum and Folcum's mechanical arm.

"Brian, your colleagues in the radar room are threatening to go to the C.O. about you. We have to do something."

He looked up at me from where he lay on his bunk and said, "They don't hear it, or they pretend they don't."

"It's that story you told me, Brian. About Betsy Ann. It's like you let it take over your thoughts or something. You're imagining things."

Brian jerked up in bed, sitting rigid, his head cocked to one side. He glanced over at the small dark window. "You heard that, didn't you? Didn't you?! Don't lie about it."

I shook my head slowly. "Wind, that's all it is. The damn constant wind we get."

"Wind can't thunk against the side of the building and then rumble down the side, slapping those corrugated valleys. You're lying, just like the others. You hear it, you know he's there, but you just won't admit it."

I walked over and took him by the shoulders and shook him hard. "Brian, snap out of it. You've been here too long, that's all. Your mind's starting to play tricks on you. Folcum's dead. You told me so yourself, you killed him, he's *dead*."

Brian wrenched free and pushed me back. "Get out of my room. I want to be alone. You never were my friend."

I sighed in defeat. I'd have to go to the C.O. myself, explain how this came about. Plead for Brian's relocation before his obsession spread any further.

Brian's first victim was an office clerk sent by the C.O. to summon Brian for an interview. From somewhere Brian had found a length of lead water pipe and after he invited the private to enter his room, he cold-cocked him right in the head. They say the man was dead before he dropped, his skull cracked right down the front over his forehead.

When the body was discovered, Brian was gone. A massive search was put on, the entire base under emergency alert. We had an escaped killer on our hands. We had a man driven by the searing cold, the isolation, and old memories who was on the rampage. It wasn't as if it hadn't happened before, but this time it was my friend, it was someone I thought I'd known intimately. I knew he had to be stopped; I just didn't want him to suffer any more than he already had.

They say in regions like the Antarctic a man comes to know his real self. Mannerisms are exaggerated over the passage of time, habits grow into obsessive behavior, and a man's mettle is tested in myriad ways. I came to understand I didn't know nearly as much about the human heart as I had once thought. I didn't really know human nature and where the limits were. I only knew Brian had been my best friend and he was haunted now by a man with a mechanical arm. Folcum was as real and present to him as any of the rest of us who shared the base compound.

Last night they found one of the radar techs who had worked with Brian bludgeoned to death in his bed. This morning the FBI arrives and the search intensifies. Where could Brian be hiding? What nightmare is he living through now?

I had just sat down on my bunk and opened the Poe to where I'd saved my place. All day long the special FBI force questioned me about Brian. I was bone weary and the wind rattling around the small window frame unnerved me. I scooted my back against the wall and lifted my legs onto the blanket. That's the moment Brian chose to speak.

"Hello, traitor," he said softly.

He was under my bed! I leaped up and leaned down to

see him. He pushed from beneath the bunk. I didn't like the grim grin that rode his lips. He looked like a man having a bullet removed, grinning and bearing it. "Brian! They're looking for you."

"I know. I'll let them find me soon. But first I have work to finish."

"What work?" I didn't mean to let the trembling reach my hands that hung at my sides. I gripped them together behind me so he wouldn't see. Brian was no longer the gameplayer and storyteller. He was insane and dangerous. I didn't think it would be smart to let him know how afraid of him I was.

"Why, your disposal, of course," he said. "You turned me in. You went to the C.O. You've wanted to get me out of here for months now. It's so petty, you know? I beat you at games, I tell better stories, and you can't forgive me for that."

"Look, Brian, you're not well. You need. . . ."

He withdrew the pipe from behind his back. "I need to send you to hell, that's what I need to do."

I backpedaled, then when he swung, I ducked. I was yelling then, out of my head with fear that made me cold all over. "Brian, listen to me! I'm not your enemy. I didn't do anything to Betsy Ann. I'm not Folcum, don't you understand that?"

He began to laugh, a wheezing, crazy laugh that filled my room and hurt my ears. "You really believed my stories, didn't you? Don't you know that's an old story people have been telling for ages? About the man with the hook? You didn't think he was real, did you?"

Then he raised the pipe over his head. I was pinned against the wall, the door too far distant to reach so I could flee.

Suddenly Brian hesitated, and his head swiveled on his neck so that he was staring at the window. "Look. There. He was never real until I told you about him. Now he's come to get revenge. He doesn't like his story told, not by anyone. People think it was just a legend, all made up to frighten teenagers and kids, but it must have really happened, he must have once been real."

My gaze was drawn to the window and for a brief second or two I swear I saw what Brian saw there. A wizened face pressed to the glass, the eyes dark and senseless with rage. And there, next to that mad face the mechanical hand clenched so that the two pincers were curved and hooked together.

Startled, I drew in my breath in a gasp, but then he was gone and nothing was at the window but snow swirling past in wind eddies.

I turned my attention back to Brian and saw he was still mesmerized by the apparition. It was my chance to make a move. I rushed forward and grabbed his arm holding the pipe, and turning my back to him, I twisted the pipe away, and got to the door to call for help.

Now that they've taken Brian away I wonder if the story he told was true or not. Had his madness made him taunt me by saying it had been a lie? And what had I seen at the window those few seconds?

I expect soon I will have to go to the C.O. and plead for a medical leave. They wouldn't let me go back with Brian.

I'm terribly lonely. I have no friend to talk to, no one to kill the time with, no one to tell me stories.

But the worst thing of all is how the Antarctic wind never ceases, how it rattles across the corrugated outside walls like . . . like a metal arm dragging past the window searching for the next victim, waiting until the time is ripe for murder, taking all the time in the world to make the next move.

What Happened Next

Adam-Troy Castro

As they sped away from Lover's Lane, Brad and Debbie must have dragged the escaped maniac down the road for the better part of a mile before his prosthetic hook snapped off the end of his right arm.

Momentum being what it is, he slid another sixty feet alongside their speeding jalopy before what was left of his momentum went the way of his dignity and he slid to a stop on his ragged, friction-burned belly.

The maniac cursed in pain and frustration as their tail-lights disappeared around the next curve. "Shit! Shit! Shit! Shit! Shit! Shit!"

They had been such promising victims.

He'd been stalking them ever since they pulled up to the shady spot beneath the trees. Brad had been blond and crewcut, Debbie bouncy and pony-tailed. They'd sat together watching the moon for so long that the maniac almost fell asleep waiting for the big lug to make his move. Then Brad put on the rock 'n' roll station, and they started to neck, their two profiles merging beneath the silhouette of the fuzzy dice hanging from the rear-view mirror—and the emboldened maniac had begun to inch forward, the razor sharp hook that he sported in place of a right hand glinting hungrily beneath the cold pitiless moon. He had just slipped the hook around Brad's door handle, already savoring the slaughter to come, when the radio station broke into the song to blast an urgent bulletin about the escaped Hook Killer and his penchant for assaulting couples parked at Lover's Lanes. Debbie had said, omigod Brad, I'm scared, we gotta go home right now, and Brad had said, don't worry, baby, I'm here to protect you, and Debbie had said, no, I mean it, Brad, this place gives me the creeps, and Brad said, oh well, if you insist, and then Brad had turned the ignition, and by now the maniac was trying really really hard to disengage his hook from the door handle, but he couldn't, because it was stuck. And Brad put the car into drive and roared away in a shower of gravel, with the hapless maniac managing to run alongside for all of twenty feet before Brad subliminated his frustrated carnal urges in a burst of wholly unnecessary speed. Leaving the maniac to endure a mile of being dragged alongside their car, shouting and cursing and scooping up the furry remains of roadkill squirrels in his rapidly ballooning pant legs.

Now, with his hook receding with the tail-lights of his intended victims, the maniac lay twisted on the pavement, in clothes worn through from friction, with an arm that ended in a stump instead of a killing implement. He had one of the world's all-time worst cases of belly rub, and he was ranting in the tone of a madman whose murderous rage had just been stoked to a fever pitch.

But what he really felt, as he unsteadily rose to his feet, was a bottomless sense of inadequacy.

Did things like this ever happen to Jason? To Freddy? To Pinhead? To Jack, the father of them all? Of course not! They had all the luck!

He slapped some of the road dust off his now-threadbare clothing—raising a cloud that probably could have been seen from orbit—and gazed hopelessly at a highway now completely abandoned by cars. He had no idea what to do next: not where to go, or how to get there, and who he should stalk once he arrived. No direction struck him as particularly promising. For a moment there he was even tempted to just screw the stalking and willingly return to the asylum, where he never got dragged behind cars and always got a second helping of pistachio ice cream on Thursdays.

And then the Gods of boogeymen smiled down on him, in the form of another pair of headlights coming down the road.

He stuck out his thumb. Or rather, he tried to stick out

his thumb, because, having bumped his head a few times during that last hundred yards or so, he wasn't thinking all too clearly. Actually, he stuck out his bloody stump.

The car stopped for him anyway.

It was a fine vehicle. Shiny and red, with the kind of expansive tail fins that had gone out of style forever three decades earlier. It was so clean that even in the darkness he could see the ghost of his own reflection in the finish.

A beautiful blonde woman leaned over and said, "You look like about two hundred miles of bad luck."

The maniac had never been skilled at witty repartee. "Huh?"

"It's an expression," she explained. "You know, like 'something the cat dragged in,' only more colorful. I just said it because you're one of the most pitiful sights I've ever seen. You're going to have to tell me how come you have all those dead squirrels sticking out of your pants—I'm sure the story's simply fascinating. Do you need a ride?"

God, she was gorgeous. The kind of kill you only saw in the movies.

But distrust of his own good fortune made him hesitate. Things had always gone wrong for him, ever since the traumatic incident that had rendered him a maniac in the first place. He had broken into a woman's apartment, intent on nothing more savage than burglary, and was met by a Doberman that bit off his right hand. He'd never live down the stories about what happened when the lady came home and brought her dog to the vet. The boys at the asylum never quit ribbing him about it—the worst among them being old man Gein, who to this day loved to sneak up behind him and cry, "Woof! Woof!"

The bastard. Like he was in a position to criticize, with his lousy taste in clothing.

The voice of the pretty blonde lady brought the predator back to the here and now. "You don't want to be walking alone this time of night," she said.

That made up his mind for him. He was an escaped maniac, dammit! Latest in a long line of noble predators stretching all the way back to Countess Bathory! Was he going to sit idly back and let a little setback like being dragged by his hook for a mile or so make him a weepy whiner? Hell no! He had zip and zowie! He was going to get back on the horse and ride!

The maniac smiled. "Sure. I could use a ride."

He reached for the door handle with his one intact hand . . . and heard a click.

The second he exerted pressure on the door handle, a pair of clamps emerged from the casing and snapped shut around his wrist, forming an unbreakable handcuff. He tried to withdraw his hand, but found it held tight. He glanced back at her, confused, and saw in her triumphant eyes the look of a predator far more experienced than he.

"Silly boy," she cooed. "I offered you a ride. I never said you could *get in*."

Through a haze, the maniac realized he'd heard about this woman before: during long lazy afternoons at the asylum, whenever he and the other maniacs got together to swap tall tales about those of their persuasion still at large.

The Door Handle Dragster.

"Hey," he said.

She blew him a kiss and peeled out.

Of course, unlike Brad, she didn't obey any speed limits.

What a Croc!

Bill Crider

(With a big tip of the Texan Stetson to Hank Davis)

The captain strode across the cobbles of Innsbruck's Old Town without regard for the tourists who wrinkled their noses as he stalked past them on Herzog-Friedrich-Strasse. His short-legged first mate hustled along behind, practically running in his effort to keep pace.

When they reached the tables outside the cafe next to the building with the golden roof, the captain sat down carefully so that his wrinkled trenchcoat would not swing open to reveal the pump-action shotgun that dangled from his shoulder by a thin nylon rope.

The mate dragged up a chair and sat beside him. Both of them glanced up at the clock on the Old Town Tower.

"Almost noon, Cap'n," the mate said. He carried a leather rucksack and wore an alpine green Tyrolean hat and lederhosen, which looked a bit odd with his calf-high rubber boots. One of his top front teeth was missing, thanks to one of the captain's temper fits, and it had been replaced with a gold tooth that flashed in the sun. The mate liked it much better than the original, and at times he was even grateful to the captain for making room for it.

"I can tell the time," the captain said, being a man who had a certain amount of affection for clocks.

He looked up, thinking how nice and practical the Tower was. It had once served as the town's jail, and the whippings

187

Urban Nightmares

administered to those inside, along with the screams of those unfortunates, could be heard by all those happening by. A good lesson for them all, the listeners and the whipped, the kind of lesson that he approved of.

The Tower bells began to clang, and just as they had struck the twelfth hour a waiter appeared to take the captain's order. The waiter started to speak, and then almost gagged. At one time the captain might have been offended, but that was long ago. Now he was used to that kind of reaction; he knew very well how he smelled. Anyone who spent as much time in the sewers as he did would smell much the same.

Before the waiter could recover and ask him to leave, the captain ordered a Kaiser beer for himself and one for the mate. The waiter scooted away, glad to put some distance between himself and the odor emanating from the two men.

"Thank'e kindly for the beer, Cap'n H—" the mate began.

The captain slammed his fist down on the table. "Shut yer gob! It's Cap'n Bob that I go by now, and don't you forget it."

The mate stared at the fist as if enthralled by it, as well he might have been, for the hand was a first-class piece of workmanship. The material that covered it was enough like real flesh to fool a mosquito, and as the captain unclasped his fingers, the mate could not hear a single mechanical sound.

"D'ye think we'll catch 'im this time?" the mate asked, looking anxiously around as if expecting someone to join them at the table. There was no one nearby, however, the only tourists having left hurriedly the vicinity shortly after getting a whiff of the captain and the mate.

"It could be so, Willem," Cap'n Bob said, though Willem was no more the mate's name than Bob was the captain's. "I wish it would be so."

"So do I, Cap'n," Willem said, a faraway look in his eye. "I'd like to go home, I would."

"And you think I wouldn't like the same?"

"It's not that, Cap'n. I know—" Willem stopped speaking as the waiter delivered the two beers. When he had hastened away, Willem continued. "—I know you'd like to get back there, too. But do you even know the way?"

"I can find the way, never think I can't. I found my way here, didn't I?"

"Oh, yes, Cap'n, indeed you did." Willem took a deep drink of his beer and set the foamy glass on the table. "Indeed you did. No thanks to—"

The fist slammed down on the table again, causing Willem's glass to hop up and down.

"Haven't I told you a thousand times never to mention that name?" the captain said.

"Aye, Cap'n, that you have. I'm sorry that I almost spoke it."

The captain drank his beer and brooded. He hated the name of the light-foot lad who had taken his hand almost as much as he hated the crocodile who had eaten it.

The mate waved his half-empty beer glass in the air, the alcohol having given him a light buzz. "We've had us some times, eh, Cap'n? Remember that day in New York, when we almost had 'im?"

Cap'n Bob remembered, all right. That had been going on forty years ago, which had been forty years after their hunt began. The only other time they had come so close had been at home, but that was when the light-foot boy sprinkled the fairy dust on the cursed reptile, which had taken flight at once and sailed away to worlds unknown. It had taken the captain five years, but he had finally had his revenge, and in the process obtained some fairy dust of his own. That pixie hussy would never be the same, he thought.

"Them were the days," the mate said, still reminiscing. "What were the names of those men we met down there in New York? I swear, one of 'em could count money in the dark, just by flippin' it past his ear. Horton? Morton?"

"Norton," the captain said. "But he wasn't a hunter, not like us."

Willem drained his glass. "No, that would be the other one. Lenny or something near it."

"Benny," the captain said. He had admired the man, who was the first to explain to the captain about shotguns.

"Swords are no good," Benny had said one morning as they rested just beneath a manhole cover. "You need something with stopping power. A shotgun is just the thing, one that fires slugs. Big ones. Why I've seen albino 'gators down here that would go fifteen feet long."

The captain asked about crocodiles, but Benny professed not to know the difference between a 'gator and a croc.

"Crocs have a notch on the sides of their blinkin' snouts," the captain explained. "It makes them look a little like they're . . . smiling."

"Wouldn't be able to tell about that, down here," Benny said. "I don't examine them that closely."

"The one I'm looking for . . . ticks," the captain said.

"Like a clock?"

"Exactly like a clock."

"Never heard a thing like that. How would a croc get down here, anyway? Flushed down the toilet like the 'gators?"

"Not exactly," the captain said.

The truth was that the croc had learned a lot in its new environment, and one of the first things it had learned was how to hide in a crowd. Some swamp 'gator in Florida had probably told him about the sewers just as the captain was closing in, and the confounded croc had flown there at once, hiding out among them for years before the captain had found out about his new place of concealment. Getting information from 'gators was a notoriously difficult business.

But gotten it the captain had, and only a few days after his conversation with Benny he had found himself face to snout with the very creature he had sought for so long. The captain had smiled and raised the shotgun he had bought that very day, taken careful aim, and then Willem, whose name had been Henry in those days, had dropped the flashlight.

Nowadays that wouldn't matter. Besides the new items that Willem carried in the rucksack, the captain had the best flashlight money could buy dangling right beside his shotgun. It held three alkaline cells and had a brilliant halogen bulb. More importantly, it was waterproof and practically unbreakable and could be snatched up from the rankest sewage still beaming brightly.

But then, back there beneath the New York streets, the bulb had shattered, the batteries had fizzed, and the sewer tunnel had been plunged into darkness that gathered 'round the captain like a thick, damp woolen blanket. The smell of the sewer reeked up from the bottom and outward from the walls, and then the captain heard the sound that had haunted his dreams for more years than he cared to recall:

"Tick . . . tock. Tick . . . tock."

The captain had turned and run. Yes, it was true. He had

been as craven as a sparrow, and it shamed him even now to think of it.

"Damn you, Willem," he said. "Damn you and your memories and your clumsy fingers."

He looked at his own hand, closed the fingers that could crush a man's bones. It was a good hand, the best money could buy, but sometimes he missed the old one. It had been crude, but it had possessed certain advantages.

Willem shrank within his lederhosen. "But them was happy days, Cap'n," he said. "You take that man Norton, now, a barrel of laughs, he was."

"I'm not looking for laughs," the captain said. "I'm looking for a crocodile."

Willem looked around the square, at the deserted tables near them, at the souvenir shops along the streets, at the brot wagon parked near the Tower, his eyes finally stopping on the heavy round drain cover that was fitted into the cobbles not far away.

"And what makes you think he'll be here?" Willem asked. "It seems an odd place for a crocodile, if you don't mind my sayin' so."

The captain smiled a thin smile. "It is an odd place, and that's exactly why he'll be here, Willem."

It had taken the captain years to figure it out, because by now the croc had learned to move around. He didn't have to mix and mingle with others of his amphibious kind. He merely had to keep moving, to places where he thought the captain would never look. A crocodile in the drains of Innsbruck? Ridiculous.

But wait. Look down that street over there. What's the name of that shop? "Crocodile's." And the flag flying out front bears the likeness of a green croc. Where had that idea come from? Had not some local sworn that he'd seen a giant crocodile sliding down a drain late one night at the tail end of an unruly Tyrolean festival?

He had indeed, but the locals had dismissed him as a drunken dreamer. A crocodile could never live in Innsbruck's climate, they told him. Imagine us some pink elephants next time. That would be about as likely.

But the captain had paid attention when the story came to his ears, as all stories eventually did if they concerned crocodiles. Not everyone knew, as he did, that to one croc, the climate mattered less than to the others. Too, deep down in the drains it was warmer than anyone might imagine. The ground was a wonderful insulator. Steam pipes leaked heat, and the sewers had an almost magical warmth of their own. A crocodile could live down there, right enough. And for a certain one, it would even be easy.

"He's there, right enough, Willem," the captain said. "You'll see. You'll see."

The captain had planned to wait a bit longer, but it was growing cold, and he knew that he and Willem would not be allowed to sit inside any restaurant or beer hall in town, no matter how disreputable. It wasn't their appearance, which was perfectly acceptable. But their smell . . . well that was another thing entirely. Besides, Willem had drunk two beers already, and he was becoming maudlin.

"Benny, Benny," Willem said. "I remember him now. He was a nice man, but a little close with his money. He was the one who showed us his vault, way down under his house. Such a nice man, he was."

"That was a different Benny," the captain said. "And Benny was his last name, not his first."

"Croc wasn't there, anyway," the mate said. "Gone again."

That had been a truly irritating episode, the captain thought. They had been about a week too late there.

"He was here, all right," Jack had told him. "But I had to get rid of him. The ticking was keeping my other guard awake."

The other guard was a very old man who wore a uniform of a type the captain had never seen before. In fact, the man was so old that the captain was frankly surprised that anything at all could keep him awake.

After that, the croc had worked for a while in a circus sideshow, where the captain once again arrived a few days too late to catch up with him.

But that was all over now. He was in Innsbruck; the captain was sure of it.

"Time to go, Willem," the captain said, standing up and throwing a handful of schillings on the table.

Willem looked up and saw the pink and white facade of the rococo building nearby. "But it's too early. The sun is still high. Everyone will see us."

The captain didn't care. The wind was cold and he was growing impatient. Besides, they needed the sun.

"Time, Willem," he said.

Willem knew that tone. He stood up and adjusted his Tyrolean hat. "Aye, aye, sir."

He and the captain walked across the cobbles toward the sewer grating. Just before they got there an old gray-haired woman carrying a sack from the Swarvoski Glass Works store leaned down and spat between the bars. Willem wished people wouldn't do that. It was bad enough going down there without having to deal with phlegm.

The captain didn't seem to mind. He reached down with his artificial hand and grasped the bars with his manmade fingers. It was at times like this that he missed his hook, which would have slipped easily and quickly between the bars, but he had lost it in a misunderstanding one evening when he and Willem (who had been calling himself Royce at the time) had lost their way and had stopped to ask directions of a young couple in a parked car. Apparently something (His smell? His moustache? His long hair? He was never sure.) had frightened them, and they had driven away with screams and squealing tires. The captain's hook had somehow gotten hung on the door, and the speeding car had ripped it right out of its socket. He had been forced to seek a replacement, and no one sold hooks any more.

The fingers worked well enough, however, and the captain set the grating aside. Willem looked around, didn't see anyone watching them, and climbed down.

The captain didn't bother to look. He didn't care who saw them. He doubted that anyone would be interested enough to pursue them, and he followed Willem without a second thought. The sewer pipe was small, not big enough to stand erect in, but that was fine. The captain was used to stooping. He reached out and pulled the grating into place.

"Are you ready, Willem?" he asked.

"Aye, Cap'n."

"Right then. Let's go."

"Which way?" the mate asked.

"West," the captain said. "Behind you."

Willem turned around and they began their trudge through the familiar darkness and the familiar foul smells, no longer so foul to them through long association.

The tunnels were not entirely devoid of light, of course. Thanks to the gratings above, there was some small illumination at irregular intervals, and it was the dim glow through those gratings that allowed the crocodile to find its way. It was not really enough for Willem and the captain to see by, however, even though they were accustomed to the dark.

After they had walked about a hundred yards, the captain called a halt. "It's time, Willem," he said.

"For what, Cap'n?"

"The goggles, you idiot. Get them out immediately."

"Right," Willem said. "The goggles. I'd near about forgotten them."

He opened his rucksack and brought them out: brand-new, high-technology, night-vision goggles. The captain had gotten the idea from a movie, The Silence of the Lambs, about a man named Hannibal Lecter, whom the captain thought to be a thoroughly amiable and engaging fellow, though none of the other characters in the story seemed to feel that way. The captain enjoyed movies, but he was sure that he would never understand them.

The goggles, however, had proved to be a sterling idea. The captain slipped his over his head, and the tunnel was suffused in a wavery greenish light. The captain could see Willem standing in front of him. He could see the walls at either side and the sludge under his feet. The goggles were infinitely better than the flashlight. And the goggles would not give away his position.

"The crocodile is doomed, Willem," the captain said. "This time, I know that the day will be ours."

Willem nodded enthusiastically. "Aye, Cap'n. It's like a miracle, it is."

"But these things will work only as long as there is at least some light from the gratings. We must find our quarry before nightfall. Otherwise we must rely on the flashlight."

"Aye, Cap'n," Willem said, remembering the embarrassing incident with the flashlight in New York. He began to walk as fast as his short legs, his bent-over posture, and the muck underfoot would allow.

The captain followed behind, his ears pricked for the sound of ticking, the weight of the shotgun comforting him. It had been many years, but he felt that he was at last nearing the end of his quest. For the first time he felt more like the pursuer than the pursued.

Even as he had that thought, his artificial hand began to throb. Or so it seemed, for the captain knew that there was no feeling there save the ghost of what once had been. The crocodile had found him tasty, but the captain knew that revenge would be tastier still, and revenge would soon be his.

It would not be nearly so sweet as it might have been had the light-foot flyer been there to see it, but peanut-butter-boy had been left far behind in a land that the captain hoped to see again one day.

And let him beware me then, the captain thought. Let him beware me then.

The tunnel they were in soon branched off into several, one of them larger in circumference than the others. Willem confidently walked into it, at last able to stand erect.

"This is the right 'un, ain't she, Cap'n?" he asked.

"Indeed," the captain said. He could see even in the odd greenish light that this tunnel was older than the others, and after only a few steps it was easy to tell that it sloped upward. There were dogs missing in the neighborhood of Castle Ambras, so he'd been told. And strange noises from below the earth. Those were signs that he could interpret without difficulty. Somewhere ahead, his ancient enemy was waiting.

"Stop, Willem," he said.

"What's the matter, Cap'n?"

"Nothing. Time to make ready."

From under his trenchcoat the captain brought the shotgun, a Mossberg Bullpup with double pistol grips. It held nine shots and was nearly a foot shorter than conventional pump models. The captain pumped a round into the chamber and took off both the manual safeties.

"All right, Willem," he said. "Lead on."

"Aye, Cap'n."

They slogged onward, the way growing steeper and steeper. The captain hoped that no great volume of water would descend on them. If it did, it would come so fast that they would not be able to resist being swept away. The grates were farther and farther apart, too, and the goggles did not work nearly so well.

"How much farther, Cap'n?" Willem asked.

"How would I know, you fool? Just keep walking."

Willem did, and they entered an area of the tunnel where primordial stinks abounded. The walls on either side were crumbly beneath a fat coating of algae, and the accumulated ooze beneath their feet seemed centuries deep. It grew so dark that the goggles ceased to function altogether. The captain called another halt while he and Willem considered the situation.

"If I turn on the light, it might be too bright," the captain said. "What do you think, Willem?"

Willem was not flattered at being asked for his opinion. He knew that the captain was asking only to have someone to blame if things went wrong.

"We could cover the lens, Cap'n," he said finally.

"With what?"

"I brought along some duct tape. It's good for nearly every emergency."

The captain handed Willem the flashlight. "Try it, then."

Willem got the tape from his rucksack and put a couple of strips over the flashlight lens, leaving the merest strip for the light to pass through. When he clicked the flashlight's button, there was only a dim glow, hardly visible but enough for the goggles to function.

"Excellent," the captain said. "Lead on."

They slopped upward until they came to a wide expanse where five tunnels branched off in different directions. Willem stopped, having no idea which one to choose.

The captain hesitated as well. He was about to make a decision when Willem whispered, "Listen, Cap'n."

They both stood still, their feet sinking into the muck, as they strained their ears. Then the captain heard the sound that had caught Willem's attention. It came faintly and from far away but with a slight echo from the tunnel walls.

"Tick . . . tock."

Adrenaline shot through the captain's veins so fast that his hair stood on end.

"There, Willem. That tunnel there."

Willem led the way, the captain right behind with the Bullpup at the ready. They tried to walk quietly, but it was not entirely possible because their feet made little sucking sounds each time they raised them from the mire.

With each step they took, the ticking became louder until it was a certainty the crocodile that they had hunted for what seemed like forever was waiting around the very next bend of the tunnel.

The captain thought about the clock and how he had thrown it to the ravening croc so many years ago and about how its sound had both saved his life and haunted his dreams until this very moment.

"Step aside, Willem," he said.

Willem hopped out of the way gladly, and the captain strode past him, raising the shotgun as he did so. A feral joy seized him and he shouted "Hah!" as he turned the corner, pulling the trigger of the shotgun and blasting into a thousand fragments the alarm clock that had been sitting on the muddy sewer bottom, ticking the seconds happily away. Hands and springs and numbers and bells flew in every direction.

"You got 'im, Cap'n, you got 'im!" Willem cried, slipping and sliding around the turn.

"No, I didn't, you cretin! He's not here! It was a trick!"

Willem skidded to a halt. "A trick? But I heard the noise, and you blasted him to kingdom come."

"I blasted a clock. That's what I blasted. The tricky devil set a trap with a clock as the bait."

"But if the clock was the bait, where's the—"

"—crocodile!" the captain screamed, turning around as fast as he could, but not quite fast enough to get off a shot at the saurian shape that slithered through the muck toward him, its mouth gaping wide in the very image of toothy destruction.

The captain leapt backward, and the crocodile's mouth snapped shut with a violent click only inches from the captain's booted feet. The captain squealed and tried to run, but he could get no traction on the slimy tunnel floor. His feet slipped from beneath him, and he fell on his back, his boots flailing in the air. The shotgun flew from his hands, banging off the wall and then sliding under the mud.

The crocodile chomped down on the captain's right foot, nipping the sole right off his boot. As the creature chewed noisily, the captain sought for purchase and managed to slip backward for nearly a yard before the crocodile realized that he was chewing rubber instead of the tasty captain-flesh he had been expecting. He spit out the bootsole and opened his mouth again, exposing his formidable gnashers.

With a quick forward step, he scooped up the captain's right foot, ankle, and calf with his lower jaw. Then he brought his mighty jaws together.

But not quite all the way. Willem, moving as fast as he ever had, stuck the flashlight between them. Before the crocodile realized what was happening, Willem whipped out the duct tape and wrapped several strips around his jaws.

The crocodile went into a frenzied dance, flopping on its side and its back, even standing on its tail, as it tried to dislodge the flashlight, but its short forelegs would not reach it and the duct tape held the jaws as if in a vise. Antediluvian scum flew everywhere, and the stink was unimaginable.

"Quick, Cap'n," Willem said, grabbing the captain's foot and pulling him along quite easily. "Let's get out of here."

The captain didn't object. As soon as they reached the junction of the tunnels, he stood up, and both of them began to run, oblivious to the thrashing that still went on behind them.

Later, as they limped past the Triumphal Arch at the southern end of Maria-Theresien-Strasse, the stench that surrounded them was almost palpable. Tourists crossed the street to avoid them.

"We should have known, Cap'n," Willem said, flicking something dark and damp from his lederhosen. "We should have known that a clock wouldn't keep ticking away all those many years."

"Shut up," the captain said.

"He'd bought himself a new one, of course," Willem said. "Or more than one. All this time, he's been leading us on, just waiting for his chance."

"Shut up," the captain said.

"He near about had you, too. Why if his mouth had closed, he'd have cropped off your foot right there. A little ragged, it would have been, considering those teeth of his, but he'd have got it, right enough."

"Shut up," the captain said.

"Lost our flashlight and our shotgun, too, and I don't know where we'll be getting another one. They're not as easy to get here as in America, I'll warrant."

"Shut up," the captain said.

"It's a bleedin' shame, is what it is. We had him in our sights, so to speak, and then it wasn't him at all."

"Willem," the captain said. "I'm going to tell you once more. I won't be responsible for what might happen after that: Shut up."

Willem nodded vigorously. "I'll shut up, Cap'n, I surely will. But tell me just one thing. What are we going to do now?"

The captain sighed. "Venice," he said.

"Venice?" Willem had heard a lot about the place. "That's to the south, isn't it? But why, Cap'n?"

"Canals, Willem, canals."

Willem had a sudden vision of the crocodile lolling in a Venetian canal, taking his ease and eating some of the better garbage as it came floating by. Listening to the gondoliers as they sang "Santa Lucia." Frightening the tourists on the vaparettos.

Suddenly Willem brightened. "Will we be in a boat again, then, Cap'n?"

It was drawing on to evening now, and the captain looked up at the sky. The first stars were beginning to appear, and there was a certain one that seemed almost to beckon him—second to the right, it was.

"Cap'n?" Willem said. "What about the boat?"

"Shut up," the captain said.

Lover's Leap

Mark A. Garland and Lawrence Schimel

Two other cars were there that night, parked close together, no lights or sound, though the moon, full and bright in the crisp, clear late autumn air, showed ample steam on the insides of the windows.

Miranda watched as Nick's blue Monte Carlo pulled up slow and the lights went out. He parked a car's length from the edge of the cliff—Lover's Leap, as it was known among the kids. Of course, no one knew of anyone who'd actually leapt from there, for love or any other reason, but it was the kind of name a place like this was supposed to have.

"My usual spot," Nick said, as he pulled into the semi-secluded nook nearer the woods, away from the other cars, and winked at the girl beside him. A fairly average girl, nice hair and clothes, a plain but cheerful smile. Miranda had seen the girl around. Her name was Ellen Gray, an inoffensive and indecisive name. That was the type Nick went for, and knew he could have. He was always so sure of himself and the world around him, that it would do exactly what he wanted it to.

Miranda knew how that made a girl feel—knew exactly how the girl with Nick was feeling right this moment. Attracted and terrified both. *Am I ready for this?* Ellen was probably asking herself, bemused by a jumble of feelings that kept her in her seat, since that was the easier thing to do than to make the decision that this was not really what she wanted, was something she only felt she ought to want. Miranda had always felt jealous of the girls who got all the attention from boys, that was what you were supposed to want at seventeen, and she wanted it desperately.

This girl, Ellen, could hardly believe that someone as popular as Nick was interested in her, which was why she'd agreed to come with him, even knowing what it would probably mean.

Nick turned toward her in the darkened car. She looked out the window, delaying the inevitable.

I know, Miranda thought, seeing it all in Ellen's eyes. *That's how I felt, sitting there, looking out at the cliff, like that moment when the earth just suddenly gives way and you're suspended for a moment, with no solid ground beneath you, and your stomach falls first.*

Ellen took a deep breath, turned toward Nick, and smiled shyly.

Miranda watched them go through the slow motions of the ritual, Nick making his corny jokes, Ellen giggling at them, both of them ceasing to speak and steam fogging the windows. She bided her time, for time was her one luxury these days.

At last, she heard movement, and the car started to crank. It cranked for at least a minute straight. She could hear Nick pumping the gas pedal as he tried the key again and again, then she heard him curse. For a moment, as they both opened their doors, she felt nervous for Ellen's sake.

She watched them as they stepped out of the Monte Carlo, Nick with his tall good looks, and Ellen, with that simplicity that took most people so much effort to achieve, attractive because of her lack of artifice. Ellen stood humming to herself, while Nick got the hood open and stuck his head under it.

Miranda moved closer, and pitched a whisper at Ellen, who heard and looked over her shoulder toward the trees. She motioned Ellen closer. Ellen glanced back at Nick, who was talking to himself, swearing mostly; she shrugged and started toward the trees.

"Hi," Ellen said. Her voice was soft and quiet, not fearful, but not willing to make itself known, either.

"I have to tell you something, your life is in danger."

Ellen's eyes went wide. "What do you mean?"

She'd frightened Ellen, she could tell; she watched Ellen pull away slightly. "Remember that girl, a couple years back, at the state overlook up the road?"

"Yeah," Ellen said, eyeing Miranda carefully. "Everyone knows about that. She fell off the cliff, or maybe jumped, and she died. They closed the overlook after that, so people started parking here."

"She didn't jump. She was pushed."

Ellen said nothing at first. She stood there, wheels spinning behind her big soft eyes. *Had this woman*, Ellen was surely wondering, *pushed her?*

"How do you know?" Ellen asked at last, her body tensed to flee, if necessary, yet frozen in place all the same.

"Because it was me. I'm that girl. I'm her ghost."

Ellen stared at her. She let out a long breath. "Yeah right," she said at last. "You're no more ghost than I am."

She pointed at Nick's car. "I did that, you know. He won't get it started until I let him."

Ellen glanced over her shoulder; Nick was still under the hood, cussing profusely, but otherwise oblivious.

"Don't you want to know who pushed me off that cliff?"

Ellen stared back at her, then slowly nodded, clearly not sure she believed the story but unable not to hear the rest of it.

"It was Nick. Which is why I had to warn you. We'd been together for a couple of months, then he started seeing another girl, secretly. We came out to the overlook one night to go parking, but then I asked him what was going on with the other girl. We had an argument about it. He's got a bad temper, Ellen."

Ellen flinched as the girl spoke her name. "How do you know me?"

"What matters is what happened next. I got out and went to the edge, to cool off. He followed me and we argued some more. He said some things, mean things, especially after I said I'd tell the other girl. He said he'd beat me if I did. I slapped him on the mouth, and he just pushed me. Right over the cliff."

Ellen stared at Miranda, still skeptical but leaning closer now. "So," she said slowly, almost whispering even though Nick was too far away and too preoccupied to hear then, "I'm dating a murderer?"

"You get him mad at you, and he'll kill you, too. The next time he calls you, hang up. When he comes over, leave out the back if you have to. Find somebody else, Ellen."

Emotions flickered across Ellen's face—she began to look almost ill. "How come they never arrested him?"

"Because no one else knows. He claims he was driving around looking for me that night, that he never found me. He cried a lot, and everybody believed him. He got away with it, Ellen, don't you see? That's one reason why he might do it again. That's why I had to warn you. He's poison. He's a murderer. He murdered me."

Miranda raised one hand and pointed at the Monte Carlo, and the engine sprang to life. Nick jerked his head out from underneath the hood, a startled look on his face.

"Ellen, what are you doing over there?" he called, once he'd spotted her. Ellen looked back at Miranda, but she saw no one there anymore. Only trees and darkness. After a moment she walked back into the full moonlight, back to Nick, and stood staring at him.

"What?" he demanded. "What are you staring at? I got it fixed."

"Nothing," Ellen said immediately, placating. "I—I don't want to start an argument."

Nick stared back for a moment longer, then shook his head, wiped his hands on his jeans, and got back in the car. Ellen got in too, and stared out over the cliff, to that space where the earth dropped away.

"You remember that girl," Ellen asked, "I forget her name, but she jumped to her death at the state overlook a couple of years ago?"

"No," Nick said, not looking at her. "I don't. Why?"

"No reason, I guess. I just think of her sometimes, when I'm out by a cliff."

"People do lots of crazy things," Nick said, keeping his head straight while nervous eyes glanced over at Ellen.

"Yes," she said. "I guess maybe they do."

The next day Ellen asked her mother to answer the phone for her, and to say she wasn't home. Her mother asked what had happened on her date last night. Ellen was unused to dating, she knew, and she'd hoped it'd work out with this boy. She trusted Ellen, she'd said so, trusted her daughter would tell her if anything bad happened.

"I'm okay," Ellen told her. "I'm just trying to go slow."

The day after that, Sunday, Ellen was alone in the house, so she didn't answer the phone at all.

"I think maybe I'd like to go visit Daddy," she told her mother, over dinner that Sunday night. He lived half way across the state, in Eastenville.

"For how long?" her mother asked.

"A few days, a week at most."

"You'll miss school."

"I know, but I'm doing great in school, and I just need to see him for a while. I need to get away, think things over. We could both go."

Ellen's mother looked thoughtfully at her daughter, waiting for her to tell her what was troubling her. "I can't miss that much work right now," she said at last.

Ellen just nodded. She waited for an answer.

"All right," her mother said. "We'll compromise. You can go till Wednesday. I'll even drive you."

Ellen told her that would be just fine. The phone started ringing, and Ellen jumped. "If it's for me, remember I'm not home," she said. Her mother, clearly wanting nothing more than to let the phone ring on and on and ask her daughter what was wrong, said she would.

On Monday afternoon, after school but before Ellen's mother had gotten home from work, Nick's blue Monte Carlo pulled up in front of the Grays' house. The house looked quiet and empty, but he went to the door and knocked anyway. All he knew was that Ellen wasn't answering his calls and he was determined to find out what was up.

When no one answered, he called out Ellen's name, then began to pound his fists into the door.

A moment later, he saw Ellen Gray open the door. "My Mom's not home," Ellen said, apologetically, "and I was upstairs."

"I've been trying to reach you all weekend," Nick said, moving forward. She stood her ground. "Where the hell have you been?"

"I got a little confused, and worried, about something someone said to me. I was making lots of crazy plans. But I guess you could say I'm over that now. Or I will be."

Nick squinted at her. "What are you talking about?"

"Nothing. I'll be okay. The night is ours, Nick. Let's go for a drive." She stepped outside, leaning into him, and pulled the door shut behind her. Nick grinned, ear to ear, and they headed for the car.

They went mall walking, then sat in the mall parking lot listening to the new CDs Nick had bought.

"Why don't we go parking up at Lover's Leap?" Ellen said. "Much more comfortable place to listen to this music."

"We can do that," Nick said, smiling a little too much.

"Good," she said, making eyes. "I think I'd like that."

"Me too," Nick said, chuckling. He pulled into a gas station, filled the tank and paid, and they headed for the hills.

By the time they arrived at Lover's Leap the sun had already set, and the full October moon had taken its place once more. There was one other car, a boy and a girl in the front seat, no steam in the windows. They were just talking, from the looks of things. Nick nosed the car into his favorite spot, then shut it off and turned to Ellen. She looked at him, eyes wet with concern.

"What's the matter?" he asked, as she sat beside him, sobbing quietly. "What's wrong with you now? I thought you wanted to do this." His tone was almost accusing.

She said, "I can't talk about it. Especially not with you. I'm just a little confused, Nick, about everything, and I get so lonely sometimes. Very, very lonely. I don't expect you to understand, really I don't."

"Oh, that's good," Nick said, with a sigh of obvious relief. "Long as it isn't me. But you sure are kind of spoiling the mood."

She started sobbing again. She opened the door and got out and went to the edge of the cliff, where she stood absolutely still, just staring out into the night.

Nick got out and came after her. "What are you doing?" he asked, trying to see her face. She kept it from him.

"I'm thinking . . . I'm thinking of maybe jumping, of ending it all, just like that other girl did a couple of years ago. You know."

"Maybe she didn't jump. Maybe it was . . . some kind of an accident," Nick said.

"Oh?" she asked. "What makes you say that?"

"I don't know. Look, don't talk crazy! Come on back to the car, will you? Enough is enough."

"No," she whispered. "I won't."

Nick set his jaw. "Yes, you will. Come on."

"You can't make me," she told him.

"Yes, I can!" Nick replied.

He reached. She stepped away from him, closer to the edge.

He reached again, but again he missed. The third time he lunged and tried to grab hold of her with both hands, but his hands passed through her. He kept falling, his momentum carrying him forward. There was nothing to grab hold of, nothing to stop him. Then nothing to put his feet on. He went over the edge, screaming as he fell several hundred feet to the rocks below.

"Did you see that?" the young boy said, his hand clutching the hand of his girl as they got out of the other car. They ran over to the spot just in front of the Monte Carlo where Nick had stood only seconds ago.

"He just jumped off!" the girl with him said in a shaky voice. "A nose dive!" the boy said, his chest heaving as he stared into the dark ravine below.

They saw no one else.

"But why?" the boy was saying, to the girl, to the night.

"Why?" the girl repeated, mumbling. No answer came.

They couldn't see the ghostly figure behind them, couldn't see the face and figure of Ellen Gray dissolving away, revealing those of a girl who had died in a ravine not far from here, two years ago. She followed the young couple's gaze, out to where the earth just suddenly gave way, no solid ground beneath you. She tried to remember feeling jealous, or scared, but already it seemed too hard. She at last let go of her anger and, as it drifted away, let herself drift apart as well.

The real Ellen Gray went to the funeral, and cried. Her mother wanted answers to certain questions, but Ellen wasn't sure she had any, and she didn't think she ever would. She made a decision that day never to go up to Lover's Leap again, which was probably just as well, since it was rumored that sometimes, on summer nights when the moon was full, a young man's angry voice would shout her name.

Tales from the White Castle

John J. Ordover

The White Castle restaurant on 21st Street in Astoria, New York had an ambiance much like all the others of its kind. The smell of grease hung around it like a London fog, the white "turrets" on the outside got grayer by the day, and the tables in the dining room were laid out carelessly, as if both the management and customers both knew most of the business was drive through or take-out, but that having tables was a corporate tradition that had to be followed.

That the dining room was deserted most of the time worked out great for me and about ten of my friends. It gave us a place to hang out after work, eat grease rockets by the dozen, and solve the problems of the world. We would get there about five-thirty and wait for Barry Dervis to make his entrance, which he usually did about an hour after the rest of us got there.

Barry was a loud, flamboyant man who dressed in dark colors that were the opposite of his Hawaiian-shirt personality. He was always ready with a joke, a dirty limerick, or some behind-the-headlines story he'd picked up working for what he called an "information processing service."

Barry was right on time this warm June evening. He stormed in, shouted his order at the counter boy, whipped off his jacket and threw it over a chair. He sat himself down with the air of a guest on a late-night talk show and asked us what we were all talking about.

That night, it was real estate. We'd been working our way

through the recent New York real estate crisis that was at last coming to an end. At its worst, properties had lost almost two-thirds of their value. We'd talked about the Japanese pulling out and other things being the reason, but Barry waved our opinions away. Told us he had the inside dope, that it was the end of the cold war that had done it.

Barry paused to wait for us to cough up the usual request for more details, we obliged quickly, and he began.

"It's supply and demand, boys," he said, "simple economics. The more supply, the lower the price. What with the cold war over, the government didn't need all those buildings on the East Side any more, you know, the ones that held the anti-ballistic missiles. When they dumped them on the market all at once, the property values crashed."

I'd heard this bandied about, but I didn't give it any weight. I mean, the entire notion that some skyscrapers on the East Side were really missile silos loaded with high-tech weapons that could down Soviet ICBMs seemed a little farfetched to me. But Barry kept talking, and I just went with the flow.

"You see," he said, "with all those buildings back on the market, the market crashed. *Ipso facto.* I suppose that was hard on the yuppie types who'd just bought condos, but of all the people I knew inconvenienced by it, it was hardest on Tex Smith.

"With a name like that, you'd have thought he'd be from oil country, and in a way he was: He was born in the Texaco station right over on Queens Boulevard. He was a mild, calm, unassuming and entirely reliable man, and he could have taught Felix Unger a thing or two about being fastidious.

"He was in his forties when the cold war ended, and he didn't have much in his life. No wife, no kids, no social life, just a small house in the suburbs he'd inherited from his mother, a small sculptor's workshop, and his Secret.

"It was his Secret that really kept him going. Tex Smith worked for the agency of the U.S. Government—not the one I work for—that oversaw the maintenance of the skyscraper missile silos. His secret was simple: He knew which buildings were fake, and where each and every last missile was.

"On his days off, Smith would go out to a local bar, sip ice tea, and wait for discussion of the missile-silo skyscrapers to come up. He'd never say anything, or join the conversation, because that would have violated his duty to his job. As the bar patrons talked and laughed and argued, Smith would sit and smile to himself. He knew the truth, that there really were missiles, and he knew where each one of them was.

"If you think that was a bit off, keep in mind that we all need things in our lives that make us feel special, and Smith's at least had the advantage of being real. He knew something that only a few others did, and it made up for a lot of things that weren't in his life.

"Then the Berlin wall came down, the Soviet Union collapsed, and word came down from Central Command—no, not the Pentagon, the people really in charge of the army. The missiles were going to be removed and dismantled.

"Now, Tex Smith wasn't the only one upset by this notion, but his reason was a little different. He realized at once that his secret was now yesterday's news, and that knowing the secret of where the missiles *used to be* was not going to get him through many cold winter nights. He had to find a new secret and he set right out to do just that.

"When the teams sent to dismantle the missiles found that the the weapon stored at east forty—uh, in the east forties— was missing its pounds of plutonium, Smith's name was the last on a list of two-hundred possible suspects. His record, his reliability, and his personality profile put him almost above suspicion. It was only when we—the agency I work for—were called in to do a 'positional analysis' that Smith became the focus of the investigation.

"What? Oh, a positional analysis is simple and straightforward. You make of list of everyone who could have accomplished your crime, then verify exactly where they were at the time of the crime. It's tedious and mindless but it solves more cases than intellect and inspiration. Where was I? Right, Smith was now the center of the investigation.

"We proceeded to his house in the suburbs and found him in the parlor, watching television. He'd expected us, and quite readily admitted that he was the one who had taken the plutonium.

"Understandably anxious to recover the highly dangerous radioactive material, a gram of which could kill a dozen people, we questioned him as to its location, and we weren't very detached and polite about it. He led us to his sculpting room.

The Geiger counters started blasting the moment we stepped through the door.

"On the wall was a full-body radiation suit, something Smith would not have needed as part of his job but certainly easy enough to acquire at his agency. Quite pleased with himself, Smith stood in the doorway and explained what he had done.

"Using his metal-sculpting equipment, he had shaped the plutonium into — what, exactly, he wouldn't say. Then he'd painted it a city-gray color and taken it into Manhattan and put it somewhere. Where, he also wouldn't say.

"And he continued not saying. He had discovered that having a secret that only he knew was far more powerful, and more heady, than having a secret that was shared with others. This was felt so deep in his psyche that no amount of questioning, at whatever level of rigor, whether or not it involved medication, proved fruitless.

"Unable to force Smith to reveal the location of the hidden plutonium, my employers started a vigorous detection campaign that continues to this day. Naturally, we don't wish to cause a panic, so our operatives wear suits, carry briefcases that are sophisticated radiation detectors, and wear "walkmen" that analyze and report the radiation concentration in the immediate area. I'm sure you've seen our agents on the streets many times, dressed in their Brooks Brothers and Donna Karan, revealing no sign of what they are really doing.

"While we've had no luck finding the plutonium that Smith stole, we have discovered many other interesting things: an underground city, an alien graveyard, and the source of the giant animals occasionally reported around the city — which turned out to be a vital economic necessity, so we left it alone.

"Smith? Oh, he's still in custody, won't say a word about the plutonium, even though he knows he could be a free man if he did. Won't even give us a hint. It has to be somewhere, of course, but it could be anything, anything gray, at least. But in this city, what isn't?"

At that point the counterboy finally appeared with the dozen sliders Barry had ordered, and he settled in to eat as the others of us looked around nervously. Barry's stories rarely left you with a comforting sense of closure, but something else was bothering me.

"Hey," I said to Barry, "the real estate market is picking up fast."

"Yes," he agreed, "government's buying back the buildings. They need them again. Not cold war stuff, though. Something more important."

"More important than nuclear war?" I asked.

"Yes."

"What is it?" we all asked.

"Sorry," Barry said, with a slightly superior smile. "That's a secret."

A Ghost of Night and Shadows

eluki bes shahar

Let us sing of arts and the woman.

Once upon a time, as the saying goes, she would have been an artist—a writer—known as something or other safe and indicative as Mrs. Goodwrite (not her real name) and been plump, respectable, grey, chaste, and a writer of improving fantasies for children.

But this was not once upon a time, and Mary Frances Godwin was neither fat nor grey—she was (reasonably) chaste but almost accidentally—Society did not compel her. She had no interest in children, or in improving them, and little interest in the tainted pool of Victorian fantastic literature. But Mary Frances was desperately lonely, and the only form of companionship the world held had no power to ease her. The trouble was, Mary Frances believed in magic.

It would have been better if she had not.

Mary Frances lived in a small apartment that dated from the time between the wars when the real world had awaited its final breaking. It was in an old city and the streets showed that it used to be a set of villages set cattywampus each to each. The streets and avenues, grown finally to connect, made sharp, right angle turns, or swept broadly around the boundaries of a village green that wasn't there any more. The apartment, as was right, was set on one of the streets most fraught with possibilities; one of the twistiest. It had been acquired—and kept, at ruinous expense—for a certain slant of light

215

through the bedroom windows in autumn and its cruel ability to over and over inspire the faint delusive hope that perhaps today, maybe. . . .

No. Never. The Eidolon Gate—never open, never extant—was closed forever. And still Mary Frances Godwin yearned for faery magic and faery lore, not knowing that in this iron age new myths were alive in the world.

It was early enough in the year for it to be raining, and late enough that the rain was cold. Some years ago on this date Mary Frances had spent the most mortifying night of her life wandering all about Glastonbury, goaded beyond rationality by heartsick hunger and the unreasoning hope that maybe, just maybe. . . .

But tonight she was not thinking about that. She was too irritated and uncomfortable. She'd had the late shift at the library and then she'd gone with Carolee for coffee—Mary Frances didn't consider Carolee a friend, but the years had taught her that never socializing at all was a species of Turning Your Back On The World, which Mary Frances knew already was not a desirable thing to do. So she'd gone for coffee, which was boring and frustrating both, and now it was nearly eleven, and raining, and no cabs to be found. They'd gone to a new place for coffee and she was slightly lost. All she wanted now was to go home.

In the distance, the lamps of a subway station glowed, floating green spheres of elflight. Mary Francis fumbled in her raincoat pocket and felt the slippery costly tokens move against her fingers; faery gold that turned to autumn leaves each time the MTA raised the fare. She didn't know what line the station served, and at the moment she didn't care. She could get out of the weather and down to 42nd or at least 34th no matter what line it was. She could get home from there.

Mincing carefully across the deserted street against the light—as if making herself small would keep her from getting any wetter than she was—Mary Frances reached the entrance and descended the steps. The glass and metal canopy over the entrance stopped the rain at once—allowing her to feel how damp and clammy her clothes were against her skin.

Past the token booth—through the wide wooden turnstile covered in peeling yellow paint—onto the platform. One end of the platform was lit by greenish fluorescents that made the brownish brick look diseased; the other by incandescent bulbs in milky, bell-shaped housings suspended from the ends of slender pipes running all the way up to the vaulted ceiling. In the middle of renovation, probably, and she was lucky the station was open at all. She didn't see any signs telling the line or the station anywhere on the platform or the green-painted pillars. For a moment she felt a surge of triumph at locating the symbolic wall mosaic common on the city lines but it was too cryptic to be of any help—a boatman poling a skiff across what must be the Hudson, no answers there.

She almost went back through the turnstile again to get information at the kiosk, but the fare was up to a dollar-fifty these days and the thought of wasting a token on a stupid question was unbearable. She'd take what came and make the best of it, although with forty years experience Mary Frances already knew that she wouldn't like it, nor would it be nice.

You went on. You waited until it was time to die. And if you wondered why, you knew better than to expect answers for your questions. That was how it was, and there was no other way it could be.

Though the station was cold—and Mary Frances was all alone in it, one small gift from the gods of urban life—she was actually starting to warm up a bit when the train she awaited finally pulled into the station and stopped with a long hydraulic sigh. For a moment she didn't recognize it for what it was; instead of the graffiti-resistant brushed aluminum cars with their uncomfortable orange plastic seats that she was used to, this train was made of *wood*. It had five cars, painted barn red, with a cream-colored curved roof like an old-time trolley car. There were open platforms on the front and back, with cream-painted poles and rails, and the row of wood-frame windows slid down from the top. Most of them were open, and as she looked inside, she could see that the rows of empty seats were iron-framed, covered in wicker, and along both sides of the roof long leather loops hung, like curves of sausage in a butcher's shop.

Straphangers. That's what they used to call commuters. Because of the straps inside the cars. Straphangers.

She felt a small uneasy thrill of discovery. Mary Frances was familiar with the past. The question was, did the past show through into the present, like rubbed-out lines of type on reused paper? The past was still here—museums and Victorian houses proved that much—but what about when you rubbed a bit of the present, intending only to touch it up a bit, and you found instead that you'd rubbed right through, and here was the past staring up at you? Was that magic?

And if it was, what then?

She stared at the subway cars, making very sure of what she saw, searching with the fear of being cheated for another explanation. But while she might be socially maladjusted and a stranger in her own time, even Mary Frances Godwin knew that the MTA didn't run trains like these any more, no matter the lateness of the hour and the isolation of the line. Antiques, refugees from the Transit Museum, familiar only through vintage photos glimpsed unwillingly in passing; a train from before the end of the world.

She took a step forward, tentatively touching the wooden side of the nearest car. It quivered faintly with the vibration of its engine, real beneath her fingers, suddenly not frightening; just the past, showing through where you tried to polish up the present, because the present wasn't made of the sort of material that could either take or hold a polish. They'd had ages of Gold, Iron, Silver, Bronze, Jet, and Atoms. This was what came after, and it didn't shine.

Mary Frances did wonder, idly and temporarily, why she should be the place that got rubbed so the past shone through. She was just an ordinary person with an ordinary life, filled with minor humiliations and faint terrors. Unhappy, but in all fairness, she did not know that every other person in the city wasn't equally unhappy. Alone, but she was used to that. She'd had no choice.

But here was a choice.

The thought came drifting in, subtle and as familiar as her privation. Here was a choice. She could change her life.

Here. Now.

Magic is afoot in the world.

Suddenly, sharply, she was afraid—of new disappointments, of fresh sorrow. In all the long years of her imprecise exile, it was always to have been enough that the magic was real— if it could be, could have ever been, real—the Eidolon Gate possible. But now here was magic: unreal, impossible, uncanny,

and by its blatancy it seemed to call for some heroic action
in return.

But she had nothing.

The subway train was here, arrogant in its dailyness. In a
moment, ghostly revenant or no, it would leave the station,
obedient to the dictates of railway nature. And behind the fact
of its appearance, as matter-of-fact as what-you-will, lay the
Summer Country whose being had in song and legend once
marched interlocked with that of Mary Frances' world. The
Summer Country whose magic had long since passed from the
world. The Summer Country that Mary Frances and her
ancestors and acolytes evoked, heart-hungry and aching.

Here. One subway, indifferent real. And with its immanence,
choices. Because to touch magic was happiness, she had always
believed that with all her withered heart, and now happiness
could be achieved. . . .

At a price.

This was no antique legend, its details softened by a hundred centuries of bleeding hearts. This was a ghost from a
new and desperate age, sent through Eidolon Gates transmuted
to cold iron, lath, and barbed wire. Board this train, and she
would . . . what?

There was a small card in the window of one of the cars.
She'd missed it before, because of the way the light from the
long hanging bulbs reflected off the windows. But she'd moved
down the train, toward the engine, and she was at the right
angle to read it now. The faded careful print said "Malbone,"
and then, out of the unasked-for memory of transit museums,
she knew.

She knew what it would cost her to ride this train.

With as much reluctance as if she hated it, though she was
far from hating it, Mary Frances turned and walked toward the
last car of the train. She had lived all her life with duty and
responsibility, with the performance of tasks that would only
bring her pain. They had honed her will, to the point that sheer
thought could override the animal treason of the body.

And she could choose.

She walked back to the last car, and slid back the wooden
gate, and stepped onto the platform, hooking the gate closed
again behind her. Then she stood there, leaning on the painted
iron railing, looking back down the tunnel, and as she did,

the train began to move, shuddering and sighing as it picked up speed. As Mary Frances watched, the lights of the station platform dwindled into the night.

Forever.

On all Saints Day, 1918, a war was just about to end in Europe at a cost of thirteen million dead, and a worldwide influenza epidemic that would in its brief season kill over twice that number was raging across the globe. In New York and its five boroughs, the subway system that would someday grow to include more than a thousand miles of track was less than fifty years old, its growth torn by factionalism and internecine disputes. And sometime late on the evening of November 1st, 1918, a 23-year-old dispatcher named Edward Lewis took a five-car train into Malbone Station.

Because the line was on strike and many were sick with the influenza, Lewis had been given two hours instruction on running a subway train and a hasty promotion to motorman—management had sworn to break the strike at any cost. He'd been on duty for fourteen hours without rest when he took the Brighton Beach local into the tunnel leading into the Malbone Street Station at 65 miles per hour.

Over a hundred people died there in the darkness, many of them electrocuted by the company's repeated attempts to restore power to the third rail. It was a disaster of such enormity that even the name of the place where it happened was blotted out. Today, you will not find Malbone Street on any map of Brooklyn.

But the Malbone Local still runs.

It's a five car train. The cars are forty feet long, short by modern standards, the old open-platform carriages of the Brighton Beach local-express. Wooden cars, painted red—they have a quaint, nineteenth-century look to them, as is only reasonable in rolling stock sent up from Virginia before the turn of the century. The last cars of that type were scrapped before World War II; none of the stock on the line now dates from much before 1960.

Once or twice a year, someone at the public relations department at the MTA gets a call from some member of the public wondering about "that funny train" they've seen. Smart PR people bury those calls deep.

No one at the MTA talks about seeing the Malbone Local, even to each other. It's been seen in all five boroughs, and runs on every line; it was in Times Square in 1928 and on Roosevelt Avenue in 1970. It doesn't run except for what they like to call, these days, "human error." Like Edward Lewis's, whose luck caught up with him fourteen hours after he'd been given the choice: work or starve.

Forty minutes after Mary Frances left the station, a Queensbound RR running on the express tracks plowed into the back end of the local standing in the station. Transit authorities were unable to say how the express had been switched over to the local track.

A preliminary investigation returned the verdict of human error. Other ages, other myths.

And the Malbone Local still runs.

The Ugliest Duckling

S.P. Somtow

But you know, he wasn't ugly exactly; in some ways he was the most beautiful of all those changelings of the twilight who blend in with the shadows of dumpsters, who flit from alley to alley, who lurk in the doorway of an all-night grocery store till, with a reticent half-smile, they find their mark and move in for the kill.

I know them well; I have been a connoisseur since I first started coming to the all-night coffee shop, thirty or forty years ago; it was still there then, though not yet owned by Greeks. I moonlighted—the way it is with me, moonlighting is the only way I *can* work—as a photographer. Exactly. *That* kind of photographer. And this part of town was the best place to find subjects for my peculiar branch of the art.

My studio was a bungalow, a guest house with a private entrance, up in the hills, ten minutes' drive from the alley with the back door of the coffee shop; that door was always locked in the 60s, but now the new owners always leave it open; it gives the homeless somewhere, inconspicuously, to go to the bathroom; Stavros the manager, son of a Thai prostitute and an Athenian bookmaker, feels that it's the compassionate thing to do.

These days, I am called Estelle de Vries; the French first name, the Dutch surname, I suppose that makes me Belgian. I appear to be in my mid-to-late forties, but in the right light I can appear ageless, and when you really look deep into my eyes you can't help knowing my real age, give or take a millennium.

"Estelle," Stavros said to me, as he poured my coffee, knowing I would never drink, "you see him too, don't you?"

"*Efkharistô*," I said, putting one hand over my cup. "You know I never drink . . . coffee."

"I am sorry," he said, as he always says, "force of habit."

"Who did you mean?" I said.

"Over there," he said, and pointed with his lips.

Across the street, in the window of a doughnut shop owned by Cambodian refugees, is where they tend to gather. The light is more flattering there. There are more boys than girls, but you can hardly tell them apart. They are colored the same, dirtied by the grime of the streets, sickly in the radiance of the lime-neon store sign. That night, though, there was one who stood apart.

"His name is Luke," said Stavros, who always knows everyone's name. "I know, I know, he's beautiful."

Human beings are nothing if not shallow. How can they be otherwise? They barely live before they are consumed by darkness. Youth is a flash, adulthood an instantaneous decay. Attractiveness, for them, is telegraphed by a few simple signals: wealth, beauty, and a frenetic pheremonal hyperactivity which they call love. The boy had at least one of the three attributes, and even through the window of the coffee shop and the tang of pollution in the night air I could smell a faint taint of another. With two out of three, it should have been easy to acquire the third.

Cars cruised the boulevard. Now and then, one stopped. None stopped for Luke. Stavros and I talked of many things. We talked about how blue the sky is in Greece. I told him how I used to sit beneath the stars in Syntagma Square . . . ride the steep highway past Arakhova to the oracle at Delphi . . . stand on Parnassus and look down at the gray-green valley. I did not tell him that it was long before he was born; I did not tell him that it was not a car I drove to Mount Parnassus; that would have confused him too much. Now and then, Stavros would try to pour me coffee. I do eat there, sometimes; you have to keep up the pretense. Tonight I didn't eat, though the special, lamb souvlaki, rare and dripping with blood and brine and lemon juice, was one of the few dishes my delicate appetites could stand. I just wanted to watch.

"There goes Gloria," Stavros said. "She finally found a

regular; he's an Indian john, I mean from India or Bangladesh or something; he pays her with one-ounce gold bars."

I had photographed her before. She wasn't that pretty, but with a chiaroscuro kind of lighting effect she achieved a certain voluptuousness. I sold the photographs to *Busty Bitches* magazine for three hundred bucks. Only paid her fifty. You get what you pay for. I was glad she'd found a steady source of income.

I watched the others as they loitered, but in my peripheral vision there was always Luke, steadfastly staring at the street, his blond hair haloed by the blinking neon, his eyes flecked with trepidation.

"In fifteen minutes," said Stavros, "he will come into the coffee shop and I will be forced to feed him."

"What do the owners say about that?"

"Oh no, scraps, leftovers, doggie-bag food really; he can get it here, he can find it in the dumpster in the morning; might as well get it while it's still 'luke'-warm, no?"

The doughnut sign fizzed; the bulb was going bad I supposed; one day there would be no alien glow for the street kids to stand in; I didn't think they'd fix it. Things do not get fixed on this street corner.

We talked about the way the water glistens in the Isthmus of Corinth. How dazzling-white the houses are on Mykonos. How the Aegean sparkles beneath extinct Thera. I did not tell him I can no longer see such things except in the cinema of the mind; I did not tell of my curious allergy to sunlight. I wonder how much he knows. Probably nothing; human beings are notoriously unperceptive; but Stavros is intelligent.

Then Luke is standing behind him. Stavros doesn't see him, can't possibly smell him—humans just aren't that sensitive— but somehow he happens to slip away at just that moment— a waitress call for his attention, perhaps.

Luke says: "You take pictures, don't you?"

"Yeah. My name's—"

"Estelle. I know. He told me."

"Are you hungry?"

He grinned. "*Fucking* hungry," he said. "Thanks." He turned, winked at Stavros, who was now puttering around with the coffee machine; gave him a thumbs-up sign. It had been a conspiracy of sorts, I suppose. Luke sat down in the booth across from me.

He was thin. I don't think he'd changed his clothes in a month. Through the holes in the sleeves of his beat-up Bulls jacket I saw scars: cigarette burns, needle marks; he put his hands on the table and I saw deep, white gouges in his wrists.

"Where are you from, Luke?" I said, expecting the usual: Oklahoma, Michigan, the Hollywood dream, the Greyhound, the disenchantment.

"I'm from Encino," Luke said.

"Oh. Then what about—"

"My parents? Fuck 'em."

"But you do have a—"

"Yeah. I'm not *totally* homeless. Don't make no difference."

"You don't talk like you're from Encino."

"Sometimes I do," he said. "When I forget I'm living on the street." His accent has shifted, almost imperceptibly, over the hill, toward the nouveau-rich valley of the valley girls.

He hadn't ordered anything, but a waitress brought Luke a plate of French fries and two slices of Boston cream pie. Luke ate both at the same time, stuffing them alternately into opposite sides of his mouth. The waitress didn't stay long, exchanged no pleasantries, hustled away as though Luke had the plague.

Which, of course, he did. I knew. Because I, unlike the others who share my world, have a sense of smell. Everyone's blood smells different, and every disease has a different taint to it, a different bouquet.

"Don't worry about it," he said. "I'm used to it."

"Are you on anything for it?" I asked him. "AZT, maybe, or one of the new experimental drugs?"

He laughed. "Need insurance for that." He went on eating, and didn't volunteer any more until both plates were completely consumed. He was beautiful. Breathtaking, except that I don't breathe. The eyes were wide, clear, blue as that same Aegean sky I may no longer look on; his skin had a familiar pallor even though I could hear his heartbeat, hear the blood sing in his arteries, sense the Brownian motion of dust-motes in the air between us as he exhaled. "I know you don't wanna fuck me," he said. "Nobody does no more. They all know somehow. Everyone talks to everyone else on the boulevard. But you could take my photograph. I'll let you take my picture for twenty, no, ten bucks, cause you bought me dinner."

"I think you're pricing yourself way too low."

"Maybe. But you're a nice lady. Who gives a shit anyways? I'll be dead soon. Ten will keep me going for another day. One day at a time." Sufficient unto the day is the evil thereof, as a wise young rabbi once told me; on the other hand, they crucified him.

"Okay, Luke. I'll take your pictures and I'll give you ten bucks. I wouldn't be able to sell them anyway; you're too young."

"Older'n I look."

Me too, I thought. "But these days, we have to have proof of age on file; otherwise, we can get busted."

"Fuck 'em," he said softly. But when he said it, he sounded curiously tender, vulnerable even; he was only playing at toughness, hiding a lifetime of pain.

We cruised around for a while in my '66 Impala. It impressed him that someone like me would have a cholo car. Actually it was bequeathed to me by an . . . acquaintance of mine. Not entirely voluntarily.

I was getting hungry now. It would be dawn in only a couple of hours. I had no intentions on young Luke. I am finicky about picking fruit before it ripens. A boy should have a chance at being a man, even if that chance was as flimsy as Luke's.

"Tell me about the dude who gave you the car," Luke said.

We turned up Highland, drove past Sunset and Hollywood, up toward the hills on the other side of which lay the life he had rejected.

"I don't know that much about him," I said. "We didn't know each other long."

"But you were, you know, intimate."

"Yeah."

The *War of the Worlds* church loomed above a Chevron station, just beneath the Hollywood Bowl. Intimate in a sense. Alfonso had tried to rape me in an alley. Thought I was just some white bitch walking around in the wrong hood, chased me down the alley in the Impala, thought he had me trapped between the front end and the graffiti; didn't know that I can't be squashed; I can make myself as insubstantial as a puff of smoke.

We were intimate for about five minutes, and I had a new car; no one really missed Alfonso; luckily, the sticker had eleven months to go. Alfonso may have been young, but he had certainly ripened enough to pluck; his existence was a dead end; I had no qualms.

"What's it like?" said Luke. I decided to eschew the freeway and go uphill toward Mulholland The streets were narrow and twisty, the houses cramped and overpriced.

"What's what like?"

"Being intimate."

"You don't know? I thought you—"

"Nah," he said. "I look like a hustler but I don't have what it takes to kill my own kind."

"But you have—"

"Born with it," he told me. "Mom was an intravenous drug user."

"In Encino?"

"Yeah. Sucks, don't it?" Oh, I thought to myself, such innocence.

By the time we turned onto Mulholland Drive, my hunger had become noisome in its persistence. But I knew where we were going, and I knew that the boy was in no danger. Here in the hills, we were above the smog. You could even see the occasional star; but the stars were almost drowned out in the lights of the city; to my right, the valley sparkled like a Christmas tree carpet, to my left, more subdued, were smears of rainbow radiance that were Hollywood, West Hollywood, even, like a wispy distant galaxy, Bel Air.

"Cool," the boy said. "But there's no stars."

"One or two," I said. Some joker had altered the speed signs from 30 to 80.

"Yeah, there's one."

We rounded a sharp bend. "Actually, I think that's a satellite."

"And then there's you. Estelle means star, I think."

"You knew that?"

"Had a book once. What to name your baby. George means 'farmer.' David means 'beloved.' Never looked up my own name, though."

"Okay. We have to stop for a moment."

After another hairpin came a lookout popular with lovers. I pulled into the lot; as I suspected, there were other cars here. There were couples, lost in each other's arms, eyes, saliva; in a convertible, a man leaned back against black leather and a tousled head bobbed up and down; above us hung the moon, huge and purplish in the alien L.A. light. No one noticed us, a middleaged woman and a boy; why would they? That would be almost the least perverse sexual combination in town.

"I've never been up here before," Luke said. "Saw it in a movie though. I think it was *E.T.*"

I ignored him for a moment. Above the parking area there was an earthy rise; a fence discouraged tourists from seeing the real view; but I knew there would be someone on the other side. Luke followed me at a distance, I could smell him. I stood awhile in the bushes. carefully listening for signs of trouble. There was always trouble on a Saturday night. The chill air sweated booze and indica fumes.

I saw trouble in a clump of oleander, a little way down the slope; I was downwind and caught a whiff of the pheromones of fear; I blended into the cold hill's side, shifted with the breeze until I was right on them. It was a woman, bound and gagged with gaffer's tape—how very Hollywood—and bruised all over; the moon made her blood all quicksilver and black. Hunched over her was one of the many serial killers who ply their trade in this town; I had had my eye on him since the last full moon, when I'd found a victim of his, dying, in an auto graveyard in Sepulveda, and sniffed him scurrying away. It was too late to save the woman, and so, regretfully, I fed. But this time, I could hunt prize quarry, hunt the human hunter of humans.

The woman saw me. She was so close to death that she could penetrate the veil of shadow I had cloaked myself with. I smiled at her. I don't know what she saw; perhaps I was a good Samaritan, perhaps an avenging angel with a flaming sword. Enough of this. I turned to the serial killer, who had just removed a hacksaw from a battered tackle box. I attenuated myself, engulfed him, sucked out all the blood in a quick whoosh through every pore in his skin so that he wrinkled up, all at once, like a dried shitake mushroom, then broke in a thousand pieces, brittle as brickle. It happened so fast, I don't know what the victim saw; I flicked the gag off her and coagulated back into my human shape, and, sated, climbed uphill to where Luke stood.

Presently, I heard the woman screaming, screaming, screaming; she had held in that scream so long, and now she could not stop.

"I saw that," Luke said. "Dude. You're a—"

I shushed him with a finger on his lips. He smarted; always and forever, my touch has the coldness of the grave about it. "There's no need to say the things we both know," I said. "Listen. Listen. You people never listen; you fill your lives with your own noise, drowning out the music that fills the space between spaces. Listen, Luke, listen."

The purr of a passing Porsche. The breeze. The screams of the woman gradually subsiding, subsiding . . . footsteps, tennis shoes on gravel on dirt, lovers breaking off their bracketed entanglement, curiosity getting the better of passion . . . I thought to myself: I know he hears these things, but can he also hear a different music? Can he hear what songs the veiled stars sing beyond the city's mist and smog? I wonder. No. Surely not. He is mortal. Beautiful and mortal.

We got back in the car. Luke was not afraid. That was strange. Perhaps not so strange; he believed himself doomed; he knew no possible redemption.

We drove a little further down Mulholland; and then I turned on Beverly Glen, took a sharp slide down Coy, heading for my bungalow. Usually they can't stop talking. They can't help themselves. I'm so alien to them, so scary, so mythically familiar. We reached the house; I had a private entrance round the back; the main house belonged to some big-name screenwriter, who had put on so many additions, turrets, minarets, and balconies, that the whole resembled a kind of Arabian nightmare.

My own humble dwelling was dingy and unkempt. Gorged, I went to the coffin—it doubles as a coffee table—and sat on the lid for a moment, letting the blood slow into a sluggish crawl, resetting my metabolism. When I looked up, Luke had already taken off his clothes.

He stood, unselfconscious, in the swath of light from the open doorway of the bathroom, against a kitchenette counter stacked with pristine coffee cups.

"I guess I forgot to ask," he said. "The pictures. You want me naked, I guess."

"Oh, yeah. The pictures. I forgot. Ten bucks."

I reached into my purse.

"Not right now," he said. "The money. I mean like, I'll take the money but, I mean, dude, I mean . . . not everything's about money. I mean, maybe I'd like to think you were just all taking my picture, just to, you know, take my picture. Like a mom would. Yeah I mean, I guess you will end up selling them to someone but, I would have done it anyway. Cause you're a nice lady."

Nobody loved him. Nobody cared.

He stood there and sure, he had no clothes on, but he wore over his scarred body so sublime an aura of purity that he seemed innocent of all those human peccadilloes they call sin. I took pictures, dozens of pictures. I used the 1600 film so I wouldn't have to use the big lights; I posed him in the natural chiaroscuro of the light from the bathroom door and the dark of the kitchenette. He was a natural. He was one of those models who stares right out of the picture, out of the printed page, whose eyes seem to have something special to say to you alone; but one of the ways you do that is to have your eyes be wide, vacant, reflexive, so that the viewer can fill the void with his own fixations, his own private delusions; perhaps that's all love really is, the art of polishing the mirrors in your eyes until you are the beloved's reflection reflected, back and forth, toward an infinite intensity.

Luke had that look. I speak of his eyes only because they drew the viewer's attention so intently that one barely saw the rest of him; the scars, the self-inflicted stigmata, the flat, firm pubis coyly figleafed by a slender hand that I had not the heart to move out of the way of my camera's uncompromising eye.

And this is what he said as he stood in the half-light. "Can you really be intimate, Estelle? I know what you are now. Can you, like, love us? Or do you only hunt us down?"

I said, "There are some things I love. The night. The dark. The cold. The first sip of blood as it gushes up from a freshly severed artery. The cadent decrescendo of a heart as it pumps its last; oh, that's a kind of music. I wish that you could hear it."

"So," he said, "do I."

He kissed me; not in an erotic way, but as a child who seeks comfort in a comfortless world.

"Be careful what you wish for," I said.

"How fucking careful do I have to be?" he screamed. "I'm gonna die, ain't I? What difference does it make?"

I didn't answer him. I just put down my camera, went over to the refrigerator, fixed him a sandwich and a Coke, and waited for him to calm down.

It was an hour till dawn; my blood was beginning to run cold.

"Do you want me to go?" Luke said. "You have time to drop me off, before, you know, the sun. . . . "

"Don't take those myths too seriously." I said. "But yeah, the sun; I don't like the sun too much."

"Or do you want me to stay?"

That was not my decision; it never could be. Not every ugly duckling is a swan. Most ugly ducklings are precisely that. To embrace eternity is a kind of destiny; it comes only to those who hear the music. I could not tell, really, if Luke could hear it.

I said to him, "Wait awhile. I'll have to retire soon. If you feel like staying, stay; otherwise you can always take the Impala."

"But how will I give it back? — I mean, I don't know if I can even find this place again."

"For me," I said, "there'll always be other cars, other rewards, other intimate moments."

"Thanks," he said softly.

"Hey," I added, "you can probably sell it for a couple of thousand, make a deposit on a place, have a real roof over your head for a while; even, I don't know, get a job; there's a law that say they *have* to hire you, they can't discriminate. Who knows, you might be able to hang on till they find the cure. And I'll still be here if you need me."

"I'll think about it," he said angrily.

I opened up the coffin. It was crush velvet inside, deep purple, with a pretty pillow of Chantilly Lace; and a velvet pouch full of soil from a place so far away and so long ago I'd just as soon forget it. I went into the back and got into, as they say, something comfortable; a nightie, a shroud, whatever you want to call it. I lay myself down in the coffin; I didn't close the lid yet. I wanted my last image of the day to be the boy; they are beautiful, you know, these humans, beautiful mostly because they are so ephemeral, because they dare not cross the river to the cold dark shore, oh, he was beautiful. Even with the dirty air between us I could feel the warmth of his skin. I could hear the trickle of his blood. I could smell all his emotions: his terror, his dread, his hope.

"In a moment," I said, "I'm going to close the coffin lid. Be a good boy, Luke. In the kitchen, in the cookie jar, there's a little more money. If you need a hundred or so, help yourself; I trust you."

He seized me by my wrists. I didn't know a human could grip so hard. His pulse pounded against my dead flesh. "Take me with you," he said.

"You don't know what you're—"

"Yes," he said, "I do. You don't know what it's like to be this way. I'm sick without even looking sick, without acting sick; I ain't come down with nothing, nothing wrong with me on the outside, everyone says I'm beautiful and then, they find out, and then I'm like, they can't look at me, can't touch me, can't even breathe the same air as me cause they think they're gonna die too. I'm nothing in this world, the world's like a fucking candy store window and I'm just standing out there in the cold with my nose pressed to the glass, I'm all craving all that sweetness and all that chocolate but I know I'm gonna die before I can taste it. Fucking Jesus, I want to *be* something—like you. The world grows up, grows old, drops dead, and you just go on and on, dude, I want to be like you."

"But you don't even like killing your own kind—"

"They won't *be* my own kind anymore, Estelle."

"If only you knew," I said.

"I don't need to know," he said. "Right now, I'm as good as dead. I feel too many things. I want to give up feeling. I want to be cold and hard. Dead is real. Dead has meaning. Dead is alive."

"But you're beautiful the way you are," I said. "Beautiful is brief. Beautiful is fleeting. Beautiful is transience."

"I love you," he cried out. "You're my hope, my future, my star."

He threw himself on top of me, slammed the lid shut, and

now there were two of us in that cramped space and he was hugging me, making love to me, trying to force my lips wide so that he could pierce his skin with my razor canines; oh, he wrapped his legs around me, thrust against me, his death wish stronger than any sex drive; he jabbed his wrists against my teeth and forced his blood to trickle down my throat, and inside the coffin's confinement the air was drenched in the perfume of his lust and fear; oh God, but he was beautiful. Even, as my tongue swelled at the touch of the warm fluid, as my sated innards gorged, even, as the heat shot through my jaded veins, even dying, he was beautiful. I wrapped my arms around his perfect body, squeezing out his half-life and sending him to a new half-death; we were intimate, for the first and only time, for such intimacy is too searing ever to be repeated. True love is as painful as it is transcendent; that's why mortals can't feel it; it would burn them up alive. But Luke had immortality in him, even though his disease bespoke mortality. That was why he would not be consumed by this love.

I knew then that he had heard the music; that he knew what song the stars sang.

So I embraced him, and I drank myself into the stupor of daylight; and at sunset I awoke, and found him still in my arms, dead yet not dead; the ugly duckling had, indeed, become a swan.

We went by the coffee shop one night, Luke and I, many days later Stavros tried to give us both coffee; and Luke would not touch his French fries or his pie. Stavros smiled a little. He did not step back in revulsion when Luke touched him, lightly, on the arm, to ask him some trifling question—the name of a new kid who had only just started working the block. The waitress, taking away his plates, looked him in the eye and was as civil to him as she ever is to anyone.

I thought: Stavros knows more than he lets on, I suspect. He set this up, somehow. I wonder if he's dropping a subtle hint. I wonder if he wants to be a swan too.

A country 'n' western love song crooned from the juke box. How strange that humans are so obsessed with love when they can experience it only once before they die . . . or metamorphose into us.

We spoke of the sky in Greece, how blue, how clear, how bright. Luke spoke of the dawn in Hollywood, purpled by pollution, tie-dyed by clouds of smog, spectacular; already there was a twinge of eternal longing. And Stavros tried to pour coffee, and I knew he was bursting with repressed envy.

"You people," he said to me, "you people."

"We people," I said.

"So full of passion," said Stavros, "so full of life. One day you'll drift away from here, and I'll be an old man minding a decaying coffee shop in West Hollywood, staring through the glass at a new crop of street kids, waiting for death."

Luke looked up at him. Touched him gently on the back of his hand. Stavros didn't flinch, even though the cold must have startled him. "Don't worry, dude," Luke said softly. "I'll send you a picture." And smiled, the subtle, sensual smile of the beautiful and the damned.

Dark of Night

Glenn Hauman

No, this is the real story. I got it from a friend of mine in college.

James VanDermeulen (one word, capital D) was having a rough time of it. Arlene, his college sweetheart wife, had just left him for *her* high school sweetheart, some fancy pants guy who invented a new e-mail program and made a million dollars a year or something and came back to take her away. She volunteered to send him alimony.

This sort of thing put James on edge—so much so that when the cashier at the Burger Bomb drive-through window shortchanged him, he drove right back and demanded his proper change. Unfortunately, he used the plate glass window the second time. And no, he didn't pay for the window—bad enough they wouldn't sell him any bourbon, the glass from the window flattened two of his tires.

His superiors at the post office noticed his levels of stress, but didn't really want to fire him, the general suspicion was that he might be one of those employees that you didn't want to fire, because he might—well, best not to dwell on it. So they relocated him. It was beginning to become a common practice: send an employee to a small laid-back town where the pace was much slower and the people much friendlier, where it was hoped that he would calm down enough to become less borderline. And if he didn't—well, at least he was away from major population centers, so the body count would be low. So James VenDermeulen was quietly transferred to the postmaster job in this quiet trance-inducing little town in Georgia called, God help him, Hicksburg.

VenDermeulen hated it.

He had no way to travel outside the city limits, since his driver's license was suspended and the bus only came through town once a day, and not on weekends when he had a day off. The average IQ of the populace barely exceeded the alcohol percentage of the local export—literally, an ex-port mixed with wood alcohol and Coca-Cola.

His co-worker was the worst of the lot. All the deliveries were done by Luther Wilson, lovingly known as "Lumpy" by the townies because of the lump on his back from carrying the mailbag around since the dawn of time. He was getting on in years now, so he used a truck now—his own pickup truck with the gun-rack in the back and his faithful shotgun Betsy in the back, because the town wasn't big enough to rate its own postal truck. Hell, the town wasn't big enough to rate its own post office, they rented out space from the local grocery store (really no bigger than a delicatessen, but nobody in town could spell that). Half the day was spent with Lumpy sorting and delivering (with Lumpy explaining how Stonewall Jackson's little brother once slept in the Cooper house over there every day on the route) and the other half was spent with Lumpy playing checkers. VenDermeulen tried to teach Lumpy chess, but Lumpy never quite got "the way the horsies moved."

Nightlife was even worse. The bar was smoky, the beer was watery, the music was country-western, and the women were unpalatable. While he had wowed one or two of them with stories of life outside of town, it was clear to him they wanted him to stay there and tell such grand stories all of his life. The rest of the female population was either devoutly religious or double coyote ugly.

VenDermeulen knew if he didn't get out of this one-horse town, he was going to go occupational.

He was contemplating this one day in the post office/deli (actually, he was contemplating whether to get an Uzi or buy American and how many people he'd have to kill to beat the current record, to be specific) when he saw Sherwood Craig lope in. Everybody knew the boy, he was the closest thing Hicksburg had to a local celebrity, as he had been diagnosed with some rare brain tumor. His momma sent him down here to pick up the mail every day. Somehow, getting mail addressed to him made him feel all grown up, since only adults got mail, particularly since it was unlikely he was going to get any real grown up pleasures out of his life. VenDermeulen always tossed a piece of "occupant" mail his way, getting the Wal-Mart circular was a joy that made his day.

Suddenly, the idea was upon him.

The letter he crafted was deceptively simple:

"Little Sherwood Craig is dying of a terminal brain tumor. His goal, before he passes into the Great Beyond, is to collect as many get-well cards as he can, to make the Guinness Book of World Records. His project is being sponsored by the Wish-Upon-a-Star Foundation, which specializes in fulfilling the final wishes of such sick little boys.

"Please copy this message and circulate it to your friends, neighbors, and co-workers.

"Only you can make a child's wish reality!

"God bless you from the Wish-Upon-a-Star Foundation!"

Then he posted it to a few computer bulletin boards.

Within days, the envelopes started pouring in from all over the country. By the end of two weeks, Sherwood was getting twenty sacks of mail a day. At the close of the first month, it had tripled.

Sherwood was ecstatic. He started to store them in alphabetical order, but gave up shortly after the first week. He kept the letters from different countries and one from each state, but his family shoveled the rest of them directly into the fire to keep the house warm.

Due to the sudden increased load on the local mail, VenDermeulen was able to requisition funds for additional employees and equipment. His excellent ability to handle the situation, to respond to the sudden change in mail service so quickly, was noted by the local supervisors. It was as if he was able to predict the influx.

Alas, it took a while for the postal bureaucracy to swing into action for the extra manpower—so Lumpy was forced to lug all the mail out to the Craigs himself. Well, he did have the pickup truck, and they needed it to lug all the sacks of mail.

The regional supervisors noted how well VenDermeulen

responded to his duties, responding to the increased pressure with further managerial flair in the face of a rather ridiculous situation. He was shortly promoted out of Hicksburg and relocated to the county hub, at an increase of rank and salary. Before he left, he even told Sherwood what he'd done and the kid practically smothered him, he was so happy to have gotten all these neat letters and stuff—and now Momma didn't even have to buy firewood, piles of it were delivered every day.

VenDermeulen was overjoyed—and wondered if he couldn't do it again.

VenDermeulen succeeded at doing it again far beyond his wildest dreams. His second scam involved a child at a fictional address (actually a local mailing list company) asking for business cards; he got a kickback for all the new leads. His third one was incredibly prolific, he asked for people to mail him spare disks that gave you ten hours free on computer networks, and then used all the new accounts to promote both the request for a) more disks and b) his fourth scam, a young nubile girl who was looking to go to college, and was asking all of America to send in all the loose change in their desk drawers to her P.O. box. That last one had netted him over eighty-five thousand dollars.

And more, he was going to be promoted to regional postmaster today. From local to county to district to regional in under four years. At the rate his star was rising, he would be Postmaster General in under a decade. Less if that commie pinko President was voted out of office.

It would have all been great, were it not for the fact that that very day Luther Wilson came to visit VenDermeulen in the office.

Lumpy, who had carried every sack of mail to the Craigs.

Who had carried every truckload to their front door for the past three plus years, six days a week.

Who had gotten a hernia from the weight of thousands of get-well cards.

Who had carried a grudge for the last year and a half.

Who had found out last week from little Sherwood Craig how his buddy Postmaster VenDermeulen had gotten all those nice people to send him get-well cards.

Who had carried the shotgun from the back of his truck into the office of the district postmaster.

Who, it was later discovered by the reporters who covered the massacre, had been transferred to Hicksburg almost twelve years ago to put him in a lower-stress position.

And that's the way it really happened. Honest.

The Bicycle Messenger from Hell

Jody Lynn Nye

"Pickup from Deenie Wurst?"

Debbie Wurtz sighed without looking up and reached for the rush parcel to the Cleo Brownie Advertising Agency. She made sure the stamp reading "Wurtz Advertising" was nicely squared on the top right of the label, just before the package was snatched out of her hand by a dirty claw. She tilted her head up to glare at the intruder and reduce him to an apologetic wreck, but was defeated. The bicycle messenger wore mirrored sunglasses. All she saw was her own angry face. Rummaging in the battered and stained carryall he wore slung across his equally filthy neon-orange vest, he produced a clipboard and pen, and then thrust them at her.

"Sign here on line 18," he said.

Debbie scribbled her name down, hoping that it was too illegible for anyone to copy and forge on faked charge card receipts. You couldn't be too careful these days of what you signed. She had heard from a client that somebody had run up five thousand dollars' worth of charges on her credit card, all on music CDs! Debbie handed back the clipboard. The messenger spun about and was moving even before she had drawn back her hand.

He was on his way, efficiently and silently. Debbie could appreciate that, even though she felt almost disgusted that such a dirty creature was walking on her carpets.

Hers, yes. Debbie settled back in her chair with her hands behind her head, allowing one moment of blissful wallowing.

Her carpets, Her office, Her agency, small, but up and coming. Fast. New contracts every day, people kissing up to her. Last year, she'd won her first industry award, a minor Clio. Since then, she'd done more and better work than the ad that took the prize, and she'd continue to shine like a supernova. Who knew what was next? Someday, in a bright fantasy filled with money and applause, she pictured herself taking McDonalds away from the indomitable Leo Burnett Agency. Yes. Glorious.

"Horrible, isn't he?" her assistant, Lorinda Mell said, interrupting her reverie. Debbie came back into the present.

"Who?" Leo Burnett?

"That man," Lorinda said. "The messenger. They drive like maniacs, you know."

"Yes." Debbie picked up the phone. Better tell Brownie that the ad layout was on the way. "They're always zooming through intersections against the light and up sidewalks, aren't they?"

"I heard they killed someone over in Brooklyn," Lorinda said. "Slammed into him, killed him dead." She smacked her hands together.

"Well, they do their job," Debbie said, losing interest in the subject. A man's voice in her ear said "Cleo Brownie." "Hello, Mark! This is Debbie. Yes, darling. It's on its way."

Another job well done. Debbie heard the words echo happily in her head as she walked toward the bus stop. Mark really loved the ad. He was sure his boss would subsidize Wurtz Agency to take the Lunch Menu part of the Munchers account. She had arrived.

Who'd have believed it? she thought, plowing through a thousand pedestrians toward the curb. Only one year and six months ago, Debbie Wurtz was in a sixth-floor walk-up office in the worst part of Queens. She couldn't have any clients drop in, lest they fall dead of heart attacks after walking up the stairs, and really couldn't afford the expensive lunches she took them to instead to woo them. Now, it was all so different.

Whoosh! She heard the sound of the tires on the pavement in just enough time to jump for it before the messenger on a racing bike shot past her, knocking her $600 Armani briefcase out of her hand.

"You should complain," a man said, as he helped her pick her belongings up.

"What's the point?" Debbie said, brushing off the smooth leather. Damn, it was scratched. "The dispatchers don't care."

"Seems like no one does any more," the man muttered as the bus arrived.

Funny thing was, Debbie seemed to hear wailing and screaming coming from the messenger's bag as he went past. Must have been wearing a personal stereo with the volume turned up to Nuclear Explosion. That's why he wasn't paying any attention to where he was going.

"Yes, this is Debbie Wurtz," she said, picking up the receiver when Lorinda signaled to her.

"This is the second demand, Miss Wurtz," the deep, throaty man's voice said. "We advise you to remit at once. Willingly. It'll go better for you if you do."

"That's Ms., Mister," Debbie said into the phone, very coldly. "I don't know what bill you're talking about. You'd better stop calling me. It's the law. If I want you to stop dunning me on the phone, you have to do it. Got it?" She slammed it down.

"What is it with people?" she asked. "We're up to date on our bills, aren't we?"

Lorinda yawned, showing yards of expensive dental work. "Of course we are. I took the envelopes to the post office myself."

But just to be sure, Debbie waited until Lorinda went home that night, and went over the books and the checkbook. No, they didn't owe anyone a thing.

Debbie put the ledger back, and arranged Lorinda's stuff on top of it so it didn't seem as if it had been disturbed. Better not let the help know you distrusted them. No, she didn't owe anybody anything. Her luck had changed all by itself. She got the breaks, and she paid her bills.

In a way, she dated her success from the day that novelty contract had arrived in the mail, one year, six months, and two days ago in the sixth-floor walkup, on a day when she'd been thinking of jumping out the window because things were going so badly.

"Sign this," read the sticky-note attached to the top of two

pages of faux parchment, "and your heart's desire will come
to pass."

Debbie had skimmed over it. Had a friend sent it to her
to help cheer her up? It read like the standard rich and famous
contract Orson Welles had offered the Muppets. As a joke,
she'd signed it, then tossed it in a drawer somewhere with a
pile of unpaid bills.

Debbie put down the success she had since enjoyed to the
power of positive thinking. All she needed was an affirmation
like that silly contract, and things began to fall into place. Her
guess was that the person who had sent it to her had found
out she'd signed it, and was harassing her out of pure obnox-
iousness. Maybe Lorinda had sent it, and was having a friend
make the calls. Debbie would have to ask, in a roundabout
way, if her assistant was happy with her job and her salary.
A marginally disgruntled employee today could become the
headline sniper of tomorrow.

"Did you hear?" Lorinda asked, picking at the flaking
mascara of her eyelashes. "They arrested some woman in
Chicago because of chain letters."

"Was she sending them?" Debbie asked. She sat over the
light table in the corner of the office. The straightedge moved
just as she was trying to lay down a Presstype border, shifting the whole thing off at an angle. Damn it. Then she sat
back on the stool to look. The layout was better that way. She
decided to leave it.

"No! She broke the chain. The newscaster said the letter
said she'd have bad luck for seven years if she didn't keep it
going. She said she burned it. Then she got arrested for tax
evasion." Lorinda shook her head, wide-eyed. "I don't believe
in these things, but I'd send it on. Just to be safe, you know."

Debbie shot a superior smile at her layout. "Right."

The mail-carrier trudged in through the door and tossed
a handful of envelopes onto Lorinda's desk. "Afternoon," he
said, offering them a big-toothed smile. "You ladies don't drive
in, do you?"

"Never," Lorinda said.

"Good," the postman said. "There's an accident down there
snarling things up all the way to the bridge."

"What caused it?" Debbie asked, pasting down more strips.

Yes, that was definitely good. Her design skills were improving every day.

"Messenger collided with somebody getting out of a cab," the postman said, opening the door. "Well, see you all tomorrow!"

Lorinda slit open all the envelopes. She put all the bills on her "IN" tray, and stacked all the real letters on Debbie's desk.

"You know, they kill people on purpose," Lorinda said.

"Who?" Debbie asked. "Oh, the messengers. Why? Kicks? Why don't they go down to Central Park and beat up joggers like everyone else?" She opened up the first envelope, of a fancy texture cream paper. Lorinda always stacked her mail in the order of the most promising prospects first. "All right, girlfriend, we have arrived!"

"What is it?" Lorinda asked.

Debbie brandished the letter. "This," she said smugly, "is an invitation to the Clio awards. We have been nominated for the 'Bright Babies' ad for Love Soap."

"Way to go!" Lorinda cheered, waving her hands in the air. "What are you going to wear?"

"Black, of course," Debbie said, immediately picturing how she would look on television. "My gold shoes and gold lace shawl. Better get me a hair appointment, darling. I need my roots touched up." She clutched the letter as if it was a hand-engraved note from God. "Oh, Lorrie, I don't believe it!"

"Who'd have thought it, huh?" Lorinda asked, grinning broadly. "We've got to be the youngest firm ever nominated."

"Probably not, but wouldn't that make great copy?" Debbie asked. She put the letter to one side, giving it an affectionate, possessive pat.

"Can I come to the awards, too?"

Debbie laughed. "Darling, the tickets are $500 a plate!" Lorinda went back to her work, pouting a little.

She opened the next envelope. The paper was just as good, but the text was less inviting. In fact, there was something she just didn't like about the feel of the letter at all, even before she read it.

"Dear Miss Wurtz," it said. "To conform to your wishes, we are now communicating with you by post. We urgently request that you remit what you owe at once. Please do not put us off any longer. In the long run, it will only make things harder." The signature was illegible. She turned over the envelope. There was no return address.

"Dammit," she said, crumpling letter and envelope together in a ball and throwing them away.

"What is it?" Lorinda asked, looking up from her word processor.

"Another crank demand," Debbie said, airily. "I tossed it." She watched Lorinda for her reaction. Either the assistant was a better actress than she'd ever thought, or she really had no connection with Debbie's mysterious harasser. Could this be some kind of long-distance stalking? She looked thoughtfully at the wastebasket. Should she keep the letter and go to the police with it? No. Better not. At best, they couldn't do anything, and at worst, they'd think she was a nut. Just leave it alone.

That night, she watched a documentary program on the Discovery Channel because one of her commercials was going to air during the second break. The show was a yawner. It was about old-fashioned deep sea fishermen who used hooks instead of nets, calling it more humane, and even managing to suggest it was somehow noble.

"It's a calling," the old captain said. He was impossibly photogenic: picturesquely weathered, with crisp white hair and sea-blue eyes. "You have to love going out to sea, riding the waves. You stay out between the sea and the stars for weeks at a time with no one around you but your crew, the dolphins and the seagulls."

Guy's a walking cliche, Debbie said, sitting up straighter on her black leather couch so she wouldn't fall asleep before her ad aired.

"Yessir," the captain went on, taking a pull at a pipe. If Debbie had put a man who looked like that into a layout, they'd never believe in him. "Yes, indeed. Sometimes you'd think you could hear the wail of tormented souls in the whistle of the wind through your rigging. Made some people afraid of being out there, but it sounded like home to me."

"With the death and retirement of men like Captain Palmer, we are witnessing the passing of an era," the earnest young announcer said solemnly, looking into the camera. "Giant commercial fishing consortia . . . " Debbie tuned out the rest of his voice.

Tormented souls, she thought, clutching a pillow to her chest like a teddy bear. That's what the bicycle-messenger's radio had sounded like when he almost hit her. She was going to have to avoid whatever radio station it was he had been listening to. The memory of it had given her nightmares for a month. She was almost glad to have a name to put to the sound.

One month later, almost to the day, Lorinda's rumors of pedal-vehicular homicide nearly came true again when Debbie climbed off the bus. This time, the son-of-a-bitch knocked her briefcase right out into the street, into a pool of snow and slush. Swearing to murder all moronic, filthy, cross-eyed messengers, she ignored the horns and middle fingers, and kicked all her papers into a soggy, frozen pile and up onto the curb. She came into the office almost a half hour past her usual time, and Lorinda signaled frantically to her over the telephone receiver.

"Yes, Ms. Wallace. She can take your call now. Thank *you*."

Debbie slid into her chair and tried not to sound breathless and angry as she picked up her phone.

"Marla! How good to hear your voice. Yes, of course. Let me see if I'm free for lunch." She snapped her fingers at Lorinda, who opened the office diary and shook her head, no. "We're both lucky, darling. One o'clock? Cardini's? Fabulous. Of course I'll buy, if you've got good news for me." She forced herself to laugh. Cheap bitch, she thought, The more expensive the lunch, the smaller the commission, but she couldn't afford to piss Marla off. It was almost always high profile work.

Cardini's cost about half again what Debbie had estimated. As she pushed out of the opulent bronze and glass doors into the cold afternoon to hail a taxi, she pictured money on wings flying out of her wallet. Never mind, Debbie thought, on the way downtown through the gray slush. She'd gotten the contract. Wallace wasn't even the first person to offer her more work on the basis of her Clio nomination.

"Aw, what the hell is this?" the cabbie moaned. Debbie looked past him out onto the street. The traffic was backed up for blocks. "Look at this."

"What is it?" Debbie asked. The cabbie picked up his radio and released a burst of static.

"Vice-presidential motorcade," he said, hooking the receiver back into place. "It's barricaded all the way to the airport."

"Dammit," Debbie said, fumbling in her wallet. "Look, I'll take the subway. Thanks." She handed him the money, enough to cover the meter with enough left over for a small tip. After all, he hadn't gotten her to her destination. Had he?

"Eh," the man said, with a resigned look on his face. Debbie climbed out of the back seat and slammed the door. Up and down the street, dozens of other people had the same idea. She tottered after them on her designer shoes, and had to wait in an endless line at the token booth.

When she hit daylight again, it was snowing. Debbie huddled her chin into her coat's fur collar, and trudged doggedly back toward her office building. Rounding the corner onto her street, she bumped into a man.

"Damn it, watch where you're going," she said, peevishly.

"Go to hell," the man growled, pulling his own collar up higher.

"It'd be warmer than here," Debbie muttered. She was reaching for the door handle, when the familiar wailing rose out of the usual city background noise. Debbie jumped to one side to miss the bicycle messenger. But she jumped the wrong way. When he swerved to avoid her, she was right in his path.

He knocked Debbie about ten feet down the icy sidewalk. With the help of clucking passersby, she got to her feet and retrieved her purse. She stomped over to glare at the messenger. He was typical of the breed, with wild hair jammed down for the season under a knit cap so dirty that you could have grown daisies in it.

"What the hell is wrong with you?" she demanded.

"Sorry, lady," he said. "It woulda been okay if you hadn't moved." He took off his mirrored sunglasses for just a second. Debbie did a double-take. His eyes were red—not the white, the irises. And the pupils. She took a hasty step backward.

"All right," she said, trying to reassert her dignity. "Just watch it."

Now her shoes were scored and scratched, and her clothes were wet where she'd landed in the snow. Debbie stalked up to her office. This was beginning to look like a deliberate attempt on her life. What was going on? Who had she pissed off?

Nobody was expected for the rest of the day, so she put her clothes across the radiator to dry and shrugged into a giant beach t-shirt one of her clients had sent her from the Caymans.

"That's it," Lorinda said, almost sounding satisfied, as Debbie examined the bruises on her legs. "That's what they do, they ride right at you. Then, pow! You're on your way to the morgue."

"That's crap," Debbie said, but she didn't sound very convinced.

"Say," her assistant said, inexorably. "Did you hear? Some assholes in England stuck a kitten in a microwave. They . . . "

"I don't want to hear it!" Debbie said, more forcefully than she had intended. Hurt, Lorinda went back to her gum and her nails. Debbie stared off into space. There had been a lot of accidents lately. It was as if someone was trying to send her a message.

So nonchalantly it hurt, she flipped through the contents of the drawer where she had last seen that fake contract. Under about a hundred packets of artificial sweetener, a pair of torn pantyhose, and the usual accumulation of inexplicable junk, she found it. Casually, with one eye on Lorinda, she leaned backward in her chair to read it.

The damned thing sounded like a deal with the devil. In exchange for her heart's desire—she remembered that part from her first, cursory reading—Deborah T. Wurtz agreed to remit her immortal soul, payment to be made within 30 days.

Terrific, she thought. I'm on 30-day net with Satan. Well, too bad. I didn't know what I was signing. It was just a joke. She tore up the paper and tossed it into the wastebasket. Lorinda looked up curiously, and Debbie gave her a casual smile.

She was just scaring herself, she knew. What I have I worked for, all by myself, she thought fiercely, and no one can take it away from me. No one!

Debbie went back to work, but it was as if she could feel the ripped pieces of paper reproaching her, so she picked up the wastepaper basket, and took it down the hall and emptied it down the garbage chute.

To hell with it, she thought. I have work to do.

At the end of the next month, Debbie got the call she had been dreaming of all her professional life. It was a member of the awards committee, suggesting that she prepare just a few words. Just in case. That could only mean one thing: she had won the award. Debbie put the receiver down like a soap bubble, then let out a whoop of glee.

"We have arrived, girlfriend!" she shrieked to Lorinda.

"Congrats, Deb," Lorinda said, holding out her mail to Debbie, her wide eyes sincere. "You're good. Now everybody knows it."

"Today, Love Soap—tomorrow, McDonald's," Debbie said, enjoying the triumph. She sorted through the mail. When she saw the cream envelope, Debbie felt a sense of dread. She almost didn't open it.

"Final notice, Miss Wurtz," the impeccable typing read. "We're sorry it had to come to this, but you have left us no choice. Our collectors will have to deal with this matter personally. We thank you for your business."

Debbie rolled her eyes, and tore the letter into confetti.

"Come and get me, suckers," Debbie said, almost snarling as she slam-dunked the remains into the wastebasket.

"What was that?" Lorinda asked, watching the particles that missed the can flutter to the ground.

"Nothing," Debbie said. "Nothing at all."

Lorinda shrugged. She believed what Debbie told her, every time. The girl was so gullible it hurt.

"By the way, your dress is ready at Cotique, and your hair appointment is at 2:00," the assistant said. "I'm so excited! I hope I can spot you on TV."

"Thanks, Lorrie," Debbie said. "I'll be the one with the gold statue." She looked at the clock. "Almost one. I'll go and get some lunch, now, then I'll go get my hair done. I won't be coming back today."

"Good luck, boss," Lorinda said, holding up crossed fingers.

"We've already won," Debbie said.

She sailed on air throughout the rest of the afternoon. Even the gray sky cleared up and beamed sunshine down on her. Everything was beautiful. In the salon frequented by dozens of professionals in her field, and in the fitting room at the dress shop, Debbie managed to let slip that she'd gotten "The Call." Word would be all over New York by morning. She couldn't wait for the scads of work that would come rolling in.

Debbie figured that what with the dress, the shoes, her purse, and her newly coifed hair, she didn't want to fight her way onto the bus and ride all the way out to Queens. She'd treat herself to a taxi. Managing to work one arm free to raise it, she stepped off the curb to hail a free cab from among the clutch coming her way. The newest, cleanest car she had ever seen slid to a stop at her feet, even managing to avoid splashing slush on her boots. Perfection, just like the rest of the day had been. It was the best day of her life.

Debbie joggled her parcels to move her arm to pull open the door. At that moment, she heard the sound of narrow tires, and the wailing of tormented souls, louder than ever, bearing down on her. Debbie's heart started pounding. It was coming for her! She couldn't see the bicycle messenger, but she knew he was bearing down on her from behind. Debbie was trapped between her boxes and the cab door. Panicking, she struggled to stuff herself and her belongings into the cab before the bike hit.

There wasn't even time for her to turn around.

My Naggilator

Lois Tilton

"Hey! They caught an alligator in the sewer!"

"They did not!"

"Yeah, look, it's on TV! The Portage Fire Department caught it."

"Hey, they did! Really, Katie, come and look!"

Kate Bixler stepped reluctantly out of the kitchen, wiping her hands on a dish towel. She was in the middle of frying chicken for dinner, and you just don't walk away and leave chicken frying on top of the stove, not if you don't want the smoke alarm going off and grease flying everywhere.

What she saw on the family room TV set was sufficient to confirm her son and husband's claim: men in high boots and heavy slickers were wrestling with the frantic, thrashing length of a reptile caught in a net.

"They spotted it down in a retention pond next to Highway 53," Hal explained. "People called in about it. Looks like it had been after the geese nesting down there. So they chased it into a culvert and used high-pressure fire hoses on the other end of the drain pipe to force it out into the net."

"Cool!" This was the opinion of Michael, the Bixler's ten-year-old son, who first had spotted the story on the news.

Kate shook her head. She didn't share Michael's attitude, and the chicken was going to burn if she didn't turn it. But before she went back into the kitchen, she noticed Corrie, her little one, raptly watching the screen with eyes that were too wide, seeing too much. "Corrie, honey, want to come into the kitchen with Mommy?"

But Corrie never followed her into the kitchen, and Kate, busy with the chicken, let her stay out there with the TV.

At the table later, Michael was still worked up about the alligator. "That was *so cool!* Man, I'll bet that thing had to be six, eight feet long! Hey, you know, maybe it coulda been the alligator Danny Fine brought back from Reptile Circus in Florida when they went on vacation! He was gonna keep it in his bathtub, but his mom got rid of it. I'll bet she flushed it down the toilet and it went down into the sewer and *grew* till it got too big to live in the pipes and crawled out!"

"On TV they said it wasn't more than four feet," his father corrected him, but Michael was considering his little sister, who was pretending to push her cut-up chicken around on her plate, and into his eyes came what Kate called The Look.

"Hey, Corrie, you know what alligators eat? They can eat cats and dogs and sometimes even deer. I saw it on TV! Remember, this alligator was waiting right by the side of the lake, and when this deer came down to drink, it went *snap!* and grabbed it and dragged it down under the water! And you know what else they can eat?"

"Michael," Kate said in her warning voice, but Michael was on a roll.

"Sometimes they eat *little kids!* They crawl back through the sewers, and when you get up at night to go to the bathroom, there they are, waiting, and they go *snap!* and drag you down back down through the toilet—"

"All right, Michael! That's it! You go to your room, *now!*"

"What!?" He looked in appeal to his father, who was prudently silent, then sullenly shoved back his chair and left the table. Kate heard the stomp of too-large shoes on the stairs, the slam of a door, and the final comment that something sucked, which she decided to ignore.

But of course it was too late, Corrie was already crying. Kate had to pick her up and hold her, feel the little body shaking with sobs of fear, and when Hal tried to appeal, "Aw, Kate, he's just a boy," she was in no way inclined to show mercy.

"I've *told* him. You know how many times I've told him not to scare her like that? Or do you want her to spend every night for the next three weeks crawling into bed with us when she has nightmares? Like last time, remember?"

Hal remembered. He lifted Corrie away from Kate. "Come on, Kitten, don't cry! Michael didn't mean it, he was just teasing you! Alligators can't crawl through the sewers. They don't eat little girls."

Corrie sniffled, looking up at him, then back to Kate, seeking confirmation. "But I saw it on TV!"

Kate only hesitated an instant. "Yes, but alligators don't eat little girls because alligators live way down in the swamps where's it's always hot, and you live here where it's too cold for alligators. So that's why they had to catch the alligator on TV and take it to the zoo, or else when winter came, it would die from the cold.

"Now, sit down like a good girl and eat your chicken."

Later, to Hal: "It's those TV shows. You know I wish you wouldn't let them watch that kind of thing."

"Oh, come on, Kate! It's the Nature Channel! It's educational!"

"It's too much blood and violence! You know they stage those scenes. Like the one with the piranhas," she reminded him pointedly. The last time Corrie had refused to go to sleep in her own bed, it was after the show where the school of piranhas tore a live goat to pieces. After Michael had thrown a dead goldfish into her bath, yelling that it was a piranha and it was going to eat her alive. Which Kate didn't hesitate to mention whenever Hal started to bring up that "just a boy" line again.

"OK, that went a little too far, I admit. But Christ, Katie, she needs to learn to take a little teasing without all this carrying on! She needs to learn to live in the real world. What's going to happen when she starts school and some boy puts a worm down her dress or something?"

"That's hardly the same thing! Besides, she's just a little girl."

But maybe Corrie was starting to grow up, after all, because she only woke up once with a bad dream that night, and afterward seemed to forget the alligator incident.

It was about six weeks later, and Kate was doing her homework for her real estate class (she meant to get a license once

Corrie was in school all day), when Corrie came into the room.
"Mommy?"

"What is it, Corrie?"

"Naggilators are real, aren't they?"

Kate put down her pen. "That's right, honey, alligators are
real, but remember, they live far away in the swamp. You don't
have to be afraid of alligators here."

"It's too cold for them here."

"That's right."

"But they have naggilators in the zoo."

"Yes, but they have to live in a special reptile house, where
they keep it warm enough for them."

Corrie frowned in thought. "Are dinosaurs real, too?"

"Dinosaurs *were* real animals, once. But all the dinosaurs
are dead now. They've all been dead for a million million years.
The weather changed, and it got too cold for them, and so
they all died."

"But not Barney. Barney isn't real."

"No. Barney isn't real."

Corrie shook her head gravely. "Real dinosaurs were green.
I saw it on TV."

"That's right." Kate thought sadly that maybe her little girl
was starting to grow up, after all. Last year, when she was
three, purple stuffed Barney had been Corrie's faithful companion, carried with her everywhere, tucked into bed with her
at night. Now, Barney was for babies, and the purple dinosaur was relegated to the toy closet. Kate couldn't exactly say
she was sorry not to have to hear that damn *song* every day,
and even less to be subjected to Michael's less innocent versions:

I love you,
You love me,
Barney died of HIV . . .

But Corrie wasn't thinking of Barney at the moment.
"Dinosaurs aren't real now. But naggilators are. So somebody
could keep a naggilator in their house, where it's warm."

"Well, somebody might have a *little* alligator in a tank. But
it would grow too big for them to keep. It could *never* get
big enough to eat a little girl."

Corrie nodded, seemingly satisfied. Kate wondered what she was thinking of. Now, if it had been Michael, she would have gone right away to check the bathtubs and sinks for baby alligators. In general, Kate was glad Corrie had been a little girl instead of another boy.

The next thing happened when they went to the store for new winter coats for the kids. At the front of the toy department there was a display of stuffed animals, and among them was a bright-green plush alligator.

Corrie saw it and stopped short. "Mommy! Look! It's my naggilator!"

Kate was so astonished she let go of her hand, and in an instant Corrie was standing in front of the display, clutching the stuffed alligator. "It's my naggilator! It is! Mommy, can I have him? Please!"

Corrie cried easily (maybe too easily) when she was hurt or scared, but she wasn't a child who usually whined, which Kate appreciated. "Well . . . " She looked for the price tag. $12.95. The alligator had a red mouth that opened and closed, with a red tongue and white felt triangles for teeth.

About this time, Michael, who'd lingered on the other side of the store in case any passing stranger might think *he* could be interested in stuffed animals, realized that money was about to be spent and showed up to demand his share of the loot. But, being Michael, he couldn't help himself, he grabbed the toy from his sister and thrust it at her face, making snapping sounds. "Hey, Corrie, look! It's an alligator, it's going to eat you up!"

"*Michael!*" Kate warned in a furious half-whisper, hating to make a scene in public, but Corrie was above being provoked.

"*My* naggilator won't eat me. He likes girls. *My* naggilator says he only eats boys!" And she hugged the toy when her mother took it away from Michael and gave it back.

Now, of course, Kate had to buy it for her, and after brief negotiations with Michael on the matter of the official NFL Chicago Bears parka he wanted, they left the store with the new purchase. From that moment, the naggilator was as constant a companion as old Barney had been. But much more of an enigma. Corrie would come up and ask the oddest questions:

"Mommy? Do naggilators take off their skins?"

"What do you mean?"

"I mean when they have to grow and their skins get too old and tight."

"Oh, you mean shedding their skins. Um, no, I don't think they do. Snakes shed their skins, but not alligators, I don't think."

Confidently, "Well, my naggilator does. He's only a little naggilator, and he has to change his skin so he can grow. And when he takes off his skin, he gets too cold, so he has to stay in my room till it's not cold any more, and he gets his new skin."

"He does?"

Corrie nodded firmly and hugged the green plush toy. "And if I get scared at night, my naggilator comes and sleeps under my bed and scares it away."

"I'm glad to hear *that*," her father remarked from his place in front of the TV.

"What a dork! What a moroon!"

"Michael, be quiet!"

"My naggilator doesn't like boys," Corrie glared at her brother. "When he gets bigger, he'll eat all the boys who try to come in my room and bother me." She opened the mouth to demonstrate. "See, he has big sharp teeth!"

Of course it was all her imagination. Imagination was supposed to be good for kids, Hal reminded Kate. She supposed so.

But she worried, anyway. It just wasn't like Corrie to invent this kind of thing. Other children, maybe, but not Corrie. Of course if it had been Michael, she might have thought there was more than imagination involved. Michael was capable of anything. But where would *Corrie* get a live baby alligator?

Still, the next time Kate was in Corrie's room to clean, she made a point of looking under the bed, in the toy closet. There was battered old Barney, there were a million random scattered Legos and puzzle pieces, but nothing to suggest the presence of any clandestine pet.

Except—well, there was this funny kind of smell. Not like something dead, thank God. More like . . . sulphur or—matches!

Of course she confronted the usual suspect first, but

Michael denied he'd been playing with matches in the house. "Jeez, Mom! What do you think I am? A little kid?"

Could he have been smoking? Kate wondered. But she knew the scent of tobacco—and other smoking materials. The smell in Corrie's room was something else.

"No, Mommy! I wouldn't play with matches!"

"Are you sure? Corrie, I want you to tell me the truth, it's important."

"It's the truth," she swore with earnest innocence. "I never had matches in my room. I never played with matches anywhere."

"Then why does your room smell like someone was playing with matches there?"

"I dunno. Maybe it was my naggilator. Naggilators don't like to be cold."

Kate frowned. "Well, I don't want your naggilator to be playing with matches, either. Do you understand me?"

"I'll tell him not to."

"Good."

That was one puzzle Kate never solved. Then a few days later Corrie came to her and said, "My naggilator doesn't have any wings. He needs his wings now. Could you make him some wings for him?"

"Wings?"

A firm nod.

"Your naggilator has wings?"

"Um-hmm. But they're still too soft for him to fly, because he's changing his skin."

Kate took the toy from her, looked at it carefully. "I suppose I could sew some wings on him. But what happened here?"

Someone had slit the alligator's tongue, half-way up from the tip. She suspected Michael, but Corrie said, "His tongue was wrong. It's really supposed to be that way."

Kate frowned. "Did you use my scissors?"

Corrie looked down at the floor. "I'm sorry."

"Didn't I tell you never to use my sharp scissors? You could hurt yourself."

"I won't do it again. I promise. But I had to fix his tongue. He couldn't talk right that way."

"Well, the next time, you come to me. Do you hear me, Corrie? I don't want you to get hurt."

"OK. But will you do the wings? Please?"

"All right. If you promise. What color are they? Green?"

"Yes. On the outside. On the other side, they're red."

"Green and red." Kate didn't know where Corrie was getting these ideas, but she dutifully made the wings and sewed them onto the toy.

"Thank you, Mommy! Now he can fly!"

"That is so stoopid! You are such a *dork!* A flying alligator! Let's see if it can fly out the window."

Kate had gone to put away her sewing box. Before she could intervene, Michael had snatched, but an instant later he was howling, "Ow! Ow!"

"What's the matter? What's wrong?"

"She bit me! The little shit bit me!" He was waving his hand in the air, Kate captured it, took a look. She was astonished to see a row of sharp, pointed bite-marks, some of them deep enough to draw a drop of blood.

"Corrie? Did you bite your brother?"

She shook her head furiously. "No! My naggilator did it. He was going to throw my naggilator out the window!"

"I was not! I never touched your stoopid naggilator! Ow! She bit me!"

"You did so!"

Furious and exasperated, Kate looked from one to the other of them. Why did kids always have to fight? "Corrie, we don't bite. That's wrong, no matter what he was trying to do."

"I *didn't* bite him! It was my naggilator!"

"Never mind. You go to your room and think about this." She turned to Michael. "Come on, we have to clean that hand. I don't want it to get infected."

But in the bathroom, washing his hand, Kate started to wonder. A child's bite marks wouldn't look like this. Would they? Should she maybe take Michael to the doctor for a tetanus shot—or something?

"Ow!" yelled Michael. "That hurts!"

"Well, if you wouldn't always be bothering your sister—"

"I never touched her!"

"Michael, I *heard* you! You were going to throw her naggilator out the window."

"I never touched her stoopid naggilator!"

"Just like you never touched her Barney?"

He lapsed into sullen silence while she dabbed antiseptic on the wounds.

"Now, you go to your room."

"*Why?* She's the one who bit *me!*"

"Because I said so." Because all this bickering was giving her a headache. Because she didn't believe Michael for a second.

Kate had gone through all this before. When Barney was Corrie's favorite, she'd had to rescue him from the garbage can, from the street, from the roof, from the Fines' doghouse. She'd had to sew back torn legs, arms, head and most often the tail. And every time, it was: *I didn't do it!*

Now she supposed it was going to start all over again with the naggilator. Except—Corrie seemed to have learned to fight back. And Kate didn't know whether she was happy about that at all.

Michael sulked in his room the rest of the day and kept it up at dinner after his father came home from work. Hal lifted his eyebrows when Kate told him what had happened. "She bit him? Good for her!"

"No, it's not good for her! What if she starts biting the other kids when she goes to school?"

"Well, she needs to start standing up for herself."

"If it weren't for her brother, she wouldn't need to stand up for herself. Really, Hal, you've got to do something about Michael."

Hal sighed, called for the boy. "Look, son. We're getting tired of this. Whenever these things happen it's always you starting it—"

"Oh, yeah? Well, what about *her?* She's been playing with matches again in her room! I can smell the smoke."

Kate started for the stairs. She *thought* she'd been smelling that strange kind of matchhead odor upstairs for the last week or so, but she couldn't ever find where it was coming from. She must have gotten too used to it.

She pushed open the door to Corrie's room. It was true, that scent was stronger than ever. "Corrie Bixler! You've been playing with matches!"

"No!"

"Don't lie to me, Corrie! I can smell it."

"That's not me, it's my naggilator! He smells like that when he gets too hot!"

"All right! That does it." Kate crossed the room and took the stuffed animal away from her. "I've told you about playing with matches. If your naggilator is going to do things like that, I guess he can't stay in your room any more."

"No!" Corrie screamed. She jumped and tried to get the naggilator back, but Kate held it out of her reach, so Corrie started pulling on her leg, instead. "No! Give him back! I need him! Please, Mommy! Give him back!"

Kate shook her head. "It's too dangerous. You have to learn to listen to me."

Corrie shrieked, "No! No! No!" She refused to let go of Kate's leg, and when she dislodged her, she rolled on the floor, screaming and screaming. Kate was appalled. Her little girl *never* did this kind of thing! But she knew how to deal with a tantrum, so she firmly shut the door and left Corrie there to scream it out.

At the bottom of the stairs was Michael, staring with a smirk on his face that Kate didn't like at all, but she said nothing. A moment later, Hal came into the bedroom where she was putting the naggilator up on her closet shelf, bright green plush stuffed toy with silly-looking wings and a toothy grin. Strangely, it didn't smell like smoke now.

"Is she ever going to stop? What did you do to her?"

"I took the naggilator away. She wouldn't tell me the truth. She said it was the naggilator playing with the matches, so I took the it away from her."

"She sure clings to that thing. It's even worse than Barney."

"I know." Kate thought she wasn't sure if she was going to give it back. Corrie had changed so much since she'd gotten it, changed in ways Kate didn't quite like. But the child kept screaming so much, without letup, that Hal finally said, "Christ, Kate, give her the damn thing back! That noise is driving me crazy!"

It was driving Kate crazy, too.

"You promise," she insisted to Corrie, "you promise never never to play with matches, you or the naggilator?"

"I promise!"

"Stoopid naggilator!"

Kate spun around, saw Michael in the doorway, sneering. "Michael! Go to bed! Now!"

"It's not even nine o'clock!"

"Go to bed anyway!"

Kate warned Hal, "She'll never learn, not if we keep giving in to her this way."

"It's just a toy, Katie! And now we can get some sleep."

But how could Kate sleep? Why couldn't Hal see that something was wrong? Corrie playing with matches. Corrie *lying* to her about it! Hal thought it was a good thing, the child using her imagination, but Kate wasn't sure.

What if it wasn't just her imagination?

What if a naggilator had red wings and a forked tongue? And smelled like burning matches?

Like burning matches . . .

Like burning . . .

Kate sat straight up in bed. "Hal! I smell smoke! Something's burning!"

She ran to Corrie's room. The smell of smoke and sulphur was so thick it made her choke, but there was no fire. Corrie was sitting up in the middle of her bed, clutching the toy naggilator, looking pale and scared.

Kate shook her. "What happened? What happened?"

"Michael came into my room! He was going to burn my naggilator! He was going to burn it!" She started to cry, a few tears.

"What do you mean? Where's Michael?"

"He was going to burn my naggilator! He had a lighter!"

Kate turned around. "Michael? Michael! Where are you?"

Just then Hal came into the room. "I called 911. What's wrong?"

"The naggilator ate him."

Kate stared at her daughter a moment. "Find Michael!" she ordered Hal. "Look in his room!"

"He's not in there. He was mean. He had a lighter, he wanted to get me in trouble. My naggilator ate him. He doesn't like boys, only girls."

"Corrie, don't *lie!* Where's Michael?"

"I *told* you!"

Hal in the doorway. "He's not in his room."

"Look for him!"

There was the flash of red and blue strobes outside the house as the fire trucks drove up. The firemen could smell the smoke inside Corrie's room, but no one could find Michael.

The police detective took Corrie into the kitchen alone, but Kate could hear what they were saying. "Tell me again what happened to your brother. And why your room was all full of smoke."

"My naggilator ate him. My naggilator gets all hot when he gets mad. He got mad at Michael when he came into my room. He burned him up and he ate him. Then he flew away."

A pause. "Is this your naggilator? Can I see him? Are these his wings?"

"Uh-huh. He was changing his skin, but now his wings aren't too soft any more, so he can fly. He flew away."

"You know, with these wings, he looks a little bit like a dragon, not an alligator."

"No, dragons aren't real. Naggilators are real. I saw one on TV. They can eat kids when they get big. Michael told me."

About the Authors

ELUKI BES SHAHAR lives in the Mid-Hudson Valley with nine cats and too many pieces of paper. She's the author of over three dozen books and short stories, including *Hellflower*, *Speak Daggers to Her*, and *X-Men: Smoke and Mirrors*. She will probably not give up writing any time soon. "The Ghost of Night and Shadows" was inspired by a genuine urban legend related to her on one of those rides through the dark on the world's largest underground railroad, and from the experience of being extremely lost in the Brooklyn subway system far too many times. She has actually been to (the former) Marlebone Station but not of her own free will.

MICHAEL BURSTEIN is the winner of the first ever Science Fiction Weekly Reader Appreciation Award for Best New Writer. His first story, "TeleAbsence" (Analog, July 1995) won the 1995 Analytical Laboratory Award for Best Short Story and was nominated for the 1996 Hugo Award. Burstein himself was nominated for the 1996 John W. Campbell Award for Best New SF Writer. He is a graduate of the 1994 Clarion Science Fiction and Fantasy Writer's Workshop, which he attended with the assistance of the Donald A. Wollheim Memorial Scholarship, awarded to him by the Lunarians, a New York City-based fan group. He also holds degrees in Physics from Harvard College and Boston University. Born and raised in New York City, he is currently living with his wife Nomi in Brookline, Massachusetts. When not writing, he teaches Physics and Mathematics at the Cambridge School of

Weston. He has wanted to write about the spider in the hairdo ever since a college friend creeped him out by telling him the story, all the while swearing that it had really happened to "a friend of a friend."

ADAM-TROY CASTRO is the coauthor of an upcoming volume in the *X-Men & Spider-Man: Time's Arrow* trilogy with Tom DeFalco. A regular contributor to *Science Fiction Age* and the author of two cover stories in *The Magazine of Fantasy and Science Fiction*, he's sold over sixty short stories in all, including prominent contributions to the anthologies *Whitley Streiber's Aliens*, *The Ultimate Witch*, *Blood Muse*, *The Mammoth Book of Erotica*, *OtherWere*, *The Ultimate Super-Villains*, *Untold Tales of Spider-Man*, and *Adventures in the Twilight Zone*. His novelette "Baby Girl Diamond" was a Bram Stoker Award nominee in 1996. To his considerable consternation, he now lives in Florida. "What Happened Next" arose out of longstanding concern over just what happened to that deformed maniac after that teenage couple drove off with his hook on their car door handle. I mean, he's still out there, isn't he? Shouldn't we be worried about this?

KATHY CHWEDYK, the published author of two Regency romance novels, has sold several fantasy short stories, both alone and in collaboration with Laura Resnick. "She of the Night" was the result when Kathy and Laura started with Kathy's favorite urban legend about serpents' eggs being sewn in to the linings of fur coats, combined it with the Ancient Near Eastern myth of Lilith, and transplanted it to the moody, Raymond Chandler-like setting Laura loves.

BILL CRIDER has been fascinated by stories of alligators in the sewers ever since reading Thomas Pynchon's *V.* After doing a fanzine articles about *V.* and other books with alligators in the sewers, he was inundated with alligator items and owns, among other things, a genuine alligator claw, an alligator candle, several wind-up alligators, and even a loaf of bread baked in the shape of an alligator. Or maybe a crocodile. Crider is the author of more than twenty mystery novels (including *Gator Kill*, in which a private-eye investigates the murder of an alligator) and several books for young readers, including *Mike Gonzo and the Sewer Monster*, which is about you-know-what.

Born in the Bronx as part of a pack of wild librarians, **KEITH R.A. DeCANDIDO** is a writer, editor, and musician. He has edited or coedited a dozen anthologies besides this—most notably *OtherWere: Stories of Transformation* (with Laura Anne Gilman)—and his other editorial duties have ranged from a highly successful line of super-hero novels to helping bring Alfred Bester back into print. His short fiction has appeared in *The Ultimate Spider-Man*, *The Ultimate Silver Surfer*, the Magic: The Gathering anthology *Distant Planes*, the *Doctor Who* anthology *Decalog 3: Consequences*, and *Untold Tales of Spider-Man*. In 1996, his band, the Don't Quit Your Day Job Players, released their first CD *TKB*; in 1998, his collaborative Spider-Man novel *Venom's Wrath* (written with José R. Nieto) will be unleashed on a panting reading public. He must share credit for several aspects of "How *You* Can Prevent Forest Fires" with the following: his wife Marina Frants, a scuba diver and underwater photographer, who first brought this legend of helicopters and scoops to his attention; Jeremy Bottroff, from whom he shamelessly stole the idea of twins named Castor and Pollux; and Howard Zimmerman, for brilliant editorial input.

MARK GARLAND read a copy of *The Sands of Mars* when he was twelve, and proceeded to exhaust the local library's supply of SF, then book stores, then magazines like *F&SF* and *Galaxy*. Eventually he tried writing some short stories of his own. Then he got interested in music, and spent the next fifteen years playing in area rock bands, writing songs (over one hundred) and recording studio demos for record companies. He also got involved in fast "street" machines, especially domestic types, like 442s and

GTOs, and enjoyed building and racing his own cars—which led to a career as a service manager at several auto dealerships. Eventually he quit auto racing, rock bands and service departments, but he still found himself compelled to do something creative with his life, so he came full circle, back to science fiction and fantasy. He's spent the last twelve years reading, going back to school, attending conventions, and writing. He lives in upstate New York with his wife (also an avid reader), their three children, and (of course) a cat. Mark has since sold five novels and more than forty short stories and poems, including two *Star Trek* novels and *Sword of the Prophets*, a May 1997 fantasy novel from Baen Books.

LAURA ANNE GILMAN grew up in suburban New Jersey knowing that she was going to be a writer when she grew up, but never doing anything about it until someone pointed out that she was as grown up as she was likely to get. In 1994 she took the plunge, sending a story off to *Amazing Stories*—and had it accepted. Since then, she has been published in a wide variety of anthologies, most recently *Highwaymen: Rogues and Robbers* from DAW, and also coedited one, *OtherWere: Stories of Transformation*, with Keith R.A. DeCandido. Her urban legend comes from firsthand experience—it happened to a friend of a friend of hers. Ms. Gilman currently lives in New Jersey with one cat and one husband.

CHRISTIE GOLDEN is the author of six novels and thirteen short stories. Her most recent works are *King's Man and Thief* and *Instrument of Fate*, both original fantasies from Ace Books, and the *Star Trek: Voyager* novel *The Murdered Sun*. Golden's particular urban legend is perhaps better known around campfires as "The Mexican Pet." In writing "The Remaking of Millie McCoy," Golden wanted to put an unexpected twist on a familiar tale. She is thrilled that the legend has hit the former Soviet Union, where tales of "The Ukranian Pet" continue to be told. Golden lives with her husband and two cats. She is presently hard at work on a second *Voyager* novel, a five-part epic fantasy series, and a mystery series set in Denver, Colorado.

ED GORMAN has written several crime novels and many short stories. The *San Diego Union* called him, "One of the most distinctive voices in American crime fiction" and *The Bloomsbury Review* said, "Gorman is the poet of dark suspense." In addition, he has written three science fiction novels under a pseudonym. See Larry Segriff's biography for more on the chosen folktale.

ELLEN GUON has published three novels (*Knight of Ghosts and Shadows*, *Summoned to Tourney*, and *Wing Commander: Freedom Flight*) in collaboration with author Mercedes Lackey and a solo novel, *Bedlam Boyz*, which is a prequel to *Knight*. Her most recent short stories are in the *Sisters of Fantasy II* and *Don't Forget Your Spacesuit, Dear* anthologies. She is the president of Illusion Machines, a computer game company, in partnership with her husband, Stephen Beeman. They develop software for Microsoft, Viacom, and other publishers. As you might guess from "Disney on Ice," she's also a former television writer, and did work for several months for the Walt Disney Company. The basis for the story is the urban legend about how Walt Disney was cryogenically frozen after his death, and that his body is a) stored at Disneyland somewhere underneath the castle or b) stored in a secret laboratory in the Angeles Crest mountains. It's a great urban legend, especially if you grew up in Los Angeles (like me) under the shadow of the Disney Empire. But, as intriguing as the idea of Walt Disney being frozen like an ice cube might be, the truth is that he's buried at the Forest Lawn Cemetery in Burbank, California.

GLENN HAUMAN'S bio hasn't significantly changed since *The Ultimate X-Men* (so buy that too) except that his company's lawsuit to overturn the Communications Decency Act has gone to the Supreme Court (for more info, see the BiblioBytes web site at http://www.bb.com) and he's finally living down that the bio didn't mention his wife Brandy or his parents, Gene and Pam. Sherwood Craig is loosely based on Craig Shergold, a ten-year-old boy who is dying of cancer. Before he dies, he would like to set the world record for receiving the most Neiman-Marcus Cookie Recipes. You can help Craig by sending an irate fax to LEXIS-NEXIS demanding that they remove all traces of your mother's maiden name from their executive washroom wall. They will respond by sending e-mail labeled "Good Times" to the computer controlling Craig's life support equipment. When Felippe Linz, the technician operating the computer opens this mail, his hard drive will be overwritten with thousands of credit card invoices for $250, erasing the last bit of evidence that Hillary was seen on the grassy knoll when JFK was shot by Kibo, thus allowing world domination by Bill Gates and his trilateral commision cronies who are eating fried peanut butter and banana sandwiches in the black helicopters with Elvis. For more info, contact the Make-A-Wish foundation at http://www.wish.org/wish/craig.html. Oh, and VanDermeulen is the name of the author's high school, not the current husband of an ex-girlfriend from high school. There is no proof indicating otherwise. None. And if you're smart, you'll stop asking questions.

BILLIE SUE MOSIMAN is the Edgar-nominated author of _Night Cruise_ and the Stoker-nominated author of _Widow_. Her latest suspense novel in the U.S. is _Stiletto_ and her latest suspense hardcover, _Pure and Uncut_, is available in the U.K. She has had stories in more than one hundred anthologies and magazines, including _Ellery Queen Mystery Magazine_, _Realms of Fantasy_, _Blood Muse_, _Diagnosis: Terminal_, _Tarot Fantastic_, and _Great Writers and Kids Write Mystery Stories_. The urban legend she wrote about claimed that a couple parking on lover's lane were assaulted by a one-armed man. His missing arm had been replaced by a hook. When the couple realized the one-armed man was a menace, they drove away in a panic. Once home and safe and narrowly escaping their deaths (although still unsure if there had been anyone trying to enter the car at all) they

discovered the would-be killer's arm hook hanging from the
rear door latch.

JACK NIMERSHEIM has written thirty-five books and over 1000
articles on technology-related topics. As a fiction writer, Jack
has sold two dozen SF and fantasy stories to various magazines and anthologies, since his first professional SF sale,
"A Fireside Chat," appeared in co-author Mike Resnick's
1992 anthology, *Alternate Presidents*. Jack was a 1994 nominee for the John W. Campbell Award for Best New Science
Fiction Writer. His 1995 short story, "Moriarty by Modem,"
was voted one of three finalists for a 1996 Homer award.

JODY LYNN NYE is the author of several science fiction and
fantasy books, including *The Ship Errant*, *Mythology 101*,
and *The Magic Touch*, and four collaborations with Anne
McCaffrey: *The Death of Sleep*, *Crisis on Doona*, *Treaty
at Doona*, and *The Ship Who Won*. Jody has lived around
Chicago most of her life, and has heard her share of urban
legends. She particularly remembers the one about the mayonnaise jar. Jody lives northwest of Chicago with her husband and two cats. Said husband's brother, a native New
Yorker, was the source of Jody's legend. Apparently, there
was a rash of rumors of a messenger knocking someone
down and killing him, and everyone seemed to know someone who knew someone whose relative was the one killed.
That seems to make it a true urban legend.

JOHN ORDOVER was born an editor, which caused him problems right from the start; in kindergarten he was censured
for complaining that "Run, Spot, Run. See Spot Run." was,
in his words, "Flawed minimalism at best, needlessly redun-
dant at worst." Ordover spent his teenage years editing such
science fiction and fantasy classics as *Stranger in a Strange
Land*, *Childhood's End*, and *The Lord of the Rings*.
However, since they had all been published long before he
saw them, his effect on the field was minimal. Realizing
this, after a short ten-year stopover in Chicago and Kansas,
Ordover returned to his native New York and took a job

as an Assistant Editor at Tor Books, where they let him edit books *before* they were published. While at Tor, Ordover studied intently for his Starfleet entrance exams, and on passing them in 1992 moved to Pocket Books where he began editing the *Star Trek* novels at a truly amazing speed. Ordover has many short story sales to his credit, and recently wrote, with David Mack, the *Star Trek: Deep Space Nine* episode "Starship Down" which aired the week of 11/06/95.

BARBARA PAUL is a mystery writer who can't quite kick the F/SF habit. In addition to five SF novels, she's had stories in *Frankenstein: The Monster Wakes*, *Werewolves*, *Celebrity Vampires*, *Castle Fantastic*, and *Future Net*. A former academic now living in Pittsburgh, she writes a mystery series featuring NYPD detective Marian Larch. The current book in the series is *Full Frontal Murder*.

Winner of the 1993 John W. Campbell Award for Best New Science Fiction Writer, **LAURA RESNICK** is the author of some thirty SF/F short stories, as well as an upcoming fantasy trilogy which will be released by Tor Books.

MIKE RESNICK is the author of *Santiago*, *Ivory*, *The Widowmaker*, and close to forty other science fiction novels, as well as more than one hundred stories. He is also the editor of some twenty-five anthologies. He has won three Hugos, a Nebula, and dozens of lesser awards. (For those keeping score at home, Mike is Laura's father.)

KRISTINE KATHRYN RUSCH is an award-winning writer and editor. She has published 13 novels, among them *Star Wars: The New Rebellion* and the fantasy series *The Fey*. She has won a Hugo, a World Fantasy award, two Locus awards, and the John W. Campbell award for Best New Writer. She is the former editor of *The Magazine of Fantasy and Science Fiction*.

ROBERT J. SAWYER is Canada's only native-born full-time science-fiction writer. His story "Gator" is, as the title suggests, based on the urban legend of alligators living in the sewers of New York. Rob's novel *The Terminal Experiment* won the Nebula Award for Best Novel of 1995; it was also a finalist for the Hugo Award. Rob has also won three Canadian Science Fiction and Fantasy Awards ("Auroras"), as well as France's top SF award (*Le Grand Prix de l'Imaginaire*) for Best Foreign Short Story of the Year, plus an Arthur Ellis Award from the Crime Writers of Canada for Best Short Story of 1993. He's also twice been a finalist for the Seiun Award, Japan's highest honor in SF. Rob's novels include *Golden Fleece* (which was named best SF novel of 1990 in Orson Scott Card's year-end summation in *The Magazine of Fantasy & Science Fiction*), *End of an Era*, *Starplex*, and *Frameshift*, plus the three volumes of his popular Quintaglio Ascension series, *Far-Seer*, *Fossil Hunter*, and *Foreigner*. Rob's work has appeared in many anthologies, including *Ark of Ice*, *Dinosaur Fantastic*, *Sherlock Holmes in Orbit*, *Dante's Disciples*, *Dark Destiny III: Children of Dracula*, and *Free Space*. His "On Writing" column appears in each issue of *On Spec*, Canada's principal SF magazine. Together with his wife Carolyn Clink, he edited the Canadian SF anthology *Tesseracts* 6. Rob and Carolyn live in Thornhill, Ontario (just north of Toronto).

LAWRENCE SCHIMEL is the author of *The Drag Queen of Elfland*, and the editor of more than twenty anthologies, including *Tarot Fantastic*, *Vampire Stories from New England*, and *Southern Blood: Vampire Stories from the American South*.

LARRY SEGRIFF is the author of several novels and numerous short stories. His first novel, *Spacer Dreams*, came out from Baen Books in November 1995. His second, *The Four Magics* (cowritten with William R. Forstchen) came out from Baen Books in October 1996. He makes his home in Green Bay, Wisconsin, where he lives with his wife and two daughters. "My Father's Son" came out of a conversation between Larry and collaborator Ed Gorman. In talking about different urban legends, and in trying to find one that connected with their own lives, both Ed and Larry realized that they both knew people who had found money at one time or another—and whose lives had been changed by that money. From buried treasure to Al Capone's vault to mattresses stuffed with greenbacks, the idea of finding a cache of cash has been a longstanding urban legend. But, as this story shows, there's no such thing as a free lunch, and even found money can come with a price tag. (The authors hasten to add that neither of them *really* owns a metal detector, nor have either of them purchased a pirate map in at least a year.)

JOSEPHA SHERMAN is a fantasy writer and folklorist. Her fantasy novels—which include *The Shining Falcon*; *Child of Faerie, Child of Earth*; the bestseller *Castle of Deception*, with Mercedes Lackey; *A Strange and Ancient Name*; *Windleaf*; the bestseller *A Cast of Corbies*, with Mercedes Lackey; *Gleaming Bright*; the bestseller *The Chaos Gate*; *King's Son, Magic Son*; and *The Shattered Oath* and its sequel *Forging the Runes*—have won the Compton Crook Award, and been selected as ALA Best Books, New York Public Library Books for the Teen Age, Junior Library Guild Selections, and ABA Picks of the List. She is also the author of the picturebook *Vassilisa the Wise* and, with Susan Shwartz, the *Star Trek* novel *Vulcan's Forge*. Her folklore titles include *A Sampler of Jewish-American Folklore*, *Rachel the Clever and Other Jewish Folktales*, *Once Upon a Galaxy*, *Greasy Grimy Gopher Guts: The Subversive Folklore of Children* (with T.K.F. Weisskopf), *Trickster Tales*, and *Merlin's Kin: World Tales of Hero-Magicians*. She is also the author of over one hundred short stories and articles for books and magazines including *Sword & Sorceress IV, V, VIII* and *IX*, *Vampires!*, *DragonFantastic*, *More Whatdunits*, *Cricket*, *The Writer*, and others, and has been a writer for the animated TV show *The Adventures of the Galaxy Rangers*. Josepha is an active member of The Authors Guild, SFWA, the American Folklore Society, and the SCBWI. She has lectured on fantasy and folklore to writers' groups around the country and told stories to groups of all ages. "The Choking Doberman" tale is a common modern urban folk theme—but probably dates to the Middle Ages!

For the past fourteen years, SUSAN SHWARTZ has been a financial writer and editor at various long-suffering Wall Street firms. For the past twenty years, she has written, edited, and reviewed fantasy and science fiction. Her most recent books are *Shards of Empire*, set in eleventh-century Byzantium, with *Cross and Crescent*, a novel of the First Crusade, to follow. Her other books include *The Grail of Hearts, Star Trek: Vulcan's Forge* (with Josepha Sherman) and, with Andre Norton, *Imperial Lady* and *Empire of the Eagle*. Her anthologies include the two volumes of *Sisters in Fantasy* and two volumes of *Arabesques*. She has published more than sixty pieces of short fiction and has been nominated for the Nebula Award five times, the Hugo Award twice, and the World Fantasy Award, the Philip K. Dick Award, and the Edgar Award once each. She has written reviews for various SF publications, *The New York Times*, *Vogue*, and a variety of other places. A lapsed academic, she has a PhD in English from Harvard University, enjoys writing polemical letters to major newspapers, and spends entirely too much time on the nets that she could use going to the opera, shopping, or even—heaven forbid—having a life. She lives in Forest Hills, New York with a computer, a lot of books, and a notorious shoe collection. The urban legend she's adapted for "Cold Shoulders" belongs to the genre known as the "Phantom Hitchhiker" and is an homage to her high school, Tailgunner Joe McCarthy, and a weird teenage death song that no Golden Oldies show plays anymore about a boy, a girl, and a letter sweater.

Award-winning novelist, composer, and filmmaker **S.P. SOMTOW** has published over thirty books, including the best-selling *Vampire Junction* series and the critically acclaimed memoir *Jasmine Nights*. His novel *The Wizard's Apprentice* won the Rocky Award for best young adult novel of the year. His most recent film is *Ill Met by Moonlight*, starring Timothy Bottoms. He commutes between his homes in Los Angeles and Bangkok. His tale was inspired by the modern urban body of vampire lore.

S.M. STIRLING was born in France, grew up in Europe, North America, and Africa, lives in New Mexico, and writes compulsively. Books include *Marching Through Georgia*, *Under the Yoke*, *The Stone Dogs*, *Drakon*, and *The Rising*. **JAN STIRLING** was born in Millford, Mass., and lived there for the first thirty-odd years of her life; stories include "Were-Wench" in *Chicks in Chainmail*, "The Mage," and "The Maiden and the Hag" in *Lammas Night*. Steve and Jan met at a World Fantasy Convention, were engaged at a World Fantasy Convention, but did not marry at a World Fantasy Convention. Their alligator-in-the-sewers story was inspired by the thought of all those baby alligators literalizing a metaphor about life by being flushed down toilets. New York's that kind of town!

LOIS TILTON is the author of more than fifty short stories and four novels, including two set in the TV universes of *Star Trek* and *Babylon 5*. She has recently completed her fifth novel, *Darkspawn*, a tale of vampires and vengeance and violent stuff. She takes a solemn vow that none of the characters in her story bear any resemblance to the members of her own family, but if Monty the garter snake doesn't stop trying to escape down the drain, there may be a sequel.

LAWRENCE WATT-EVANS is the author of more than two dozen novels and over a hundred short stories, including the Hugo-winning "Why I Left Harry's All-Night Hamburgers." He's a full-time writer living in the Maryland suburbs of Washington with his wife and two kids. "Sit!" is based on a tale (described in the story) that's been told with any number of black celebrities as the dog-owner in an elevator, but the most common version is about Reggie Jackson.

Bibliography

For those readers who would like to read more about urban folklore, including compilations of the folktales themselves, the following titles offer a variety of tales, rhymes and illustrations:

Brunvand, Jan Harold. *The Baby Train & Other Lusty Urban Legends*. New York: W.W. Norton & Company, 1993.

————. *The Choking Doberman and Other "New" Urban Legends*. New York: W.W. Norton & Company, 1984.

————. *Curses! Broiled Again!* New York: W.W. Norton & Company, 1989.

————. *The Mexican Pet*. New York: W.W. Norton & Company, 1986.

————. *The Vanishing Hitchhiker: American Urban Legends and Their Meanings*. New York: W.W. Norton & Company, 1981.

Dresser, Nornine. *American Vampires: Fans, Victims, Practitioners*. New York: W.W. Norton & Company, 1989.

Dundes, Alan and Carl R. Pagter. *Never Try to Teach a Pig to Sing: Still More Urban Folklore from the Paperwork Empire*. Detroit: Wayne State University Press, 1991.

————. *Sometimes the Dragon Wins: Yet More Urban Folklore from the Paperwork Empire*. Syracuse: Syracuse University Press, 1996.

————. *When You're Up to Your Ass in Alligators: More Urban Folklore from the Paperwork Empire*. Detroit: Wayne State University Press, 1987.